Gracefully Grayson

Gracefully

Grayson

Ami Polonsky

HYPERION

LOS ANGELES ☆ NEW YORK

Copyright © 2014 by Ami Polonsky

All rights reserved. Published by Hyperion, an imprint of Disney Book Group. No part of this book may be reproduced or transmitted in any form or by any means, electronic or mechanical, including photocopying, recording, or by any information storage and retrieval system, without written permission from the publisher. For information address Hyperion, 125 West End Avenue, New York, New York 10023.

First Hardcover Edition, November 2014
First Paperback Edition, June 2016
10 9 8 7 6 5 4 3 2 1
FAC-025438-16074
Printed in the United States of America
Library of Congress Control Number for Hardcover Edition: 2014010155
ISBN 978-1-4847-2365-4

Visit www.hyperionteens.com

SUSTAINABLE FORESTRY INITIATIVE
Certified Chain of Custody
Promoting Sustainable Forestry
www.sfiprogram.org
SFI-01054
The SFI label applies to the text stock

For Ben and Ella,
who have great faith in stories

Part

One

Chapter 1

IF YOU DRAW a triangle with a circle resting on the top point, nobody will be able to tell that it's a girl in a dress. To add hair, draw kind of a semicircle on top. If you do this, you'll be safe, because it looks like you're just doodling shapes.

I was in third grade when I realized I could draw princesses without anyone knowing and, for more than three years, I've been sketching the same thing in the margins of my notebooks at school. I look up at the board. Mr. Finnegan has already given us almost an entire page of notes, more than most teachers, but I don't mind. Humanities is the best class of the day, and besides, it's no problem for me to take notes and draw at the same time. I sketch another triangle dress in my notebook, circle on the top point, thin semicircle of hair. I try to look at it like I've never seen it before just to *confirm* that nobody else would know that the sketch is really a princess. But I'm good. It's too abstract.

My pen is a glitter pen—silver. I have a gold one in my backpack, but I always leave the purple and pink ones in my drawer at home with the rest of my art supplies. If anyone asks, I can always say I found the silver and gold ones on the floor in the gym or something, but probably nobody will. I want to fill in the dress with the shining silver, add big eyes and a smile and long shimmering hair, but I never would because that's not what boys are supposed to do. I squeeze my eyes almost shut to try to see the princess the way I want to. All I can see is her silver outline, though, so I rest my head in my hand and look out the window instead.

Outside, a giant truck barrels down the street and a city bus honks as it turns the corner. Mrs. Frank, the gym teacher, is bringing some little kids out to the soccer field. They're skipping and running across the grass. Beyond them is Chicago's skyline. Even though the leaves are starting to change color, it still feels like summer, and it's way too hot in the classroom. My bright yellow basketball pants are sticking to my thighs. I push my bangs to the side as I adjust the sweatband on my forehead.

Finn is awesome, and I'm lucky I got him for Humanities, especially since Mrs. Tell is the other humanities teacher and she's probably ninety years old and supposedly horrible. My cousin Jack had her last year and was always in trouble in her class. He blamed it on how boring she was, but lately he's in trouble in every class, and most of what he says these days is bull.

I look back to my notebook as Finn asks Anthony to read a paragraph about the Holocaust aloud. I think of my drawing pads at home, in my top desk drawer. Usually I draw the castles and landscapes huge and then make the people tiny, so they're barely noticeable—the queen, the king, and the little blond princess. When I was younger, my mom was an artist, and I wonder for the millionth time what she would have thought of those drawings and of the sketches in my notebooks at school, and I wonder what she drew when she was my age. The one painting that she left behind especially for me is of the earth surrounded by a wave of trees and sprinkled with smiling animals. Behind the earth is the sky, brightening from darkness into light, and at the top of the sky, one bird that's red, yellow, and blue is soaring, all alone. The painting hangs on the wall next to my bed, so I fall asleep each night looking at it, especially at the bird. And I wake up to it every morning.

Finn writes the names of some places in Europe on the board. I turn to a clean page. "We're going to start talking about people in specific cities who risked their lives to help Jews escape the Nazis," Finn says. He sits on his desk as he waits for us to finish writing.

I look up at him when I'm done. He looks relaxed, as usual. His white dress shirt is tucked neatly into his dark jeans, and he's holding a red dry-erase marker in his hand. "These people had to keep their involvement in the Resistance *secret*." He emphasizes the word by walking back to the board to write it above the other notes.

I doodle a new princess and sketch a jagged circle around her. "How would it feel to hide an enormous, important, life-threatening secret from your friends, your neighbors, and maybe even members of your own family?" Finn continues. I bend down and take my gold glitter pen out of my backpack. His question makes me forget all about the Holocaust and think, instead, of when we were in elementary school, back when we had recess every day, and how, for so many years, I sat on the side steps alone, watching everyone else play. I draw a ring of gold flames outside of the jagged circle. They surround the princess. She suffocates.

The clock ticks on the wall, and somebody coughs behind me. Otherwise, the class is still.

"Grayson? Any thoughts?" Finn finally asks. He usually calls on me if nobody answers; I guess because I can always come up with something to say. "What do you think?" he goes on. "How would you feel if you were going about your life, day to day, all the while hiding a dangerous secret?"

I try to seem calm, like I usually feel in Humanities, but my heart is starting to race. I hesitate and look down at my notes. "I mean, I guess I'd feel like it would be safer to stay away from other people," I finally stumble. Finn waits for me to say more, but I'm kind of hoping he'll call on someone else now.

"Can you elaborate?" he asks.

I adjust my sweatband again. It's damp. "Well," I say, "I'd just stay away from people because I'd be worried I'd accidentally tell them my secret." It sounds like a question, the way I say it. I feel my ears turning red, and I flatten down my hair to hide them.

The class is quiet, and I look down at my glitter pens. The pause feels like forever.

"Okay," Finn finally says slowly. Then he's silent for another second. "Interesting. Does anyone have any thoughts on Grayson's comment?"

I avoid his eyes and glance around the room at the faces I've known pretty much since kindergarten. For a minute, I only look at things, not the people, like the thin braid hanging down the side of Hailey's head that's clasped at the bottom with one of those tiny heart clips, Meagan's pink backpack on the floor next to her desk, the shining wooden desktops.

Then I let my brain adjust and I examine the people. Ryan, who is a complete jerk, sits right across the aisle from me. He glances in my direction, and I look away. On the other side of me, Lila is twirling her long, brown hair into a bun. She seems quiet, but she's completely in charge of the girls. My eyes rest on Amelia, who started at Porter last week. She looks like she belongs in high school, not sixth grade. Her long, reddish hair hangs over her huge chest. Slowly, she puts her hand up.

She seems nervous, and I feel kind of bad for her. It's probably not easy to move once the school year has already started, and especially not to a school like Porter, where most of us are lifers.

"I'd actually make friends with more and more people," she

says sort of softly when Finn calls on her. "I wouldn't stay away from people, because that might look suspicious. I'd just try to act normal, you know, like everyone else." Her pale, freckled cheeks look pink.

"So," Finn says, "on one hand we have Grayson's idea to isolate oneself, and on the other hand is Amelia's idea to surround oneself with lots of people in order not to appear suspicious." Next to the word *secret*, he writes *Isolate v. Integrate* in quick, slanted writing.

I look up at the clock. It's almost time to go, and I can't wait to get to my next class. I copy the last notes quickly. The bell rings, and I stand up with everyone else. "We'll pick up here tomorrow," Finn yells over the sound of rustling notebooks. He glances my way. I concentrate on my shoes as I walk to the door.

Chapter 2

WHEN SCHOOL IS OVER, I get out of the building fast, like I always do. Lots of kids stay after for activities or sports, but I never have. When I was younger, Uncle Evan, Aunt Sally, and my teachers always tried to get me to join debate or the boys' chorus or whatever, but finally they gave up and left me alone. I didn't feel like debating anything in front of an audience, and, even though I have a pretty good voice, I *definitely* wasn't trying out for the boys' chorus.

I look around as I walk to the bus stop. The streets are empty, and it's pretty quiet outside of school. I relax. Jack does football fall quarter, and Brett goes to the After School Club with a bunch of the other second graders, so they won't get home for a while. Luckily, we're the only ones who take the 60 home, so as long as Jack and Brett have activities after school, I don't have to know anyone on the bus.

My back is completely sweating through my yellow T-shirt, and I sit on the edge of the shaded bench at the bus stop so my mammoth backpack can fit behind me. I always end up taking home books I don't need, but it's easier to get out of the building quickly if you just take everything. I squint in the sun. My mind wanders to the Resistance.

The Chicago street fades away, and I see a young girl, just my age. She's hiding alone on a dirty blanket in the dark, cold basement of the little house where I live with my mom and dad. When the world sleeps and it's safe, I knock gently on the basement door and bring her something to wear and what stale bread we can spare. She is thin and cold. Her deep, dark eyes meet mine as I loan her my gray, woolen dress.

"Hey, Grayson," a voice says softly, and I snap my head up. Amelia is standing next to the bench. Her dark eyes meet mine. "Do you take the 60?"

I jump up and accidentally knock my shoulder on her chest. Oh, God. "Sorry," I mumble. She looks down and takes a little step back. "Yeah. Um, do you?" I ask nervously.

Her cheeks are pink again. "Yeah, we live at the end of Randolph, right across from the lake."

"Really? What's your address?"

"One twenty-five Randolph," she says.

"I live right across the street from you," I tell her. You can see Amelia's building from our dining room window.

"Oh, cool. This is my first time riding the bus," she contin-ues. "My mom drove me up till now. She said she'd drive me until I got used to things. So nice of her. Like that could make up for anything . . ." Her voice is sarcastic, and it trails off. She holds her red hair out of her face. The warm wind blows around us and becomes even hotter as the 60 pulls up at the stop.

I don't really know what to say, so I force myself to smile as I fish my bus pass out of my backpack pocket. Amelia unzips her messenger bag, takes out a tiny, hot-pink change purse, and finds her fresh, never-been-used pass. We climb the steps, and I walk to an empty seat. She wobbles over as the bus starts to move and sits down next to me. I look out the window and watch the cars and trucks pass by.

The bus ride is short and will be over soon. Out of the corner of my eye, I can see that Amelia is looking at me. I'm sure she wants to make new friends. I mean, nobody wants to be lonely—unless they *have* to be. Unless it's their only choice. So, I take a deep breath and turn to her. "What do you think of Porter?" I ask.

She seems relieved. "It's okay," she says. "I guess it's hard to tell. It seems pretty much like my old school, so far."

I nod. "Where'd you move from?"

"Boston," she says. "My mom got a promotion so we had to move here."

"Oh." I look down at Amelia's hands and try to think of what else to say. Her nails are all chewed up, like mine, and I can feel her body bumping and swaying next to me as the 60 makes its way over the potholed streets. We sit quietly for a couple of minutes, and I pretend to be interested in looking out the window.

"This is where we get off," I tell her when the bus finally slows down. Together, we stand up and walk to the doors. They open, then close behind us. We stand on the corner saying goodbye and see you tomorrow. She heads off down the street.

I cross the street slowly, watching my shoes as I go. Aside from talking about school stuff, that was probably the longest conversation I've had with anyone from Porter since second grade. When I get to the other side, I turn and watch Amelia's back as it disappears into the front door of her building before I walk the rest of the way home.

On the fifteenth floor, I unlock the door to our empty apartment. It's cool inside, and the air conditioning is humming away. I go to my bedroom, close the door, and stand in front of my mirror. My shoulders are sore from carrying my overstuffed, gray backpack, and I watch myself drop it by the foot of my bed.

My bangs cover my white sweatband, and my hair, which hangs just past my ears, has gotten all tangled up in the wind. I take the sweatband off, grab my brush from my desk, and comb through the knots. I put the sweatband back on so it pulls my bangs off my face, like a headband, but I know I can't keep it like that so I take it off altogether and throw it onto the bed as hard as I can. It lands silently. I study my sandy blond hair, thick and straight, and my blue eyes. I'm skinny enough that I seem lost in my shiny, bright yellow basketball pants and T-shirt, but my jaw doesn't look as pointed as it used to, and my shoulders seem more obvious underneath my shirt. I look down at my hands and think of Jack's hands and Uncle Evan's, and then I try to push these thoughts away.

I search the mirror for what I was able to see when I got dressed this morning—the long, shining, golden gown and the girl inside of it—but the image has completely vanished, just like I knew it would, because since sixth grade started, this has happened *every single day*. My imagination doesn't work like it used to. The basketball pants and T-shirt left in the gorgeous gown's place are pathetic.

I can practically hear the blood racing through my veins. Aunt Sally and Uncle Evan told me I used to have gigantic temper tantrums when I first moved here. I would rip the curtains off the windows, throw my desk chair across the room, and break everything I could. Everything, obviously, except for the old toys and pictures on my bookshelf. I'd never hurt those.

The urge to explode is rising in me now. I want to smash something into the mirror until I'm a million pieces on the ground, but I'm stuck in front of my reflection and I tell myself to breathe, to try harder.

I spin in a slow circle and my wide pants legs puff out like sails. I watch myself. They're still pants, and my chest tightens. I spin again, not like a dainty princess, but like a tornado. I'm making myself nauseous and dizzy, but I don't care. And finally, with the wave of a magic wand, with glitter flowing in its trail, in a blur of gold and a rush of hot blood and wind, my clothes transform, the way they have for so many years, into a dress.

I breathe deeply now. I know my pretend dress won't last for long, and tears sting my eyes. I sit at my desk and open the top drawer. The castle in my sketch is almost done, and I sharpen my gray colored pencil, lean over the sketch pad, and shade in the empty spaces. I draw the king and the queen outside in the garden, holding hands, and then, in the top window of the castle, so small that you can barely even see her, I draw the blond princess.

Suddenly, my bedroom door slams open and Jack barges in. I snap my sketch pad shut. I hadn't even heard anyone come home. "Dinner, loser," he announces.

I stand up in a fog. I am Cinderella. I follow my evil stepbrother to the dining room, wearing a golden gown that only I can see.

Chapter 3

THE WARM OCTOBER days fade into plain old November in Chicago. Some of the leaves still cling to the branches outside the tall, freshly cleaned windows at Porter. They're fiery orange, red, and yellow against the gray-white sky. They're like flames dangling from the trees—like something you'd see in a painting.

I'm sitting at my desk, doodling in the margins of my notebook. "We're starting a new novel today," Finn is saying, and I look up to watch him excitedly carry a stack of books to his desk from the bookshelf.

"Are we going to have to write a paper on it?" Lila calls out. She glances around the room, probably to make sure that everyone's watching her. And for the most part, everyone is.

"Great question, Lila, thank you!" Finn says, smiling. "We are!"

Practically the whole class groans.

Meagan, who sits right in front of me, tucks her thin, black hair behind her ears and fixes her eyes on Lila, who is still glancing around the room. Meagan looks interested, but also sort of annoyed. She and Lila have been friends forever. All of a sudden, I wonder what she thinks of her.

"We'll have lots to discuss as we read," Finn continues. "Starting today, all of my classes will be working in pairs for the rest of the quarter. You're the lucky ones who get to rearrange the classroom. Once you're paired up, everyone will have a built-in discussion partner!"

I look up quickly, then down, as my hands get clammy. "So," Finn continues, "everybody up! Find your partners! Once you've pushed your desks together into pairs, I want the pairs lined up in rows!" He's yelling now over the noise of the class. It's like someone broke a piñata, and everyone is frantically searching for candy. Except for me. I stand up slowly, and I don't move. *It's not such a big deal!* I want to scream. But I'm frozen.

I've done this so many times before. Teachers at Porter are always making us choose partners for projects, or choose groups for discussions. By now, I've figured out what to do. I stand still. I watch kids pair up frantically. They look so stupid. I wait. In the end, the teacher will suggest that I join up with Keri or Michael or whoever is left over.

Across the room, Ryan motions for Sebastian to join him, and

Hailey and Lila are already laughing about something as they push their desks together. Amelia is in the middle of the room, looking around nervously. She always sits next to me on the bus now. I'm starting to feel jittery. She says something to Maria and then looks down, her face flushed. She glances around again. It almost looks like she's about to cry.

She starts walking in my direction. Now my heart is racing in my chest. *Nothing* is working for me the way it used to, and all the sounds around me start to disappear, like someone is turning the volume button on the radio almost to off. The only noise I can hear is an annoying hum, and suddenly, it's like I'm watching myself watch the class, as if I'm a bird perched on the high wooden bookshelves lining the classroom walls. I see myself below, biting my lip, clumsily untying the oversize gray sweatshirt from my waist. I watch myself look down and retie it, trying to stretch it so it hangs around my waist completely. I see myself study the small gap in front. The sweatshirt isn't big enough to be a skirt. And, then, from my perch up above, I start to feel like someone's watching *me*, like I'm a bird in a cage. I look over to Finn. He's sitting on his desk, his head cocked to the side. He looks at the sweatshirt around my waist and back up to my eyes.

With a thump, I'm back on the ground. Amelia is standing in front of me. The volume has been switched back on. Desks and chairs scream across the floor.

She looks nervous. "So, do *you* already have a partner, too?" she asks.

"No," I mumble.

"Do you want to pair up, then?" she asks quickly.

I can't think of a reason to say no, so I nod. "Yeah, okay." We push our desks together at the back of the room behind Ryan and Sebastian, and sit down. Finn is dancing around the classroom directing pairs to move six inches this way or that. I smooth out my hair and look down at my nails. I can feel Amelia's eyes on me.

"So, I never see you at lunch," she says. Her voice is loud over the sounds of the classroom, and I cringe. She continues, "Do you have a different lunch period or something?"

In front of us, Ryan and Sebastian grin at each other and turn around. Sebastian adjusts his glasses. "He's eaten lunch in the library since, like, third grade," he says.

I try not to flinch, and I look at Amelia. She's blushing. "Oh," she says quietly.

"I bet he's doing extra homework," Ryan says, smirking. "Like the teachers don't already love him. What a freak." I look back down at my fingernails.

Finn is back in the front of the newly arranged classroom, yelling for our attention. Ryan and Sebastian turn around, and I look up at Amelia out of the corner of my eye. Her cheeks look pink, and she's staring straight ahead.

"We only have a minute left," Finn says once the class is quiet. "Here are your books. Please read chapters one through three tonight." He hands out stacks of novels quickly at the front of the room, counting out the right numbers for each row.

Sebastian passes two books back to me without turning around. I hand one to Amelia, and she puts it into her backpack. I do the same.

The bell rings. Once Ryan and Sebastian are out of earshot, Amelia turns to me. Almost whispering, she says, "I think you should meet me in the lunchroom fifth period. We could eat together."

I think, suddenly, of second grade, before Emma moved away, and of the table in the corner of the lunchroom where we always used to sit. I look at Amelia's round face and dimpled cheeks.

I feel myself stepping out of my skin again. "Okay," I say. I have no control over myself. "I'll meet you there."

Chapter 4

I HAVEN'T SET FOOT in the lunchroom in forever. It's crazy how loud it is. I guess the entire middle school is jammed into one room, so what did I expect? Everyone is crammed in, close together, leaning over tables, throwing brown paper bags, getting up, sitting down, yelling, laughing. The smell of hot lunches and old sandwiches is so disgusting that it's almost unbearable. I look over to where a bunch of seventh graders are sitting, and I scan their faces quickly for Jack, but luckily, I don't see him anywhere.

The ceiling of the lunchroom is high, and long rectangular windows line three sides of the room completely. A flood of blinding light pours in from outside. The noise bounces like a million invisible Ping-Pong balls from the floor to the ceiling to the windows to the tops of the lunch tables over and over again.

I stand in the doorway, feeling completely ill. I wonder where Jack is. The strap of my backpack is cutting into my shoulder, and I can't take it anymore. I turn around to head to the library. But I take one step and walk right into Amelia.

"Good, you came!" she says. "Come on." She steps ahead of me, into the lunchroom. I take one more look around, and I follow her in.

She walks slowly down the aisle in the center of the room, looking carefully at each table she passes until she finally stops when she gets to a pretty empty one near the back of the room. Lila, Meagan, Hannah, and Hailey are sitting toward the middle of the long table, huddled together in a little clump, their lunch bags in front of them and their lunches spread out on the tabletop. "Let's sit here," Amelia says quickly, and she plops her backpack down on the end of the table. "Are you buying lunch?"

I slide onto the bench and unzip my backpack. "No, I brought one." I take out the brown bag that Aunt Sally packed last night.

"Yeah, me too," Amelia says, taking a pink lunch bag out of her backpack. "You couldn't pay me to eat hot lunch." She glances over to the four girls and looks quickly back to me. I peer over at them to see what she's looking at, but they're just sitting there, eating and talking.

"I know," I tell her, and smile a little. I watch her unwrap her sandwich. She takes a bite, and I wonder who she ate with before today. Probably nobody.

My stomach is fluttery and empty feeling. Up through second grade, Emma and I used to eat lunch together every day. Across the room, some eighth-grade boys are sitting at the table near the glass doors where we always used to eat. Looking between them to the empty playground outside makes me think of friendship bracelets made out of colorful yarn and the way Emma would tuck her shirt into her jeans before we'd hang upside down on the jungle gym. I smile to myself thinking about her messy blond hair, red-rimmed glasses, and missing front teeth.

It doesn't feel like I'm supposed to be here, in this loud, crowded room filled with shouting and laughing, but a part of me—the part of me that also wonders how Emma's doing in Florida, if that's even where she still lives—is happy to be back.

I bite into my sandwich, chew slowly, and wonder what to say to Amelia. She's glancing around. Her eyes jump from one group of sixth graders to another. She looks again at Lila, Meagan, Hannah, and Hailey, and smiles this time. When I look over, I see that Lila is waving to her.

Amelia turns back to me, beaming, and takes another bite of her sandwich. "So, it's cool that Finn lets us pick our own groups," she says, her mouth full. "We never got to do anything like that at my old school."

"Yeah," I say, as I dig through my lunch bag for my water bottle. "We always get to do that kind of thing."

"That's awesome," she says, opening her pretzels.

She starts telling me about Boston, and I wonder if she had lots of friends at her old school. It's like I stepped inside a bubble with Amelia. The bright light, noises, and smells bounce off of it.

Amelia is still talking when the lunch monitor gets to our table and tells us to line up at the glass doors for sixth period. It's strange to think that life in the lunchroom went on without me during all the years I was eating by myself in the library. I wonder for another second if I'm making a mistake, but I smile at Amelia anyway, stuff the rest of my lunch into my backpack, and follow her to the double doors.

☆

After school, I watch for Amelia at the bus stop. She shows up a few minutes after me, and we get on the 60 together. We always sit in the same seats now.

"So, what do you do after school?" I blurt out, and immediately look out the window. I don't want to see her reaction.

She doesn't seem fazed. "Nothing. Watch TV, homework. My mom comes home at, like, six, and we have dinner." I picture Amelia alone in her fancy marble apartment, and I feel sorry for her. It seems lonely, and I look at her eyes to see if I can find the sadness.

"Where does your dad live?" I ask.

"Just outside of Boston. I used to go to his house every weekend, but now that we moved I'm going for the summers instead." She says it as if she's telling me about a math assignment, like it's no big deal.

"Do you like him?" I ask.

"He's nice when it's just me and him, but I can't stand his wife and I have two prissy little stepsisters who everyone thinks are perfect." She's talking fast now. "They're five and seven, and they're such brats. And his wife is so whiney and obnoxious. I can't stand them." She spits the last sentence out like it's a piece of old, disgusting gum.

"Oh." I look at her. Her body bounces as the bus bumps along. Her jeans are kind of frumpy, and her arms are folded over her dark pink fleece, like she's trying to hide herself. I envision two perfect little girls in perfect matching outfits, and I am positive that Amelia feels like an outcast. I understand how she feels, and I look out the window again and squeeze my eyes shut.

I think back to all the other kids in the lunchroom, sitting together in clumps, huddled around their own shared secrets. I take a deep breath and turn back to Amelia. "So, do you want to go shopping with me this weekend? There's this great thrift shop in Lake View that I've been wanting to go to."

She looks at me for a second, her head tilted to the side. She seems curious and surprised. "Really?"

"Yeah!" I say. I'm excited, but I catch myself. "Our old nanny used to take us all the time, but I haven't been in forever. I need winter clothes." The bus is slowing to a stop. We stand up, make our way to the door, and jump down. "My aunt and uncle usually just give me money and let me shop by myself. They don't really care what I do." I'm surprised that I say this; I'm not really sure if it's true.

She pauses again and watches my eyes as the bus disappears down the street. She pulls her hair away from her face. "You live with your aunt and uncle?"

"Yeah," I say, jamming my hands into my pockets. I look down the street, away from Amelia. "Listen, I have to get home. Ask your mom if you can come with me. Tomorrow or Sunday. It doesn't matter. Call me. You have the school directory, right?"

"Yeah," she says, still studying me as I turn quickly to cross the street. I run across as the bright hand starts to blink. My giant backpack suddenly feels like two hands collapsing my shoulders. It thuds against my back as I run. The wind has picked up off the lake at the end of the block, and it wails through the tall buildings like the siren on an ambulance. I turn around when I get to the corner and look back at Amelia through my long, windblown bangs. She's still standing where I left her. She raises her hand slowly and gives me a little wave. I smile quickly, then turn and walk home.

Chapter 5

I LET MYSELF into the empty apartment and go straight to my room. I throw my backpack onto my bed as I watch my reflection in the mirror out of the corner of my eye. My black jeans are jeans. My oversize, long-sleeved T-shirt is a T-shirt. The girl in the leggings and dress who I struggled to see this morning was gone by the time I'd finished breakfast. I slam my bedroom door and walk to the kitchen for some cereal. *You're getting way too old to pretend,* I tell myself.

I shove what I wish I saw in the mirror out of my mind and think back, instead, to my conversation with Amelia. I wonder if she'll call me. Maybe I'll have a real friend again. I think, for the first time in forever, of Emma's apartment and how her mom would give us lunch on the kid-size wooden table in her living room. I remember pink plastic bowls of macaroni and cheese, and juice boxes. My body feels strange, like it's someone else's, and I shudder, because I could be making a huge mistake.

I bring my cereal to my room, avoiding the mirror this time. Instead, I pull out my sketch pad and colored pencils, and focus on the field of flowers that I'm working on. I draw the flowers on their stems—each one different from the one next to it. I think about adding two girls in the middle of the field, but I hear the front door click open and Jack and Brett talking, so I slide the drawing into my drawer, take my math book out of my backpack, and start my homework instead. I glance at the clock. Aunt Sally and Uncle Evan will be home soon, too.

There's a knock on my door, and Brett pokes his head in. "Hi, Grayson," he says through the crack. "Whatcha doing? I need to show you something."

"Cool, what is it?" I ask, putting down my pencil. He walks over to me until our noses are practically touching, and he opens his mouth. "You guess," he says as best he can with his mouth open wide. "What's different?"

I peer inside. "Looks like there's a tooth missing," I say. He grins and pulls a tiny red plastic treasure chest out from his pocket. He pries it open to show me. I remember getting the same thing from the nurse's office at school when I was younger. "That's awesome," I tell him even though the tooth looks gross. "Don't lose it."

He snaps the treasure chest shut. "I won't." He shoves it back into his pocket and walks over to my bookcase. "Can I?" he asks. I nod. He picks up my old brown teddy bear and the small greenish one, and jumps onto my bed with them.

"What's Jack doing?" I ask him, and he shrugs as he adjusts the T-shirt on the brown bear. Probably lying on the couch with his eyes closed, listening to music again.

I do my math problems while Brett plays on my bed. Eventually, I hear the front door open and close, and then dinnertime noises. Uncle Evan is talking to Jack. "Don't you have homework?" he's asking, and Aunt Sally is saying something about setting the table.

Brett puts the bears back onto the shelf carefully, right next to my old picture books, and we walk to the dining room. White boxes of Chinese takeout are scattered on the gleaming glass table. Uncle Evan asks us how school was and did we do our homework—the same questions every day. I sit next to Brett and start opening containers as he shows Aunt Sally, Uncle Evan, and Jack his treasure chest and the hole in his mouth.

"Make sure you put that tooth under the pillow for the tooth fairy," Uncle Evan reminds Brett as Jack rolls his eyes.

"Jack," Aunt Sally warns, shooting him a look. "So," she says, "aside from Brett finally losing his tooth, did anything exciting happen today?" She pauses, looking at us expectantly, but no one answers. Her eyes look tired. "Hey, Ev," she says like she just remembered something, "my prediction about Felix and that brief was absolutely right on. Can you believe that?"

"I can," Uncle Evan responds. "So, what happened?"

And they go on, discussing some legal situation while Brett shows me how he can poke his straw into the new window in the side of his mouth and drink his milk through it. Eventually, he almost spills, and Uncle Evan makes him stop. I stare out the floor-to-ceiling windows at Amelia's building and the darkening sky.

Aunt Sally is stacking our plates into a pile when the phone rings. Jack jumps up and darts into the kitchen.

"Hello?" he asks. There's a pause, and he comes around the corner into the dining room with the phone to his ear. He has a giant, annoying grin plastered on his stupid face. "Who's calling?" he asks, his eyes sparkling. "One moment please," he sings, in a phony, polite voice.

He keeps the phone next to his face. "Um, Grayson, it seems your girlfriend, Amelia, is calling?"

I jump up. "Shut up, Jack," I say. I hold out my hand for the phone. He isn't budging. I look at Aunt Sally and Uncle Evan for help, but they're just looking back and forth between me and Jack, shocked.

"Jack, is it really for Grayson?" Uncle Evan finally asks.

Jack grins. "I'm serious; it is!"

"So why aren't you giving it to him?" Brett asks, and Uncle Evan startles.

"Yes, Jack, just hand him the phone," Uncle Evan says, glancing over at Aunt Sally, who now has a pleased smile on her face.

Jack extends his arm slowly, and I snatch the phone from his hand. I walk to my room and sit on the edge of my bed.

"Hello?" I almost whisper.

"Hi, it's me, Amelia," she says. "Who was that?"

"Just my cousin Jack. Ignore him. He's a complete jerk."

"Yeah, seriously," Amelia says. "How old is he? Does he go to Porter? Did you tell him I'm not your girlfriend?"

"What?" I ask.

"He called me your girlfriend. Did you tell him I wasn't?"

"Oh—no, I will," I say.

"Okay." She pauses. "Grayson?"

"Yeah?" I realize I'm holding the phone to my ear with both hands.

"So, I'm free tomorrow. What time do you want to go?"

"You can go?"

"Yeah, but my mom wants to know what time the bus leaves and where exactly we're going."

I smile. "Okay! Great! We can leave whenever you want. The express buses run all the time on the weekends. It's in Lake View, on the corner of Broadway and Belmont. I don't know the exact address, but I can find out. It's called the Second Hand. Want me to look it up?"

"No, that's okay. I'll tell her. Do you want to meet at the bus stop at ten?"

"Yeah, that's perfect!" I say.

"Okay, see you tomorrow."

"Great. Bye."

I end the call and sit back down on my bed for a minute, beaming. I stay that way until I feel up to explaining to Aunt Sally and Uncle Evan that I have plans with a friend for the first time since second grade.

Chapter 6

I ZIP MY dark purple sweatshirt to my chin and put up the hood to block out the Chicago wind as I head for the bus stop. I glance down at my wide, gray, shiny track pants. The foggy image of the skirt that I saw in the mirror this morning is already flickering and fading. I think I can feel Aunt Sally, Uncle Evan, Jack, and Brett watching me from the living room window fifteen floors up, but I don't turn around to check.

Amelia is making her way down the street, and I try to forget that my pants are still pants as I wave to her and smile. Her chin is buried in the neck of a red peacoat. I really should have worn something warmer. It's freezing out.

"Hi!" I say as she joins me under the glass enclosure. Her eyes look pink. "Do you have a cold or something?" Then I realize that she's been crying, and I feel like an idiot. She takes a crumpled, used-looking piece of tissue out of her pocket and blows her nose.

She takes a deep breath. "Sometimes I just hate my mom," she says, blowing her nose again. She shoves the tissue and her hands into her pockets.

"Oh," I say. It's like the words are nothing to her. *My mom.* I look at her blotchy face, and for a second, I try to imagine what it would be like to be able to hate your mom, but I don't even want to think about it. "Why?" I finally force myself to ask.

"She's just constantly hounding me about the way I look. She was so excited when I told her I was going shopping. She was like, 'Be sure to get some tops to flatter your figure.' She may as well just tell me I'm fat and ugly." She sits down on the bench and slouches forward.

"That's ridiculous," I tell her. "That's so obnoxious." I search for the right words, but I don't know exactly what to say.

"Whatever," she says. "It doesn't matter. I'm used to it."

The bus pulls up. We sit in the back. She takes a deep breath and pushes her hair out of her face.

"So, why do you live with your aunt and uncle?" she asks as the bus starts to move.

I feel like I've been hit from behind by a wave of lava, and even though I'm still freezing, I'm suddenly sweating. I'm an idiot for not knowing the question was coming, for not rehearsing. I know I can't avoid answering. *This is what having friends means,* I tell myself.

I haven't had to talk about it for so long—not since Aunt Sally and Uncle Evan made me do those sessions with that stupid therapist in fourth grade. I think about his office and the paintings and drawings on the walls that other kids made for him in his "art studio." What losers, I remember thinking. What pushovers. What could this guy possibly be doing for them that's so great? The thought made me furious then, and it makes me furious now. *You need to stop isolating yourself at school,* he used to tell me. He didn't know anything about me.

But maybe Amelia could. She's studying me. I have to say something, so I take a deep breath, stare at the seat in front of me, and start to talk.

"When I was four, my parents died," I tell her. I talk fast. "We lived in Cleveland. There was a car accident. It was really bad. It was on the highway. There was this truck that swerved into their lane, and they were killed instantly." I glance at her quickly. She's staring at me, and I look down at my feet, at my dark blue gym shoes that are almost purple. "I was at preschool when it happened."

I feel like I'm reading from a storybook, and I want to slam it closed now and throw it out the window like it's on fire. I look at Lake Michigan. The waves are white and wild next to the gray highway. Two trucks fly past us. I realize I'm not breathing, and I force myself to.

"Oh," Amelia says quietly.

I stare at the dust and dirt that's shoved into the crevice around the metal window frame next to me, and for some reason,

I think of my old blue house. I don't remember it, but I have a picture of it on the bookshelf in my room. There's a FOR SALE sign on the front lawn with one of those SOLD banners crossing over it. Uncle Evan told me that he tried to get the real estate lady to take the sign down for the picture, but she said it was too much trouble. I don't know why, but I wonder about the people who bought it. I wonder if they painted it, or if the house is still blue.

"It was bad," I say. "But I don't remember it at all. My uncle Evan is my dad's brother, so I came to live with them."

"Oh my God," she says, and then she's quiet again. It seems like I should say something else.

"My grandma Alice lives here, too. She's really sick now. Anyway, I guess it made sense for me to come to Chicago."

"Oh my God," she says again, and I don't know what else to say.

For a while, both of us are quiet. I watch out the window as the bus pulls off the highway. "So have you been to Lake View?" I finally ask her as we slow down at the bus stop, thankful to have something else to talk about.

"What? No," she says, as she follows me off the bus. We stand at the corner in a crowd of people. "Maybe I should consider myself lucky," she says as we cross the street. She stares straight ahead as she talks. Her long, red hair is blowing across her cheek.

"I guess so," I say.

"I mean, maybe I don't have it as bad as I thought."

I look at her round, solid face, and I open the door of the

Second Hand. She walks in, up the sloped wooden floor that looks like it has survived a thousand floods, between the circular racks of clothes, and toward the YOUTH sign that hangs crookedly at the back of the store. I follow her.

A guy behind the counter with a shaved head, earrings, and a nose ring says hey to me as I pass him. Two women dressed in black layers and wearing bright lipstick sift through the clothes on a rack.

We're the only ones in the back of the store. There are fewer racks of clothes back here, and the back door is cracked open so the air isn't quite as thick with the scent of mothballs, which is good because the smell makes me want to vomit. To the side are three minuscule dressing rooms with old bedsheets for doors and a giant mirror is propped against the wall. I stand in front of it and study my skinny body. My purple hood is still up and I take it down, unzip my sweatshirt, and run my fingers through my hair. I push my bangs carefully to the side of my forehead. My eyes sting from the cold air outside, my nose is pink, and I notice again how my chin looks squarer and less pointed than it used to.

Uncle Evan has shown me pictures of Dad when he was my age, and I know I look like him. The thought makes me want to smash the mirror. I shove my fists into my pockets because what I *really* want is for Dad to be here, and I wonder for the millionth time if I'd still have to be this lonely if Mom and Dad were alive. In old black-and-white pictures, Grandma Alice looks just like

Mom did. I search my face in the mirror for any hint of her or Mom in me, but I can only see Dad.

I quickly walk to where Amelia is browsing in the girls' section. Her coat is in a neat pile on the floor near one of the dressing room doors, and she's searching through a rack labeled GIRLS' DRESSES AND SKIRTS in messy writing on a laminated sign. "What do you think of this one?" she asks, pulling out a deep purple, floor-length skirt. The fabric is thin and scrunched, like an accordion, and is interrupted three times by bands of deep purple lace. The lace pulls the fabric in and makes soft swells. I stare at it.

"It's great," I say, and I reach out to touch the fabric.

"Are you looking for anything?" Amelia asks. She quickly drapes the skirt over her arm. "I thought you needed winter clothes."

"Oh, yeah," I say, and walk to the boys' racks, still watching her out of the corner of my eye. I filter through the hangers, but really I pay attention to Amelia on the other side of the room. She's collecting a pile of clothes—deep pinks and purples, laces and embroidered flowers, and they're draped over her arm like shimmery gowns from a fairy tale.

The clothes I run my fingers over are way less majestic. I search halfheartedly for shirts that are narrow but extra long, colorful plaids, and bright fabrics. I pull out a green, metallic-looking Green Bay Packers jersey. The sleeves glisten in the artificial light, and I walk to the mirror with it and hold it in front of my chest. It's too long, and would come down almost to my knees. I could ignore the lettering on it. With my old jeans that are too tight now, I could imagine it's a sparkling dress over leggings.

"What'd you find?" Amelia asks, walking over to me with her soft pile of clothing still hanging tenderly over her arm.

I study the image of the football jersey in the mirror. *Green Bay Packers* screams at me from the chest. "Ah, nothing," I say, and hang it on the rack closest to me. "It's too big." My imagination is failing me. I'm way too old to play dress-up. I look down at my feet. My purplish blue shoes look completely blue in the bright lights.

"Are you sure?" Amelia asks. "Do you want to try it on? I'm going to try these on."

"Nah," I say, taking a deep breath. "It's okay. It's hit or miss in secondhand shops. They don't have much in my size this time."

"Okay," she says, walking away. She lets herself into a dressing room, and I sit on a stiff, metal chair next to the mirrors where I don't have to look at myself. I study the scratches on the wood floor. Amelia comes out to examine how she looks in each new dress, skirt, and top. She stares at herself for a long time in the purple skirt. "I don't know," she says, cocking her head to the side. "Do people at Porter wear things like this?"

I sit up straight and look at her carefully. "I mean, not all the time," I tell her. "But I think it's fantastic."

In the end, she puts it back on the rack. She buys a shorter black skirt with a flouncy ribbon around the bottom and a white T-shirt with flowers embroidered around the neck. I am empty-handed as we leave the store. I didn't realize it had started to rain while we were inside. I pull up my hood against the drizzle, and we board the bus for home.

Chapter 7

AMELIA AND I go to the Second Hand every Saturday in November. She tries on clothes and sometimes finds something to buy. Unexcitedly, I search the boys' racks. One windy morning, I give up on the idea of finding anything I'll like. I leave Amelia behind and walk away from the boys' section to the shelves of knickknacks at the front of the store.

"Who buys this stuff?" Amelia asks, suddenly by my side.

"Are you done shopping?"

"Yeah, they don't have anything good today." Amelia runs her hands over dusty vases and grimy statues of sleeping cats and prancing horses.

"Hey, look at this!" I pick up an old golden birdcage with a blue plastic bird on a perch inside. I turn it around in my hands. On the side is the thing to wind it with.

I twist the knob and put it back on the shelf. Amelia and I stand there. For a minute nothing happens, but then the bird slowly starts to flap its dusty, feathered wings, like it's finally waking up from a super-long nap. Old-fashioned, rusty-sounding music chimes. The notes are creaky and uneven, and the fluttering becomes jerkier as Amelia and I watch. It looks like the bird is trying to fly through glue, but its wings keep getting stuck. We glance at each other, and Amelia starts to giggle.

Suddenly, the bird freezes, its wings outstretched, and, in slow motion, it tips over and falls off its metal perch. Amelia grabs my arm. "Oh my God, I think we broke it," she whispers, fixing her mouth into a frown, trying hard not to laugh. The bird is lying on the floor of the cage, one of its wings still twitching, as the music continues to ping. It almost looks like the bird is trying to get up and fly away.

It's kind of depressing to see it lying there like that, but I smile at Amelia anyway. "Let's get out of here!" she whispers, laughing. I look behind me. The man at the register is staring at us. Amelia is hysterical now, and I quickly drag her outside. I can hear the still-dying chirps of tinny music until the door clicks shut behind us.

Outside, the cold air is sharp. Amelia collapses in laughter on the concrete steps of the Second Hand, and I sit down next to her. I guess it's stupid to feel bad for a plastic bird, and watching

Amelia laugh so hard makes me start to laugh, too. "We totally broke it," she finally says, trying to compose herself.

"Come on," I say, standing up, still laughing. "It's freezing. Want to get hot chocolate? There's a coffee shop down the street." I grab her hands and pull her up.

When we get to the coffee shop, she saves us two seats at the bar by the window while I order our hot chocolates and a marshmallow square to share. We hold the paper cups in our freezing hands. Our reflections are pale and blotchy in the giant window. The people walking on the sidewalk pass through them. They're so close that we could touch them if the wall of glass wasn't there.

Amelia takes the lid off of her paper cup and dunks a piece of marshmallow square in. I watch her and do the same thing. "Next Saturday, I'll take you to this other coffee shop a few blocks that way," I tell her, pointing out the window. "Our nanny used to take us all the time. They have way better snacks."

"Cool," she says, as she swivels back and forth on her stool and smiles.

☆

Back home, Aunt Sally looks up from her laptop when I let myself into the front door. "Grayson," she says, lifting her reading glasses onto her head. She puts the laptop next to her. "How was your morning with Amelia?"

"It was great," I say.

"I'm so glad." Aunt Sally smiles at me and then looks down at her fingernails for a second.

"Grayson, honey?" she says, looking back up, her face serious now. "Your uncle Evan is planning to go over to the nursing home. He got a call from Adele when you were out. Your grandma . . ." She pauses and tilts her head softly to the side. My heart jumps. "Well, you know she's been more and more confused, lately. And Adele said she took a nap this morning and when she woke up, she had a fever. The doctors are worried that she might have pneumonia."

"Oh," I say, and I feel sort of guilty because I should be thinking of Grandma Alice, sick in her bed at the nursing home, but I'm not. She's had Alzheimer's for practically as long as I can remember. I'm thinking instead of the black-and-white picture on my nightstand of me, Mom, and Dad. You can only see our faces, but you can tell that Mom was tickling me. My back is smushed into her, and I'm laughing. Dad's arm is around us both.

"'Kay," I say. I know I sound nervous, and I can tell Aunt Sally is waiting for me to say more, but my brain feels stuck. I don't feel like standing there anymore, and I head for my room.

A few minutes later, Uncle Evan quietly taps on my door. He lets himself in and sits on my bed. I'm standing in front of the mirror tying my hooded sweatshirt around my waist. I'm trying to see it as a purple skirt, but I can't focus. I keep thinking again of how in all the pictures I have of Mom, she looks like a young version of Grandma Alice.

"Grayson?" Uncle Evan starts.

"Yeah?"

"Why don't you come with me to the home to see your grandma?" I give up on the sweatshirt and throw it onto my bed. It lands on my pillow next to the picture on my nightstand. Uncle Evan and Aunt Sally aren't even related to Grandma Alice. They wouldn't be taking care of her if it weren't for me.

"Okay," I say.

"Good. Do you think you can be ready in fifteen minutes or so?" he asks. I nod, and he drums his fingers on his knees as I sit down at my desk chair. I pull my colored pencils and sketch pad out of the top drawer and stare at my half-finished drawing of a rose bush. I hate the nursing home. It's so depressing.

"So, Grayson," Uncle Evan finally says, "Aunt Sally and I were talking last night. We want you to know how glad we are that you've made a new friend. You seem happier now that you're hanging around with Amelia, and we think it's really fantastic." He smiles. "Did I ever tell you that your Aunt Sally and I met when we were in sixth grade?"

"Really?" I ask, but then I look down quickly. I know what he's getting at. "It's not like that," I tell him. "We're just friends."

"Of course," he stammers. "I didn't mean . . ."

"It's okay," I tell him, and I smile to try to make him feel better. In pictures of Mom, you can see that she had the same wrinkles on the sides of her eyes that Grandma Alice has. Once, a long, long time ago, Grandma Alice told me they were matching smile wrinkles. I reach up and touch the side of my face, but it's smooth.

"Well, okay, then," Uncle Evan says, getting up off my bed. He stops behind me on his way to the door and pauses, placing his hand on my shoulder as I pick up a red colored pencil.

"Really, son, we're glad you're happier." I cringe. He gives my shoulder a little squeeze. "I'll let you know when I'm ready." He shuts the door quietly and completely behind him.

☆

Even though the nursing home is supposedly a nice one, it's gross, and it smells like rubbing alcohol, Band-Aids, and old people. In the elevator there's a nurse and an old man with a walker. I try not to stare at him. He's trying to talk, but no words are coming out. It's like he's chewing on air, and my eyes sting.

We walk down the long hallway to Grandma Alice's room. Inside, everything is the same as it has always been, only this time instead of sitting in the rocking chair next to the window, smoothing out the blanket on her lap over and over again, Grandma Alice is in her bed. The back is propped up, and someone attached the metal rails to the sides. Her eyes are open but I can tell that she's not looking at anything.

Uncle Evan and I stand next to her for a minute. "Hi, Grandma," I say, but she doesn't answer and Uncle Evan puts his hand on my shoulder again. Adele reaches over and gently picks up Grandma Alice's arm so she can wrap the blood pressure cuff around it. She takes her blood pressure, writes something on a clipboard, and then she and Uncle Evan start to talk.

I wander around the room. "She still hasn't eaten. . . ." I hear Adele start to say. I try to ignore them, but it's hard to in such a small room.

I look at the pictures on Grandma Alice's dresser. They're kind of dusty and I wipe them off on my shirt one by one as Adele keeps talking to Uncle Evan in a hushed voice. "Her symptoms definitely point to pneumonia," she's saying. Grandma Alice has the same photo as I do of our blue house in Cleveland. Mom and Dad met in Chicago and moved to Cleveland just before I was born so Mom could take a job teaching at the university. I wonder again what my life would be like if she hadn't gotten that job and they'd stayed in Chicago. And I wonder again about the house, if it's still blue.

I pick up a picture of me with Grandpa Lefty. He died when I was two. I'm sitting on his lap on the front porch of their old house in just a diaper. There's a black-and-white picture of Grandma Alice when she was a baby with dimpled cheeks, short bangs, and a round belly, and one of Grandma Alice and Grandpa Lefty on their wedding day.

Then I pick up my favorites: Mom riding a bike when she was about my age, her eyes squinting in the sun and a shirt tied around her waist, floating behind her in the breeze; Mom and Dad kissing in front of their wedding cake; and the one of me as a baby, mostly hidden under a blanket, lying on Mom's chest.

"I don't think it will be long now, but you know Alice—she's a fighter," Adele says as I drift back over to them. Grandma Alice is sitting in the same position, but now her eyes are closed, and she's breathing deeply and kind of raggedly.

"Well," Uncle Evan says. Gently, he straightens the blanket on Grandma Alice's lap and doesn't say anything else. A clump of her white hair has fallen over her face, and I braid it loosely and tuck it behind her ear so it won't unravel. I can feel Uncle Evan watching me as I pick up her soft, bumpy, paper-thin hand. The skin droops between the bones, like a row of tiny bridges. Mom grew inside of her, I think to myself, and I replay the feel of her skin on my hand the whole way home.

Chapter 8

IT'S DREARY on Monday morning. Finn is standing in front of the windows, trying to start a discussion as gentle snow swirls outside behind him. I watch him, my chin resting in my hands. Amelia is doodling lazily on the cover of her notebook next to me, and I'm thinking of Grandma Alice's room—of the dusty pictures and the hospital bed. And of what Adele said.

Finn keeps asking the class questions, but nobody's talking. "Okay," he finally sighs, "enough of this! You obviously don't want to talk to me. Everybody, stay with your partner and pair up with another group to make a foursome. You guys can discuss the passages from the book in small groups. Remember, next Monday I'll be assigning your big papers, so stay focused!"

Everybody, including Amelia, starts looking around nervously.

"Go ahead," Finn says, hoisting himself up onto the window ledge, looking amused. "Let the mad dash for partners commence!"

I pick up my book and backpack, and follow Amelia's lead. Her eyes are fixed on Lila and Hailey across the room, and she walks quickly over to them. I feel like a dog on a leash following her.

"Hey, guys," she says, approaching them. "Can we join you?"

Lila glances across the room to where Meagan and Hannah are already sitting with two other girls, their backs to us. "Sure," she says, after a second.

"Pull up Jason's and Asher's chairs," Hailey adds, smiling. We sit down, and I turn my chair so I don't have to look at Ryan and Sebastian, who are at the desks right next to us.

"So, what do you guys think of these passages?" Lila asks, looking at the three of us. Of course she wants us to do all the work.

"I thought the second one Finn was talking about was the most interesting," Hailey says, flipping back in her book to find it.

I watch her as she searches through the pages. The summer before third grade, I did art camp with her and Hannah. I remember stringing beads onto pieces of elastic with them at the playground. By then, Emma was already gone. I suddenly wonder why I didn't stay friends with them once third grade started; I suddenly wonder why Emma was the *only* one.

"Here it is!" Hailey says. "Page fifty." I flip to it in my book. She starts to read but I barely listen.

At art camp, sometimes we'd go to the park with our little easels and paints. I remember kids making paintings of the swing set, the giant trees, and the flowers and vegetables that some other camp groups had planted. This one time Hannah and Hailey and I were painting together at the edge of the garden. I was trying to make a gigantic orange tiger lily with watercolors, but both of them just wanted to paint these little sprouts that were poking through the dirt.

I look at the tiny freckles on Hailey's nose as she finishes the passage. When she's done, she takes off her turquoise head-band and runs her fingers through her light brown hair. Then she puts it back in, making tiny, delicate comb marks, collecting the wisps.

I touch my sweatband on my forehead and take it off as Amelia starts writing down notes in big, loopy handwriting. I turn the sweatband around in my hands. It's grayish-white with sweat stains. I try to imagine it's turquoise, but it's still grayish-white and disgusting.

I think back to fifth grade when all I had to do was *pretend* and everything would be okay.

Outside the window, the powdering of snow is still making its way down to the ground, and Finn is still perched on the win-dow ledge. His eyes wander to the sweatband in my hand. He smiles gently when our eyes meet. I look away and put it back on. Finally, he hops down and makes his way around the classroom to listen in on everyone's discussions. When the bell rings, we pack up our stuff. "So," Lila says, looking mostly at Amelia, "you should sit with us at lunch." She stands up and straightens her pink shirt under her backpack straps.

I look to Amelia quickly. "Okay, great!" she says, smiling up at Lila.

I swallow hard and Lila looks at me. "You, too, Grayson," she adds. "If you want."

I look from her to Amelia, nod and smile. "Okay," I say.

"Great," Amelia adds, beaming. "We'll see you fifth period."

☆

At lunchtime, Amelia and I sit with the girls in the middle of the table. We spread our lunches out in front of us. The table-top is crowded with water bottles and half-filled plastic bags. Hannah takes a rubber band off her wrist and gathers her curly brown hair into a ponytail. She glances at me for a second and smiles. I wonder if she still paints, and I almost ask her, but I don't. Amelia rests her elbows on the table next to me as she talks to Lila. Meagan bounces her knee across from mine. She almost seems a little bored. Even though I'm happy to be sitting here, I can't stop thinking about how weird it must look from the outside—five girls and a boy.

We sit with them every day that week, but I hardly say anything. It kind of surprises me to hear all of them, but espe-cially Lila and Amelia, gossiping about kids from our class. I wonder if, before Amelia and I joined them, they ever used to talk about me.

☆

On Friday after dinner, the phone rings. It's Amelia.

"Hey, Grayson," she says. "Do you mind if we don't go to Lake View tomorrow? It turns out there's something else I have to do."

I swallow hard. "Oh. That's okay," I tell her, trying not to sound disappointed, as I walk quickly to my room with the phone. I close my door. "Do you want to go Sunday instead?"

There's a pause. "Um, I think my mom said my aunt and uncle are coming to town to visit us on Sunday, but I'm not sure."

"I guess we could just go next weekend," I tell her.

"Okay," Amelia says. "Sorry about that. So, have a good weekend. I'll see you at school, okay?" I lean back on my bed.

"Sure, great," I tell her, staring at my blinding white ceiling. We say good-bye, and I hang up and throw the phone onto my pillow. I try to tell myself it's not a big deal, it's just one weekend, but disappointment settles over me like icy snow. I look at the bird in Mom's painting. I try to focus on it to keep myself from crying.

Chapter 9

IT TURNS OUT that I wouldn't have been able to go with her anyway. The next morning, Uncle Evan comes in just as I'm waking up to tell me that Grandma Alice is dead. "Adele told me that she went very peacefully in her sleep," he says as he sits on the edge of my bed.

"Oh," I say, because I can't think of anything else. I think of her soft hands and blue eyes.

"I just got off the phone with the funeral home. We'll bury her tomorrow. Okay?" he says, watching me carefully. I feel like I should be doing something, like crying, but all I can do is nod.

Uncle Evan waits for a minute before saying, "Okay," one more time. "So, if you don't want to talk, I guess I'll give you a little space. Aunt Sally and I are in the dining room if you need us." He gets up and watches me for a few more seconds before gently closing my door.

I look at Mom's smiling face in the picture next to me. Her hair is blowing around her cheeks. On my bookshelf with my old toys and books from Cleveland are the framed pictures: the blue house, Dad holding me outside of my preschool, Mom pushing me in a swing at a park. I get out of bed and look at them, one by one. I keep waiting to feel sad about Grandma Alice, but I can only think of Mom's face, and how, if she got to be a grandma, she probably would have looked just like Grandma Alice did.

The truth is that Grandma Alice had been pretty confused for as long as I could remember. It had been years since we really talked when I visited her. Mostly I'd just sit in her rocking chair and draw while she wiped down the clean countertops over and over again.

I guess there *were* those really thin lemon cookies that we used to eat together at her kitchen table when I was younger. I remember them now. And the narrow tin of freshly sharpened colored pencils that Adele always had ready for me. And there was the way the sunlight would come through the thin, waving curtains in the summertime when the windows were open. The gross nursing home smell would blow away, and the light would paint waves on the dark blue rug. They would move whenever the wind rustled the curtains. I used to bring my stuffed animals in my backpack, and Grandma Alice and I would sit in the middle of the waves and pretend my teddy bears were swimming all the way across a rough, giant ocean.

I'd kind of forgotten about that until now.

I don't want to go to the funeral, but in the end, Aunt Sally and Uncle Evan convince me that it will be okay. It's freezing at the cemetery and the sky is gray. I stand between them in the swirling snow and watch Grandma Alice disappear into the ground.

Chapter 10

ON MONDAY MORNING I sit in Humanities, organizing my notebooks and folders and watching everyone file in. I keep thinking about Grandma Alice's coffin being lowered into the dark hole. I'm looking for Amelia, and finally, just as the bell is about to ring, she walks in with Lila. I wave to her, but she doesn't see me. The two of them are too busy talking and smiling at each other, and, as they come closer, I notice that they're wearing almost identical outfits.

Their sweaters and skirts are crisp and new looking. The skirts flow to the ground, and the deep-red fabric looks bright against their black Uggs, especially Amelia's brand-new ones. The skirts are made of thin, gathered fabric that swishes and flows as they walk, and looking at them makes me remember

Grandma Alice's curtains in the summertime. And the purple skirt at the Second Hand.

I stare at my fingernails as Amelia walks over to our desks. I think of her phone call and how she said there was *something else* she had to do on Saturday. My brain races faster than my mouth can work. "Hey, Amelia" is all I can manage to get out.

"Hi!" She's whispering now under Finn's voice. "Did you have a good weekend?"

How could she just ditch me for Lila and then pretend that nothing is wrong? I'd been planning to tell her about Grandma Alice, but I just force a smile and nod. Luckily, I don't have to talk anymore because Finn is telling us that he's giving us quiet, independent work time all week since our big papers are due on Friday.

I take out my notebook, but I can't concentrate. I wonder if Amelia and Lila will spend every Saturday together from now on. I'll be stuck at home, doing nothing, just like before. And now I can't even go to the stupid nursing home to visit Grandma Alice. I think about the funeral, about how it was only the five of us and Adele there, and I realize that I'm the only person left from Mom's side of the family.

I feel like I'm disappearing.

Once fifth period comes, I know I can't go to the lunchroom. The thought of listening to everyone talk about their weekends and sitting there with Amelia and Lila in their matching skirts— the skirt that Amelia ditched me to buy—seems completely unbearable. I turn toward the library instead.

Walking through the wooden library doors at lunchtime feels strange, but also familiar. Mrs. Millen looks surprised to see me. She's sitting at her desk, eating a steaming bowl of some sort of Weight Watchers meal, just like she's been doing for years.

She puts her fork down when I walk in. "Hi, Grayson!" she says, studying my face. "Are you back to have lunch with me today?" She takes a sip of her Diet Coke.

"Yeah," I mumble, and hoist my backpack onto a desk. I sit at the empty cubicle next to it and unzip the outside pocket. I'm not hungry, but I take out my lunch bag anyway and let it thump onto the desk. I rest my chin in my hands and avoid Mrs. Millen's gaze. I wonder if the girls will ask one another where I am, and if they'll even care that I'm not there. Maybe they'll be glad I'm gone: the freak boy who eats with the girls. Amelia was probably just hanging out with me this whole time until she could find *better* friends—*girl* friends. I'm such an idiot.

I try to calm myself down. *It's not a big deal,* I tell myself. *You've eaten in here for years.* I stare at the cubicle walls where kids have carved their names into the wood. I never understood what would make someone do something like that, but suddenly, I want to take out a pen and do it, too. I picture the carving, *Grayson was here,* and I unzip my pencil bag and glance over at Mrs. Millen. She's still watching me curiously and she gives me a little wave, so I zip the pencil bag back up and squeeze my hands between my knees.

There's old tape stuck onto a wall of the cubicle in the shape of a smiley face. A wad of pink gum is shoved into one of the corners, and, right in front of me, hangs a crooked flyer. I look at it. MIDDLE SCHOOL SPRING PLAY TRYOUTS! it says in red computer print. There's a dumb picture of an opera singer underneath the heading. I keep reading.

WHEN? MONDAY AND TUESDAY, DECEMBER 15TH AND 16TH, 3:15–5:30.

WHERE? AUDITORIUM

WHAT? *THE MYTH OF PERSEPHONE*

SIGN UP FOR TRYOUTS OUTSIDE OF MR. FINNEGAN'S OFFICE

COME ONE, COME ALL!

I stare at the flyer. We learned about the Greek gods in fifth grade. Aunt Sally and I made flash cards together before my test, with the gods on one side and a description of each one on the other. I think the myth of Persephone is the one about how the seasons were created, but I can't remember for sure.

My mind wanders to the kids who have always done the plays and musicals at Porter—mostly older kids who are seventh and eighth graders now. Then I think about the quiet, kind of weird kids who do crew. I can picture them sneaking around behind the scenes dressed in black, invisible. Maybe I could do crew. But my mind shifts back to all the plays I've seen, to the spotlight, the deep burgundy velvet curtain and the solid, wooden stage. And to how it might feel to have everyone watching you.

I picture Amelia sitting at the lunch table this very second, laughing at every stupid thing that Lila says, and then I picture the empty place next to her, where I sat. I feel like a ghost.

I stand up, grab my uneaten lunch, and throw my backpack over my shoulder. I burst through the doors into the empty hallway, leaving Mrs. Millen and her Weight Watchers meal behind me.

The hallway on the fourth floor is dark and empty. Finn's office is the first one on my right and a piece of paper is taped neatly to the closed door. TRYOUT LIST FOR *THE MYTH OF PERSEPHONE* is printed along the top. I scan the list quickly for an open slot until I get to the very end. The last line is the only one that's empty: 5:15–5:30 on Tuesday.

A blunt pencil is dangling from a piece of yarn that's taped to the sign-up sheet. I pick it up and dig my fingernails into the worn, yellow paint. I study the imprint of my nail—proof that I'm still here—and write *Grayson Sender* on the line. When I drop the pencil, it sways like the pendulum on Aunt Sally and Uncle Evan's grandfather clock as I walk away.

☆

I watch for Amelia at the bus stop after school. Eventually, I see her walking quickly over to me, her skirt bright against the thin layer of snow covering the ground.

"Hey, Grayson," she says, her breath thick in the icy air. "God, it's freezing out. Where were you at lunch today?" I study her face as she tucks her hair behind her pinkish ears. She's so clueless.

"I just had a lot of homework," I tell her, hiding my frozen hands in my jacket sleeves. "I went to the library." I can't bring myself to say anything more.

"Oh," she says. "Were you working on the Humanities paper? That's going to take forever to write."

"Yup," I say, relieved to have the excuse. "I might go to the library all week to work on it."

The bus pulls up, and Amelia and I get on. She runs her fingers over the creases in her skirt as we bounce along. At the Randolph stop, we say good-bye. I cross the street and don't look back.

☆

That night, I'm jittery. I've never tried out for anything before, and I have no idea what I'll be asked to do the next day. In first grade, our class put on *The Lorax*. Everyone had a part, and Emma and I were pink trees. I don't remember much about it except for the two of us standing together in the background. This play won't be anything like that.

Jack used to do the plays in elementary school. He's supposed to be helping Brett with his homework, but he's watching TV in the living room. I guess I could ask him about tryouts, but I don't want to. Aunt Sally and Uncle Evan are downstairs in our storage room organizing the boxes of Grandma Alice's stuff from the nursing home, so I can't ask them. Anyway, I don't feel like telling them I'm auditioning, so I just pull out my sketch pad and try to concentrate on my drawing.

The next morning, as Finn promised, we have the double period to work on our papers. I wonder if he noticed my name on the tryout list. I know I should speak up and just ask him what I'm going to have to do. So when the bell finally rings, I leave Amelia packing her things and stop in front of his desk.

"Grayson," he says, "I was just about to ask you to stay behind for a minute."

"Okay," I say. The class is gushing through the door now, and I look down. I study my shoes as the voices and laughs drift into the hallway. The classroom is almost still and silent now, except for the echoes of other kids' voices and a freezing breeze that has suddenly appeared. I look behind me. Somebody must have cracked one of the windows open at the back of the room and the cold breeze is rustling the poems and stories that Finn has tacked to the bulletin board on the wall.

"So, Grayson," Finn begins, leaning toward me a little bit in his chair. I watch his hands as he fiddles with a pen, and when I look up to his face, I see that he's smiling at me. "I saw that you signed up for auditions. I was really, *really* happy to see your name on that list. I'm wondering," he continues. "Can I ask what inspired you to try out? I mean, don't get me wrong, I think you'll be great on stage. Theater seems like an amazing fit for you, actually, but I'm curious. You've never shown an interest in any of the plays before."

I shrug. He watches my eyes, still smiling, and I don't know what to say. I picture the walls of the wooden library cubicle— old, dirty, and engraved with carvings of other kids' names. "Um," I stumble, "I don't know. I guess I just felt like joining an activity." I probably sound like an idiot, but he's still leaning forward, listening. He waits, but I don't know how to put it into words: how Amelia ditched me, and Grandma Alice died, and how I wanted to carve *Grayson was here* into the cubicle but I couldn't, so I signed up for play tryouts instead.

"Well," he finally says, "I think it's great. The play that I chose for this year's performance is magnificently written. It's really something special, so it's a good year for you to come aboard." I think about how cool that would be—to be a playwright and to get to decide what happens to all of the characters. The thought makes me smile. Finn is still looking at me eagerly, like he's waiting for me to say something else.

"I guess I just wanted to ask you what I'll have to do at the tryout," I finally say. The second bell rings and I jump.

"I can give you a pass. Don't you have study hall third period?"

"Yeah," I tell him, smiling. I drop my backpack at my feet.

"Great. It's very simple," Finn says, taking a pad of hall passes out of his top drawer and setting them on his desk. "When you signed up, you took a packet from the folder outside my office door, right?"

I swallow hard. "A packet?"

"Not to worry, not to worry." He rummages through his desk,

takes out a red folder, and hands me a thin, stapled packet from inside it. He must have read my mind because he says, "You definitely don't need to have anything memorized. There's a brief synopsis on page one followed by some one-to-two-page excerpts from the play. They're labeled with each character's name. During study hall or lunch, just read through them all and choose who you want to try out for. We'll have copies of the script on stage, or you can read from the packet when you come up to audition."

He pauses. I must look nervous because he says, "Grayson, your ability to analyze text and understand characters is excellent. Read the parts. Choose the one that feels right. I know you'll be able to do a very thoughtful reading."

I glance at the hall passes. Study hall is such a waste of time. "What's the play about?" I ask.

"It's a mythological story. Do you remember Persephone from your unit on the Greek gods last year?"

"Sort of," I say. "It's about how the seasons were created, right?"

"Exactly. In this version, Persephone is a girl who's about your age. She lives with her mother on Mount Olympus until she gets kidnapped by Hades, the god of the Underworld. The play *is* about how the seasons came to be, but it's also the story of her struggle to return home."

I nod. "And anyone can try out for any character?"

"Absolutely!" He looks over at the clock, puts my name and

the time on the hall pass, and rips it off the pad. "Here you go," he says. "And, Grayson?"

I take it from him. "Yeah?"

"I'm glad you're trying out. I know it's not easy to do something new." I pick up my backpack and try to picture myself on stage.

"Thanks," I say to Finn, and I smile at him and at the thought of not disappearing again.

Chapter 11

WHEN THE THREE o'clock bell rings, I throw all my books into my backpack and grab my jacket from my locker. The halls are bustling, and I'm surrounded by people as I make my way to the auditorium. I feel like I'm swimming in a crowded school of fish.

The giant room is empty when I arrive, except for some commotion behind the curtain on the rounded wooden stage, so I sit in the front row of fold-down chairs and flip through the packet Finn gave me. I've already read through the whole thing three times, but I flip through it again anyway.

The thick velvet curtain is partly opened, and I can hear Finn's voice from behind it. "I think I want to rearrange this today," he's saying. "I prefer the chairs on the opposite side, and this long table over here."

"I agree," a woman's voice answers, and furniture rattles across wood.

Some other kids start to file in. Most take seats near the back of the auditorium, but a few make their way over to where I am. I think again of *The Lorax*. I remember how the bright stage lights made it impossible to see the audience, and it felt like it was just the kids, all alone, up on the stage.

Andrew Moyer sits down right behind me. He's an eighth grader who has been a lead in every play I've seen for the past few years. I glance at his black T-shirt, open flannel button-down, and serious green eyes. Paige Francis and Reid Axleton, two more eighth graders, inch their way in next to him. I'm sure the three of them will get the biggest parts. I face forward quickly so they don't think I'm staring at them. They probably have no idea who I am, and I wonder if they think it's weird that I'm sitting up front, all alone.

Finn comes out from behind the curtain. He's disheveled looking, and he smoothes back his hair. When the noise in the auditorium dies down, he smiles at us. "Welcome," he calls out. Ms. Landen, one of the seventh-grade humanities teachers, comes out from behind the curtain with a microphone stand. Jack always says how much he hates her class, but she seems nice. She's smiling and young looking, and her long blond hair is pulled back into a low braid. She puts the microphone stand in front of Finn and hands him the mic. "Thanks, Samantha," he says to her back as she disappears behind the curtains.

"Welcome to play tryouts." Now his voice booms and fills every corner of the auditorium. Every crevice. My heart thumps. "I'm eagerly anticipating your auditions for *The Myth of Persephone* today. I am grateful to Dr. Shiner, as always, for supporting the arts programming here at Porter and for giving me the opportunity to direct this play."

Finn looks to the end of the front row of seats and smiles a stiff, polite smile. I glance over to see Dr. Shiner, the principal of Porter, sitting calmly in the last seat of the front row. His long, bony legs are crossed neatly, and his thin body looks like it has been swallowed up by his perfectly ironed suit. Everyone starts clapping, so I clap, too. Dr. Shiner stands and waves to the auditorium. His eyes are dark black, like they've sucked up all the color from the room.

Finn continues. "One by one, Ms. Landen and I will call you up for your audition. Once you're done, you're free to leave. All we ask is that you remain relatively quiet while you wait your turn. If you want to practice with a friend or talk softly, that's fine. We'll have the curtains partially drawn, which will block out a good deal of noise, but we can't have the volume level getting out of hand."

He looks around at us and smiles in my direction. I turn again to look at Andrew, Paige, and Reid behind me. "The cast list will be up on my office door Monday morning when you return from break. I want to stress to you," he continues, "that *everyone* will be cast in a role. There are many small nonspeaking parts in this play, between the Elves and the Souls of the Underworld, so if you want to be on stage for this performance, you will be. Nobody will be cut."

Finn takes the microphone off the stand and sits down on the edge of the stage with it. "And now for an extremely brief overview of *The Myth of Persephone,* for those of you who can't remember what you learned in fifth grade or didn't read the synopsis on page one of your packet." Andrew, Paige, and Reid giggle behind me.

"So, Persephone lives with her mother, the goddess of the harvest, Demeter. Her grandfather is Zeus."

"Zeus!" Andrew calls out in a loud, low voice, and everyone in the auditorium laughs. I turn around to look at him again. He's smiling at Finn.

"Moving along," Finn says, amused, "Persephone is kidnapped by Hades, the god of the Underworld. When this happens, Demeter becomes so depressed that all the crops begin to die." I think for a minute of Mom and Grandma Alice as Finn continues. "Zeus goes to Hades and tells him to free Persephone, which he does, and in the end, it's agreed that she'll spend half the year in the Underworld, at which time no crops grow, and the other half of the year with her mother, during which time the world will be in full bloom."

"And that's why we have the seasons!" Reid calls out.

"Exactly," says Finn.

He looks us over. "If there aren't any questions, we'll get

started." He waits for a minute and then nods at us. "Good luck to you all; I know you'll do great. First up, Andrew Moyer."

I look down at the packet in my hands. "Wish me luck," I hear Andrew say as he inches his way out. He leaps up the stage steps, two at a time.

I can't make out everything he's saying up there, but I hear him tell Finn that he's auditioning for Zeus, and I watch him take a red script from Ms. Landen. He flips through it, takes a deep breath, and starts to read. It looks like Ms. Landen is reading some of the lines, too, and I turn to page four in the packet, Zeus's part, and strain to hear what line Andrew is on.

I figured I'd try out for Zeus, but I know there's no way I'll get it over Andrew. He's older and taller and would obviously make a way better Zeus than me. I flip through the packet nervously and skim through the other parts again. I chew on my nail.

Up on stage, Andrew is handing the red script back to Ms. Landen. He takes a little bow and laughs, and I hear Finn tell him he did an excellent job. Paige scoots out behind me and grins at Andrew as she walks up the steps onto the stage. She seems so confident in her long, black skirt, shimmery with sequins, and I look down at my shiny black track pants that I used to be able to imagine so easily into a skirt just like hers.

Up on stage, she tells Finn she's reading for Persephone. Of course. I listen as she begins. Hades has kidnapped her, and she's demanding to be taken back to her mother. Her voice is loud and clear, and she sounds super dramatic. I look at the second page of the packet, at Persephone's part, and then around the auditorium again.

When Paige finishes, she and Andrew wait for Reid to audition before the three of them put on their coats and walk out the auditorium doors together. I glance at the clock on the wall and watch everybody in the room try out, one by one. I turn through the pages of my packet slowly. I should be rereading Zeus's part, but I can't focus on it.

It's almost my turn. My heart starts pounding, and when Finn finally calls my name, I'm the only one left except for two seventh-grade girls packing up at the back of the room. I watch them whisper and laugh as they put on their jackets and gather up their long hair, and I think about Lila and Amelia. The familiar longing races through my body—the familiar *wish*.

My heart thumping, I walk slowly up the stage steps and through the opening in the curtains into the small, makeshift room that Finn and Ms. Landen created. The auditorium doors slam as the two seventh graders leave. The lighting is dim on the stage, and the heavy burgundy velvet surrounds us. Finn and Ms. Landen sit behind the long table smiling at me, notebooks open to blank pages in front of them.

I try to smile back at them, but my legs feel suddenly weak, and now I feel like my thumping heartbeat is coming from somewhere else, somewhere outside of me. I look at the script that Ms. Landen is holding out to me. It looks like it's floating toward me. I take it.

"Grayson, you've been waiting forever," Finn says. He turns to Ms. Landen. "Samantha, this is Grayson, one of my sixth graders."

"Hi, there," she says, and I watch her write my name in her notebook. "Is this your first time trying out for a play?"

I nod and look down at the red script. *The Myth of Persephone* sparkles on the cover in shimmery gold writing. Beyond it are my black track pants and just one more time I try—I try to see them like Paige's sparkling skirt, but I can't. My heartbeat is like a drumbeat. It surrounds me. Each gentle thud creates ripples all around me.

I flip through the script. The word *Underworld* jumps out at me from the page, and I think of Grandma Alice's coffin, light brown and disappearing under shovelfuls of gray dirt and snow. I think of Amelia and Lila and their matching skirts, and of Paige's sequined skirt. And then I think, again, of my track pants.

"So, Grayson, who have you decided to read for?" Finn asks. His words come to me softly through the thick, warm air, and I look up at him, but I can't answer. All I can do, for some reason, is think about the years and years that I spend *pretending* my pants into skirts just like Lila's and Amelia's and Paige's, and how, for all those years, I just *pretended* that everyone else could see what I saw. And I think about how doing that used to make everything okay.

At home, my track pants and basketball pants hang in my closet, silky and shiny in a row of bright yellow, black, gray, silver, and gold, but they're only pants to me now. My too-long

T-shirts don't look like dresses. Without them, I'm nobody, and the idea takes shape in my mind. It takes shape and floats into my mouth, and it waits there.

I look down at my hands, at my chewed-up fingernails, and then back at Finn's face. The stage is silent and still. Finn and Ms. Landen are waiting for me to say something, so I do. I ask the question: "Can I try out for Persephone?"

Chapter 12

NOBODY MOVES and nobody says anything and my words hang in front of us like fog. My heart is pounding all around me. I watch Finn watching me, and Ms. Landen watching him. His face is calm, but he's studying me carefully now. I want to look down again, but I don't let myself.

He takes a deep breath. "Well," he says. And then he doesn't say anything for another minute. He picks up his gray pen and studies it, like he's trying to decide how to start the story that he's about to write.

I can't move, and I can't tear my eyes away from him and Ms. Landen. I don't know how much time passes, but it feels like forever. Finally, Finn opens his mouth to talk. "I suppose," he says slowly, like he's thinking aloud, "I suppose that there's no reason why you couldn't try out for Persephone." I nod. My heartbeat sinks back into my chest and I start to breathe evenly again.

"I mean, a tryout is just that, right? A *tryout*," he continues, and then he pauses again before saying, "What I mean is, yes, of course you can. Why shouldn't someone be able to try out for whatever character they choose? But, Grayson," he continues, looking at me carefully, "I should add: if we do feel that you're right for this role, we'd, well, of course we'd need to sit down and talk about things—about how people might react."

An image of Ryan's and Sebastian's faces pops into my mind, and my heart starts pounding again. I hadn't even thought of that, of what everyone else would think. "Yeah, maybe I—" But Finn's voice interrupts me.

"But it's premature to talk about that now," he says, and nods his head a final time. "Go for it, Grayson. Let's see how you do, reading for Persephone."

Persephone. I let the name bounce around my mind. I don't even want to imagine what people would say—a boy cast as a girl—and I think again of Ryan and Sebastian. And Jack. And everyone else, and for another second I think that maybe I should just try out for Zeus, or forget tryouts and join crew, but Finn's brown eyes are deep and kind. I'm frozen in front of the long table. And the faraway shadow of a hand from another lifetime has slowly rested itself upon my shoulder, like an echo. It smells like hand lotion and the clementine it just peeled and broke into pieces in front of me. *Stay*, it offers. I close my eyes for a second.

I see endless black dotted with glimmers of gold. I focus on them—on the sparkling lights, and then I open my eyes.

"What page?" I ask.

Ms. Landen looks at Finn one more time. He nods at her, and she clears her voice. "Twenty-seven," she says. "This is where Hades is trying to convince Persephone to be happy in the Underworld. We're having people who try out for Persephone—" She stops for a second and clears her throat again. "We're having you read this section because it's a part where Persephone shows a lot of passion and emotion, and we want to see how you would manage this intensity."

She opens her copy of the play. "I'm going to read for Hades. You may see us taking notes while you're reading. This is nothing to be alarmed about. You can start at the top of twenty-seven whenever you feel ready. And, Grayson?" she says.

I nod and swallow hard.

"Good luck."

I scan the words, and before I know what I'm doing, I start to read. Persephone paces around Hades's throne. She's peering out every window, one by one, and choking back tears. I envision myself in her shoes. It's not that hard to do, and I can practically see the dark gardens of the Underworld in front of me.

"'You must release me,'" I state firmly, finally turning to face Hades. I try to hide my emotion from him. Evil seeps from his menacing eyes, and I don't want him to think he has won.

"'My mother cannot exist without me,'" I read, but I know that what Persephone must really mean is *I can't exist without her,* and I hear my voice catch as I think of Mom's face in the picture on my nightstand.

"'Of course she can,'" Ms. Landen reads. "'And she will.'"

"'No.'" My voice is steady now, but I can sense Persephone's longing. "'I need to leave.'"

"'I will bring you everything you want,'" Ms. Landen states. "'Within reason, of course,'" she adds.

I look into Hades's cold eyes. "'My mother will figure out a way to come for me. Zeus will help her. Or I'll figure out a way myself.'"

Hades laughs a horrible laugh. I'm trying to scare him, but the truth is that his powers are much greater than mine.

"'Please,'" I beg. "'Just let me return home!'"

Hades grins, sensing his victory. And suddenly, I realize that I still have some control. I step forward, firmly.

"'All right, then.'" I make my voice cold, to match his. "'I will remain. But as long as I am here in this cold, dark, evil land, I will never smile. I will never eat. I will never do anything but try to get home.'"

Suddenly, Finn tells me I can stop. I look up from page twenty-eight of the script, and I feel almost surprised to be back in the burgundy room.

Finn and Ms. Landen stare at me and then, slowly, they look to one another, smiling. "Thank you, Grayson," Finn finally says, turning back to me. "That was very, *very* well done." In a daze, I hand him the script. He takes it, and for a minute, nobody says anything.

"So, I'll see you tomorrow morning in Humanities," he finally adds, and I nod.

I walk through the passageway in the curtains into the cold air. My eyes sting in the light as I walk across the stage and down the wooden steps. I gulp air awkwardly. I notice the hard floor beneath me. I feel like it's the first time my feet have touched the earth.

Part

Two

Chapter 13

I GRAB MY STUFF off the seat where I left it. I don't feel like myself as I put on my jacket and backpack and walk out the side doors of the school and into the darkness. My breath is a puff of fog in front of me in the frozen air.

Across the street, I turn around and look at Porter. Most of the lights are still on inside, and the whole school practically glows against the black sky. The door of the east gym opens. A group of girls walks out, talking and laughing, and I wonder what time football practice will be over. I watch three teachers come out the giant arched front doorway holding overflowing tote bags. They walk down the steep steps to the parking lot.

I'm suddenly exhausted, but I force myself to think about what happened on stage. I try to remember exactly how I felt before I asked Finn if I could try out for Persephone, but it's a blur.

But then I think about reading Persephone's lines with Ms. Landen. That's not a blur. I can remember that; I remember how perfect it felt. I felt like I *was* Persephone, and I start to smile. The gym door opens again and a few more girls walk out, basket-balls in hand. *That was very,* very *well done,* Finn had said, and it seemed like he meant it. And I felt that way, too. I felt like it *was* very, very well done.

There's a huge pile of snow next to the sidewalk behind me, and I run up it and jump off the other side onto the snow-covered lawn. "Yes!" I call out, and two old ladies walking down the side-walk next to the bus stop look my way. I run across the snow, my ankles burning with cold, just as the bus pulls up. I skip up the steps. The driver is watching me with a little smile on her face. I look at her name tag. "Hi, Dori," I say. I wonder if she has kids.

She looks amused. "Good evening." I smile and sit down in the empty seat behind her. I plop my backpack onto the seat next to me, and think of Amelia.

Suddenly, I can barely breathe. *I just tried out to be a girl in front of the entire school.* I imagine Amelia, Lila, Meagan, Hannah, and Hailey at the lunch table, huddled together, their heads touching. I can practically hear their voices and laughter floating up from the jumble of headbands and braids and long, just-brushed hair—*He did what? What a freak.* I take my back-pack off the seat next to me, hold it on my lap, and rest my head on it as the bus pulls away.

At home, the apartment is empty. I bring my backpack to my room, drop it on the floor, and look at myself in the mirror. I wonder what Finn and Ms. Landen saw at tryouts. I felt like I *was* Persephone. Did they see me standing there in front of them? Or did they see her?

I try not to let it, but the image of the girls' faces bursts into my mind again. Ryan and Sebastian join them, and Ryan's gaze stabs at me. I rub my eyes with my fists, hard, to create bursting firecrackers to burn the picture away. I should just forget about it and type my Humanities paper, but I don't feel like it, so I lie on my bed and try to think about the tryout and the feeling of *being* Persephone. I try to remember it exactly.

Eventually, I hear the front door open and close, and the sounds of Aunt Sally, Uncle Evan, Jack, and Brett in the other room. Jack pounds on my door and tells me it's time for dinner.

At the dining room table, I sit down next to Brett and scoop some takeout lasagna onto my plate. I'm too wound up to eat, so I push my food around while Uncle Evan reaches for the pitcher of water in front of me. "It's really too bad we couldn't make that trip to Costa Rica work, isn't it, boys?" He pours water into all of our glasses.

"Tell me about it," Jack says. "Every single one of my friends is going somewhere awesome. Did you know the Aarons are going to South Africa?"

"Huh," Uncle Evan answers, sitting back down and blowing on his lasagna. "Well, I'm sorry, guys. There was just no way. Not with the craziness that's ensuing at the office." He turns to Aunt

Sally. "At least you'll get some time off, huh, Sal? What are you going to do with yourself?"

"Now, there's the question," Aunt Sally says, chuckling. "I never know what to do with free time."

"So, how was school?" Uncle Evan asks.

"Whatever," Jack says. "It's almost break, so there's nothing much going on." I'm sure this is Jack's latest excuse for not doing his homework. For a second, I think back to his winning science fair project in fourth grade. The summer before school started, he set up all different kinds of birdhouses at Aunt Tessa and Uncle Hank's lake house in Michigan to see which ones the birds preferred. I remember them hanging in the overgrown rose bushes, little house wrens flying in and out of the tiny doorways. I try to remember exactly when Jack stopped caring about everything, but I can't pinpoint it.

"Brett? How was your day?" Uncle Evan probes.

"Good. It was good. Lucia spilled her water bottle on the computer table at After School Club and got in big trouble because you can't bring water bottles to the computer table. And there was an assembly."

"Is that right?" Uncle Evan asks him, and Aunt Sally smiles and leans over to cut up the green beans on his plate. "What kind of assembly?"

"I don't know. Some people in weird costumes with instruments."

"It was a string quartet from the Children's Symphony

Orchestra," Jack says quickly. "They did a holiday concert, but just for the elementary school."

Aunt Sally stops cutting Brett's food and looks up. For a second, she and Uncle Evan stare at Jack. "What?" he finally asks. "I saw a flyer in the hall."

Uncle Evan clears his throat. "Grayson?" he asks. "How about you? Anything interesting happen with you today?"

I hesitate and push my lasagna around my plate some more. I think of the soft curtains on stage and the warm, thick water-air. "I tried out for the spring play," I say.

Uncle Evan, Aunt Sally, and Jack stop eating and stare at me. They look stunned. Brett looks around at everyone. "What?" he asks. "That's cool, Grayson. We're doing a play soon, too." He looks around again. "What?"

A smile starts to creep across Jack's face, and I look back down at my plate. "Doesn't Mr. Finnegan direct the middle school play?" Jack asks.

"Yeah," I say. "So what?"

He shakes his head. "That guy is so gay." He's grinning like an idiot, and I have the sudden urge to get up from my chair and kick him. But I never would, so I dig my nails into the black leather seat instead.

"Jack!" Aunt Sally and Uncle Evan yell at the same time.

"What is wrong with you?" Aunt Sally goes on.

"I heard Mr. Finnegan's the best teacher in the whole school," Brett says.

"He is," I say, still staring at Jack. My ears feel like they're on fire. "The play he's directing? It's amazing. He's a genius."

"Whatever," Jack says, as he wipes his mouth with the back of his hand. "I'm sure it will be a snoozer." He looks at Aunt Sally and Uncle Jack, than back at his plate. He puts his fork down. "What's the big deal? All the school plays are."

"My goodness, Jack. Let's not forget that you were in almost every single play when you were in elementary school," Aunt Sally says. "You loved Drama Club." Jack rolls his eyes. Aunt Sally turns to me, smiling. "Grayson, I think it's great that you tried out. Don't you, Ev?"

"I do," Uncle Evan says, sounding proud. "I definitely do. So, when do you find out if you made it?"

My heart skips a beat. "Everyone makes it," I stammer quickly.

"I'm going to be the mayor in our play," Brett says. "When do you know what part you have?"

I can't talk about it anymore. "Monday after break," I tell them, pushing my chair back. "I have a big paper to type. Can I go to my room?" I ask. I put my plate on the kitchen counter and leave them and their curious gazes behind me.

☆

The next morning in Humanities, I'm restless. One part of me feels like doing the mile run in gym, and the other part of me wants to go to the nurse's office and lie down on one of those little cots. I prop open my notebook in front of me and watch Finn at his desk at the front of the room. I scream silent messages to him: *I need this role!* Then my stomach drops. How could I be wishing for this? He looks up once and catches my eye. I feel my face flush and look quickly out the window. The old snow looks gray.

I watch Amelia out of the corner of my eye throughout the double period. She and Lila exchange looks and mouth words to each other. Amelia writes something in huge letters on a piece of notebook paper, rips it out, and holds it under her desk where Lila can read it from across the room. Lila starts laughing and buries her face in her hands. By the time the bell rings, Amelia's paper is still only half a page long.

I lean down to pack my backpack. "So, where were you yesterday?" Amelia asks me. "Did you get picked up after school?"

"Oh, no," I say, pretending nothing's wrong. I take a deep breath and look her in the eyes. "I actually tried out for the spring play."

Her face lights up. "Really?"

"Yeah, Finn's directing."

"I think that's great, Grayson!" she says. "I bet you'll meet a ton of new friends!" She swings her backpack over her shoulder and gathers her long hair in her hands. I swear, she looks relieved. "Will I see you at lunch? Or are you going to the library?"

"Library," I mumble as she walks to Lila's desk. I can't imagine ever sitting down with them at the lunch table again. When I pass Finn's desk, I avoid his eyes and walk out the door alone.

Chapter 14

I STAND, HUDDLED in the corner of the glass enclosure at the bus stop on Friday after school. Even though I can't stop thinking about whether Finn is going to cast me as Persephone, I'm glad that for two weeks I won't know. Everything feels hopeful and safe now, and I wish I could just stop time. I can't stand the thought of a crowd of anxious faces waiting to see the cast list on Finn's office door on Monday morning.

The wind is whipping like crazy. Amelia joins me at the bus stop. I don't know what to say to her. I know I'll never be able to tell her how I *really* feel about her and Lila's matching skirts. What could I possibly say: *I should have been the one wearing the same skirt as you?* I take a deep breath. I'll just be nice to her, I think. Nice, but not *too* nice.

She seems upset. "Are you okay?" I ask her.

"I'm so annoyed with Lila," she spits. "She told Asher that I have a crush on him."

"Oh. Do you?" I don't mean to ask the question, but I do. I feel like I'm covered in a layer of ice that is starting to melt. I can practically feel it loosening around me.

"That's so not the point. Since when are friends supposed to do things like that to each other? It's so obnoxious." She looks down the street for the bus.

"She probably just likes him, too," I say, pulling my hat down farther over my ears.

She glances at me. "I don't like him."

"Okay."

"I mean, I guess he's kind of cute."

I smile. I don't want to, but I can't help it. Amelia laughs a little as the bus pulls up. We get on together.

As we sit side by side, it starts to feel like fall again. I can almost hear dry leaves crunching underneath our feet on the sidewalks in Lake View. For a minute, I imagine the girls whispering at the lunch table again, but I force myself to stop. "Are you going away for break?" I ask.

"No, I was supposed to go to Florida with my dad and step-mom, but at the last minute they had to cancel. I guess she has this work thing."

"Oh." I wonder how stupid it would be to give her a second chance. "Do you have any other plans?"

"Not really," she answers. "Everyone's going somewhere."

"Yeah." I take a deep breath. "We should go to Lake View."

"Sure," she responds quickly. "Or, actually, we could go to this new thrift shop that my mom and I found in Wicker Park. It's kind of nicer, you know. I mean it's not so grungy. It's cool."

"Okay, great!" I say.

"So, do you want to go tomorrow? I think we took the 23. I have to ask my mom. But I can find out the schedule and call you later, okay?"

"Great!" I say again. "That sounds good."

The next morning I wake up to the sound of the wind whipping past my window. Outside, the ice on the lake is covered with fresh snow. A snowplow is making its way up the side street, but the sun is shining. It's already almost nine o'clock, and the bus leaves at nine forty-five. I take a quick shower and walk through the sleepy house to the kitchen. Aunt Sally is sitting on the love seat in the family room. She's wearing sweatpants and a T-shirt and reading something on her laptop. The muted TV is turned to CNN.

She pushes her reading glasses onto her head. "'Morning, Grayson," she says. "Did you sleep well?"

"Yeah," I say, glancing at the grandfather clock.

"You're taking a nine forty-five bus?"

"Yup."

"Okay. Are you sure you don't want to take a cab from Wicker Park afterward and meet us at the Planetarium? The timing would be perfect. Uncle Evan and I need a few more hours to organize the rest of your grandma's paperwork down in the basement, so we're not planning on getting there until eleven thirty or so."

Hearing Aunt Sally mention Grandma Alice makes me feel like leaving. "No, it's okay. I'll just come back here when I'm done. I don't know how long I'll be, anyway."

"Okay. Well, will you call my cell if you change your mind?"

I nod.

"You know, Grayson, Uncle Evan and I were talking last night after you went to bed," she says. "We're really glad you tried out for the play. Are you nervous?" She smiles gently.

Yes, I want to scream. *I'm dying. I don't know what I'm doing.* "Yeah. I guess two weeks is a long time to wait."

"It's almost cruel for him to make you kids wait all break!" She smiles again, but something snaps in me.

"He's not doing it to be cruel," I say quickly. "I'm sure he just wants to make a careful decision. He knows what he's doing, you know." And as soon as I say it, I wonder if it's true.

Aunt Sally looks a little hurt, and I look up at the clock again. I feel bad for her, but I don't know what to say. "I have to go," I tell her. "I have to meet Amelia."

"Okay, have fun," she says, watching me carefully. I walk into the kitchen and grab a granola bar and bottle of water from the pantry before I head out the door.

☆

The sidewalks in Wicker Park are covered in dirty snow. We get off the bus at the corner, and I follow Amelia half a block down the street to the thrift shop. The displays in the windows are bright and trendy looking. We arrive just as a lady is unlocking the door from inside and turning the CLOSED sign to OPEN. She holds the door for us.

"Good morning!" she says, smiling, as we walk in, and raising the blinds throughout the store. The countertops and tile floor glisten in the sunlight.

Two other saleswomen greet us, too. "Are you looking for anything in particular?" one asks. She's dressed neatly in a red turtleneck sweater, and her hair is wound into a tight, black bun.

"We're just browsing," Amelia answers expertly. She turns to me. "Our section is back here." She grabs my arm and guides me to a second room that's empty, except for us.

This store is definitely nicer than the Second Hand. There's a much better selection, and it seems cheerful. I don't know why, because the Second Hand is kind of gross, but for a minute I miss it—its familiar sloped, wooden floors and musty mothball smell. I think of all the time I spent looking for clothes in the boys' section—shirts that were too long or especially radiant.

I run my hands over the newer-looking clothing on the racks. I find a deep purple sweater that looks like it will fit and hang it over my arm. I roam around the quiet room and stop next to another rack.

I study the skirts in front of me and pull out a long one. XS, $15.00 is written on the tag. I hold it up, close to my face.

The fabric is thin and creamy yellow. It looks like an antique. It's decorated with dainty embroidery and, around the bottom, tiny, amber beads hang delicately from a lace ribbon. I run the palm of my hand beneath them and smile. It looks like something Persephone might wear.

My mind wanders back to the deep-burgundy curtains on the stage, the warm, thick air, and the smooth indentation of the golden letters on the script. The rhythm of the drumbeat pounds distantly in my ears. I drape the skirt over my arm on top of the purple sweater and walk into a dressing room.

I hang the sweater on a hook on the wall. In the corner is a small stool covered in disgusting-looking green fabric. There's a rip on its surface where yellow foam pokes through. I put the skirt on top of the tear and take off my pants.

Amelia parts the curtains of the dressing room next to me. "Don't they have such a better selection?" she asks. I see her feet through the space below the thin divider that separates us. Her metal hangers clang on the hooks.

"Definitely," I tell her. I shake my damp shoes off my feet. A ball of icy snow on the tan carpet soaks through my sock. I'm in a daze. It's like I'm somebody else.

"My mom got an amazing dress here," Amelia says from her dressing room. I pull on the skirt and zip it up the side. It fits me perfectly. I take a step toward the mirror. The tiny beads tickle my ankles and make a gentle shaking sound, like two dice in a hand, or raindrops.

"Did you find anything good?" Amelia asks.

I pull my socks off. "Yeah," I tell her absently. I turn to see how I look from the side. The dice knock together again, softly. More raindrops and my beating heart. I look up. The mirror seems as tall as a building, and I suddenly feel like someone is behind me, but I can see there's only the beige back wall of the dressing room. I turn around to be sure, but I'm all alone.

I reach for the curtain. There's a bigger, three-way mirror on the wall next to the windows. All that exists now is me and this skirt, and I need to see how I look in the light.

The carpet is damp beneath my bare feet, but I don't mind. I stand in front of the mirror and examine myself. My hair is getting long. I lift up my white T-shirt so I can see the top of the skirt. It rests perfectly against my stomach. The lace is completely magnificent.

And suddenly, Amelia's image joins mine in the mirror. Her old socks are bunched around her pale ankles. She's wearing a blue jean jacket over her pink T-shirt and a long, flowery skirt. She's smiling. Her eyes glisten and dance. I don't breathe.

She throws her head back and laughs. Her hair swings behind her. "Grayson! What are you doing? You're hilarious!" I watch her eyes in the mirror as they travel down my body, and up again, from the amber beads to my eyes. I keep my eyes fixed on the image of hers as, with her grin fading, she scans my body, looking for clues. Our eyes meet again in the mirror.

Her face is suddenly serious. "Grayson," she whispers, "what are you doing?" She looks forward in the mirror toward the back of the store. I can hear the saleswomen in the distance. We stand side by side, staring at each other. She pushes her hair out of her face. "What are you doing?" she asks again. "Do you want people to think you're crazy?" I can't move.

"Grayson!" she whispers.

I think of Lila's crimson skirt. That should have been my skirt. I turn and look at Amelia, at her wide eyes and pale, freckled skin. Her voice returns to its normal level, and she looks out the window. "So, I better get home," she says. "There's a ten-thirty or an eleven o'clock bus, but I told my mom we wouldn't be long, so I better head out."

"Okay," I tell her. I can barely feel my own mouth forming the words.

She looks at her feet. "So are you coming, or are you staying longer?"

"I'm coming."

We change into our own clothes quickly. I leave the skirt in a heap on the dressing room floor, and we walk outside into the freezing air.

It's snowing again by the time we get on the bus, and we sit next to each other, looking ahead. My fingers and toes are freezing, but the back of my neck is on fire. I can't get the image of a cast list on Finn's office door out of my mind. Suddenly, I can't bear the thought of getting the role. But when I think of *not* getting it, I can't bear the thought of that, either. I wonder if I'm getting sick, and I rub a circle on the window. I need to see out, but it immediately fogs up so I stare at the cracked blue seat cushion in front of me instead.

We ride in silence, and I think about how loud the quiet is; I think about what it means. Finally, the bus slows to a stop on Randolph. I'm desperate to get off, but I can barely bring myself to move. My legs ache, and I know everything is over. Even if Finn doesn't cast me as Persephone, Amelia will tell the other girls. They'll be talking about me at lunch, about the boy who tried on a skirt—a beautiful, beautiful skirt. The gossip will spread down the lunch table like a disease, and nobody will ignore me again.

I stumble off the bus and walk across Randolph. Snow blows down my collar. I picture it turning to steam on my burning neck.

Chapter 15

THE DOORMAN opens the glass doors for me, and I stagger through. I immediately see Aunt Sally and Uncle Evan across the lobby standing close together, waiting for the elevator. Uncle Evan is holding one of those big manila envelopes, and they're talking excitedly.

I take a deep breath and try hard to pretend that everything is normal, but I feel wobbly when I walk. I can't stop thinking about Amelia's eyes staring at me in the mirror. "Hi," I say softly, coming up behind Aunt Sally and Uncle Evan. They turn around quickly.

"Grayson, you're home already!" Uncle Evan says, and they look at each other, smiling. I watch their eyes wander to the envelope in his hand. There's a *ding*, and the elevator doors open. I'm boiling, and I take off my jacket. Inside, Aunt Sally pushes the button, and we start to move.

"What's going on?" I ask, studying their strange-looking grins. Just talking makes me tired, but I try to act normal. I try to block out everything that just happened.

Aunt Sally gives Uncle Evan a little nudge. "Well, ah, we found something in your grandma's things that you're going to be *very* interested in," Uncle Evan says. My heart leaps, and my face feels even more flushed than before.

"What?" I ask. "What is it?"

"Look," Uncle Evan says, and he holds out the envelope. I reach for it. On the outside in red pen it says *Letters from Lindy (Save for Grayson)*.

I can feel sweat on my forehead now.

"Your grandmother obviously put these aside for you," Aunt Sally says, beaming. "Probably a long time ago. Can you believe it, Grayson?"

The doors open, but I can hardly move. Aunt Sally puts her hand on my back, guiding me out of the elevator.

"Grayson, honey," she says suddenly, stopping in the hallway. She studies my face. "Are you okay? You feel warm!" She holds her hand over my forehead. I think again of Amelia's wide eyes and clutch the envelope in my hand. *Letters from Lindy.*

I want to lean into Aunt Sally's hand. But instead, I tell her, "I don't know. I feel weird." My eyes are hot. I look at the envelope. I turn it over in my hands. "Where was this?"

"Is he okay?" Uncle Evan asks, touching my forehead. "I can't tell. Is he warm?"

"Where was this?" I ask again.

"Honey, it was in your grandma's files, the ones that Adele packed up for us." Aunt Sally fumbles with the keys and unlocks the door. "Get out of those wet clothes and we'll talk about it. We assume your grandma must have put those aside for you before she got sick. We were going to read them, but we decided not to." She pauses. "They belong to you."

I feel like I'm floating across the hall. I stare at the envelope, at Mom's name, *Lindy*, written in Grandma Alice's wobbly cursive, and I stumble to my room. My footsteps don't match the swish of surroundings passing me by and my legs don't feel like mine. I take my damp pants off, leave them in a pile on the floor, and get into bed. My feet are icy between the cold sheets.

I lay the envelope in front of me. My heart thumps, and my eyes burn. The door opens slightly, and Aunt Sally pokes her head in. Uncle Evan is behind her. "Can we come in?" she asks.

I nod.

Aunt Sally has a thermometer in her hand. "Open," she says. I do, and Uncle Evan sits on the foot of my bed.

"We're happy to read those with you if you want," Uncle Evan says. "We know it will probably be strange for you—"

The thermometer beeps, and Aunt Sally takes it out of my mouth. "It's slightly high, but barely," she says, and looks at my eyes again. "Grayson, how was your morning with Amelia? You're home awfully early."

I look away from her, at the painting on my wall. I focus on the bird. "It was fine," I say.

She pauses, and I can feel her watching me. "Okay," she says. "Should we read those letters with you? We know it might be difficult."

"No!" I say quickly, and I pick up my envelope. "No. It's okay. I'll be okay." I'm suddenly desperate for them to leave me alone.

"All right," Aunt Sally says. Uncle Evan gets up off my bed. "You'll let us know if you need anything?" he asks.

I nod, and they close my door behind them.

I turn the manila envelope over in my hands a few times before I open it and slowly tip the contents onto my bed. Three light blue envelopes slide out. They're addressed to Grandma Alice. I run my fingers over the handwriting, squint at the dates stamped over the postage stamps, and put the letters in order from the first one written to the last. I line them up neatly, their corners touching. I realize I'm not breathing and I force myself to.

I pick up the first envelope and turn it over. The return address on the back is our blue house in Cleveland. Grandma Alice didn't open the sealed flap. There's a neat, even slit across the top. I can imagine her slicing it open with the shiny metal mail opener that she kept in her kitchen drawer, and I wonder where that letter opener is now. The flap is licked shut. I know it's Mom's spit on the envelope. I run my finger along it, tearing open the flap. I close my eyes. I try to feel her.

Suddenly, it's like I'm floating, cross-legged, on my bed. I can't hear the TV or footsteps in the other room anymore, and everything is black. I feel the envelope, sturdy and thick. I open my eyes and peek inside.

The paper is pink inside the blue envelope. It's bright, almost fuchsia, and I pull it out. Tucked inside the paper are some photographs. There's a sudden crack in the blackness, and I feel like someone is watching me. I look at the door, but nobody's there. I unfold the paper and take out two pictures. I put them in front of me, one by one.

Once, at Tessa and Hank's lake house, I let myself sink to the sandy bottom in the shallow end of the lake. I plugged my nose and crossed my legs and opened my eyes. All around me was dark green and brushstrokes of light. The sound of nothing was very loud. It's what I hear now. I'll look at the pictures first, just for a minute. Then I'll read the letter, I tell myself. Then look at the pictures again.

The silence is roaring in my ears. I scan the pictures, not wanting to see too much yet. In the first one, Mom is holding a baby in a hospital bed. It's me. Her hand is cupped around my tiny back. In the other one, I am a little kid, looking up at the camera. My face is crisp in a surrounding blur.

I clutch the pink paper. My hands are sweating and I'm sure I'm wrinkling it, but I know Mom wouldn't mind. I open the card. On the top is says *September 6* and I look back to the date marked on the stamp. Mom wrote this almost exactly a year before the accident.

September 6

Dear Mom,

    How are you? I miss you and hope you're well! Today's the big day—Grayson's first day of preschool! I'm a little nervous about it, but I'm sure he'll be fine. They have plenty of dress-up clothes and art supplies, so what could go wrong, right?!

    Here are copies of the pictures I told you about. His teacher said they'll be working on the "All About Me" books for a while, but when he brings his home, I'll make a copy and send it to you right away.

    Enjoy the pictures! Sending love from us all!

        XO, Lindy

I put the pictures next to me. The air feels too thick. I want to read the other letters before I look at them again. Mom chose them. I want to save how she saw me for last.

I try to smooth out the wrinkles I made on the pink paper, and I put it back into the envelope. My hand is shaking as I open the second one. Inside is another bright pink card. The front of it is covered in purple scribbles. I unfold it carefully.

December 30

Dear Mom,

    Grayson wants to say thanks for sending him the fantastic book of Greek myths for children! Can you read

*what he wrote? (Ha!) I'll translate: "Gran, Christmas
book, thanks!"*

*In all seriousness, he absolutely loves it. He begs me
and Paul to read it to him all the time. Actually, that's
not accurate—he begs us to read him one of the stories
over and over. He's completely obsessed with "Myth of the
Phoenix." So much so that I'm going to add a phoenix
flying above the earth in the painting I told you about.
I'm finally almost done with it!*

Thanks, Mom! Love you!

XO, Lindy (& Grayson)

I look up at Mom's painting—at the red, yellow, and blue
bird that I've been staring at for all these years. It's a phoenix. I remember the story from fifth grade. I imagine a bird
bursting into flames, its ashes in a heap on the floor until they
finally take the shape, like magic, of another bird. My eyes
are on fire. I can picture Mom's hand holding a small, wooden
brush and dipping it gently into the red, then yellow, then blue
paint to create it. Did she use a palette to hold the colors? Paper
cups? I want to hold her hand. I want to study its creases and
paper cuts.

But obviously I can't, so I pick up the last blue envelope that
Grandma Alice put aside for me. It feels like there's another photograph inside, and I pull out the last pink card. The picture falls
onto my lap, face up.

In it, my eyes are bright. I'm in front of a mirror. I'm wearing a pink tutu.

September 3

Dear Mom,

Here's the fantastic picture I was telling you about. Doesn't he look adorable? Thanks for talking to me last night. I know, in my heart, that Paul and I are doing the right thing, but it's been so hard for the past year since Grayson started going to school. I feel like we're always being judged for how we allow him to dress.

What you said the other day is true: Grayson is who he is. If he continues to insist that he's a girl, then it's our job to support him. All I want is for him to be true to himself.

Anyway, thanks for continuing to keep this quiet. Paul and I both still want Grayson to have the power to show the world who he is—whoever that may be—on his own terms and in his own time. Sending hugs and kisses.

XO, Lindy

Chapter 16

DARKNESS IS MOVING IN, and now the room is too dark and too bright all at the same time. Someone is holding the paintbrush, and they're flip-flopping between the colors of the darkest night and the brightest day. When the light comes, the world is a crystal. I can smell the hand lotion and clementines again.

I stay in this world, and I study my pictures. I look at how Mom and Dad saw me, and this is what I see: I'm a baby in Mom's arms in a hospital bed. I try to feel Dad's hands; I know they're holding the camera. My eyes are slits, and I'm wrapped in a white blanket. Mom is looking down at me. Her eyes look tired and heavy, but her smile is huge.

In the next picture, it's just my face. I reach for Dad's hands again. I want to pry them off the camera and hold them. Light is flowing in from somewhere, and it makes my eyes bright blue and my hair blonder. My face is calm, like I don't care what anyone thinks. Beneath me, my shirt disappears into a blur of purplish blue and for some reason the thought enters my mind— the thought that this is the picture of what *could* have been.

When I look closely at the last one, I stop breathing for a minute. I'm in front of a mirror and in the corner of it a flash of light hides Mom's and Dad's faces. Dad is holding the camera, and Mom's arm is around his waist. My back faces them and, in the mirror, I can see my smiling face. I'm wearing jeans and a white T-shirt underneath a pink tutu. In my hand is a plastic wand, its silver streamers swaying.

I close my eyes now, and I let the memory come to me—the only whole and complete one that I've kept from my first life. I let it float out of the velvet-lined box where I've kept it, locked carefully in my mind.

Mom and I are on top of a grassy hill. There's an ocean below us, and hot, humid air holds us. I'm wearing red, yellow, and blue. The thick air is like warm water. It puffs out our shirts and lifts our hair. "Let go of my hand," Mom says. "Put out your arms. Maybe this is how it feels to be a bird."

Chapter 17

MY EYES ARE the first part of my body to start working again. I look at the outlines of things: a glass of water on my bedside table, but not the water inside; window frames, but not the windows; picture frames, but not the pictures.

Then sounds come. The phone rings far away. Voices, loud and hushed, all at the same time. "Mr. Finnegan, hello!" Aunt Sally's muffled voice rising and falling, then rising and rising. It pounds on my eardrums.

Long, gentle silence.

"Sally, we need to just talk to him about it." Uncle Evan. Did Dad have a similar voice? Doors closing. TV. Footsteps on wood. I'm back-floating in still, warm water.

It's like those first nights after I moved here, and I remember them now—the strange smell of the pillowcase, the sliver of light that fell through the opened doorway at night and how it bent over the corner of the bed and onto the rug and faded into darkness near the dresser, like a road to nowhere.

My body is burning. I'm asleep and awake all at once, and images come in snippets. The bedside lamp is suddenly on. I can see the light like an explosion through my eyelids. Paper rustles. Silence.

"Oh my God, Evan, read this."

Whispering. Paper unfolding, folding.

Someone sitting down, pressure on the bed, wire on foam.

"Look at this picture."

More rustling and the sounds of quiet and breathing.

Whispers again. "Oh my God, Evan. What do you think she meant?"

Nothing. "Evan!"

"It's perfectly clear what she meant, Sally. *Perfectly.*"

Silence.

I barely know if the voices are real. My blanket scratches at my neck. My feet can move now, and they kick the covers off. I open my eyes. Uncle Evan's face is close to mine. His gaze shifts from my eyes to my chin. His eyes are soft, and they study my face.

I see the tiles around the toilet now, gleaming—bright, clean white. I'm sick, and Uncle Evan's hand is on my burning back. The toilet is flushing. I look away and hold on to the sink. A cold washcloth is on my neck. It's like I'm sleepwalking, and I'm back in my bed, asleep in the darkening room.

But, eventually, I can tell that morning is coming. Someone has put the covers back over me, and the room is brightening. When I finally open my eyes, the first thing I look at is the phoenix flying in the painting over my bed. Nothing that happened feels real, but when I turn away from it, I see the three sturdy blue envelopes propped neatly against my lamp.

Chapter 18

I SIT UP SLOWLY. My mouth is dry, and my body is weak. I stare at the blue envelopes, and I can't believe what happened. It feels like a dream, but the envelopes are there, right in front of me. I pick up the last one, the one Mom wrote just before the accident, and I pull out the pink paper again.

Grayson is who he is, she said. Who am I? I want to *hear* her tell me. I look at the picture of me in the tutu. *All I want is for him to be true to himself.* My mind races, but I keep coming back to what I know is true: they knew. They knew, and it was okay.

I swing my legs carefully over the side of my bed and stand up. My blood rushes to my feet and I'm dizzy. I haven't had anything to eat or drink since yesterday morning. As I walk to my closet for a pair of pants, I see myself in the mirror in my white T-shirt and underwear, and I suddenly remember Amelia's dark eyes in the store mirror. Darkness starts to seep in again, and I turn back to my bed. The springs squeak as I sit down, and Uncle Evan's head pokes through the cracked doorway.

"Grayson? You're up! How are you feeling? Sally!" he calls. "He's up."

I hear quick footsteps, and Aunt Sally appears beside him. She takes a cautious step into my room. "Grayson!" she says. "Are you okay?"

"I think so," I tell her. But when I think about yesterday, feelings of sickness and dread come to me like words trying to make a sentence. I sit on my bed and watch Aunt Sally and Uncle Evan standing in the doorway.

"Grayson," Aunt Sally starts awkwardly. "Those letters. Uncle Evan and I read them last night. When we gave them to you, we didn't know. We didn't know what they'd be about." She looks down at her feet. "We should have read them first," she says, still not looking at me. "That must have been very difficult for you." Her voice fades away. "We're sorry." Uncle Evan is watching her. I wait for her to go on, to tell me what exactly she's sorry about, but she doesn't say anything else.

"Son, why don't you get dressed and come to the living room so we can talk?" Uncle Evan says. "Tessa came about an hour ago to take the boys to the lake house for the day." He glances at Aunt Sally uncomfortably. "And, well, there's one other thing that we need to talk about, too," he says, still watching her.

I can't feel a thing. Half of their words bounce off of me like light on a mirror. I pull on my pants and brush my hair. My face is pale, and I'm dying of thirst. I walk to the living room, numb, the feeling of cotton behind my eyes. I feel like I'm four again.

I sit on the couch across from them. On the end table next to me are a glass of water and a mug of tea that Aunt Sally must have made. I drink the water carefully and pull a red pillow onto my lap. I hold it there like a shield.

Uncle Evan runs his fingers through his hair, studies his hands for a minute, and begins to talk. "Grayson," he says, "I guess there are a couple of things we need to discuss with you." I don't move.

"The first thing is that, like your aunt Sally said, we know it must have been very difficult for you to read those letters from your mom. We didn't know what they'd be about. And what your mom said, well, we're not quite sure what to make of it." He looks at me carefully. "Or what *you* make of it."

Nobody says anything. "You know," he finally goes on, "how she talked about wanting you to be who you are, and how she included that picture of you in the, uh, the pink dress," he says.

"Tutu," I correct, automatically.

"I'm sorry?" Uncle Evan asks. .

"It's called a tutu."

"Right. Well. That was obviously a very long time ago."

I'm starting to feel sick again.

"And we don't have to talk about anything right now if you don't want to, but we do want you to know—Aunt Sally and I *both* want you to know that you can always come to us. With anything."

"Of course he knows that," Aunt Sally stammers quickly. I look at her flushed face and nod automatically. Uncle Evan watches me expectantly, but I'm frozen. The room is quiet except for the ticking clock.

After a minute, Uncle Evan clears his throat and continues. "Well, then. I know this is a lot—a lot to think about, and you probably feel very overwhelmed, but the other thing that we need to talk to you about, Grayson, is that yesterday when you were in your room, when you were, ah, reading the letters, Mr. Finnegan called."

A tiny wisp of memory of Aunt Sally's voice weaves its way back into my mind, and my heart starts to race.

"He called to ask us—"

"He didn't call to ask us anything," Aunt Sally interrupts. "He called to *tell* us."

"Okay, well, he called to say that he was thinking of—"

"Not thinking of, Evan. He had made the decision." I realize that Aunt Sally is fuming. Her face is hard, and her eyes are cold. I don't think I've ever seen her like this before.

I can't contain myself. "Why did he call?" I yell.

Uncle Evan looks shocked. "Well, apparently you tried out for the lead *female* role in the play, Grayson?"

My heartbeat is wild. I nod.

"Grayson," Aunt Sally pleads, her forehead wrinkled in concern, "why?"

"Take it easy, Sal," Uncle Evan says to her softly.

"I'm sorry," she continues. "It's just that, well, Grayson, I'm worried about you. Why would you want to set yourself up to be teased like that? Kids can be very cruel, especially in middle school. I'm just trying, Grayson, I'm just trying to protect—"

"But what exactly did he say?" I interrupt.

"Now, hang on a minute," Uncle Evan says. "We'll get there. But what Aunt Sally said—it *is* something to think about. If you want to do this, to play a girl's role, well, you should do it. That's how I feel." He looks at Aunt Sally. "But, Grayson, what your aunt is saying is true. Kids are not going to be kind about it."

"So, did he say—?"

"You know," Uncle Evan says, "we, ah, we didn't know until we read your mom's letters that you'd also been like that before you came to us."

"Also?" I ask.

"When you first moved here, you used to dress up as a girl all the time," Aunt Sally says. "I suppose that's what your mom was referring to in her letter."

I tighten my grip on the red pillow. "I did?" I ask.

Uncle Evan nods. "We didn't know what it meant." He pauses. "Your dad and I had grown apart quite a bit by the time you moved to Cleveland. It's one of my biggest regrets—that we didn't talk to each other more." He takes off his glasses and rubs his forehead.

"Oh," I whisper.

"But it was just for a little while that you dressed up," Aunt

Sally adds quickly. "Like your mom said, you actually insisted for the first couple of months that you lived with us that you *were* a girl. But your teacher, Mrs. Stern, assured us that it was all a normal phase, or possibly a reaction to the trauma, and that it would pass. And it did."

Uncle Evan looks at her. "It did, Sally, but only after we explained to him that Jack would stop tormenting him if he just acted like a boy." He turns back to me. "You used to wear my undershirts like dresses. They were way too long on you. You used to trip over them. I don't know. I suppose . . . Maybe we should have gotten you—"

"Evan!" Aunt Sally interrupts. "All it took for him to stop the behaviors was a simple explanation that this is not something that boys are *supposed* to do."

My hands are sweating. I swallow hard. "And then I stopped?" I ask.

"Of course you stopped," Aunt Sally says quickly. "You had no problem stopping."

"Well, Jack wasn't exactly easy on him," Uncle Evan says to her, as if I'm not sitting right across from them. "Maybe *that's* why he stopped. Maybe he didn't want to deal with Jack teasing him about it anymore." He pauses. "And you and I, well, it's not like we exactly supported Grayson the way it seems Lindy and Paul did." His voice catches when he says his brother's name.

Aunt Sally takes a deep breath. "It was a hard time for everyone." She turns and looks at me again. "Jack felt very displaced when you arrived. He was only five and a half. He didn't know right from wrong, and Brett was just a tiny baby. We had so much—"

Uncle Evan cuts her off. "Anyway, you and Jack eventually became great friends," he says. He glances at Aunt Sally, and it looks like he's trying to force himself to smile. "It just took a few years."

I stare at them. I feel like I've just read the prequel to my life story, like I'm understanding things for the first time. "Why didn't anyone tell me about this before?"

"Oh," Aunt Sally says, "I guess I thought you remembered."

I stare at her blankly.

"But, Grayson, the point is that we need to make a decision together here," she continues. "About whether or not it's a good idea for you to do this. To play the role of this, ah, Persephone character. Mr. Finnegan said he already cast you, but before making it official, he wants to confirm that you're still up for it. So we have a very easy opportunity to just tell him—"

"So I got the role?" I ask them, standing up. The red pillow falls on the floor.

"Yes, Grayson, that's the whole point," Aunt Sally says. She looks at Uncle Evan and back at me.

All of a sudden, I can't help smiling. I don't mean to, because Aunt Sally looks like she's about to cry, but I can't stop. I say it again, just to hear how the words sound one more time: "I got the role."

"This is completely ridiculous," Aunt Sally says, looking up at me, her voice rising. "Mr. Finnegan has absolutely no business putting you in a position like this!" Now she doesn't look like she's going to cry anymore—she looks furious again. Beside her, Uncle Evan seems small and defeated. He rubs his hands on his knees as he looks up at me. And even though all I can remember about Mom's and Dad's faces is how they look in pictures, it's like they're standing next to me now. Their hands are on my back, and I can't turn my thoughts away from a vision of myself on stage, in the spotlight, in a beautiful, flowing gown.

"Grayson, are you okay?" Uncle Evan asks, watching me strangely.

"Yeah," I tell him, still grinning. "I'm perfect."

Chapter 19

TESSA AND HANK drop Jack and Brett off after dinner.

"I hope you're not contagious," Jack says, passing me on the way to his bedroom. He slams his door. I think back to when we were younger and he would open his bedroom door for me when I did our secret knock—*tap, tap, bang, bang, bang.* I remember the time we went sailing with Tessa and Hank while Brett sat on the pier with Aunt Sally and Uncle Evan in the whipping wind and blinding sun. The sailboat capsized in the reeds on the far side of the little lake. Jack and I were laughing in the water, bobbing up and down in musty-smelling lifejackets. He reached for my hand and helped me crawl up onto the slippery, white bottom of the boat.

Brett looks down the empty hallway and then sits on the couch next to me. "Are you still sick?" he asks.

"Nope, I'm good," I tell him. I wonder what Aunt Sally and Uncle Evan told Tessa and Hank. They wave to me from the doorway. Do they know about the play? The thought horrifies me.

We sit on the couch together for the rest of the night. Even after it gets late, Aunt Sally and Uncle Evan don't make us go to bed. I pretend to be watching *Star Wars* with Brett, but really I'm lost in my thoughts. Whenever I used to imagine Mom and Dad, I'd think of their faces in the framed picture on my nightstand. But now it's different. Having those letters—now it's like I can actually *feel* them next to me.

Winter break drags on. I can tell that Aunt Sally and Uncle Evan are trying to give me space, but I catch them staring at me strangely all the time. Aunt Sally gets us a week's pass to the museums, but there's no way I'm going. Every day, she, Jack, and Brett head out after breakfast. I lie on my bed a lot and look at Mom's painting. I especially look at the phoenix. I read the letters over and over again. I study my pictures. Mom and Dad *knew*. They knew, and it was okay.

One night after dinner, Aunt Sally and Uncle Evan come in. "Grayson," Aunt Sally starts, "we just want to check in with you—to see how you're doing. And to see where you're at with this, ah, play thing. Mr. Finnegan left another message on my voice mail today. I think he really wants us to call him back."

I sit up in bed. "You haven't called him back yet?" I ask.

"Well, your uncle and I wanted to give things a little time. You know, to settle." She looks at Uncle Evan.

"So," he asks me, "are you still thinking that you'd like to take on the role?"

"Yes!" I say. "Definitely."

"Why?" Aunt Sally sounds desperate. "Why do you want to set yourself up to be teased? Other kids could make your life miserable if you do this, Grayson. You could get bullied. You could get *hurt*."

I don't feel like myself anymore; it's like I'm acting in a performance already. "I don't know," I say. "I guess it's just that I feel . . ." I take a deep breath and look at them. "I mean, I've been thinking about what you said, about how I could talk to you, and about how I was when I first moved here. . . ." They both stare at me frantically, their eyes wide. "I guess I still feel—"

"You feel *what*, Grayson?" Aunt Sally interrupts anxiously.

I look from her unblinking eyes to Uncle Evan's. "Nothing," I say, lying back down. "I just wanna do it. That's all. If I get teased, I can handle it." I have no idea if this is true.

"Well," Aunt Sally says flatly, "I think we should tell Jack and Brett. Just so they're prepared." She looks hurt and my stomach tightens. Prepared for what?

"Fine," I say. They stand there for another minute before closing my door.

☆

The next morning I stay in bed as long as possible. After a while, though, I know I need to get up. I'm starving, and I have to go to the bathroom. Besides, I can't hide out forever. I think of what Aunt Sally and Uncle Evan said about how Jack treated me when I first moved in. When I walk to the dining room, I feel myself bracing for an attack.

Aunt Sally, Jack, and Brett are at the table eating breakfast. "Hey! Look at the pretty lady!" Jack calls out. Brett watches him, his spoonful of cereal frozen halfway to his mouth.

"Jack, this is exactly what I'm talking about. You need to leave him alone," Aunt Sally warns, looking up from the paper. "How'd you sleep, Grayson?" she asks automatically.

"Fine," I tell her, watching Jack out of the corner of my eye. I sit down next to Brett and pour myself some cereal.

Brett turns to me, his mouth full now. "Dad told me the story about Persephone and why there are seasons," he says, chewing. "So, you're gonna be Persephone?"

"Yeah," I tell him, forcing a smile.

"Is it a true story?" he asks.

"Nah," I say. "It's made up."

He nods.

"Well, *Grace*, I think you'll make a perfect girl," Jack says. "But what am I supposed to tell all my friends when they ask me why my cousin is totally gay?" His face turns pink when I meet his eyes, and he looks down and plays with his cereal.

"Jack," Aunt Sally says sternly, but she sounds exhausted.

Brett watches us, confused, and I think again of how I'll look to everyone else, onstage, in a dress, and I understand, suddenly, that this question is out there, this question of what it all means. I think of what Mom wrote—*All I want is for him to be true to himself*—and in this exact moment I wish for her harder than ever before. I need her to tell me who I am. I need her to say it, because I know what Jack thinks, and I know it's not that.

"What does—" Brett starts, but Jack interrupts him.

"Well, what am I supposed to say to everybody?" He glares at me.

"I don't know," I mumble. Anyway, I *don't* know. "I'm sorry," I say.

"Well, obviously you're not sorry enough. If you were really sorry, you wouldn't do it. You're a total embarrassment."

"That's enough, Jack," Aunt Sally says quietly.

"Whatever," he spits. He gets up from the table and storms out of the dining room. I hear his bedroom door slam.

Brett looks back and forth between me and Aunt Sally. "I don't get it," he says. "Why can't Grayson be Persephone?" Aunt Sally looks out the window as Brett continues, "It's just a play."

Even though I want to, there's no way I can explain that it's so much more than that. Brett's words just hang there, half-true, in the air.

☆

That night, I lie awake in my bed in the dark. The house is still except for muffled voices coming from Aunt Sally and Uncle Evan's room. I look at my clock; it's almost eleven o'clock. I creep quietly through the hall and sit on the cold, wooden floor across from their closed door. They're arguing.

"Just tell me everything he said, Sally, for Christ's sake, without interjecting your opinion every second!" Uncle Evan is saying.

"Would you lower your voice? You're going to wake everyone up!" Aunt Sally replies in a loud whisper. "I just told him he had overstepped his bounds as a teacher, that's all. I told him that Grayson still wanted the role, but that no teacher, no *one person*, should be allowed to make a decision like this without a serious conversation with everyone involved!"

"And?"

"Then he said that he'd like to sit down with Grayson to talk about how people might react to everything, and to coach him through how he could respond. I told him no way, not to bother, that we were talking *all* about the possible ramifications at home."

"Sally, are you sure that was a good idea?" Uncle Evan asks. But it's like she doesn't even hear him.

"Then, he just said that he didn't mean to step on anyone's toes, but he believes that any teacher who is really going to make a difference in the life of a student is going to blur the boundary between the kid's academic and personal life. Or something like that. Utter nonsense. I told him he was creating a monster. This entire situation is spinning out of control, and I can guarantee you that Grayson is only going to get hurt as a result."

My heart is thumping. There's silence.

Finally, Aunt Sally starts to talk again. "I suppose we could just tell Grayson he *can't* do the play." My stomach ties itself into a blazing knot.

"No," Uncle Evan says abruptly. "Absolutely not. Grayson has not involved himself in *anything* for how many years? And then the first thing he finally decides to get out there and do, we forbid? No way." Aunt Sally doesn't respond. "Anyway," Uncle Evan continues, his voice quieter now, "I mean, maybe this whole play thing *means* something. Maybe the dressing up wasn't 'just a phase.' You read Lindy's letter."

"Of course it was a phase!" Aunt Sally replies quickly. "And who knows what *exactly* she was talking about. But you know what, Evan? Let's just say it wasn't a phase. That's not the point. It's not Mr. Finnegan's place to get involved. *That's* the point. He is completely inappropriate. I'm calling Dr. Shiner Monday morning. I'm sorry if you disagree, but I am. He needs to know how I feel about this decision. Maybe there's something he can do. Mr. Finnegan is setting Grayson up for something too big for anyone to handle. Grayson is a *child*—he's in no position to make a decision like this on his own."

The knot in my stomach tightens.

"God, I can just see Lindy encouraging this in him, you know?" she says.

"Jesus, Sally," Uncle Evan whispers.

"I'm sorry, Ev," Aunt Sally goes on, softer now. I strain to hear. "Honestly, I don't think I'm cut out for this type of thing." There's another long silence, and then she continues. "Remember that time when he first moved here and we all went to the Clarks' for dinner? Remember the kids were all playing dress-up, and we had to practically drag him out of Allie's dress to get him home? God, I just remember the way Alex and Esther were looking at us while he was lying on the floor screaming—like we were completely incompetent."

"Sally," Uncle Evan says again, even softer this time.

"Anyway," she continues, "he's going to get teased horribly. That's really the point."

I can't listen anymore, so I creep back to my bedroom and close the door quietly. My hands are shaking. I tuck my covers in tightly around me and shut my eyes against the darkness.

Chapter 20

AS I WALK UP the empty stairway to the fourth floor in the early morning winter light, I hear voices drifting through the closed door at the top of the steps. I already know my role. *So, why are you doing this?* I suddenly scream to myself. But, the thing is, I *want* to. I want to stand in a crowd, huddled at Finn's closed office door, reading the cast list, seeing who got what part.

I adjust my backpack and study the doorknob for a minute before I finally open it and walk slowly over to the small crowd of mostly seventh and eighth graders. Tommy is there, and Reid, Paige, and Andrew, of course. Meagan, Hannah, Hailey, and a few other sixth graders stand in front of the list, too, studying it, whispering and pointing. I didn't even realize they had tried out.

I inch my way into the crowd quietly and focus on the white paper on the closed doorway. I don't look at anybody, but I can feel everyone all around me. And there it is:

Persephone—Grayson Sender

Ink on paper. Permanent. My heart beats firmly, and I smile to myself as I read through the rest of the list:

Hades—Reid Axelton
Zeus—Andrew Moyer
Demeter—Paige Francis
Hermes—Tommy Littleton
Lead Elf 1—Meagan Lee
Lead Elf 2—Audrey Booker
Lead Elf 3—Natalie Strauss

I'm surprised to see Meagan's name as one of the smaller leads. She's so quiet in class. I wonder how she'll do. I scan farther down the list to the smaller roles, the other Elves and the Souls of the Underworld. I see that Hailey and Hannah are Elves numbers eleven and twelve.

I stare at the paper for as long as I can. A buzz of whispers surrounds me. I don't want to turn around, but I know I can't stay here forever. So I stuff my hands in my pockets, lower my head, take a deep breath, and turn to leave. I try to feel Mom and Dad next to me like I did at home over break, but I can't. I'm completely alone.

"Congratulations, Grayson." The voice sounds sharp. I cringe, thinking of Aunt Sally's warning, and look up. It's Paige. "It's pretty impressive that a sixth grader got the lead." She adjusts her backpack and folds her arms over her chest.

"Thanks," I say, forcing a smile. Reid walks over to us, and I feel like getting out of here fast, but Paige keeps talking.

"I thought that was going to be my role. Usually eighth graders get the leads."

"Oh." My face is hot. I don't know what to say. "Sorry, I, uh . . . I guess I didn't think I'd get it," I finally mumble.

She takes a deep breath and looks quickly up at Reid. "Well," she says, looking me over. It sounds like she's giving in. "I guess you better call me 'Mom' from now on."

The room wavers. Just once, and just for a second. I steady myself and focus on Paige's layers of brightly colored, silky shirts. A clump of tangled necklaces and chains hangs around her neck. Nobody else at Porter dresses like her. "Right," I say.

Andrew joins us. The three of them look at me curiously. "I better get to class," I say quickly.

"What do you have first period?" Andrew asks.

"Um, Humanities, with Finn."

"Best class *ever*," he says, smiling at me.

"Yeah, definitely," I say. "So, I better go."

"See you tomorrow at rehearsal," he calls as I walk to the staircase. Before I get to the doorway, I turn around and look at the three of them once more. Reid and Andrew are standing close together, talking quietly, and Paige is still staring at me. Then I see Meagan, Hailey, and Hannah off to the side, not saying a word, and I realize that they were probably listening to our conversation.

"Hey, Grayson?" Meagan suddenly calls. She glances quickly at Hailey and Hannah, and then back at me.

"Yeah?"

"Wait up; we'll walk with you. Come on, guys."

I almost tell them that I'm fine, that I'll just go on my own, but I don't. Hailey and Hannah follow her, and the four of us walk down the stairs to the first floor.

☆

I pause for a minute outside the door to Finn's room and watch Meagan, Hannah, and Hailey go in. I know Amelia will be inside. I wonder if she's told everybody about the skirt yet. The thought makes me hate her.

Finn isn't sitting on top of his desk, greeting everyone the way he usually is, and I realize how much I'd been looking forward to seeing him. I hunch my shoulders forward to try to make myself as small as possible as I walk to my seat.

Across the room, Amelia is sitting on Lila's desk. They're

laughing hysterically. Hailey joins them. "Hey, guys," I hear her say. "What's so funny?" I strain to hear them.

Amelia leans over toward Lila to whisper something in her ear, her hair falling across both of their shoulders. Hailey stands back a bit and watches. They could be talking about anything, I tell myself, but my heart is pounding.

Ryan and Sebastian sit down in front of me. Ryan turns around as Sebastian starts to unpack his backpack. "Hey, Grayson," he says in a too-sweet voice. Sebastian glances at him, and I stare ahead. I can feel my face turning red. "What'd you do over break?" He pauses. "Your auntie take you shopping for some new flannels?" He glares at my shirt. "Oh, you're gonna ignore me? What a shock."

Sebastian taps Ryan's shoulder and points to Finn, who is walking through the doorway, a stack of papers in his hands. He plops them onto his desk, smoothes down his hair, and looks us over.

"In your seats, everybody," he says above the talking and laughter. "Sorry I'm late. Welcome back, welcome back! I hope everybody had a relaxing break." The class quiets down and I keep my eyes fixed on Finn as Amelia takes her seat next to me. She doesn't say anything, and neither do I. Out of the corner of my eye, I notice that she's wearing a new bracelet. Tiny hearts dangle from a silver chain. For some reason, I want to touch it, but I never would.

"I know it's been a long two weeks, and your heads are probably still in the clouds, but I assume you all remember that before break, we completed our unit on the Holocaust," Finn says, smiling. "I'll return your papers at the end of class. Today we're going to shift gears. I want you out of your pairs and back into your original rows from first quarter. I've got new plans for us for this unit. So, let's get up and move. Try to remember where your desk was. If your memory has failed you, come see me!"

Everyone starts to rustle around. "As soon as you're back in your places, I'll pass out our new novel." He holds a copy of *To Kill a Mockingbird* above his head. "It's a difficult novel, but it's one of my all-time personal favorites!" He practically has to yell to be heard over the sounds of people talking and pushing their desks and chairs across the floor. I shove my desk away from Amelia's without looking back.

It's a relief to be away from her. I look around at the rest of the class and notice Meagan watching me with her almond-shaped eyes. She looks down when my eyes meet hers, but after a second, she looks back up and smiles. I smile back.

"Okay!" Finn shouts. "Quiet down! Let's get started! We're going to jump right in. Notebooks out!" He scribbles *To Kill a Mockingbird* on the board. I copy it down in my notebook and sketch a princess as I listen to him talk. I study her for a minute, and then add a king on one side of her and a queen on the other.

Chapter 21

I'M IN A RUSH to get to the auditorium after school the next day. Just as I shove my last book into my backpack, I feel a tap on my shoulder. My stomach tightens, and I take a deep breath. Slowly, I turn around. Lila is standing in front of me. Across the hall, Amelia watches us as she buttons her red peacoat.

"Hi, *Gracie*," Lila says, throwing her long, brown hair over her shoulder. I shift my eyes to Amelia, but she looks down and turns around to close her locker. *Coward!* I want to scream. "I just wanted to say hi," Lila continues, giggling. I watch her laugh. I don't know what to say.

"Well, bye, Gracie." She runs across the hall, grabs Amelia's arm, and pulls her down the hallway. Neither of them looks back, and as I watch the back of Amelia's red coat disappear, I know that she's gone.

I slam my locker shut and try to breathe evenly as I walk to the auditorium, my eyes stinging. *It's starting,* I tell myself. Aunt Sally was right.

I shove the auditorium doors open, hard, and walk over to the stage where a bunch of people are already sitting, their legs dangling over the ledge. "Hey, Grayson!" Paige calls out, as if she was waiting for me. "So, Grayson?" she goes on, and Aunt Sally's voice explodes into my head again: *He's going to get teased horribly.* I brace myself and look up at her.

"Yeah?"

"Listen, I'm sorry that I was kind of a jerk yesterday morning." I don't say anything. The room is getting quieter, and I don't check to see, but I'm sure everyone is watching us. My face is probably bright red. I *think* she's being serious.

"That's okay," I mumble. I want to look away, but I force myself to focus on her long, feathery earrings.

"No, really, it was rude. I talked . . . I mean, I thought about it last night, and I think it's really brave that you tried out for a girl's part. I'm sure you're going to make a great Persephone." She pauses. "What are you waiting for?" she finally asks. "Come on up. We leads need to stick together." She pats the stage next to her.

Her apology sounded almost rehearsed, but she's smiling now, so I make my way up the stage steps and scoot into the spot next to her. "Thanks," I say, glancing at her bright pink sweater. "So, do you know where Finn is?" I ask.

"I'm not sure," she says. "Late for our first rehearsal, I guess." She smiles at me again. I should look away. I think of Amelia. I should protect myself. But I smile back.

"There he is," Meagan says, pointing to the auditorium doors. He and Dr. Shiner are in the hallway talking, their faces just inches apart. I swallow hard and wonder if Aunt Sally actually called the school. Dr. Shiner, his face flushed, is still saying something as Finn turns and walks toward us as if nothing happened. When Dr. Shiner storms off, I glance at Paige. She shrugs and I look away.

The crowd around me has grown; everyone must be here by now. "All right, guys and gals," Finn says, taking a deep breath and walking up the steps. It looks like he's forcing himself to smile. "Sorry I'm late. Let's get started." At the back of the stage is a long table, and we turn around to face him as he sits on top of it.

"First off, congratulations! I can't tell you how excited I am about this play. We have a very impressive cast this year, and I'm confident that this performance is going to be one of the best ever."

"Woo-woo!" Paige calls out. She starts clapping, and everyone joins in.

"Thank you. Thank you very much," Finn says jokingly. "Okay. Now for logistics: the rehearsal schedule is on the bulletin board behind the stage steps. Some days only leads come, and other days everyone comes. I've already e-mailed copies of the schedule to your families."

He looks us over. "As those of you who've been in a play before know, every rehearsal we start off with a warm-up activity before turning to the script."

"That's the best part," Paige whispers to me, and I nod like I know what she's talking about.

"This week is the read-through," Finn continues. "It will take two days because we're going to discuss as we read. We want to figure out *why* these characters are doing what they're doing. So we'll warm up, and then we'll get to work. Questions so far?" He looks around at us. I want to ask him what he means by warm-up activities, but nobody else is raising their hand, so I don't, either.

"Great, then." He jumps off the table. "Let's walk the stage. Almost everyone here is a theater veteran, but for those of you who are new, I want you to feel free to observe for as long as you want to, and jump in whenever you're comfortable."

I have no idea what he's talking about, but I stand up with everyone else. I notice Finn nodding in Paige's direction, and she quickly takes my arm. "Come with me," she whispers, and guides me to an empty space at the back of the stage by the table.

"All right," Finn says over the chatter and giggles. "Everyone, quiet down and think for a minute. Who are you today? A person? An animal? A male or a female? How old are you? When you've chosen your character, start walking."

I look quickly at Paige. "Just choose someone to be," she whispers. I stare at her.

"Anyone?" I ask, starting to smile.

"Yeah. A person, an animal, anything."

She stands still for a minute, and then starts flapping her arms like they're wings. I almost start laughing. She looks completely crazy. I feel someone moving behind me and turn around to see Tommy gorilla-walking past the burgundy curtains. Meagan struts by us, her nose in the air. I feel like I'm in another world. Everyone looks completely serious and completely stupid at the same time—but stupid in a really good way.

Paige stops flapping her wings for a second and reaches over to grab my hand. I start to walk next to her. I close my eyes and try to imagine the long skirt with the amber beads swaying.

"Very nice," I hear Finn saying as we move around the stage. Paige flies off, and I keep walking. I keep imagining my skirt.

"Freeze!" Finn finally calls out, and everyone does. "Who's sharing today?"

"Oo oo, ah ah," Tommy grunts loudly, his knuckles still on the floor. He starts hopping up and down, and when Finn calls on him, he tells us that he's Tom the Gorilla and that he's super-crazed because he just escaped from the San Diego Zoo. And that his knuckles are definitely injured, and will someone please take him to the vet? I smile and clap with everyone else as Tommy stands up, shaking out his hands.

"Ouch," he says, and we all laugh.

"Great job," Finn says over our laughter. "I wish we had more time for warm-ups, but we have to get down to business. We'll walk the stage again next time." He walks over to the table.

"I'm going to pass out your scripts." We gather around him as he opens a cardboard box. "Don't lose these, please," he says, lifting a stack of red scripts out. "I don't have extras." The gold inscriptions twinkle in the overhead lights, and I hold mine carefully when Paige passes it to me.

"There are folding chairs stacked behind the curtain," Finn tells us. "Once you've gotten your script, go ahead and grab one. Carefully. I don't need an avalanche here. We're going to make a circle on the stage and start the read-through."

One by one, we inch our way behind the curtain and pull our chairs onto the stage. I stick by Paige's side, and she doesn't seem to mind. She unfolds her chair and scoots it over so I can fit in next to her. Reid pushes his chair in on the other side of me and bounces his knee up and down as he flips through his script.

"Okay," Finn says, once we're settled. "Let's start. As I said, we're going to discuss as we read." He hops up onto the table again. "Page one!"

I open my script. The spine is stiff, and the paper smells new and fresh. Tommy starts reading the prologue. "'A long time ago, in a country far away, stood Mount Olympus, the home of the Greek gods,'" he begins. "'The gods were beautiful and good, and they were not alone. Horrible creatures lived among them.

These beasts existed so gods and mortal heroes could go to war with them—so goodness and light could struggle to win.'

"'In the fields of Mount Olympus lived Persephone. She was a lovely, young girl. . . .'"

I smile to myself as he continues, but I barely pay attention to his words anymore. *She was a lovely, young girl.* The line races through me over and over again, like electricity. *A lovely, young girl.*

I look around at the cast as Tommy reads. Everyone is following along, even Finn. Meagan, Hannah, and Hailey are across from me, concentrating on their scripts. Hannah is playing absentmindedly with her long ponytail. Meagan scratches her nose. I can't believe I'm actually here. I can't believe I'm Persephone.

When Tommy finishes, Finn asks him why Hermes would want to share this story with an audience. I flip through my script as they talk. I scan my name, *Persephone,* on practically every page. *You* are *the lead,* I tell myself, smiling. I have no idea how I'm going to memorize it all.

"Grayson?" Finn calls. I look up from my script. "Earth to Grayson." He smiles. "Your line."

"Page three," Paige whispers to me, tucking her script under her thigh and reaching her hands over to help me flip back to the right page. I look up at her soft, eager face, and then over to Finn. He's still smiling, waiting patiently.

I read my monologue and, when I'm done, I look up in a daze. I glance around the auditorium. The door to the hallway is propped open now, and Dr. Shiner is leaning against the door frame. He looks like he's staring right through me, and I wonder how long he's been standing there. I look down at my fingernails quickly as Tommy reads Hermes's response to my monologue. "'Persephone had no idea what fate awaited her,'" Tommy concludes.

When I look back up, Dr. Shiner is gone.

Chapter 22

I'M HEADING TO another rehearsal, trying to make the past few days stop swirling in my head. I'm almost to the auditorium doors when I hear a voice calling my name. The hall is crowded, but right away I see Ryan and Sebastian approaching me in their identical black winter jackets.

"Hey there, Gracie," Ryan says. "You on your way to play practice?" I can't move and I glance at Sebastian, but he's looking down. "Well, I hope they have lots of pretty dresses for you to wear, freak," he says. He shoves his elbow into my side as they walk past me. I stumble a little, my eyes suddenly on fire as I turn to watch their backs disappear around the corner. I take a deep breath and try to picture myself on stage between

Paige and Reid instead of here, in the hallway, my side burning. *Ignore him,* I tell myself, and I walk to the auditorium. *Always ignore him.*

It started the other day after Humanities. When the bell rang and I got up to leave, I saw him staring at me. Finn was across the room, digging through a cabinet. I headed for the door, but Ryan got up and stepped in front of me. I walked around him, tucking my long bangs behind my ears. "You letting your hair grow out, Gracie?" he asked, watching me go.

The next day, he and Sebastian appeared silently at my desk before Finn came in. Ryan had a fake-sweet look on his face. I looked away and watched the door. Where was Finn? "I'm not trying to be rude, Grayson," Ryan said, even though I wouldn't look at him. "We're just wondering—I mean, *everyone's* wondering— why are you playing a girl? Are you gay or something?" The room shook, like the first rumblings of an earthquake. I looked at Sebastian. I don't know why. Maybe to see if he felt it, too, but he was looking out the window. A minute later, Finn walked in and shooed everyone to their seats.

I push open the doors to the auditorium. Hard, to shake these memories out of my head. Today is practice for leads only, and Tommy, Reid, Audrey, and Natalie are sitting together on the ledge of the stage, talking to Finn. They wave to me as I walk toward them. "Hey, Grayson!" they all call out together. Then they look at each other, surprised to hear their voices in unison, and collapse practically on top of one another, laughing.

I feel my body relaxing as I join them. Paige isn't here yet, so I sit down next to Reid, who's still hysterical. The auditorium doors bang open. Paige and Meagan walk in together and toss their backpacks onto the wooden seats. Finn looks at his watch. "We'll give it a few more minutes. We're just waiting for Andrew, right?"

"He's coming," Paige says. "I saw him at his locker. He was totally freaking out because he couldn't find his English binder. Have you ever seen his locker?" she asks us. I smile at her when her eyes meet mine. "It's beyond disgusting. I think he has old lunches in there from, like, September." She climbs the stage steps and sits down right next to me. Meagan follows her. I glance at the other empty spaces where she could have sat instead, and I smile.

"Hey," I say to her.

"Hey, yourself," she replies. "So, Finn?" she asks, suddenly turning to him. "Have you been to the Shakespeare Theater?"

"Of course! I was just there last week," he answers. "Why do you ask?"

"My dad got us tickets to *Romeo and Juliet*," she says. "Is that what you saw?"

"It was," he answers. "Opening night."

"Did you like it? I've heard it's *amazing*."

"It *was* amazing," Finn answers. "We'll discuss it, but *after* you see it. I can't wait to hear what you think!"

"Cool," Paige says.

I watch them talking. Reid is on one side of me, and Paige

· 142 ·

is on the other. They're like bookends, and I concentrate on the feel of their arms on either side of me as we wait for Andrew.

When he finally slams through the door, apologizing, we take our places for Act One. Tommy has his entire monologue memorized, and, when it's time for me and Paige to go onstage, she leaves her script on top of her backpack in the chair next to Finn. I wonder again how I'm going to memorize everything. "Ready?" I ask Finn from the stage, my script in hand.

"Whenever you guys are," he calls up to us.

I turn to the right page. "'Mother,'" I call, and it feels so weird to say it out loud. I try to not smile and to stay in character, like Finn told us to. Paige is pulling pretend weeds in the corner of the stage. "'I'm going to the stream,'" I tell her.

"'Be careful, Persephone,'" she says.

"'Yes, Mother.'" I look down at my script. It's her line, but she's looking at me expectantly. *What time will you be back?* I whisper to her.

My line? she mouths, surprised. I nod, and she almost starts laughing.

"'What time will you be back?'"

"'Before dark,'" I read. The stage is quiet. *Persephone, I'd like you to bring some of the Elves along,* I whisper. I burst out laughing. I can't help it. Obviously, she doesn't have her part memorized as well as she thinks. I take a deep breath and try to compose myself.

"'Persephone, I'd like you to bring some of the Elves along,'" Paige repeats. Suddenly, a red script sails through the air, like a

Frisbee, and lands at Paige's feet. We both look out at the auditorium, hysterical now. Finn waves at us from the front row of seats.

"Maybe we'll take our snack break early today?" he asks. I can't stop laughing as I dig my brown paper bag out of my backpack.

☆

At home, I eat dinner quickly. I want to get to my room so I can finish my math homework and memorize lines. I don't have too many problems left—I've been getting so much done in the library at lunchtime. "You're on a *mission*," Mrs. Millen said to me earlier today as she sat at her desk with her steaming lunch and Diet Coke and watched me fly through my assignments. It's true. I want to be able to focus on memorizing lines once I'm home. "Getting into Persephone's skin," as Finn puts it, is the best part of my day.

And anyway, I don't want to be around Aunt Sally. I look up from my food. She's watching me eat, and I look out the window at the black sky. I heard what she said. She thinks I'm a monster.

"So, Grayson," Jack says, as he shoves rice into his mouth, "do you know what Tyler asked me in gym today?" I freeze. Jack's new best friend, Tyler, is Ryan's older brother.

"No," I mumble.

"He asked me if being gay is genetic."

I accidentally drop my fork onto my plate.

"Jack! We're not getting into this with you again," Uncle Evan warns.

"Whatever," Jack mumbles. "Of course you're not. It's all about what *Grayson* wants. That's how it's always been. You don't even care about me." I can't believe he could possibly think that.

"Don't be ridiculous," Aunt Sally says quickly.

"Why don't you just try ignoring Tyler?" Brett asks. "At school, Mr. Smith always says if you have a conflict with someone, you can try ignoring them."

"Shut up, Brett," Jack says.

"Why? Anyway, I still don't get it. I mean, it's just a play."

I can't listen anymore. "I'm finished," I say as I get up from the table. "I have to work on my lines."

☆

In my room, I sit on my bed under Mom's painting with my script in my lap. I've got to get this memorized by rehearsal tomorrow, but it's hard to concentrate. Jack's words echo in my ears. I can't believe how stupid he is.

There's a gentle knock on the door, and Uncle Evan comes in. He sits at my desk. "So," he says softly, "you have a lot to do?"

"Yeah," I tell him. "Everyone's starting to get their lines memorized but me."

"You know," he says, "when I was in law school, I had to figure out how to remember thousands of pages of information."

"You did?"

"Sure. It was pretty intense. What I would do is try to visual-ize the pages in my mind, you know? Like, I'd read a section of information, and then close my eyes and try to actually see some of the key words. It really helped." He pauses. "You want to try that? I could help you—you know, read along to see if you're getting it?"

I look at him. Dad looks so young in the pictures that we have of him, and I wonder: if he were alive, would he and Uncle Evan still look alike? Would his hair be turning gray above the ears, too? Would he push his glasses up with his knuckle when they slipped down on his nose? I hear dishes clanging in the kitchen, and the TV is on now. Uncle Evan gets up and quietly closes my door all the way.

"Sure," I tell him, and hand him my script.

"So, Act One, huh?" he asks, scanning the words.

"Yeah."

"Great. Whenever you're ready, Grayson."

"Uncle Evan?"

"Yes, son?" he asks, without looking up.

The words are like a slap, but I try to ignore the feeling. "Thanks," I say.

"My pleasure." He looks up and smiles at me. "Your line."

Chapter 23

THE AUDITORIUM IS CHAOTIC. I'd forgotten that the whole cast, including all the Elves and Souls of the Underworld, would be at rehearsal today. Reid, Andrew, and Tommy are on the stage with a couple other boys. They're talking, and then laughing too loudly at something one of them is saying.

The girls are in the front rows of auditorium seats. Paige is already there, and, of course, she's in the middle of the group. Hailey, Hannah, and a bunch of the Elves are gathered around her. Natalie and Audrey walk in together. They say hi to me on their way to the front of the auditorium. A few more people hurry past, but I hang back.

Finally, Meagan walks in. "You coming, Grayson?" she asks.

I glance at the boys onstage again, their movements quick and their voices booming.

"Yeah, I'm coming," I say, and I follow her to the wooden seats.

I keep my eyes fixed on Paige, who smiles when she sees me. "Hey, Grayson!" she calls. Everyone looks up at me, and I let my eyes scan their faces for a second. "Come sit with me," she says, moving her jacket and backpack off of the seat next to her. I wonder if she saved it for me.

I scoot past Sofia, one of the Elves. Hannah is leaning over her, holding a tiny pink clip between her lips and making a thin braid down the side of her head. Her fingers move quickly, like they know what they're doing, and when she's done she clasps the braid at the bottom.

"'Kay," Hannah says, "who's next?" I notice that she has a pack of tiny clips resting on top of her pink backpack. They're arranged in the package like a rainbow—pink, peach, yellow, light green, light blue, and lavender, the colors lined up in neat plastic rows.

"Me!" says Meagan from the row in front of her.

"Color?" asks Hannah. I watch them talk. Their voices crisscross easily, back and forth, and the rhythm of their words reminds me of "Miss Mary Mack, Mack, Mack" and "Bo Bo Ski Watten Totten" and all the years of recesses I spent sitting on the cement step outside with a book in my hands, pretending to read, but really watching the girls. Wishing.

"Um, do two next to each other. Blue and purple."

"Lean over," Hannah says, and Meagan does.

I watch Hannah's hands fly until two perfect, long, black braids appear on the side of Meagan's head. I reach up, run my fingers through my longish hair, and I look over at Paige. She's glancing at her watch. "It's already almost three twenty-five. Where's Finn?" she asks, to nobody in particular. He's come in late almost every day.

"Here he is," someone says, and I look up to see him jogging down the auditorium aisle.

"Afternoon, ladies," he says, nodding in our direction, and I glance at the other girls quickly. I doubt he noticed me huddled in the middle of the group, but Sofia giggles.

"*Shh,*" Paige says.

"Gentlemen," Finn nods to the boys on the stage. "Sorry I'm late. I'd like everyone to join the boys up here," he continues. "I need you all to grab a mat from this pile and find your own space on the stage. We're doing something new for warm-up." He points to a stack of yoga mats that someone must have brought in from the gym. The mob of girls surrounding me starts to move, and I'm part of the clump. We walk together onto the stage. "It's going to be kind of tight with all of you here. Spread out as much as you can! Lie down on a mat on your back," Finn calls up to us. "We're doing a relaxation exercise!"

I unroll a mat and smile to myself when Paige puts hers right next to mine. She lies down and closes her eyes. I lie next to her. Above me, the ceiling looks like it's about a million miles away. The stage lights are bright, so I close my eyes, too. The mat smells gross, and I hear people walking and talking above me. When the stage finally starts to quiet down, I look to my right and see that Andrew is next to me now, too.

"I could fall asleep," he whispers.

"Definitely." I smile.

"Okay," Finn finally says quietly from somewhere on the stage. "Today we're going to start building some relaxation exercises into our rehearsal routine. Many actors use relaxation and visualization techniques to help them settle into their characters. We're going to start by relaxing each muscle group in our bodies, one by one. We'll begin with our toes and work our way up to our necks."

I listen to Finn's voice. He tells us to tighten our muscles, and then feel them relax. By the time he has gotten to our necks, the room is completely silent.

He's practically whispering to us now. "Now that you're relaxed, we're going to begin our visualization exercises. Keep your eyes closed. Picture yourself on stage rehearsing. You are no longer yourself—you *are* your character." He pauses, and then continues, even slower. "How do you want to see yourself?" he asks us. "Look down and imagine your body, your clothes. What do you see?" He pauses. The quiet is long and still. "What, as a character, do you need to learn, and what do you already know? Think about this. Make a mental list." He waits, the silence hanging over the stage, heavy now. I can practically feel it seeping into the open spaces around me. "What are you afraid of?" Another long pause. "And, finally, what do you wish for?"

My muscles suddenly tighten. I open my eyes and stare at the track of lights dangling far above my head. My heart is racing, and I try to focus on the pattern—black, light, black, light, black, light, but the light is seeping into the black spaces and everything is too bright to look at for so long. I close my eyes again, but I'm still blinded by the bursts of light floating in front of me. I feel dizzy, like I'm spinning, and I'm starting to feel like a bird again, like I did that day in Humanities so long ago when Amelia asked me to be her partner.

The auditorium is silent, but Finn's voice echoes in my head. *What do you wish for?* I'm flying above myself now, looking down at the stage that's slowly swirling beneath me. I'm like the phoenix in Mom's painting. All the colors beneath me are blending together. Paige and Andrew are on either side of me. Their eyes are closed. My eyes are open. I'm clutching the sides of my yoga mat.

What are you afraid of? I hear Aunt Sally's voice ripping through my head again: *He's creating a monster!* But I don't look like a monster. I look the way I'm *supposed* to look—the way I need everyone else to see me. I'm wearing the long, lacy skirt with dangling amber beads. It's like an antique. It's something Persephone would wear. My blond hair is a fan around my face. I look scared, but also pretty. My heartbeat surrounds me like the drumbeat that I heard at tryouts. I remember it now—how it felt when I first knew that I was supposed to be Persephone.

What do you already know?

I am a girl.

Part

Three

Chapter 24

AUNT SALLY'S HAIR *is blond like mine. I wonder if she wore it in braids when she was a girl.* This is what I'm thinking, and I don't know why, as I feel the gentle *tug tug tug* on my head. I imagine Paige's fingers crisscrossing quickly, like they know what they're doing. "Pass me a clip," she says to Meagan. It's Tuesday after school, leads only, and when Paige said she'd make me a braid, I shrugged and smiled.

I feel one last *tug*, and warm plastic against my cheekbone. "Cute," Paige says, and smiles. It's like she can read my mind, because she adds, "I'll make you another one." She gathers my hair at my scalp, and the gentle tugging starts again. When she's done, I can hear the two plastic clips clanking together. I see the pink and purple out of the corner of my eye when I turn my face.

"You look fabulous, Grayson," Natalie says, grinning. I can't tell if she's kidding or not, but either way, her face looks kind, so I smile back.

Finn won't be in for a few more minutes even though rehearsal is supposed to start at three fifteen. I reach up to touch the bumpy braids and plastic clips.

"So, Meagan," Paige suddenly asks, "what's up with you and Sebastian?"

"Oh my God," Meagan says, rolling her eyes. "Why does everyone keep asking me that?" She sounds annoyed, but I can tell she's trying not to smile. "Who told you?"

"Um, Liam?" Liam is Sebastian's older brother. I follow the conversation carefully with my eyes, trying not to seem too interested or shocked, but I can't believe what Meagan is saying. Sebastian? Ryan's loser sidekick? What is she thinking? A thought wrestles its way into my mind—have Meagan and Sebastian ever talked about *me*?

"So, what's going on?" Paige nudges. "Are you guys together or something?"

"I don't know!" Meagan squeals.

"Well, I think he's cute," Paige says, just as Finn slams through the auditorium doors.

"Sorry," he yells. "Sorry I'm late."

"As usual," Audrey mumbles under her breath, and the girls stand up to move onto the stage for relaxation.

I stay where I am for a minute and reach up to touch the two plastic clips hanging next to my cheek. Meagan's long, black hair swings as she walks toward the aisle.

Andrew, Reid, and Tommy are already on the stage, laying out their mats, and Finn is talking to them. The four of them are laughing. I pull the clips off the ends of my braids, tuck them into my pocket, and run my fingers through my hair. I feel the braids unravel as I join the others onstage.

☆

On Friday Paige is absent, and I stand in the aisle for a minute, studying the growing group of girls in the auditorium seats. Meagan is in the middle of the clump. Hannah and Hailey are on one side of her, and Audrey and Natalie are on the other. They're bunched together, talking. I walk over to them and sit down in front of Meagan. I feel lost without Paige, and I open my backpack to take out a book to pretend to read.

"Hey, Grayson," Meagan says, so I turn around. I've been watching her and Sebastian this past week, and if they really are together, they spend a lot of time ignoring each other.

"Grayson, lean over," Natalie says, and I see she has a handful of clips. "Let's braid your hair again."

"Okay." I smile, put my book back into my backpack, and turn around on my knees to face the girls behind me. She reaches for my hair, and I feel her fingers gently scratch my scalp.

"Um, are you braiding Grayson's hair?" a sixth grader named Kristen asks from behind me. She's one of the Elves.

"Yeah, he looks fab with braids," Natalie says as she works, and I glance back at Kristen while Natalie hangs onto a clump of my hair.

"*Okaaay*," Kristen says. I can't tell what she's thinking.

Nobody says anything for a minute. Finally, Kristen asks, "Want some help?" and I see Audrey pass her some clips.

Kaylee is sitting next to me now. "Can I have a few?" she asks, laughter in her voice. I look at her out of the corner of my eye as Natalie tugs at my hair, and soon a million hands are flying over my head. Someone's pulling too hard. I don't know who, but I don't say anything. I reach my hand up to feel what's going on, but Natalie tells me to wait, so I do.

Meagan gives me a thumbs-up as Natalie, Kristen, and Kaylee work, and I notice that Hannah and Audrey are both talking to her at the same time. She's looking back and forth between them, like she's stuck in the middle of two worlds, and for some reason, this makes me smile.

By the time Finn comes in, the girls are done. I reach my hands up and feel my head. It's completely covered in braids and clips and, all of a sudden, I feel almost guilty—like I just cheated on a test and didn't get caught. But I push that thought away. "So? What do you think?" I ask, turning my head from side to side. I know I must look like a clown, but everyone's smiling at me now, so I don't really care.

"Super adorable," Natalie says, and we walk up to the stage. Finn smiles at me as I take my yoga mat off the pile. It's kind of uncomfortable to lie on top of a million clips during relaxation, but I leave them in anyway.

☆

When rehearsal is over, I stand in the aisle pulling clips out of my hair and unraveling my braids. I watch everyone zip themselves into their winter jackets and put on their backpacks as I work.

"Need some help?" Meagan asks from behind me. I turn around. She's standing with Hannah and Hailey. They look like an ad for the Gap in their pink and purple shiny jackets, their hair smooth and long.

"Nah, I'm almost done," I say. I think of the girls' voices and grins as I let them braid my hair, and the feeling washes over me again—that I did something wrong and got away with it. I let them treat me like I was a stupid doll or something. Anyway, what *real* girl wears a million crooked braids all over her head, sticking out all over the place? *Real girls* wear regular shirts, pants, skirts, jackets, and shoes, not crazy, exaggerated porcupine braids that make them look like an idiot. This was all just a big joke to everyone. I pass Hannah my handful of clips, and she zips them into the outside pocket of her pink backpack. I suddenly feel like crying, and I pat my head to make sure I got them all out.

"I think you're good," Meagan says, examining my hair. "Ready to go?"

"Yeah," I say. I swing my gray backpack onto my back and tuck my jacket under my arm.

"You taking the bus home?" Meagan asks as we walk out the auditorium doors.

"No, my uncle's picking me up on his way home from work," I tell her. "You?"

"My mom's getting us."

"Cool."

"So, do you still go to the library at lunch?" she asks.

I look down at my shoes. "Yeah, I try to get my homework done so I can memorize lines at night. My uncle's been helping me." I run my fingers through my hair one more time.

"Well, if you ever want to eat with us, you should," she says as we approach the double doors to the parking lot.

I look at Meagan and smile. Hannah and Hailey are standing on either side of her, watching her. "Thanks, Meagan," I tell her. And I mean it, but I know I'll never be able to sit at the same table as Lila and Amelia again.

Outside at the circle drive, Meagan's mom is waiting in a silver SUV. "Bye, Grayson," the girls say, and they pile into the car, one shining jacket at a time—first pink, then purple, then pink again. Meagan's mom rolls down the passenger window and leans toward me.

"Hi, Grayson!" she calls, and I suddenly feel panicky. I'm sure she knows I'm Persephone. "Are you getting picked up?"

"Yeah, my uncle should be here any minute."

"Okay, as long as you have a ride. Have a good weekend!"

I stand in the cold, damp air and wait for Uncle Evan. I should put my jacket on, but I don't want to. I look at it, hanging over my arm—dull and black—and I try to picture what I wish were there instead. *Real girls wear regular shirts, pants, skirts, jackets, and shoes.* I think about the braids again. I don't want to look like a freak. I want to be a real girl.

Uncle Evan pulls up, and I get into the car. The heat is blasting, and the news is on the radio. "Hey, Grayson," he says as I buckle my seat belt. "How's everything?"

"Good," I tell him.

"Great. So listen, I hate to say this, but I'm not going to be able to practice lines with you tomorrow morning. Sorry about that. Something came up at work, and I need to go in to meet with Henry." He looks distracted. "We'll definitely do it Sunday, though, okay?"

"That's fine. It's not a problem." I almost feel relieved. *Real girls wear regular shirts, pants, skirts, jackets, and shoes.* "Actually, I was thinking of going to that thrift store in Lake View tomorrow, anyway. Is that okay?" The words tumble out of my mouth.

Uncle Evan looks at me quickly. "You going with Amelia?"

"Nope," I say. "No. Just me."

"Sure. I'm sure that's fine," he says as he pulls onto the street.

Chapter 25

THE NEXT MORNING, it looks slushy and gray out. I crack my window open. It's way too warm for the end of January, and the wet air floats into my room, through the screen. I get dressed in my jeans and a sweatshirt, and grab my light blue fleece from my closet.

It feels strange to be riding the bus alone to the Second Hand. I haven't done this since last summer, since before Amelia. The bus bumps and bounces through potholes as I watch out the steamy window.

In Lake View, the crowd feels familiar as I make my way down the sidewalk. I don't look up as I pass the floor-to-ceiling window at the Coffee House, but a shudder zips through my body anyway. The wind is blowing like crazy behind me, and it practically pushes me through the doorway of the Second Hand.

Inside, everything is the same. It's dreary and dim and smells like mothballs. I pass the shelves of knickknacks. I want to look, to see if the broken bird is still there lying at the bottom of its cage, but I don't. I doubt it, anyway. I walk to the empty youth section.

I glance at the racks of boys' clothes, and I remember all the time I spent sifting through them, looking for things that I could easily pretend into dresses and long, flowing shirts, and, for a tiny second, I miss doing that. It seems so safe. But, on the other side of the room are the racks of girls' clothes, and I go to them.

I look behind me at the guy at the register with the shaved head, and at the few people shopping in the front of the store. *It's my sister's birthday this week,* I silently rehearse. *She asked for clothes for a present.* I look through the racks of T-shirts hanging on the wall and pull out a pink one with a sequined heart on it. It looks like it will fit me. I want to browse slowly, to feel the fabric of each T-shirt on the rack; I want to try them on, but I tell myself to hurry. I quickly find two others that I like, a lavender one with a light ruffle of lace around the bottom, and a fuchsia one with colorful butterflies embroidered on the sleeves. I take a deep breath and walk with them to the register. *It's my sister's birthday this week. She asked for clothes for a present.*

There's someone in line ahead of me, so I drape the shirts over my arm and run my fingers through a bowl of silver rings on the front counter. One looks like a braid, and I try it on. It makes me think of Paige. Next to the rings, necklaces dangle from a metal stand. I examine them—the crosses, hearts, and colorful beads, and I look carefully at a bird charm hanging from a silver chain. Its wings are spread; it's mid-flight. I turn the tag over. Ten dollars.

"You all set?" I look up. It's my turn.

"Um, yeah." My hands kind of shake as I put the shirts on the counter. I put the necklace on top of them. The guy pulls out the tag on each shirt. He doesn't look up, and it crosses my mind for a quick second that maybe he wouldn't care that the clothes are for me.

"You find everything okay?" he asks.

"Yeah."

"Cool," he says, finally looking at me. He smiles.

"It's, uh, it's my sister's birthday this week," I stammer. "She wanted clothes for her present."

"This is a cool necklace," he says as he rings it up.

"Yeah."

"Twenty-four eighteen," he says, putting everything into a plastic bag.

I hand him twenty-five dollars and wait for my change. "Hope your sister has a good birthday," he says, handing it to me. I put the coins into my pocket, grab the bag, and head out the door.

Chapter 26

THE REST OF the weekend crawls by. When Monday morning finally comes, I wake up early in my dim room and put on my jeans. I take the plastic bag out from where I hid it behind the summer clothes in my closet, pull out the necklace and pink shirt with the sparkly heart, and carefully snap off both tags. I crumple them up and throw them in my garbage can before tucking the bag back behind my shorts.

Standing in front of my mirror, I watch myself pull my pajama shirt off and put on the T-shirt. The heart lies flat on my chest. I clasp the necklace behind my neck, brush my hair and tuck it behind my ears, and stand there for a long time, looking at myself. I wonder what Paige would think.

When I hear the shower running across the hall, though,

panic gushes through me. I open the other side of my closet, pull out my dark purple hoodie, put it on quickly, and zip it up all the way to the top. I look like my old self in it, but still, I can't help smiling as I wait for my turn in the bathroom.

☆

At school, Finn is late to Humanities again. I pretend to be looking for something in my backpack so I don't have to make eye contact with anyone. I pay attention to the feel of the T-shirt underneath my hoodie while I wait for him to come in.

When the bell finally rings, I look to the door. Still no Finn, but Ryan is making his way to my desk now. I touch my hand to the top of my zipper and look back down to my backpack.

"Hey—*Grace!*" Ryan whispers. I keep my head down. "*Gracie!*"

And then, Finn's voice. "All right, class! Sorry I'm late. Everyone, take your seat. Ryan? In your seat please." I take deep breaths. "Notebooks open!" Finn picks up a dry-erase marker. "Everybody's copy of *To Kill a Mockingbird* should be out. Let's get started." I press my fingers to the bird flying under my sweatshirt as I listen to him talk.

☆

When Science is finally over at three o'clock, I lean down to pack my backpack. Meagan and Hannah are lab partners right behind me, and when I stand up, I see Sebastian walking toward them with a little smile on his face. His hands are in his pockets. "Hi, Meagan," he says shyly. I look back and forth between their faces.

"Sebastian!" I hear from across the room, and I turn around. Ryan is pushing his way toward us, through everyone who's heading for the door. "Watch it," he says to Sofia as he shoves past her. "Sebastian, let's go. My mom always picks me up out front." I head for the door and glance behind me one more time as I pass Mrs. Leo's desk. Sebastian is saying something to Ryan. His face is flushed.

Suddenly, I hear Mrs. Leo's voice. "Grayson, do you have a moment?" I look over to her. She's always asking people to stay behind to help her clean lab supplies.

"Oh, sorry, I have to get to rehearsal," I call from the doorway.

"Oh, that's right. Well, it will only take five minutes or so. Don't after-school activities start at three fifteen? I wanted to talk to you and Sebastian for a minute."

My heart jumps. Why?

I glance up at the clock on the wall. "Okay." I head back to her desk.

"Sebastian?" she calls across the room. He looks over and his eyes widen.

"Yeah?" he asks.

"I need to talk to you and Grayson for a moment." Ryan looks at Sebastian and smirks. Then he covers his mouth with his hands and fake-gags. Mrs. Leo seems totally oblivious.

"'Kay," Sebastian mumbles, and Ryan, Meagan, and Hannah head out the door. Sebastian joins me in front of Mrs. Leo's desk. She takes her glasses off and pushes them up onto her white curls.

"So, boys," she starts, and I feel like she just punched me in the face with her tiny, knotted, veiny fist. I look down at my shoes. "You know, I've been a teacher here at Porter for almost forty years."

I nod and swallow, and glance over to Sebastian. What does she want?

"Well," she continues, "in all my years here I've never . . ." She pauses and looks almost embarrassed. I glance down to make sure my zipper on my sweatshirt is still up. My heart is pounding in my ears.

"Well, I've never been able to get enough kids together who are interested in starting a Science Club."

My breathing evens, and I feel my body relaxing. I look at Sebastian. He seems relieved, too.

Her face lights up. "So, you fellows are interested?" she asks quickly. "I'm looking for a few kids from every grade to head it up—good students who have a solid understanding of science."

I speak up first. "Um, sorry, Mrs. Leo. I can't. I'm too busy with rehearsal." I glance at Sebastian, and then over to the clock on the wall again.

"Yeah," he mumbles. "I, um, I have guitar after school. And homework." His voice trails off, and I smile to myself as I listen to him trying to come up with an excuse.

"Oh, okay," Mrs. Leo says, disappointed. "You kids are all so busy these days."

I inch backward to the door. "Sorry about that, Mrs. Leo," I say. "If I change my mind, I'll let you know," I tell her, my hand on the doorknob. I need to get to rehearsal.

Sebastian is by my side. "Yeah, sorry," he says awkwardly.

The hallways are emptying out as we walk to our lockers downstairs. I glance over at Sebastian. I picture him at Ryan's side, but then I think of the way he smiled at Meagan after class today. "That was close," I say.

He keeps his eyes on the floor. "Yup." He's quiet for a minute before he looks at me and smiles. "Seriously."

At my locker, I grab my books and jacket and shove everything into my backpack. Sebastian shuts his locker across the hall from me, and when I start to walk toward the auditorium, he's by my side again.

I touch my bird charm through my sweatshirt as we turn the corner away from the main hallway. The hall outside of the auditorium is almost empty. It looks like everyone is either at their after-school activity by now or has left the building, except for Sebastian and me and a couple of kids down by the front doors.

When we get closer to the auditorium, though, I stop walking. I see now that the two figures at the far end of the hallway are Ryan and Tyler. For the billionth time, I think about Aunt Sally's prediction, and I turn to look at Sebastian. He's watching them, too. They're coming toward us, and I can see the smirks on their stupid faces. And even though a little piece of me still hopes they're just here to meet Sebastian, the truth is that I know they're not. I know they're here for me.

The four of us are so close to each other now. Tyler is bigger than Ryan, but aside from that, they look almost identical with their straight bangs and hard faces.

"Hey, Sebastian," Ryan says once we're face-to-face. But he's looking at me. "Mrs. Leo didn't want to make you and Gracie lab partners, did she? 'Cause who would I be with, then?" Sebastian is looking toward the doors at the end of the hallway. He shakes his head no.

I keep my fingers on my zipper. "So, Gracie-girl," Ryan continues, "why were you ignoring me in Humanities today?"

I don't say anything. My mouth won't work.

"Grace," Tyler pipes in. "Why won't you just talk to us? Jack told me if we wanted to talk to you, we could find you here after school. So why aren't you talking to us?"

I feel like I'm in a cloud. Sebastian takes a few steps back until he's leaning against the lockers. "I've gotta go," I say to Ryan and Tyler. The words spill out. I don't even feel myself talking. My hand is still holding my zipper. But Ryan takes a step closer, blocking me.

"You going to the auditorium to play dress-up?" he asks as Tyler comes to his side. "I bet they have lots of pretty things for you to wear." He glances up at his brother and smiles.

My mouth opens and closes. I'm dizzy. I hold tight to my zipper.

"Hey, look, Ry," Tyler says, pointing to my hand on my zipper.

"You're right. He's all ready to put his dress on." He turns back to me. "Why are you such a freak?" he asks.

I can't get my hand to move. He takes a step closer and grabs my sweatshirt. I stumble forward into him. He smells like sweat. I look over to Sebastian again, but he's standing with his arms hanging limply at his sides.

Suddenly, I hear shouting behind me. Ryan and Tyler look over my shoulder, and I turn around. Paige is rushing toward us, her backpack thumping against her side. "Hey! Hey! What's going on?" she yells, and in a second, she's by my side. She wraps her arm around mine.

Ryan and Tyler don't say anything. "Well," Tyler finally says, "we were just talking to Gracie." He smiles at Paige. Her face turns bright pink, and I can practically feel the heat rising from her body. I lean into her a little.

"Why don't you just get away from him?" she yells, even though they're standing right in front of us.

"Whoa, calm down, psycho," Tyler whispers. He glances around the hallway, and he and Ryan start to back away. I look at Sebastian. He's watching Paige, and he looks relieved.

"That's right," Paige continues. "Just get away from us, you coward idiots. Run on home. Losers!"

I stare at her. I don't know what to say. I can't believe the words flying out of her mouth. Ryan and Tyler look around nervously. "Come on, Ry," Tyler finally says. "We've gotta go anyway. Dad's picking us up at the west door."

"I thought it was Mom's week," Ryan stumbles.

"Well, you thought wrong," Tyler says, and grabs him by the arm. They turn and run off, banging through the side doors of the school, and are gone. The hallway is silent except for my breathing and the sound of the blood racing through my veins. Sebastian hasn't moved.

The auditorium doors suddenly slam open, and Finn barges through. "Paige!" he yells from down the hallway. "What on earth is going on?"

I grab her hand and look her in the eye. "Don't tell," I demand. I don't know why I say it.

"Are you insane?" she whispers.

"I'm serious," I say. "Please."

"Why?" she asks as Finn walks toward us. A crowd of heads is poking out of the auditorium door behind him now.

"I . . . I don't know," I say. And I don't. I feel dangerously close to a cliff. "Just, please?"

She looks at me like I'm crazy. "Okay," she says. I don't want to let go of her arm, but Finn is standing over us now.

"What is this screaming about?" he asks. "Is everything okay?"

"Yeah," Paige answers, looking him in the eye. "Sorry, Finn."

"All right, then," he says, studying us as we stand there, side by side. His eyes rest on mine for what seems like forever. *You sure?* they beg.

I'm sure. I drop Paige's arm and shove my fists into my pockets.

Finn still doesn't move. "Grayson, you know if you ever need to tell me anything, you can, right?" he asks.

"I know," I mumble. I can't say anything else.

We stand together in silence. "All right, then," he finally says again. "We should get to the auditorium."

I glance back as we follow him down the hall. Sebastian is gone.

Chapter 27

EVERYTHING KEEPS flip-flopping back and forth, from bad to good, over and over again. Sometimes everything is light. Other times, everything is dark.

In class, and with Aunt Sally and Jack at home, I keep my head down and my fingers on the zipper at my neck. During these times, I want to become invisible again, the way I used to be.

But at rehearsal, it's totally different.

I'm sitting with the other leads, our feet dangling off the stage. I look up at the stage lights hanging above us and at the spaces between them—the blackness fading into light over and over again. Paige is on one side of me, and Andrew is on the other. "Ladies and gentlemen!" Finn is saying. "I never thought that by February we'd be so far along. This is going to be a very, very strong performance!" I picture myself as Persephone, onstage in the dark, crowded auditorium, and I smile.

"Last time, we were talking about Act Three," Finn goes on, and Reid raises his hand to ask him something about the scenery in the Underworld. I can picture myself sitting on Hades's bench in my golden gown.

"Hey, what's so funny?" Andrew whispers, nudging me playfully.

"Huh?" I ask, looking up at him. He starts to giggle. I must have been staring into space, smiling. "Nah, nothing," I grin. I know if I keep looking at him, I'm going to burst out laughing, so I look down at my feet.

All of our shoes are hanging over the stage ledge, and the trip that Aunt Sally and Uncle Evan took us on to the Grand Canyon two summers ago pops into my head. I remember standing at the edge of the cliff, looking over the railing, and feeling so close to falling. Once, when we were hiking, I tripped on a rock and stumbled toward the edge of the path that dropped off into a steep, rocky hill. It was Jack who reached out his hand to grab mine.

I listen to Finn's voice as he continues to talk, but I can't hear his words anymore. The feeling of the crystal light fades into blackness as I envision myself, onstage, as Persephone again. Now I feel like I'm a step away from that cliff.

I automatically check the zipper on my sweatshirt to make sure that it's up all the way. I try to clear my mind and focus on Finn's words: "If there aren't any questions, we'll jump right in!"

Everyone scrambles for their places. I push the memory of the cliff out of my mind as I walk to center stage. The Souls of the Underworld are wandering the stage, watching me. They're waiting for me to give my line. Uncle Evan and I practiced this scene last night, and I know it perfectly.

I sit down on the bench next to Kristen and watch the deathly Souls as they roam around us. Everything is damp and dreary. "'I'm so lonely in the Underworld,'" I say to Kristen, and I try to describe the *feeling* of happiness up above, but I can't put it into words. I forget about the evil in her eyes. I'm daydreaming, thinking of my mother in her garden, and, distracted, I reach for a pomegranate from the cardboard tree next to us. I break it open with my thumbs and put a seed into my mouth, not noticing Kristen's slight smile.

Finn interrupts just as Zeus and Hades are coming into the garden to find me. By then, I've eaten six pomegranate seeds. "Listen up for a minute here," Finn says. "I want you to notice how well Grayson has gotten into character. Well done, Grayson." Everyone looks at me and I can't help smiling, even though I try to tighten my lips. "That was golden," Finn goes on. "Golden."

Across the stage, Paige is nodding, like she agrees with him. She catches me looking at her, flashes a smile, and gives me a thumbs-up.

☆

When I get home after rehearsal, Jack and Brett are already there. An open cereal box and two dirty bowls are on the dining room table, and I can hear their voices from across the apartment. On the way to my bedroom, I pass Jack's closed door. His Nerf ball thumps against it, and he and Brett suddenly burst into laughter. I swallow hard. I know they're on Jack's bed shooting baskets from across the room. Someone jumps onto the rug and scrambles for the ball.

I quietly close my bedroom door against the sounds and take out my math book. Uncle Evan promised me we'd practice lines after dinner again and I want to be ready, but it's hard to concentrate. Even with my door closed, I can hear them jumping and laughing, and I remember when Jack and I used to play this same game together, bare feet on messy blankets, the orange Nerf ball soft in our hands.

The weeks pass by. It's bitter cold out now. I spend every second that I'm not at rehearsal or practicing my lines wishing that I were. One Friday, after Paige meets me at my locker and walks me to the auditorium like she always does, Finn comes in with a small cardboard box in his hands. The other girls and I join the boys on the stage. I notice that Dr. Shiner is taking a seat in the back row. He must have walked in a step behind Finn.

Finn stands in front of us with a wide smile on his face.

"We're about a month away from the big day!" he tells us. "I got you all something. Thankfully, we came in just under budget, so . . ." He opens the box, takes out a brightly colored rubber bracelet, and holds it up. It's red, yellow, and blue swirled together—primary colors. "Just a little symbol of our solidarity. It says *The Myth of Persephone* on it," he announces proudly, putting it on his wrist. He holds his arm up for everyone to see.

"Cool," Paige whispers next to me.

Finn hands the box to Kaylee. She takes a bracelet and passes the box down. When it comes to me, I take one out, pull it onto my wrist, and look at the slanted inscription: *The Myth of Persephone*.

"Definitely cool," I say to Paige. She holds her wrist up in front of me.

"Cheers!" she says, smiling. We clink bracelets.

For a second, I think about how perfect it would be if I could freeze time. I'd stay right here forever.

But obviously, that's impossible.

At home that night, I change into my pajamas and bring my three dirty T-shirts across the hall to the bathroom with the small baggie of Woolite I took from the laundry room. My fingers become red and numb as I knead the shirts in the icy water in the sink. I can feel the bracelet on my wrist dragging against the water, and I watch my face in the mirror as my hands work automatically.

The water turns a cloudy gray. I drain it, wring the T-shirts out, and bring them back across the hall to my room. I push my clothes to the right side of the rod in my closet to clear a space for them to dry on hangers, and I lay the towel that I took from the linen closet on the floor to collect their drips. I close the closet door and lie down on my bed to wait for Uncle Evan to come in and practice lines with me so I can feel alive again.

☆

The days are endless patterns of darkness, light, darkness, light, darkness, light. One Monday in March, I'm at rehearsal, off-stage, waiting for my cue. It's the last scene of the play, and Zeus is about to take me out of the Underworld. Everything around me is light. I reach up to the zipper on my sweatshirt. I know that as soon as rehearsal is over, the darkness will move in again.

I don't want to let it.

I unzip my sweatshirt. Just a little, an inch, maybe two, and pull my necklace out. I look down at it. The bird reflects the stage lights, and I smile.

"Grayson?" I look to Finn. "Your line, kid," he says, and I walk out to the center of the stage.

☆

When rehearsal is over, Paige comes over to me. I'm leaning over, pulling my jacket out of my backpack, and I can feel the bird dangling on its chain under my neck as I watch her glittery shoes approach. I automatically reach my hand up and touch the charm. I could tuck it back into my sweatshirt, but I can't let the darkness move in again. So I stand up.

"Hey," she says.

I lower my hand. "Hi."

"Oh, cool necklace!" she squeals, and, for a second, she raises her hand to her own necklace—a colorful circle of red and orange glass hanging on a piece of brown leather. "Is that new?"

I straighten out the chain while watching her eyes. I can feel the neckline of my lavender T-shirt behind it. "Thanks, and not really," I say carefully.

She keeps looking at me and reaches her hand out to touch the charm. I feel a gentle tug on the back of my neck. She turns the bird around with her fingers. She studies it. I picture her sparkly, blue fingernails on top of the shining silver, and the lavender T-shirt behind. "So," she finally says. "Is your uncle getting you?"

"Actually, my aunt's supposed to meet me outside. She was at some PTA meeting."

"Cool. I didn't know she was on the PTA."

"Well, she used to be. She quit a while ago, but I guess she's rejoining."

"Should we go?" she asks.

"Yeah, sure." We walk outside. It's not as dark out now at five thirty as it used to be. Spring is coming, but it's still freezing. We stop at the top of the cement steps, and I zip my sweatshirt, put on my jacket, and pull up the hood.

"There's your dad," I say as his car pulls into the drive.

"'Kay. See ya, Grayson." She slides her mitten along the metal railing as she walks down the steps two at a time. I shove my frozen hands into my pockets.

"Hey, Paige?" I call, and she turns around at the bottom. I'm shivering.

"Yeah?" she asks, pulling her knitted hat farther down over her ears.

I want to say something, but I don't know what. "Nothing," I say. "See ya."

She smiles at me and waves. I sit down on the icy step to wait for Aunt Sally. A few minutes later, she rounds the side of the building, and we walk through the parking lot to her car. "How's everything, Grayson?" she asks.

"Fine, I guess," I say, watching my feet trudge through icy snow.

"Anything interesting happen at school?" She digs through her purse for her car keys, her frozen breath hanging in the air between us as she speaks.

I shrug as she unlocks the doors. Part of me wants to hug her and show her my necklace and T-shirt. But a bigger part of me feels like a freak standing there next to her. I get in the car and we ride home in silence.

Chapter 28

THE NEXT MORNING I sit in Humanities and watch the door for Finn. Ryan walks in, and I immediately put my hand up to my neck to cover the bird charm resting against the outside of my sweatshirt. Thankfully, Finn is right behind him. His lips are pushed together tightly, and the look in his eyes reminds me of Uncle Evan when he's stressed out about work. He throws his briefcase onto his chair. It lands with a slap.

"Seats," he yells over us. I watch him carefully, my hand still covering my charm. I've never seen him like this, and a distant memory comes to me in broken pieces. I'm holding a smooth porcelain cat in my tiny hands. A thin, winding crack covers its back, like a gray spiderweb. I feel Mom's presence high above me. A hand reaches down and grabs the cat.

"Silent reading," Finn practically whispers to the now-quiet class. "For the double period." I hear groans. "You can complain all you want," he continues. "I know lots of you are probably behind in *To Kill a Mockingbird*, anyway. And for those of you who aren't, you can reread until you truly understand it."

I look around and see that everyone else is doing the same thing. We've never had silent reading for more than twenty minutes in Humanities, and nobody's ever seen Finn angry about anything. I unzip my backpack quickly and take out my book.

I try to read, but I can't focus. Finn is pacing up and down in front of the board, chewing on a pen. The class is silent except for the sounds of pages turning. The quiet hangs over us like a cloudy sky.

A few minutes before the end of the double period, there's a tap on the door. The whole class looks up quickly. Dr. Shiner is standing in the hallway, glaring through the small, rectangular window. Without saying anything to us, Finn quickly walks out to the hall. As soon as he closes the door behind him, the class explodes into chaos. I look at the clock. The bell is about to ring anyway, so I lean over to zip my book into my backpack. I barely reread a page. When I sit back up, Ryan is standing over my desk. I immediately reach up and touch my bird charm.

"Nice necklace, Gracie," he says. "So." He pauses. "How's it feel?"

"What do you mean?" I ask weakly. I wish Paige were here.

"What I mean, freak, is how does it feel to know that Finn's getting fired because of *you*?"

I stare up at him. The floor starts to shift under me, slowly, like a canyon is about to open up right under the school. The room is becoming too quiet again.

"What are you talking about?" I whisper.

Ryan turns to the row next to us. Everyone is staring. "He doesn't even know!" he says, smirking. "My mom told me your aunt was there," he says. "At the PTA meeting? Man, you are totally clueless."

Suddenly, things are coming together in the too quiet, stale air—puzzle pieces are floating, connecting. *I'm* why Aunt Sally wanted to rejoin the PTA. And so is Finn.

"My mom wouldn't tell me what happened," Ryan continues, "but I'll get it out of her. She tells me and my brother *everything*. All she said was it had something to do with you. My guess? Finn's being booted for making you into a fag like him!" The canyon beneath us is getting wider. Ryan bends down and put his face in front of mine. The bell rings, but nobody moves. "He do something to you, Gracie?" he goes on. The classroom is silent.

My body is frozen and on fire, all at the same time. I think back to that day in the hallway when Paige ran over and saved me. I wish that she were here. I know I could never scream at Ryan like she did, but I don't have to stay here and listen to him. I reach down for my backpack.

There's a rustle next to me, and I look over. Meagan is making her way through the desks. Her face is flushed, and she's looking at the floor. Her thin, black hair is hanging down the sides of her cheeks like black curtains. She stops next to Ryan, in front of me. A second later, Hannah and Hailey are by her side.

Meagan pushes her hair back from her face. "Ready to go, Grayson?" she asks as I throw my backpack over my shoulder. Her voice is quiet, but the room is silent; everyone can hear her.

"Yeah," I whisper. I feel like I'm floating over the floor as the four of us walk to the door. In the hallway, Finn and Dr. Shiner are talking in quick, hushed voices. They stop when we pass by them. I look up at Finn's deep, brown eyes. He looks away.

At rehearsal, everything is different. Dr. Shiner is already in the front row of the auditorium when Paige and I get there, and none of the girls are sitting around gossiping about Meagan and Sebastian. Nobody is passing around a hairbrush or digging a handful of clips out of their backpack.

We join the others on stage, and I hear two seventh graders, Stephanie and Lindsey, whispering something about what Lindsey's mom told her last night. "We should just ask him what's going on," I hear Stephanie say, and my heart skips a beat. I look down at the bird charm hanging against my blue sweatshirt as I sit on the stage between Paige and Meagan to wait for Finn. Paige puts her arm around me. I notice that she's looking right at Dr. Shiner, and the feel of her bony arm over my shoulder makes me want to cry.

Finn finally shows up, and we start rehearsal. I scream

to him silently: *Look at me! Tell me what's happening!* But he doesn't. I can't get the picture of Ryan's stupid face out of my mind. The darkness hangs over the stage, and I think everyone can feel it. I look at Stephanie and Lindsey. They're still whispering to each other.

On stage, Andrew is telling Paige that he's going to help her find Persephone. Paige is supposed to be upset that I'm missing, but I can tell she's distracted. She keeps glancing down at the tattered script in her hands.

Finn is pacing up and down in front of the stage, his hand over his mouth as he watches. When Paige and Andrew finally stumble through to the end of the scene, they look over to him. "Sorry, Finn," Paige says. She fiddles with the script in her hands. He doesn't say anything for a minute.

"You know what, guys?" he finally says. "It's okay. It is okay." He repeats it, looking thoughtful, but it kind of feels like he's talking to himself. "It's a hard scene. And if it's not perfect, it's not the end of the world."

I watch from where I'm standing at the side of the stage, halfway behind the burgundy curtain. I twirl my plastic bracelet slowly around my wrist.

"We'll get it, Finn," Andrew says. "You don't have to worry. We'll both work on it more."

"No, Andrew, don't worry. Like I said, it's a hard scene. Let's just move on, okay? Act Three, Scene Two. Let's do it." He claps his hands together once, and the sound echoes through the auditorium before it drops onto the stage and dies. The massive room is silent. I look at Dr. Shiner. His legs are crossed neatly, and his face is sharp. He's biting his lower lip.

"Come on, Scene Two. Let's do it." Nobody moves, so he says it one more time, and we take our places.

☆

After rehearsal, Uncle Evan's car is waiting for me, and I run down the steps, get in, and slam the door.

"Grayson?" he asks. "What's going on?" But he asks it weakly, like he already knows the answer. I have so much to say, but my mouth won't work. My throat is tight, like my own body is trying to suffocate me.

"Why would she? Finn's the best teacher." It's all I can manage to get out.

Uncle Evan is quiet, and he punches the radio off. I can hear the wind whipping around the car. "Well," he finally begins, "I think she just felt that he overstepped a boundary." I know him, and he's choosing his words carefully. He's protecting her.

"But I want this!" I scream.

"I know, Grayson, I know you do."

"Is it true that Finn's getting fired now?"

"Fired? Oh, I don't think so. I think the question on the table is whether it was within his right to unilaterally make the decision to cast you as Persephone."

I can't talk anymore, so I lean my head back and close my eyes as Uncle Evan pulls out of the parking lot. And the thought

· 187 ·

suddenly comes to me: what if I quit? I open my eyes and sit forward in my seat. If I quit, would all of this just go away? Uncle Evan looks at me. "You okay, Grayson?"

I don't want to quit. "No," I tell him.

"I know. I'm sorry."

That night, I dream of the Grand Canyon. I'm walking on the rim next to a funnel cloud. It spins wildly next to me. It's so close, and I know it's going to push me in. I can't stop it. I peek into the swirling cloud, and I see my own face staring back at me, my hair arranged into even blond braids.

Chapter 29

EVERYBODY HAS HEARD the rumors. The next morning in Humanities, nobody is talking or laughing. Nobody is sitting on top of anyone else's desk waiting for Finn to tell them to hop off and get to their seats. Everybody thinks Finn is getting fired—all because of me.

I think about what Uncle Evan said in the car. I don't know what's true and what's not. Finn is at the front of the classroom, staring at us like he doesn't know what to do with us.

Across the room from me, Asher waves his hand in the air. "Yes, Asher?" Finn asks. He sounds exhausted. Asher looks at Jason and then back to Finn. My body tenses. I know he's going to ask him what's going on. *Do it!* I scream silently. I can't believe I want him to say it out loud, but I'm dying to know.

But Asher suddenly looks embarrassed. "Never mind, Finn," he says, and Finn nods and looks out the window as he rubs the dark stubble on his cheeks.

"I'm sorry," Finn finally says, looking back at us. "I'm sorry about yesterday. I shouldn't have made you sit for an hour and a half doing silent reading. That was not the right thing to do." He looks like he wants to go on, but he doesn't. He turns his attendance binder around in his hands absently.

"Today, we're going to get back to business. We're going to start working on our debates based on *To Kill a Mockingbird*. For this assignment, I need you in groups of four."

The class is fidgety. Everyone knows what is coming next.

"So," Finn continues, "I can feel your vibe. It's fine. Find your groups and push your four desks together to create small tables. You're going to be sitting here through the end of the quarter." The classroom is getting louder. I watch a truck drive through a pile of slush outside the window. "Once you're sitting with your groups, we'll discuss which themes we should debate. Go ahead. Find your partners."

There's commotion around me—desks and chairs moving, and people finally laughing and talking. But I keep my eyes on my desk. I don't care who I end up with.

"Grayson?" I look up. It's Meagan. "Come on, we saved you a spot." On the other side of the room, in front of the cabinets where Finn stores all the extra books, Hailey's and Hannah's desks are pushed side by side. Meagan's desk is across from Hannah's, and there's an empty space next to it.

"Thanks," I mumble. I pick up my backpack and start to push my chair and desk across the floor. I pass Finn's desk. He's sitting on it, watching the class, fiddling with his pen. I smile at him weakly as I pass by him, but he looks away.

My eyes start to sting. He hates me. Maybe Uncle Evan doesn't know what he's talking about. Maybe I *am* getting Finn fired. Of *course* he hates me.

Amelia and Lila are in the other corner of the room side by side, across from Asher and Jason. They're giggling. Ryan is carrying his chair over his head as he walks from one end of the room to the other. "Come on, Sebastian, just join our group," he's yelling. Sebastian is standing next to Anthony, looking helpless. Finally, he picks up his chair and follows Ryan.

I fit my desk into the open space next to Meagan's just as Finn hops off his desk and starts to weave his way through our clusters, directing us to rearrange this way or that. "I'm looking for six tables of four desks each. Straighten yourselves up! It looks like a tornado swept through here!" He stops in front of Ryan and Sebastian's group and has them all get up and move their desks closer to the windows. When he finally has us the way he wants us, he stands in front of the chalkboard and scribbles *Debate Topics* on the board.

"Notebooks out!" It feels, in this moment, at least, like the real Finn is back. I pick up my gold glitter pen and write the date in my notebook. The outside light bounces off the shimmering writing and it's kind of hard to read, but I don't mind. It makes me forget about the darkness and think about the light.

I try to hold on to this feeling for as long as I can until I look at Ryan across the room and remember everything else.

☆

At rehearsal on Friday, we're all sitting in a clump onstage. Dr. Shiner must have come in during our relaxation exercises. He's in the front row again, watching us. Finn sounds tired, but he is still upbeat as he reminds us that the performance is now less than two weeks away. I rub my burning eyes and look up to the ceiling at the bright stage lights as he talks.

"Please remember, and remind your parents, that a week from tomorrow we're having a Saturday rehearsal," Finn is saying. "Our parent volunteers will be coming in to put the finishing touches on the costumes they made. You can tell your families that I need you at twelve thirty, and I promise to have you out of here by three."

He pauses and looks us over. "We're going to pick back up with the final scene when Zeus escorts Persephone home. Ms. Landen has agreed to help us out here, and we're honored to have her assistance." He glances over to where she's sitting in the second row, kind of hidden by Dr. Shiner. I hadn't even noticed her there, and she smiles and waves at us. I've barely seen her since tryouts.

"As you may know, Ms. Landen has a great deal of experience directing Porter's musicals, and she's going to help us figure out our spacing and timing since, for the last scene, we're

· 192 ·

going to have the entire cast onstage." He nods at her. "Thanks, Samantha," he says. She gives him a little salute, and we take our places.

I sit next to Andrew in a cardboard horse-drawn carriage. Reid and the Souls of the Underworld are supposed to be on one side of the stage, and Paige and the Elves on the other, but nobody is where they're supposed to be, and Finn is directing people this way and that. It feels like forever before the scene actually starts. But the stage lights are bright. And even though Finn probably hates me, I can't help feeling happy. I'm in the crystal light now.

"Remember where you're standing! Remember who you're supposed to be next to! Keep away from center stage! That's the space that Grayson and Andrew need to use!" Finn yells.

Finally, Ms. Landen steps in. "May I?" I hear her ask Finn.

"By all means," he says, sighing.

"Okay, guys?" she says calmly, and everyone quiets down. "I need to tell you something. I know this feels like chaos now, but I want you all to listen to me." She pauses, and it looks like she's trying to figure out how to put something into words.

Finally, she starts again. "Something I've learned over the years is that often, as the production date approaches, the rehearsals become more and more difficult. I'm not exactly sure why," she continues, "but I have a theory that sometimes, everything needs to fall apart before it can come back together the way it's supposed to." She pauses and looks us over. The room is silent. "Does that make sense to you?" Everyone stares at her.

She looks us over and nods. "You'll see. Just wait. Let's take it from the beginning of this final scene, okay?"

We make it through to the end, and I look to the auditorium seats as Hermes gives his closing monologue. Finn's hand is covering his mouth, and he looks beaten down. He has dark circles under his eyes.

The scene was a complete mess, and no matter what he says, I know he wants it to be perfect. It's the last scene of the play. And it's probably the last play he'll ever direct at Porter, I think to myself.

All because of me.

Chapter 30

I CAN'T STAND the thought of the weekend. A few summers ago at Tessa and Hank's, they put out a raccoon trap next to the opening under the back steps. They stuffed it full of boysenberries and left it out overnight. In the morning, there was a baby raccoon huddled in the corner. The boysenberries were still scattered on the floor of the trap and matted into the baby's stiff fur. Jack, Brett, and I sat there forever on the itchy grass watching it until the guy from Animal Control finally came and took it away. This is what I think about as I lie on my bed after dinner, my wrinkled script in my hand.

I can hear Aunt Sally and Uncle Evan talking in the living room. I can tell they're trying to be quiet, but their voices keep exploding. I creep out of my bedroom and listen to them as they yell in whispers. "I didn't *mean* for everything to happen like this, okay?" Aunt Sally says.

"Well, what on earth did you expect, Sally?"

"What did I expect? I expected Mr. Finnegan to give Grayson a different role. Or he easily could have just agreed to switch Persephone into a male character—directors do that all the time. At the very least, he could have agreed that Grayson's costume shouldn't be a *gown*, for heaven's sake. All I expected was for everyone to do the right thing—to keep Grayson *safe*. I didn't expect anyone to talk about *firing* Mr. Finnegan." Her voice rises as she talks.

"Would you quiet down? And besides, you're being dramatic. It was a handful of parents who brought up the idea of firing him, not Dr. Shiner." Uncle Evan pauses, and I imagine him staring out the window. "Regardless," he goes on, "I wonder if he'll stick around after this." For a minute, nobody says anything. "If he leaves Porter, for whatever reason, those certainly are some big shoes to fill. He's one of the most popular teachers there."

"Great, that's great, Evan. Just make me feel as guilty as possible. Anyway, I don't care about any of that. This is about what's best for *Grayson*."

My stomach lurches, and before I know what I'm doing, I step into the living room. Uncle Evan is standing by the window, like I imagined, gazing out over the black lake. Aunt Sally looks up at me and opens her mouth to say something. Then she closes it.

Suddenly, words are flying out of my mouth. "You don't care

about what's best for me," I say, quietly at first. "I *want* this role." But before I know it, I'm screaming. "Anyway, you think I'm a monster!"

Aunt Sally sits down on the love seat. It looks like she's about to cry. Good. Uncle Evan comes over to me and puts his hand on my shoulder. "Grayson," he says, but he looks at Aunt Sally as he talks, not at me. "Sit down. Of *course* your aunt Sally doesn't think you're a *monster*. You're upset—and rightfully so. You must have a lot of questions."

I look at him through burning tears. "How could someone get fired for giving somebody a role in a play? I wanted that role. I tried out for it!" I scream these last words. I won't sit down. I stare at the two of them.

Uncle Evan finally sits on one of the brown leather chairs across from Aunt Sally. He crosses his legs and uncrosses them, and takes a deep breath. "The question on the table, Grayson, is whether or not Mr. Finnegan acted in line with Porter's philosophy of properly teaching and guiding the whole student."

"What are you talking about?"

"Well, some parents on the PTA," he says, glancing at Aunt Sally, "think it was irresponsible of Mr. Finnegan to give you a role that has, well, implications, without consulting with the administration, the guardians, and the rest of the teaching team."

"But I wanted that role," I scream again. I talk slowly, pausing after each word. "I. Tried. Out. For. It."

For a minute, nobody says anything.

"What are they going to do to him?" I ask, my heart pounding.

"We don't know, Grayson," Uncle Evan says. "There's talk among some parents on the PTA that he should be fired, but Dr. Shiner certainly hasn't said anything about that."

"Could they cancel the play?" I ask quickly.

"I can't imagine they'd do that. But I do imagine they'll at least monitor his theater productions much more closely from now on. I just don't know how it will unfold." He pauses. "It would be a shame for anyone to get in the way of someone who really does have his students' best interests at heart," he continues as he looks over at Aunt Sally.

She stands up, glares at him, and storms out of the living room. I hear the front door of the apartment slam.

Uncle Evan flinches but doesn't say anything about it. I walk down the hallway toward my room. "Grayson," Uncle Evan calls after me, but I keep walking. I can't bear to have him looking at me. I go into my bedroom and slam the door.

At school, Finn acts like nothing's wrong, and I can't understand it. We have the whole double period to work on our debates, and he's writing out the topics and teams on the board. I scream silent messages to him—*Look at me!* But he won't.

I unscrew the top of my gold glitter pen, take out the thin cylinder of ink, lay all its pieces on my desk, and absently put it back together. I glance quickly across the room. Ryan is daydreaming, and Sebastian is waving his hand in the air. Finn finishes writing and turns around. "Yes, Sebastian," he asks, rubbing his stubbly chin.

"Can we switch teams?"

"For what reason?"

"Well, what if we got assigned to debate something we don't agree with?"

Finn looks at Sebastian with heavy eyes, and finally, his face softens. "Something I believe in," he says, looking around the room, "is that it builds character to stand in someone else's shoes. You know, to try to see things from another perspective." He nods, like he's thinking about what he said, but Sebastian just sighs, rests his head in his hand, and looks out the window.

Chapter 31

THE WEEK CRAWLS BY. Every time I walk into Humanities
or rehearsal, I expect Finn to pull me aside. I want him to tell
me this isn't my fault and explain what's happening. Instead, he
acts like everything is fine—like the whole school isn't talking
about the fact that he might get fired because of me.

Thankfully, our dress rehearsal is on Saturday, so at least I
have an excuse to get away from Aunt Sally. Uncle Evan hardly
ever goes to the office on the weekends, but he says he's happy to
get some work done there, and he'll drop me off at twelve thirty
and pick me up when I call him.

At school, I walk down the quiet, dark hallways. At the
entrance to the auditorium, I stop and lean against the door
frame. It looks hectic inside. Finn and Ms. Landen are scooting

around from person to person. Costumes, most of them only partly finished, are draped over the auditorium seats, and a few parents are sitting behind sewing machines that are set up on a long table in front of the stage. Meagan's mom is in one of the aisles, draping thick red velvet around Andrew's shoulders. I take a deep breath and walk inside. She and Andrew smile at me as I pass them.

Paige hops off the stage and meets me halfway down the aisle. "Hey, Grayson," she says, "You're here! Wanna meet my mom?"

"Yeah, cool," I say. She pulls me up the stage steps. "Do you know if she finished my costume?"

"I think so. The lady loves to sew. She's so bizarre." A woman with an older version of Paige's face is unfolding a huge piece of pink satin in the middle of the stage. I look from Paige's shimmery turquoise leggings, gold scarf, and colorful shirt to her mom's brown corduroys, green sweater, and dark-rimmed glasses. A pin hangs out of the corner of her mouth, and she takes it out as Paige and I approach her.

"Mom, *this* is Grayson," Paige says.

"Hi, Mrs. Francis," I say.

"Grayson, please," she says beaming. "I feel like I already know you—call me Marla." I look at Paige. "I've really enjoyed making your costume," she adds.

"You have?" I ask, smiling back at her.

"Of course I have," she says, nodding. "Very much so." The underneath side of her hair is damp, and she smells like shampoo.

There's a list on the ground, and she picks it up, studies it, and then she looks back to me. "So, Persephone's gown just needs a few final adjustments."

"Great! What do I do?"

"Oh, nothing, sweetie. I have your measurements that you turned in to Mr. Finnegan a while ago, but as long as I'm here, let me just remeasure you. You might have grown in the last month. It'll just take a minute. Take off your jacket."

I do, and I drop it behind the curtain. Paige sits down at her mom's feet. I look from Paige's sparkling silver shoes to her mom's brown suede loafers. "Okay, Grayson," Marla says. She pulls a paper tape measure out of her pocket. "Let's see what we've got." She measures my leg, from hip bone to ankle, and squints at the piece of paper on the ground. "Wow!" she says, smiling. "According to this measurement, you've grown over half an inch in a month!" She measures one more time and eyes the paper again. "Yup," she says. "Growth spurt!"

She gently lifts up my sweatshirt and measures my waist. I close my eyes. My heart is racing now and my chest feels tight, like a rubber band that's being pulled and pulled and is about to snap.

"Okay, honey, let me get your arm and chest measurements. Why don't you take off your sweatshirt?"

I open my eyes. I can see myself reflected in her glasses, and I watch myself as I slowly tuck my hair behind my ears. I don't have a choice. What am I supposed to do, tell her I refuse to take it off? So I watch my hand reach for the zipper, and I shift my gaze to her other lens to watch the sequined heart appear. I drop my sweatshirt onto the floor by my feet.

Beyond her glasses and the hearts, Marla's brown eyes blink gently. Once. Twice. She lifts her hand to my chin, and I think of my bird charm between Paige's fingers. I watch Marla's eyes as she drags the tape measure from my shoulder blade to my wrist bone. When I glance down at Paige, I see that she isn't looking at me. She's looking at her mom.

"I'll do the other arm, too," Marla says. "Just to make sure you're even." She measures my right arm. "Perfect," she says. "Now, lift up your arms a bit. Let me get your chest." She wraps the tape measure around me. It hugs the sequined heart. Tight.

Finn is walking up the stage steps now. I look at his face and I miss how things used to be. I remember standing in front of him on stage, way back in December, asking if I could try out for Persephone. I remember the burgundy curtains and the warm water-air and the first time I held the script. I can't imagine what I must look like to him now, standing on stage in a girl's shirt. I glance behind him to see if anyone else has noticed, but everyone seems busy with something else.

He walks over to us, his eyes fixed on my shirt, and stands in front of me for a minute until, for the first time in weeks, he looks at my face. He looks happy. I realize I've been holding my breath, and, carefully, slowly, I start to breathe again.

He turns to Marla. "Everything going okay?" he asks.

"Samantha and I can't tell you how much we appreciate all you've done."

"Honestly, Brian, I love this kind of project. Paige keeps telling me I'm obsessed with my sewing machine." She laughs a little. "Really, it's my pleasure."

"Well, thank you. It means quite a lot to us to have your help."

"I'm happy to do it," Marla says as Finn walks down the stage steps. He turns around when he gets to the bottom, looks from my shirt to my face one more time, smiles, and walks away.

Marla finishes measuring me, and I look down at my sweatshirt. Nobody is looking at me, and it doesn't seem like anyone else has noticed what I'm wearing. I know Paige won't care. Finn's back is to us. He's searching for Natalie, who is next on Marla's list. I don't know what to do, so I put the sweatshirt back on. I don't zip it, but I wrap it around myself and fold my arms over it to keep it in place.

Natalie hoists herself up onto the stage, and I pull my bird charm out and sit down next to Paige. "I like your shirt," she says, nudging me.

I look at her—at her clothes and scarf that are so different from what other people at Porter wear. "Yeah, thanks," I say.

"I mean, I think it's cool of you to wear something so unique."

I look at my feet. I don't know how to explain to her that she's missing the point, but I smile again, anyway. We sit there, side by side, and watch Marla trim the golden belt on Natalie's lavender robe. It's only a little after one o'clock, and I could call

Uncle Evan to tell him I'm done, but I don't. Paige and I clean up fabric scraps as Marla works, and Paige braids my hair. She talks a lot about Liam and how he asked her to be his science partner. I study her face and her hand gestures and look at her fingers. They're covered in silver rings, and I think of the one I tried on at the Second Hand. I wonder if it's still there.

When Marla is done, we help her fold up the leftover fabric and put it into plastic bags. "Do you need a ride home, Grayson?" she asks me.

"No, thanks," I tell her. "I told my uncle I'd call him when we were done. He's at his office."

"It's no problem for me to drive you," Marla says. "Why don't you call him and tell him we'll drop you off? We could go get something to eat on the way. I'm starving. Are you guys starving?"

"Absolutely!" Paige says. I look from her to her mom, shrug, and smile.

"Great!" Marla says. She looks excited. "Paigey said you live downtown, right?"

Hearing her say "Paigey" makes me imagine a little girl in a diaper and a sparkling T-shirt. I smile to myself. "Yeah, on Randolph," I tell her. "By the lake."

"So, you know where we should go? Paigey, remember that sushi place we went to with the Wilsons last summer? Wasn't that downtown, near Randolph?"

"You want to go for sushi at three o'clock?" Paige asks. She looks at me and rolls her eyes, but Marla is still smiling. I think of Mom's face in the picture on my nightstand. I try to imagine how it would look today, but I can't; I don't know how to. All of a sudden, it feels like the car accident was a million years ago, and I don't know if that's a good or a bad thing.

"Who cares?" Marla asks. "That place was amazing! Where's my phone? I'm going to look it up." She digs through her purse. "Do you need to borrow my phone to call your uncle, Grayson?" she asks.

"No, I've got mine," I tell her.

"Oh, okay."

"Mom, I'm going to the bathroom before we go. Grayson, come with me," Paige says, pulling me off the stage.

"Okay, Paigey," I tell her.

"Watch it." She grins. I hold my unzipped sweatshirt in place, and we walk out the doors of the auditorium together. The hallway is empty and quiet, and I stop walking outside of the auditorium doors as Paige continues across the hall and into the girls' room. "Be right back!" she calls over her shoulder. The light green door closes slowly behind her and clicks into place.

I stand there. I'm frozen.

On the door is a black stick figure in a dress. GIRLS, it says. I want to push the door open and go in with Paige. I want us to stand next to each other at the sinks while we wash our hands and talk about how she thinks Liam is cute. I want to borrow her hairbrush. It's hard to breathe and my heart is thumping, and all of a sudden, I'm worried that it might explode from all these years of *wishing*. I'm worried that it might explode into a million tiny pieces, and that then I'll be gone—invisible again. But this time, for real.

I look around. The hallway is empty, and I walk toward the light green door. I touch the cold metal. I'm so *close* to what I need. But I can't open it. Even Paige would think I'm a freak if I walked into the bathroom with her, so I zip my sweatshirt and go to the boys' room instead. I try to hold on to the feeling of the cool door on my fingertips. I try to breathe carefully so my heart will slow down. I pay attention to the air coming in, the air going out. I go to the bathroom. I wash my hands. I rub my eyes and splash water on my face. In the dirty mirror, my cheeks look flushed. I blot them dry with rough paper towels, and when I come out, Paige and Marla are waiting for me.

In the car, I text Uncle Evan to tell him about the change in plans. I feel shaky as I watch the low, dark sky outside the window. There's a bright circle buried behind the gray. The sun is trying to peek through, but it can't.

The sushi place is empty except for us, and we sit by the window. I fiddle with the white tablecloth that hangs onto my lap as Marla orders us edamame to share. The waitress walks away. "You know," I blurt out, the words forming suddenly in my mouth, "the reason everyone's talking about Finn getting fired is because of me. He'll barely even talk to me anymore." It's a relief to say it out loud. Paige looks to her mom. Marla picks up her chopsticks, snaps them apart, and studies them for a minute.

"Well, Grayson," she finally says, "usually, when it comes to political matters at Porter, I try to stay out of things. But this," she goes on, "well, Paigey and I have spent a lot of time talking about how this is different."

I look at Paige as Marla continues. "I know that there are some parents who want Mr. Finnegan fired because he gave you the role of a female character." She pauses, and it looks like she's trying to decide what to say. The waitress comes and puts a bowl of edamame in the middle of the table. Marla thanks her, and finally, she continues. "Sometimes people make important choices that happen to be risky. I agree with Mr. Finnegan's decision. And I think it was an extremely noble one to make," she says. "Paige and I both do. We've talked a lot about it. And as for him not talking to you . . ." She studies my face carefully. "What do you mean, honey? Are you sure about that? I'd imagine he's just distracted?"

Hearing her words makes me feel better even though I know she's wrong about that last part. But I can't talk about it anymore, so I just shrug. Marla looks out the window and squints a little. "Look," she says, "the sun is finally peeking through!" She turns back and smiles at me. "Let's order a bunch of things to share, okay?"

"Okay," I say. I watch her hair fall to the sides of her face as she studies the menu for us, and I wonder again about Mom, and how she'd look if she were sitting here with us, too. Then I think again of how weird it is to miss someone I can barely even remember. Across the table from me, Paige squeezes her edamame until the bean pops out. It lands in my glass of water, and I laugh.

☆

When we pull up in front of my building, I thank Marla for the sushi and the ride. I want to say more, but I don't know how to put what I'm feeling into words. I look at Paige as she sits in the passenger seat and adjusts the gold, silky scarf around her neck.

"So, I'll see you Monday," I say to her.

"Sounds good."

"Grayson," Marla says, "I just have to say—we want you to know that you are welcome at our house anytime you need anything. *Anytime.*"

"Mom!" Paige says rolling her eyes. "Why do you have to be such a drama queen?" But she's smiling.

"I'm sorry, I'm sorry. I know. I can't help it." She looks back at me as I climb out of the car. "But I mean it, Grayson."

"Thanks," I say. I mean it, too.

Chapter 32

THE PLAY IS ONLY three days away. When Paige and I walk into the auditorium after school on Monday, the crew kids, a few of the moms, Finn, and Ms. Landen are already there. This is the first day in forever that Finn hasn't been late, and he and Ms. Landen are standing next to two science lab carts piled high with colorful, flowing costumes. I scour the fabrics with my eyes until I find the golden gown Marla made for me.

Paige and I jump onto the stage. Finn looks our way, says something to Ms. Landen, and walks over to us. When he stops in front of me, I smile at him weakly, and this time he doesn't look away.

"Grayson, do you have a minute?" he asks. I can't make my mouth work, but I nod. He motions for me to follow him, and I jump down. Everything is a blur. We walk over to the side of the auditorium. I notice the dark circles under his eyes again, and I'm suddenly embarrassed. I can't believe what I've done to him.

"Grayson," he says, looking around quickly, "I'm going to make this brief because a while ago I agreed to a request from Dr. Shiner that I not spend one-on-one time with you."

"What?" I interrupt.

"I'm not really at the liberty to talk to you about it in detail, so all I'll say is that Dr. Shiner and I made an agreement, and I wanted to be able to continue directing this play." He glances around the auditorium again. "I've probably already said too much," he adds carefully.

I look at his eyes, and he looks down at the paper clip he's been turning around and around in his hand. *This* is why he hasn't said a word to me in weeks? I feel my heart is beating in my throat. And suddenly, Ryan's words pound in my ears: *He do something to you, Gracie?* I feel like breaking something. I feel like crying.

"I'm sorry, Grayson," Finn continues. "I just want you to know that this outcome is not what I intended when I told you that you could try out for Persephone."

"I know," I say. "Of course I know that."

He looks relieved. "If it's okay with you, I'm going to talk frankly with the cast today about my future here at Porter. There are lots of questions swirling, and I feel that people deserve to know what's going on." He pauses and looks at me carefully. "I know you're aware of the rumors. I'm not going to mention anything about you," he continues. "I'm just going to tell everyone what's happening with me. I wanted to make sure you were okay with that. I want you to know that I am aware of how this affects you, too."

I can't say anything. I just nod. I glance over to the stage where everyone is gathered. They're watching us, and the auditorium is too quiet. This is what I've been hoping for, to know the truth, and now I feel like I'm on trial and the jury is about to deliver my verdict.

"Listen, you better go join everyone else." Finn looks to the auditorium doors. Dr. Shiner is walking in. But he doesn't shoo me away. He turns back to me slowly. Deliberately. "I'm sorry, Grayson."

"No, I'm sorr—" I start to say, but he cuts me off.

"No," he says, and points his finger at me. "You have nothing to apologize for. Remember that. Now go join your group." I walk back to the rest of the cast. I don't want to, but I don't know what else to do. I feel too weak to jump up and sit next to Paige again, so I slide down onto the floor alone and lean my back against the wooden cabinets that line the front of the stage.

Everyone is already silent, but Finn asks us for our attention anyway. My heart won't stop pounding, and I look up to where he's standing right in front of me. "Cast and crew," he says, "this is it. This is our last week of rehearsal before the big performance. You all have worked so hard, and I know this is going to be an amazing show. This afternoon, we are doing the performance in full costume. The crew is here, and we need to give them all a big round of applause. They designed and created all the scenery, and they're going to be working the curtains as well as the lights, and doing the scene changes. Without them, there would be no show." Everyone claps. I sit on my hands. Finn looks like a giant from down here, and I focus on the brown leather of his shoes. The soles look worn out.

He pauses. "There's one other order of business that I want to talk to you about before we take our places and begin." He looks us over and glances down at me for a second. I hold my breath and focus on his feet. He continues. "Many of you have probably been wondering about all the rumors swirling around this production for the past few weeks. I believe that rumors are unhealthy. You deserve to know the truth."

The room is still. I look at Dr. Shiner sitting in the front row. His fingertips are pressed together, and he's watching the back of Finn's head as he talks. I look at Finn's feet again as he continues.

"I've made a decision," Finn finally says. "It will soon be time for me to move on." I suddenly feel like I'm in a dark tunnel. Finn's shoes are being sucked away from me by a giant vacuum until I'm on one end and he's on the other. Everything between us is narrow and black.

He goes on. I squeeze my eyes shut and listen. "I've been a teacher at Porter for almost ten years now. Recently, I've been in touch with a small playhouse in New York City called the Central. It's actually a very historic, famous theater. Their current assistant director will be leaving soon, and I'm going to take over her position. It's an amazing job at an amazing theater, and it's something that I can't pass up. So *The Myth of Persephone* will be my last production here at Porter. I feel honored to have gotten to work with all of you on it."

I look away. The tunnel is gone, and all that is left is me, sitting on the floor for everyone to see. *What about me?* I want to scream.

For a split second, Finn looks down at me again. Everyone above me seems frozen, like they're glued in place. "Okay. Places! This is a dress rehearsal. Give it all you've got." His words ring through the silent auditorium.

I stand up in front of him. I can feel the stillness behind me. Slowly, it bleeds into chaos, like someone turning the volume up on the radio. There's whispering, then shouting, then scrambling for costumes. "Grayson," Finn says, taking a step closer to me, "I believe that you can do this without me." He pauses, and then continues. "All of this."

I nod and float backstage. I don't make eye contact with anybody. Ms. Landen helps me step into my golden gown for Act One. And even though Finn is leaving because of it, and even though Aunt Sally thinks I'm a monster, when I look at myself in the giant, floor-to-ceiling mirrors, I finally see myself the way I'm *supposed* to be—my inside self matched up with my outside self. And now, everyone else will finally see it, too.

Chapter 33

IT'S LIKE I'VE been waiting my entire life for this day. The brushstrokes surround me—the bright crystal and the darkness. Tonight I will be a girl in front of an audience. I'm supposed to be a girl, and tonight I will be. And Finn will leave Porter because of it. White and black. Light and dark. And me, in the middle of it all. Gray.

There's nothing else for me to do but walk through these columns of dark and light, so I do; I go through them to the library after fourth period. I have my lunch in my backpack, but there's no way I'll be able to eat it. I have a science project due tomorrow, too. I'm almost done, but I don't know how I'll be able to concentrate enough to finish it. My script is in my backpack, and I smile when I think of it. It's beaten up and worn out, and the cover is taped on now.

"Gracie!"

I don't know why I turn around. In front of me, the late morning light slants through the hall windows. It paints bright rectangles on the tile floor. Next to the rectangles are Ryan and Tyler. And, off to the side, a few steps away, is Jack.

I want to crack open and scramble out of my body. I want to become a bird again and fly up to the ceiling, but I'm stuck on the ground. My eyes are glued to my cousin, and all I can think of is the secret knock I used to use to get into his room—*tap, tap, bang, bang, bang.* Ryan starts to talk, and I shift my eyes away from Jack, onto him.

"You ignoring us, Gracie?" he asks.

"No," I say. It's all I can think of.

"You gonna blow us off again? Why didn't you answer us?"

I shrug.

Tyler's voice now: "You're looking pretty today. Where are you going?"

"Library."

Darkness, Light, Darkness, Light, Darkness, Light.

"Why don't you come with us to the lunchroom? We wanna hang out with you."

Tyler and Ryan are next to me now. Jack hasn't moved, and Tyler looks at him. He claws at him with his eyes, but Jack takes a little step back. Tyler's hand is on my arm now. Ryan grins next to him.

"I'm sorry," Jack suddenly says, and he reaches his hand toward us awkwardly. I don't know who he's talking to. I think of him reaching for my hand at the Grand Canyon. I remember the feel of his palms, callused from baseball practice.

My heartbeat feels like it's coming from outside of me again.

I break free and run through the empty hallway to the staircase. My feet pound another beat on the floor, and my heartbeat and all the footsteps bounce like millions of bullets inside my head.

At the top of the empty staircase, I turn around. Tyler and Ryan are right behind me, and Jack's back is disappearing down the hallway. I feel somebody's hands on my backpack, pulling and then pushing. I steady myself. Hands grab at my hair. I shake my backpack off, and it falls onto the stairs. Someone's feet are under mine now, in between mine, and I feel the hands—pushing again. I grab for the railing, but it's too far away and I'm falling.

First, my forehead. My wrist explodes into flames. Then my knee. Slower now. Finally, the ceiling.

There's no other movement on the stairs, and I turn my head away, toward the open lunchroom door. As I stare into the lunchroom, the first thing I notice is the unbelievable level of noise. Then, I feel the floor pounding. Footsteps are coming my way. I don't try to sit up. I don't want to.

Sebastian's face is suddenly above me. A second later, Dr. Shiner's. "I told you to hurry," Sebastian whispers.

"Thank you, Sebastian," Dr. Shiner sighs.

More pounding. High heels.

Mrs. Nance is kneeling next to me now. Behind her are faces. They lean in toward me, over her shoulders, like weeds.

"Back to the lunchroom!" Dr. Shiner yells.

They disappear, flattened by a tornado. I blink. There's a sharp fire burning in my left wrist.

Mrs. Nance holds something to my forehead. She moves it away. It looks like red paint.

Dr. Shiner kneels down next to me. "Who?" he sputters.

"I already told you what Ryan said." A voice from behind.

The back of Shiner's head. "Didn't I tell everyone to get back to the lunchroom, Sebastian?"

More burning. Flames in my bone.

Mrs. Nance's hand is behind my back now. "It's enough, Ed. I'm taking him to my office. You can ask your questions later."

I'm dizzy when I stand up, and she keeps her hand on my back. My left hand hangs at my side, numb, burning, lifeless.

In the nurse's office, I lie on a cot and look at the tiny black holes on the ceiling tiles. I hear Mrs. Nance in the other room on the phone.

"I'm terribly sorry, Mrs. Sender. He's resting now. Yes, of course. Dr. Shiner's investigating. Well, it is quite swollen. Definitely. It needs to be checked out. Okay. We'll be here. See you soon."

I close my eyes, and I see the aura of the ceiling light. It reminds me of the spotlights, and I push myself up on the cot with my good hand. "Mrs. Nance?" I call.

Her head appears in the doorway. "Yes, honey. Lie down. You really need to take it easy."

"The play's tonight." The darkness is trying to take over.

"I know, dear."

I don't want to let it. "I'm still doing it."

"Lie down, honey. We'll figure it out."

I'm dizzy anyway, so I listen to her.

Finally, I hear Aunt Sally's voice. Why couldn't Mrs. Nance have called Uncle Evan? I turn away from her when she walks in. "Grayson," she says, rushing to my side. She leans over me, but I keep my eyes on the windows. She walks around to the other side of the cot and lowers her face until it's next to mine. "Grayson, honey. Are you okay?" The rims of her eyes are pink. "Oh, Grayson. This is *exactly* what I was worried about."

"Mrs. Sender?"

"Yes, what is it, Mrs. Nance?"

"I think he's been through a lot."

"Of course he has." She turns to me. "Your uncle is meeting us at the ER. Do you need help getting up?"

I don't, and I follow her out the door. Mrs. Nance squeezes my good hand as I go.

☆

Uncle Evan meets us outside the front doors to the emergency room. It's humid out, and the snow is melting off the roof. A river of dirty water runs along the curb. Uncle Evan and I walk in while Aunt Sally parks the car. I feel like I'm floating, so I sit down in the waiting room while Uncle Evan talks to the receptionist. I don't want to see anything else that's going on around me, so I study the blue-and-white tile floor. I smell rubbing alcohol and hear commotion. I don't look up.

It takes forever to get the X-ray. I sit between Uncle Evan and Aunt Sally while we wait. "I'm still doing the play," I say once, but Uncle Evan tells me to just concentrate on relaxing.

"We'll figure it out," he says.

In the X-ray room, I'm alone with a nurse and a giant, humming metal machine. I catch a glimpse of my wrist. It's pink and swollen, so I look away at a painting of a robin on the wall.

We get to wait in a different room now. A white curtain surrounds a cot, and I lie on it while Aunt Sally and Uncle Evan sit in blue chairs, whispering. Finally, I hear the screeching of metal and a doctor pushes the curtain open.

"Grayson?" she asks, looking down at a clipboard in her hand.

"Yes." Aunt Sally answers for me.

"Good afternoon. I'm Dr. Mitchell," she says, and extends her hand to Aunt Sally, and then Uncle Evan.

"Sally and Evan Sender," Aunt Sally replies. "Is it broken?"

"Well, it's not broken, but it is fractured." She slides the X-ray films out of an envelope and onto the flat, rectangular light on the wall. I look away as she flips the switch. "We call it a hairline fracture. Here it is—you can see it. It's not too bad, as far as fractures go, but he'll need to be in a cast for about two months."

"Jesus," Aunt Sally whispers.

"It could have been a lot worse," the doctor assures her. "What happened, now?" she asks, turning to me. "You fell down the stairs at school?"

I nod.

She studies me, and nobody says anything. "Okay. Well, I'm going to have Allison prepare the plaster for your cast. I'll be back in a few minutes." She walks out.

I look at Aunt Sally and Uncle Evan. "Are you in pain?" Uncle Evan finally asks.

Just then, the curtains open again and a nurse with short, blond hair comes in. "Grayson, right?" she asks, smiling. "I'm going to be helping Dr. Mitchell with the plaster. You want a fancy color for the cast?" She's talking to me like I'm four. I stare at her.

"What's it gonna be, big guy? We've got black, blue—"

"Pink," I say.

"Oh, Grayson," Aunt Sally sighs. "That is just what landed us here in the first place! *Why* would you want a pink cast?"

"Sally!" Uncle Evan hisses it like a warning. "Would you step outside with me for a moment?" He looks at Allison. "Excuse us, please. Grayson can choose whatever color he'd like." The metal rings on the curtains scream as they leave. I can hear their hushed voices coming from the other side. I look at Allison and try to focus on her face. I concentrate on her slightly shifting contact lenses. She studies me.

"So, pink?" she asks. I nod. "Okeydokey." She disappears and I'm alone.

I rest my head on my right hand. Aunt Sally and Uncle Evan's voices have gotten louder.

"Why, after everything that just happened, would we allow him to walk into school with a pink cast on his wrist?" Aunt Sally is saying.

Uncle Evan says something I can't hear, and then nobody says anything. "Well," Uncle Evan finally whispers, "I think I better call Mr. Finnegan."

"Mr. Finnegan? How about Dr. Shiner?"

"We need to discuss what's going to happen tonight, with the play."

Allison comes back in. Dr. Mitchell is a step behind her. She glances back at Aunt Sally and Uncle Evan, and then looks me over.

"Dr. Mitchell?" I ask.

"Yes?" Her eyes are soft and brown.

"I'm the lead in our spring play tonight."

"Hmm." She looks thoughtful. Aunt Sally and Uncle Evan are still yelling at each other in loud whispers.

I'm so sleepy, but I don't want to let the blackness seep into the light places. I feel like a tired soldier. "I need to be in it."

She doesn't say anything for a minute. "I hear you," she finally says.

"Can you tell them it's okay?"

"I'll tell them. As long as you promise to rest up and take it easy after it's done."

I nod. "Thank you," I whisper. I look away. I feel their hands on my arm, on my hand. My wrist is freezing, then hot, wet and then dry. In the end, they say they're done. I finally look down. My hand is resting peacefully by my side, my fracture enclosed in a hard, pink shell.

Chapter 34

The Myth of Persephone

Prologue:
Programs rustling, whispers in the dark
Suddenly: silence
A circle of light frames a messenger
White robe, golden wings
He talks of things
Like good guys, bad guys
And heroes who win
When the curtains slowly rise
Creaking, crawling
And light floods the stage
We stare

Act I, Scene I:

Because inside the costume waits the boy
Who everyone's talking about
Leaning forward, ready
Pink cast swollen on his wrist
His golden gown glows under overhead lights
We smirk
As he frolics through his cardboard garden
(Tiger lilies, willow trees)
Somebody should take that boy for a haircut

Act I, Scene II:

We know backstage
That teacher is guiding, directing
It's like the circus came to town, a freak show
In the still dark
We watch the bright stage
Hades's black robe flows
As he ponders the wanting, the abduction, the capture
Of light

Act I, Scene III:

It's funny, we have to admit
The boy looks graceful up there
His face smooth and calm
His voice a clear bell
When he's whisked away to Hades

The cardboard horses dragging
The sturdy silver carriage
His gown a glorious golden circle around him
We hope he'll jump out: *Run away!*
We scream in our heads
We start to forget he's a boy

Act II, Scene I:

Trapped in the Underworld
Tied down by evil Souls
Persephone watches, helpless
Demeter tears through wilting gardens
Nature dies in her wake
Willows wither, flowers droop, dead leaves
Fall
They fall and they carpet the earth

Act II, Scene II:

In the Underworld, Hades paces
Explains to the Souls
Who hold Persephone down
That they will guard her
Keep her
Forever in the Underworld
But together we smile in the dark
On her face, we see objection
In her eyes, we sense protest

We sit forward in our seats, all at once
Flowers blown forward by a breeze
We want the good guy to win

Act II, Scene III:
We glance side to side at one another
As Persephone drifts through black cardboard trees
The plastic Spring of Lethe
The Underworld
We are:
The little kids, the moms, the dads, the sisters
The brothers
The girl, red hair, the man, red beard
We are:
The grandmas and grandpas from out of town
Kleenex in our pockets, glasses around our necks
We are:
Everyone, in different shades of white and brown

Act III, Scene I:
We are one
We are squinting to see
We are the judges
When Zeus approaches Demeter
Royal, noble, deep red cape
An offer to help in his mighty hands
We clap

Act III, Scene II:

In the Underworld
The girl winces, just once
She rubs her hand over her cast
Surprised it's there
When she lingers at the bench
Absently plucks some fruit off a tree
We know what's coming
We brace ourselves

Act III, Scene III:

Good guys are supposed to win
But she only wins halfway
She'll live six months in light
Six months in darkness
Light
Darkness
Light
Darkness
Light
Lights from behind
Light up the stage
Everyone surrounds her now
The Souls, the Elves, the poor kids who didn't get bigger roles
They're staggered, a wall
Like soldiers

Surrounding the girl
Who rides her carriage home

Epilogue:

In the end the deep-red curtain billows and drops
Lights off, sightless night, still
Then, the spotlight again
A beam of sunlight through crystal
The girl walks out cradling her arm
She must be in pain
The door to the parking lot is open next to the stage and
She feels the humid wind that's holding her up and
She takes her director's hand while
He bows and she curtsies
Gracefully.

Chapter 35

BY THE END of spring break, my wrist doesn't throb anymore, but I'm still not used to the cast. My light blue, long-sleeved T-shirt sticks to it as I pull it on with my right hand. I stand for a minute, looking out my bedroom window at the treetops below, and I adjust my pink T-shirt underneath the blue one the best I can. My charm is resting against my shirt, a silver bird flying against a light blue sky.

Uncle Evan drops Brett off at the elementary school doors and then drives Jack and me over to the circle driveway. We walk through the double doors together and down the hallway.

Ryan won't be in Humanities. Dr. Shiner came to talk to us over break. From my bedroom, I listened to the muffled sounds of adult voices around the dining room table. After more than an hour, Uncle Evan asked me to come out and sit down with them.

"So, Grayson," Uncle Evan had said, all the while staring at Dr. Shiner with sharp eyes, "Ryan has been switched to the other sixth-grade section, per our request. Dr. Shiner has assured us that your paths will cross very infrequently. And Grayson can count on that, Dr. Shiner?" he had asked.

"He can," Dr. Shiner nodded, looking at his hands instead of at me. "Both Ryan and Tyler are prohibited from setting foot anywhere near you again. As you know, they're suspended until the week after break. Once they return, one slipup, and they'll be expelled."

"Sound okay, Grayson?" Uncle Evan had asked me anxiously.

I nodded.

"And, Grayson," Dr. Shiner had gone on, still looking away, "are you sure you don't have anything to add to your statement? Ryan and Tyler *jointly* chased you down the hallway and *jointly* pushed you down the stairs?"

I looked down the hallway. Jack's bedroom door was opened a crack. "I'm sure."

The hallways at school are bustling. "See you after school," Jack says to me when I stop at my locker outside of Finn's door. He carefully looks around at the crowded hallway for a minute. I don't know what to think about him, and I watch his back as he disappears around the corner into the seventh-grade wing.

The idea of taking the bus home instead of going to play practice is the most depressing thought in the world. I wonder what next year's play will be and who will direct it. I take my books out of my locker, load them carefully into my backpack, and walk into the classroom with my head down.

When I get to my seat, I finally look up. Everyone is standing around, talking in strange whispers, and my heart jumps. I follow Meagan's gaze to the front of the room, to where Dr. Shiner is watching us out of the corner of his eye as he hands a young teacher a stack of binders and overflowing manila folders. She is nodding intently as he talks to her.

Finn has left us. I stumble into my seat.

Meagan sits down next to me, but I can't look at her. My throat is dry, and my heart thumps. When the bell rings, Dr. Shiner walks out the door and closes it behind him.

The class explodes into laughter and shouting, but I can barely hear a thing other than the sound of flames roaring in my ears. He didn't even finish the year. He didn't even say good-bye.

Numbly, I watch the new teacher. She walks in front of Finn's desk and looks us over. A paper airplane sails through the air. Some people are sitting in the wrong seats, and Jason and Asher are still sitting on top of their desks.

"I'd like your attention, please," the new teacher says. Her voice is solid and she actually looks calm, like her day is going as planned. She keeps talking, even though only some of us are paying attention.

"When I told my husband that I was going to take a long-term subbing position in a sixth-grade Humanities class, he told me I was nuts." The class is getting quieter now. I hear a few giggles. "I asked him why he would say such a thing," she continues. Everyone has switched back into the right seats now. "He said that sixth graders are animals! I told him I wholeheartedly disagreed with that. Sixth graders are people. So, he wished me luck and told me to embark upon this job at my own risk." She pauses and flashes a big smile. Her teeth are even and white. "And here I am."

I look around as I rub my arm above my cast. "My name is Amber LaBelle," she continues. She turns and writes it on the board—her first name, too. Her handwriting is nothing like Finn's. The letters are neat and solid.

She faces us again, looking serious now. "I know that you are probably confused. It is my understanding that it's a surprise to you that your teacher is not here. I'm sorry to say that I don't know much about the situation. I do know, however, that he left me extremely extensive notes about your current unit." She holds up a thick binder, and then opens it to the first page. She studies it for a minute while we all watch her.

"According to Mr. Finnegan's instructions, we are going to have a discussion today on some of the major themes that you all identified before break in *To Kill a Mockingbird*. This is, I must add, one of my all-time favorite books." She smiles and looks back down at the binder. She bites at her bottom lip as she reads something. "And it seems like we have some big debates to present tomorrow," she finally adds. She looks up again. Her eyes are dark blue, like deep water, and the sound of the flames roaring in my ears is gone now.

She turns and faces the board. I look at her brown leather cowboy boots and her long purple skirt. *Bravery*, she writes on the board to the right of her name. She turns back around and faces us.

"Okay, let's take our notebooks out!" There's a sudden rustling in the classroom. I lean over and take out my notebook and *To Kill a Mockingbird*. "So, tell us, who is brave in this book? Who isn't?" she asks. The class is silent. "Well, don't be shy! What do you all believe the author was trying to tell us about bravery?" More silence. Finally, a few hands wave in the air.

"Thank you! Finally!" Mrs. LaBelle throws her head back and laughs. Her long curls bounce. "Tell me your name before you speak," she says, her voice still bubbling. She points to the back of the classroom.

"Sebastian." I turn quickly and look.

"Okay, Sebastian, go ahead."

"Well, I think to be brave, you have to be scared at the same time. To be brave means there's something important you have to do and you're scared, but you do it anyway." I think of his face, peering out at me from behind Dr. Shiner as I lay at the bottom of the staircase, my wrist in flames. "That's all," he says.

Mrs. LaBelle studies Sebastian thoughtfully for a minute. "Okay, very good." She writes on the board, *Take important action despite fear.*

I listen and take notes. I look up to the clock. It's eight fifty-three, which means nine fifty-three in New York. I look out the window and wonder what Finn is doing now.

Chapter 36

AT HOME THAT NIGHT, Uncle Evan comes into my room after dinner. I've been at my desk, staring at my science textbook for so long that I can barely even see the words anymore. "Hey, Grayson," he says as he sits on my bed. "So, Aunt Sally tells me you said everything was uneventful on your first day back?"

I know what he's getting at. "Yeah, I don't think I have to worry about anyone else." I look down. The TV is on in the other room now, and Aunt Sally is asking Jack if he finished his homework.

"And everything else was okay?" Uncle Evan asks.

"Yeah," I say as I reach up and touch my charm. "Finn's gone."

"Well." It looks like he wants to say something, but he doesn't say anything else. The silence ticks in my ears like a clock.

Finally, he stands up, takes his wallet out of his back pocket, and opens it up. He pulls out two tickets and sits back down. "Today at work Henry asked me if I could use two tickets to the Shakespeare Theater this coming weekend. He and his wife are going out of town. Aunt Sally's not particularly interested in Shakespeare, so she thought maybe you and I could go. It's *Romeo and Juliet*—it's a matinee on Saturday."

I smile at him and nod. "I've heard it's great," I say.

"Yeah? You heard about this? You know, it doesn't surprise me that you're becoming interested in theater. Your parents both loved this kind of thing."

"They did?" I ask.

"Sure." Uncle Evan looks around my room, almost like he's seeing it for the first time. "You know," he says, "when we were kids, your dad and I did absolutely everything together. We were best friends." I didn't know that. "As we grew up, though, I guess we had our own lives, our own paths."

I nod.

"My biggest regret in life . . ." He takes his glasses off and rubs his face. "My biggest regret in life is that we didn't talk much as adults. Your aunt and I got married, your dad and your mom got married. We grew apart." He puts his glasses back on. "It kind of reminds me of you and Jack sometimes." I look down at my hands in my lap. "Your parents loved each other very much, you know," he adds.

"I know."

"They loved you."

"Yeah."

"So, Grayson, there's something that came for you in the mail last week," he says, standing up and opening his wallet again. "Aunt Sally didn't . . . Well, I think your aunt is still searching for a way to process things. I felt, well, I feel that this belongs to you."

The only letters that have ever meant anything to me are the ones from Mom. For the tiniest, split second, I feel like Uncle Evan is about to pull out another letter from her. But I know this is ridiculous. I glance at the painting on my wall as Uncle Evan takes a white envelope out of his wallet. It's folded in half and kind of molded into the shape of the wallet. The return address says *Brian Finnegan*. It's from New York.

"It's from Finn," I say.

"I know." He pauses. "Well, I'll leave you alone," he says. It looks like he wants to say something else, but he doesn't. He gets up, walks out of my room, and closes the door carefully behind him.

I stare at the envelope for a long time. I know that as soon as I read what he wrote, I'm going to forgive Finn for leaving, and I sit and let myself feel furious for another minute. Then, I can't wait any longer, and I carefully rip it open.

March 18

Dear Grayson,

You were amazing in the play tonight, and I'm so proud of you. An old acting teacher of mine in college

used to say that "risk taking is free." He was so wrong.
It's not free. You took a risk, and now I'm sure you're
contending with everything in its wake. Risk taking is not
free, but I can assure you, it's worth it.

Grayson, I'm sorry I wasn't up-front with you about
when I'd be leaving for New York, and I'm sorry I left
without saying good-bye. I guess I was just dealing with
too many of my own emotions to do the right thing.

I know it may feel like there are people who are
against you, but I want you to remember that most people
in the world are good. Look for the people who extend a
hand to you. And when they do, take it.

I'm so proud of what you've done this year. And always
remember, Grayson, to be brave.

Fondly,

Mr. Finnegan

I read the letter three more times before I put it in my top
desk drawer with my letters from Mom. I wish Finn were still
here. I'm tired of people leaving me, and I'm tired of the letters
they leave behind. I don't want to be left behind anymore.

☆

The next morning in Humanities, I roll my gold glitter pen back
and forth between my fingers. Someone has cracked a window
open, and a warm, damp breeze is weaving its way through the

classroom. The air feels heavy. The world outside is green-gray. It's about to pour.

"We're almost ready for the first debate!" Mrs. LaBelle announces as everyone settles into their seats and quiets down. "Let me see . . ." She leans over the desk and looks at Finn's binder. "Grayson, Hannah, Meagan, Hailey, Ryan, Sebastian, Steven, and Bart. Are you guys ready?" She looks up.

"Ryan switched classes," a voice calls out.

"Ah, that's right." Her face flushes, and she pauses for a minute. "Not a problem," she finally says. "Everyone else, find your note cards and come on up. Does everyone else have a notebook out? I want you all to make sure you're taking extensive notes on each debate. I'm not sure if Mr. Finnegan told you, but you're each going to be choosing one of these topics to write a paper on."

The class groans. Mrs. LaBelle grins. "And, they'll be due at the end of next week. I can't wait to read them!"

Thunder rumbles outside the windows, and the wind is picking up now. Everyone whispers and points at the swaying trees. I dig through my backpack for my note cards. The wind gusts again, and the poems and stories that Finn tacked to the bulletin boards suddenly rustle and jump like they're trying to escape from the wall. Amelia closes the window next to her, and they settle back into place.

I find my note cards in my folder and think again about what Finn said in his letter. Then I think about how Marla called him *noble,* and for some reason, I think about what Ms. Landen said about how, sometimes, everything needs to fall apart before it can come back together the way it's supposed to.

"Okay, what are you waiting for? Group one, come on up!" Mrs. LaBelle says, opening her grade book.

"I can't find my note cards," Bart announces, and Steven and Sebastian get up to help him dig through his backpack. I look past them to where Amelia is sitting next to Lila. Her eyes meet mine. She starts mouthing something, and I turn away. I don't want her to think I'm eavesdropping on whatever she's trying to tell Meagan, Hannah, or Hailey. I look at them, wondering what they're talking to Amelia about across the room. They're all looking through their note cards, though, and I look back at Amelia. She's saying something to *me*. I squint at her lips.

Good. Job. In. The. Play. She smiles. Behind her the rain is starting to slam against the windows. I smile back.

"I think my note cards are in my locker," Bart says to Mrs. LaBelle.

"All right, then, go take a look," she says as the thunder booms again. Everyone squeals.

I turn my note cards around in my hands, and I think about Jack. We didn't say much to each other over break. He seemed kind of quiet, actually. Part of me wanted to talk to him. Part of me wanted to ask him why he left the hallway on the day of the play, but I didn't. I think about it again—his hand held out awkwardly before he ran off. I thought about it all break; I tried to figure out what it meant.

I see his hand in my mind again as he reached for my wrist

that day at the Grand Canyon. I remember the feel of his palms, callused from baseball practice, and his startled smile as he pulled me away from the edge. I see him walking a step ahead of me to the park across the street, his skinny ankles disappearing into his gym shoes. He's standing over the kitchen sink, eating wet raspberries out of a colander. He's handing me a red pillow from his bed to reinforce our fort. He's clutching the slippery side of the sailboat. Lake water is running off of his hair and into his eyes in tiny rivers. He's laughing. He's reaching through the warm water for my hand. I raise my hand.

"Yes? Grayson?" Mrs. LaBelle says.

"Can I go to the bathroom?" I ask.

"Of course you can. Just hurry."

I get up and duck out of the classroom. There's nobody in the hall but me, and I can hear voices coming from behind the closed classroom doors. Name tags hang crookedly above some of the lockers, though lots of them fell off months ago. I stop in front of the drinking fountain. Water is dripping from the bottom of it into a dirty, yellow bucket. I stand there. I listen to the quiet noises around me.

In front of me are the two bathroom doors, and I look back and forth, from one sign to the other. BOYS and GIRLS. I remember Paige's back disappearing into the girls' room across from the auditorium, and my wish fills me again like a fire.

I walk into the boys' room. It's empty. The urinals are disgusting, and they smell like pee. I pass them quickly and go into a stall. It's hard to do it with my cast on, but I peel off my gray thermal and then my pink T-shirt with the sequined heart on it. I'm freezing, and my hands are kind of shaky. I hold my pink T-shirt between my knees and put the thermal back on and then put my forearms into the body of my T-shirt to stretch it out a little. The dried plaster of my cast catches on the T-shirt as I pull it over the thermal. I look down.

I walk out of the stall and stand in front of the tall, dirty mirror that looks like it's about a million years old. There are smudges of rust on it, in the corners and around the edges, and someone has scribbled all over it with a green Sharpie. I think of all the years that I spent wearing boys' clothes and pretending that I looked like I do right now, and I think about how I wished and pretended that everyone else could see me the way I'm supposed to be, the way I *really* am. I take the two tiny hairclips that I've been carrying around out of my pocket and arrange them neatly behind my ears. I smooth out my hair and walk out the doorway and into the hall.

The door to the classroom is closed. I stand in front of it for a minute and look through the window. Bart is holding his note cards now, and he, Sebastian, Steven, Meagan, Hannah, and Hailey are next to Finn's desk. They're talking and laughing with Mrs. LaBelle. They're waiting for me.

I look down at the doorknob. I'm scared, but I do it anyway— I open the door and walk inside.

Acknowledgments

ENDLESS GRATITUDE...

To my early readers who expressed enthusiasm and took the time to talk to me and ask me important questions. Your excitement upon reading (some *very* unpolished) drafts of this book kept me moving forward. Joyce Heyman, Laura Bleill, Christy O'Brien, Dale Lipschultz, GraceAnne DeCandido, and Lisa Pliscou—thank you for embracing me and Grayson early on in my journey.

To my fellow workshoppers at StoryStudio Chicago for being present at the start and providing thoughtful, much-needed feedback.

To Molly Backes for your generous gifts of time and insight. Thank you for giving me the confidence to call myself a writer.

To Caryn Fliegler, my oldest friend and trusted reader—you read multiple drafts and gave me invaluable feedback from day one. Thank you for looking out for Grayson and telling me once that nothing should matter but the experiences she was created to endure.

To Lydia Polonsky for being my first editor, Kenneth Polonsky for your feedback and excitement, and the entire Polonsky clan for eagerly anticipating each new stage with me.

To Susan Caruso for giving me days upon days to write and for your insights into the life of a drama geek. Thank you for your never-ending support of me as a parent, writer, and person.

To my parents for your unflagging enthusiasm about my writing career and for your all-around backing during this new phase of my life: Barbara Hurwitz, thank you for many things, but especially for being my number one fan. Martin Lipschultz, thank you for teaching me to always look for the gray. And to Dan Lipschultz, thank you for being my childhood partner in observation, analysis, and crime.

To my trusted agent, Wendy Schmalz, for taking me and Grayson under your wing with such quick enthusiasm that I am still pinching myself. Thank you for always being there to answer my many questions and to support me as a writer and a human being.

To my talented editor, Lisa Yoskowitz, for believing in Grayson and paving the path for her entry into the world. I am forever grateful for the questions you asked and for your help in making this book what it is now. And to the entire team at Hyperion, especially Suzanne Murphy, Stephanie Lurie, Dina Sherman, Liz Usuriello, and Julie Moody—thank you for your important contributions and amazing support.

And, finally, to my family, the inspiration for everything: Benny, who is all love and only light; Ella, my sensitive, fierce, and brave little friend; and Daniel, my first reader and first love.

Two lives tied by one brave act

Threads

a novel by
Ami Polonsky

Also by Ami Polonsky:

Threads

To Whom It May Concern:
Please, we need help!

THE DAY TWELVE-YEAR-OLD CLARA finds a desperate note in a purse in Bellman's department store, she is still reeling from the death of her adopted sister, Lola.

By that day, thirteen-year-old Yuming has lost hope that the note she stashed in the purse will ever be found. She may be stuck sewing in the pale-pink factory outside of Beijing forever.

Clara grows more and more convinced that she was meant to find Yuming's note. Lola would have wanted her to do something about it. But how can Clara talk her parents, who are also in mourning, into going on a trip to China?

Finally the time comes when Yuming weighs the options, measures the risk, and attempts a daring escape.

The lives of two girls—one American, and one Chinese—intersect like two soaring kites in this story about loss, hope, and recovery.

Acclaim for **Patrick McGrath's**

Dr. Haggard's Disease

"Reverberate[s] with echoes of previous masters of horror, from Poe to Hitchcock to Brian DePalma . . . McGrath is a writer of generous gifts."
—*The New York Times*

"Patrick McGrath has never before written with such accuracy or passion as he does on these pages . . . [a] splendidly achieved performance."
—John Banville, *The European*

"Since we are now threatened by a dark age, the new Gothic as wielded by McGrath seems the perfect diagnostic tool for an age newly troubled by the moral monsters and hideous dilemmas our science has produced."
—*Chicago Tribune*

"A novel in which the terrible and the beautiful are melded . . . a myth of the creator sacrificed to his creation. As *Dr. Haggard's Disease* demonstrates, the Gothic genre, far from being restrictive, is as capacious as the mind of the writer employing it."
—*The New York Times Book Review*

"I haven't read a novel as piercingly truthful about the loss of love since Greene's *The End of the Affair*."
—Anthony Quinn, *The Independent*

"A deceptively familiar tale of doomed love, set in London at the outbreak of World War II . . . . [A novel] of noble love mired in disease and decay."
—*Vanity Fair*

Patrick McGrath

Dr. Haggard's Disease

Patrick McGrath is also the author of *Blood and Water and Other Tales*, *The Grotesque* and *Spider*, and is co-editor with Bradford Morrow of *The New Gothic*. He now lives in New York and London and is married to the actress Maria Aitken.

Dr. Haggard's DISEASE

Patrick McGrath

VINTAGE CONTEMPORARIES

Vintage Books

A Division of Random House, Inc.

New York

CELEBRATING

10

Years of

VINTAGE CONTEMPORARIES

FIRST VINTAGE CONTEMPORARIES EDITION, 1994

Copyright © 1993 by Patrick McGrath

Library of Congress Cataloging-in-Publication Data
McGrath, Patrick, 1950–
Dr. Haggard's disease/Patrick McGrath.—1st Vintage
contemporaries ed.
p. cm. —(Vintage contemporaries)
ISBN 0-679-75261-7
1. World War, 1939–1945—England—Fiction. 2. Physicians—Fiction.
I. Title
PS3563.C3663D7   1994
813 '.54—dc20   93-43492
CIP

Author photograph © Anthony Crickmay

Manufactured in the United States of America
10 9 8 7 6 5 4 3 2 1

Acknowledgment

For the immense help he's given me—
medical, psychiatric, and literary—
not only on this book but on *Spider* as well—
I'd like to express my love and gratitude
to my father, Dr. Patrick McGrath.

For Maria

We two being one, are it.

JOHN DONNE

I WAS IN ELGIN, upstairs in my study, gazing at the sea and reflecting, I remember, on a line of Goethe when Mrs. Gregor tapped at the door that Saturday and said there was a young man to see me in the surgery, a pilot. You know how she talks. "A *pilot*, Mrs. Gregor?" I murmured. I hate being disturbed on my Saturday afternoons, especially if Spike is playing up, as he was that day, but of course I limped out onto the landing and made my way downstairs. And you know what that looks like—pathetic bloody display that is, first the good leg, then the bad leg, then the stick, good leg, bad leg, stick, but down I came, down the stairs, old beyond my years and my skin a gray so cachectic it must have suggested even to you that I was in pain, chronic pain, but oh dear boy not pain like yours, just wait now and we'll make it all—go—away—

I crossed the hall, you'd have heard the floorboards, and opened the surgery door. Always full of shadows that room, no matter how bright the day, and stinking of ether, but there on the far side, over by the cabinet, a figure. And the figure turned. And it was, indeed, a pilot, this I could now see clearly, a dark-haired young man of eighteen or nineteen in a blue uniform with wings over the left breast. You approached me rather formally and held out your hand. "Dr. Haggard?" you said.

What did I do, nod? Sigh?

"My name is James Vaughan," you said. You didn't falter. You said: "I believe you knew my mother."

Oh God. *I believe you knew my mother*—had you *any* idea the effect those words would have on me? I don't believe you did. I don't believe you did.

I closed the door and limped over to my chair. You sank gracefully into the chair on the other side of the desk and crossed your legs, and I couldn't help observing how you crossed them, in the exact same way that *she'd* always crossed her legs, with the one ankle pulled in close to the other and the foot pointing at the floor. I could hear nothing but the throbbing of blood in my head and the cry of a gull from the cliffs. As calmly as I could I offered you a cigarette but was unable to light it, for my hands were shaking. You half rose from your seat and lit both cigarettes with a small flat silver-plated lighter. "Tea?" I said.

"Lovely." You even *sounded* like her!

I went to the door, stepped into the hall and called Mrs. Gregor, who appeared from the kitchen wiping her hands on her apron, and asked her for tea. Everything seemed to be happening so slowly.

"Look, is this a bad time?" you said, suddenly suspecting that my unease was caused by your interrupting me in the middle of something important.

"Not at all," I said. "Excuse my agitation, I don't—that is, I haven't seen your mother since—"

The sentence died in the surgery's gloom. Neither of us said a word, and the uneasy fluster of the first minutes subsided as we pondered the immense unspoken world that filled the silence between us like a gas. Then our eyes met across the desk and locked for an instant, just as Mrs. Gregor turned the doorknob, pushed the door open with her bottom and backed into the surgery with the tea tray. We smiled. "I'm awfully sorry doctor," she said, "but we're out of biscuits."

"Oh dear," I said, my eyes still upon you, "I don't think we can manage without biscuits."

DR. HAGGARD'S DISEASE   13

"There's never anything in the house on Saturdays," Mrs. Gregor remarked, setting the tray on the desk then leaving the surgery and closing the door softly behind her.

You continued smiling as I lifted the lid off the teapot and peered at the contents. That you should be *here*, her *son*, in *Elgin*—! As I poured the milk I glanced over and saw you suddenly scratch at the fabric of your trousers—the smile vanished—you frowned—and I tried to remember the last time I'd felt her presence as acutely as I felt it then.

It was at a funeral I first saw her, did she ever tell you that? And do you know, I can't remember whose it was! Who was dead, I mean. It was October 1937, a fine, crisp day, and the air in London had a sort of smoky quality to it. The leaves drifting off the chestnuts along Jubilee Road heaped themselves on the pavement and between the iron railings and crunched underfoot as I hurried along. I'd been up all night in Accident and Casualty, so I arrived ten minutes after the service began. I was wearing my black suit of course, and my black overcoat, and I slipped into the pew at the very back of the church and sat down clutching my hat (a black homburg) and adopted the sort of demeanor one does at funerals. There was a ripple of disturbance and a few heads turned, then it subsided. I'd been working at St. Basil's only six weeks or so, but I recognized a number of the doctors, including Vincent Cushing, and, in the pew in front of me, the senior pathologist. Him I knew only slightly, and I'd formed no particularly strong impression of the man. This would change, of course; as you know, your father was to have a profound impact on my life (Spike is with me still, if proof were needed) though at the time, as I sat with my homburg in my lap and gazed at the broad black back and the roll of pink flesh at the collar, I naturally had no inkling of any of this. But here's the curious thing, and I've thought about this often and I still don't know why, I'm still no closer to an explanation—what was it that immediately riveted my attention on the woman by his side?

Oh, I hardly need describe her to you! When I first came into the church hers was one of the heads that turned, and I believe that the sight of me—panting, disheveled, and late— amused her, and so I had my first brief glimpse of her smile. Dear James, that smile! It seemed to say that nothing should ever dampen one's spirits not even the ghastly grim pomp of a medical funeral! She was a tiny gamine creature all bundled up in a big black coat with a fox round the neck and a smart black hat with a folded-back brim. The face in the fur was pale and heart-shaped with delicate bones and eyebrows fine and black as pencil lines. Her eyes were startlingly clear. They seemed to be wetly shining, somehow, and it was impossible not to respond, and I did, I returned her smile, but was that enough? Enough to start the germ in me? Funerals have always affected me strongly, and this may at least partly explain it; but to captivate me so utterly with a smile, and a smile, at that, amid the stiff black backs of a churchful of mourners— is the heart really so impulsive, so mercurial an organ as that? Perhaps it is. Afterwards, when we milled around outside the church, I lost sight of her, nor did I see her later in the graveyard, but there was a moment when the coffin was being borne down the aisle to the waiting hearse outside, and we turned toward it, that I stole a glance in her direction, and again our eyes met; and I think you might say that from that point forward I was done for. I was lost.

Since that day I have changed in ways that I think would astonish you. The man you know—the man I have become— is but a phantom of the man who first glimpsed your mother in a north London church, and caught her eye, and fell in love—that man is dead, and in his place there's just this, oh, this limping shadow—

Don't move, darling boy. Don't fight it.

• • •

So yes, I did know your mother—though when you sat there
in the surgery that Saturday afternoon, and asked the question,
I'm afraid I was unable to say a word—the resemblance was
so uncanny! "Yes," I said at last, "I did. We knew each other
well."

A pause, a hush, as you gazed at me expectantly. "I'm
sorry, would you like more tea?"

"No thank you."

"We knew each other for several months," I said, "and
then I moved down here, down to the sea."

Down to the sea. The lonely sea and the sky. Down to this
small, forgotten sea resort, this is where I came, broken in
body and spirit, to practice general medicine. Here I felt I
could find peace and obscurity, here in this quiet seaside town
with its esplanade and its pier, its Marine Park Gardens, with
every lunchtime in the summer a performance of light sym-
phonic music by the Municipal Orchestra. It suits me here,
it's kind to broken men like me. I fell silent. Shadows deep-
ened, evening was coming on. You wanted to know much
more but you couldn't pour out your questions, you were far
too reticent, or too well-mannered, for that. So you struggled
to find a way, and though a few gambits suggested themselves
there was, to you, something distasteful about the whole tac-
tic, and finally you opted for plain candor. "Were you," you
said, "her lover?"

Was I her lover? What was I to tell you? You were her son,
after all, and I suddenly felt that the moment was one of
extreme delicacy, and that what I said next would profoundly
influence the nature and course of our relationship. Was I to
tell you the truth, and arouse—what? The rage of the child
who sees his family riven and holds the intruder to blame?
But if I lied to you, or somehow blurred the outline of the
thing, wouldn't that be worse? Wouldn't I then forfeit any
chance I had of winning your trust? And I wanted your trust,
for I wanted to hear you speak of her, just as you wanted to

hear me; we wanted the same thing, though it would take time to acknowledge this to one another, hence our unease. But there was more to it than this, there was the uncanny resemblance you bore her, which gave me the faintly eerie sensation, in that first conversation, that if I allowed my imagination to drift at will it would be *her* who was with me in that shadowy room—and indeed, when you'd gone, and it grew dark (I stayed in the surgery for hours), I could have sworn she'd been there, the same aura, somehow, lingered that I knew from Jubilee Road. So it was this idea that through you I could glimpse again something of her that made me so desperately afraid that if I said the wrong thing you would vanish, leaving me doubly bereft. "I loved your mother," I said. "She was the most fascinating woman I ever knew." (I didn't say I love her still.) You nodded. You appeared satisfied with this. It seemed to be enough, for the time being.

We talked then of less consequential matters and I was glad of that, it allowed us to be at ease with one another. We talked about the war, and I remember at one point you said, "Oh well, but we always seem to win things, don't we?" I remember thinking such blithe optimism was probably necessary, for a Spitfire pilot. I'm afraid I don't share it.

You rose to leave after half an hour or so and I showed you out. You stood on the front door step and then, seemingly quite on impulse, you turned and said, "May I come and see you again?"

"Of course," I said—a surge of joy and relief—"you're always welcome." A quick nod of gratitude, then you were walking down the drive, small sprightly figure in a smart blue uniform, and I watched you till you'd turned out onto the road and were lost to sight. I stood a moment longer. Dusk was coming on, and the starlings gathered in the trees by the wall at the end of the drive had started their evening chorus. I stepped off the porch and went a small way down the drive, then turned and regarded Elgin against the evening light.

• • •

I'd bought the house in the autumn of 1938, some months after the affair had ended, and the Munich crisis was at its height. I was in a very bad way then, as low as I've ever been, stagnant, depressed, in severe physical pain, and it felt to me as though the world were a distorting mirror in which I discovered only my own reflection: the inexorable drift into war—an echo, merely, of my own imminent disintegration. Elgin changed all that. It enabled me to act. I stood at the end of the drive I remember, the first time I saw it, and gazed in dawning wonder at its steeply gabled roofs, its tall chimneys, its many windows, each one high and narrow, with lancet arches and slender leaded frames. The stone was streaked with salt, and what paint there was was everywhere flaking off to reveal weathered, cracking woodwork beneath. Out in front the grass was knee-high, the hedge untrimmed, and the flower beds overrun with weeds, such that an air of neglect, of decrepitude, almost, clung to the place, but none of that could for one moment detract from the effect it had on me: there was something monumental about the house, something massy, but at the same time it *soared*—the arches, the gables, the steep slate roof and slender chimneys—they drew the eye upward and in doing so aroused a *blaze* of ideas and feelings in me. Oh, it was a romantic house, a profoundly romantic house, it didn't suggest repose, this house, no, it suggested the restlessness of a wild and changeful heart; and its power was immeasurably enhanced by its siting. For Elgin stood close to the edge of a cliff that dropped a sheer hundred feet to black rocks and a churning sea.

Black rocks and a churning sea . . . How many hours have I spent in Elgin dreaming of your mother? Her spirit often seemed more in possession of the house than I was, as though I had haunted it with her memory. I did haunt it with her memory—a museum of nostalgia, this is what I made of Elgin, though at the time I believed it would enable me to forget.

As if the heart ever forgets. But that was what was in my mind that day, as I made my slow way up the drive to the front porch, the roof of which was as steep and pointed as the rest of Elgin's roofs, and knocked on the door. Silence. I knocked again (I've never told you this) and with an audible gasp and a scream of dry hinges and swollen carpentry the door swung open, to reveal an old man in carpet slippers and dressing gown blinking from the shadows at the light of the day. His head was deathly pale and almost hairless, and he peered at me through bleary eyes as with trembling fingers he lifted a cigarette to his bloodless lips. It was Peter Martin. "Yes?" he whispered. I introduced myself and reminded him that we had an appointment. He seemed a little astonished at this, nonetheless he led me into the surgery. "What appears to be the trouble, Dr. Haggard?" he said.

The surgery was the first room off the dark-paneled hallway at the front of the house; a passage led into the back parts, and a carved staircase ascended to the upper floors. I was reminded of the doctor's surgery my father took me to when I was sick as a boy—the examination couch, the glass-doored cabinets full of dressings and medicines, the screens behind which patients undressed—dear boy you've undressed behind those screens yourself! And like the doctor's surgery of my boyhood there were two doors, one giving onto the hallway and the private parts of the house, the other into the waiting room.

Poor old chap. I realized at once that he'd forgotten our appointment and assumed I was a patient—a fair assumption, given the limp, the stick, and my general condition. I corrected his misconception and he showed me over the place: it was as though I'd entered the house I was born in. The furniture was draped in heavy velvet, the mantels were crowded with ornaments and clocks, and heavy lace curtains hung on all the windows. As we moved from room to room he told me about Mrs. Gregor and said he expected that I'd want to keep her on. On the top floors several of the bedrooms were closed up, the furniture sheeted and cobwebs in all the corners, and that's when I started to envision how it all would be once I was installed. "I've let the garden go, rather," he said as we paused at the window on the second-floor landing, which looked out over the back of the house onto a jungle of weeds and bushes, more overgrown flower beds, and the sea beyond; "but I daresay you'll be able to take it in hand."

"Yes indeed," I said. Oh, I didn't care about the flower beds or any of that—I just wanted the house! I asked him a few questions about the practice, about what sort of income it could be expected to yield, admitting rights to the hospital, the patients. Old people mostly, he said.

"Fair bit of cancer then?"

"Fair bit."

Then I asked him what he wanted for it, Elgin included. "Hugh Fig didn't tell you?" he murmured.

"No."

We sat outside the back door in old white wicker chairs and talked medicine, a couple of doctors having a drink. He told me a few stories about the practice, odd little tales that usually ended with the words: "Lost him, I'm afraid, nothing I could do." I contained my excitement with difficulty. I learned that this was a community of the frail and elderly who had come to the sea to die, and as the old man rambled on about a nasty case of rheumatic fever he'd treated last winter it occurred to me that for forty years the sick of the district had looked to him for the comfort and support that a physician must dispense when all his technical resources are spent. This is not the science of medicine, this is its art, and I said this to Peter Martin. He wheeled about in his chair and peered at me closely through those bleary old eyes. "Got a family, Dr. Haggard?" he said.

"No." My father died while I was at medical school; my mother when I was a child.

"Not married?"

"No."

"Ah." He sank back. "Anyway," he said, finishing up his tale of the encrusted heart valves, "lost her. Never did have much joy with rheumatic fever."

When it came time to leave we still had not discussed money, or indeed whether he was willing to sell to me, though I believed he was. "Oh, talk to Hugh Fig," he said, as my taxi appeared at the end of the drive, "I'm sure he'll be able to sort it all out."

I thanked him warmly.

"Not at all, doctor," he said. "Too old for it myself anymore. Wife died ten years ago, never quite saw the point of things after that." He turned back inside and closed the door behind him.

Hugh Fig was indeed able to sort it all out, and we quickly came to terms. My mood remained buoyant. I met Mrs. Gregor, and again looked over the house, this time in the full knowledge that it was mine. I was able now to think soberly about where I would sleep, where I would read, and I imagined my late evenings in Elgin, those quiet hours spent listening to music with a book in my lap—how pleasant all that would be, in this large, quiet house! I imagined too how my pictures would hang on the walls, where my books would go, on and on—it is a happy pursuit, the inscription of oneself, as it were, upon some fresh blank tablet like this. Elgin, I decided, would become an expression of myself, or of the self, rather, that I would rebuild here; for I had been shattered, I had been broken in body and in spirit, and I needed a haven to heal in.

Eventually we settled on a date by which the house would be vacated, and I organized the removal of my possessions to Griffin Head. There came a day in the early autumn when I stood in my room in Jubilee Road and surveyed it for the last time, the room that had known such joy, and lately such pain. Books all gone, walls bare of pictures. A single suitcase stood by the door, and leaning against it my cripple's stick. A faint last stab of loss, hastily suppressed, and I left. I was becoming adept at suppressing loss. At the bottom of the stairs I said goodbye to Desmond Kelly and gave him a fiver. He thanked me warmly. "You'll come back and see us, will you, doctor?" he said.

"Oh, I doubt it," I said, "I doubt I'll be back."

I came into Elgin late in the afternoon. There was still much to do: my boxes were unopened, my books unshelved, my pictures unhung. All that could wait. I limped through the empty house, then out to the back. The sea was running briskly and the sun had begun its descent to the horizon. I picked my way down the garden path, beating back the weeds with my stick. I went through the gate in the hedge at the bottom, and so along the short path to the cliff's edge, where a set of rickety wooden steps made a steep and perilous descent to the narrow pebbled beach below. The tide was coming in; it foamed and roiled about the black rocks at the foot of the cliff, then rushed back with a hissing sound, dragging with it scraps of seaweed and driftwood and other briny detritus. The breeze was stiff, it felt fresh and salty in my face and in my hair, and carried the cries of gulls from the pier, which was obscured from view by a jutting headland a hundred yards or so along the cliffs. There I stood, breathing the good sea air, and reveling still in a powerful sense of well-being.

After some minutes I decided to attempt the climb down the wooden staircase to the beach below. I grasped the handrail and took the first step down, but as I did so a sharp twinge from Spike made me gasp with pain, and I abandoned the idea, and instead made my way, in no small discomfort, back up toward the house, and so into the surgery. There I slipped off my jacket, unfastened my cuff link and prepared to relieve the pain; a moment later came the familiar glow of spreading peace, and Spike just faded away.

It was a strange, rather unearthly adventure, that first night in Elgin. The sky was clear and the moon hung low over the sea, spilling yellow light on the barely heaving surface. I stood in the upstairs back bedroom, by the window, with the lights off, and gazed out toward the horizon for many minutes. The morphia had silenced Spike, replaced his ache with that pervasive vital warmth that seemed somehow always to compose me, and enabled me to concentrate my faculties, which quickly became attuned to the myriad tiny sounds all around me on the very edge of imperceptibility, all the creaks and rustles, the sighs and hissing of the woodwork and plumbing of an old house. It occurred to me then that Elgin was starting to breathe—it was an odd sensation, uncanny, though curiously exhilarating, the sensation of something old, something massive that has lain inert and dormant for years, being roused, shuffling to life again. I limped from room to room in a state of some excitement, believing, you see, that it was I, Edward Haggard, who had provided the spark now animating the frame through which I moved!

It was close to dawn before I felt I could sleep. I had gone back down through the garden to the cliff, though this time I didn't try to descend. I watched the sea crashing about the rocks below, which were shining wetly in the moonlight and festooned with clumps of bulbed and blackly glistening seaweed. Then I turned, and regarded Elgin for the first time from the back by night—again that sense of soaring mass, that upward sweep of the structure, up into the sharp pointed gables and the high narrow chimneys, a sheen of moonlight sliding across the slates—I had left every light lit, and the house shone like a beacon against the night sky. A beacon: for too long I had been a craft adrift upon a dark and empty sea, and her the only star I'd had to steer by.

Oh where to begin? Dear James, these few short weeks we've had—memory has this quality, that it can yield its material with such remarkable *speed*— a tragedy remembered in the blink of an eye, a lifetime over a bottle of gin. In these last few seconds—all this: my relationship with your mother; its end; the aftermath; you—then strangest of all perhaps, what happened after we met, my efforts to help you—all of it vividly present to me *at this moment*. Morphia helps, morphia excites memory, displays to the inner eye great vistas of experience, lived life, felt life, all in an instant, precise in every detail. You'd be surprised if I told you how much I looked forward to our next meeting. Or perhaps you wouldn't—I know you were eager to talk more about your mother, for what we had accomplished in that first encounter was merely an opening of the subject, a breaking of the ice, no more. It was enough for you to know, that Saturday, that I had loved her. The rest would come later. As for me, I felt that I must allow you to dictate how quickly our intimacy developed. You were the younger man, less sure of yourself in the emotionally fraught territory that we were about to explore—explorers, this is what we were, at the start of our journey, and you, I decided, should set the pace. At the beginning, at least, you would lead.

You telephoned a few days later. Mrs. Gregor was doing the spring cleaning I remember, for after talking to you I left Elgin on my afternoon rounds, and as I climbed into the car I saw her throw open the window of one of the upstairs rooms that had been shut up all winter, and the gesture spoke directly to what I was feeling: my heart was a musty chamber, long closed, but good clean fresh air was starting to blow through.

You came round to see me after dinner that night. You were reticent, but it was not the reticence of a weak or uncertain character, far from it. I felt, rather, that underneath, the character was firmly developed. There was authority, yes, and hope, too, and a quiet courage—all I've lost, in fact, since Spike. So while you were often silent, and blushed easily, there was at the same time a sureness in the way you moved across a room, the way you sat in a chair, and particularly, in the way you spoke about what you knew best, which was flight. But at the same time you were so *young!* With your unruly black hair, your clear, burning eyes, your white skin, red lips, the fine clean bone structure of your small dark head—you were still in many ways a boy. I did not take you into the surgery but upstairs to my study and there, after a cursory airman's glance at the sky (evening was shading quickly into night) you sank into an armchair and smoothed the fabric of your uniform trousers while I poured you a glass of beer. "Anything interesting today?" I murmured. I had my back to you, standing by the drinks tray on the table by the door; I glanced over my shoulder and saw you shrug. "Not a lot," you said with a frown, brushing at a speck of dust on your knee.

Later I would learn what it meant, that frown, that clipped dismissive reply: it meant the squadron had lost a pilot. In those first months of the war such loss was still a novelty, but even so, not a thing any of you would make a fuss about. "Poor old Johnny," you might say, "bought it, poor chap"— and that was all. I don't suppose you could afford any greater emotional expenditure than that—a man in a perpetual state of mourning isn't much use in the cockpit of a Spitfire, I can see that.

So I sat down, watched you for a moment, and then put to you the question that had intrigued me since you first appeared in my surgery. "James," I said, busying myself with a cigarette so as to deflect, rather, the weight of the question—"why did you come here?"

"To Elgin you mean?"

I nodded.

You brought together those fine dark eyebrows in a delicate frown—how often I'd seen *her* frown in precisely that manner!—and for a second or two turned your head to gaze at the window at the far end of the surgery. "You loved my mother," you said.

Again I nodded.

"And you knew my father."

"Yes."

"I was never close to him," you said—oh, I could well believe it!—and then you paused; this was not easy for you.

"Go on," I murmured.

"My mother never hid from me the fact that she was unhappy."

All this I knew.

"Sometimes I heard them arguing. I heard your name. I asked her who you were, but she wouldn't tell me."

That scene I could well imagine—I could see her crossing the room, taking your troubled face in her hands, saying, "Now darling, you mustn't ask me questions like that"— she'd spoken the same words to me!

"Then she fell ill, and I felt as though it were connected, somehow. I could never talk to my father about this." Another pause. "I'm sorry doctor, I don't know what it is I'm trying to say. I suppose I feel she left without saying goodbye—is that absurd?"

The way you looked at me then, in an agony of perplexity but at the same time resolute, unafraid—you wanted to understand, even if you risked looking a fool, even if it was painful. You were without guile, this was what charmed and moved me, and I knew it was my responsibility to ease the uncertainty, that sense of incompletion.

"I only joined the squadron a couple of weeks ago," you said, "and it was just by chance I learned that a Dr. Haggard was practicing down here. Stroke of luck, really."

You smiled—James, it was *her* smile!

"Stroke of luck indeed," I said. "But tell me, what do you mean, 'connected'? What was her illness connected with?"

Silence. "I don't know," you said at last. "Connected with the atmosphere at home. With the arguments. With my father being so angry all the time. I felt as if she were being punished."

I was beginning to understand. "Illness isn't a form of retribution," I said gently. "It's not a sign of moral failure."

"Oh I know."

You sighed then, and it tore my heart, that sigh, so great a weight of suffering was in it. "I know that," you said, "so why do I still feel so dreadful about it?"

I had an idea why you felt so dreadful, but I did not voice it. I would have to handle this with great tact and delicacy, I realized. It was time, I decided, to give you what your father never could, some sense of the background of the affair.

I was living at the time, I told you, in a small flat in a large house about a mile from the hospital, in Jubilee Road, one of those long drear north London streets of tall dark houses whose windows, at dusk, uncurtained and unlit, make them look hollow and haunted within. The front door, four or five steps up from the pavement, behind high spiked iron railings, was inset with a panel of stained glass and opened into a dark hallway dominated by a sideboard like a catafalque. At the end of the hallway stairs with threadbare carpeting ascended to the gloom of the upper regions. I had a big, high-ceilinged room on the second floor at the front, overlooking the street, with a fireplace surmounted by a marble mantelpiece and a large mirror. The shelves were crammed with volumes of medicine and poetry, and the faded floral wallpaper was hung here and there with landscapes and sunsets I'd collected as a student. And apart from two armchairs drawn up to the fireplace, and the table I worked at, this was it. There was a small bedroom, almost completely filled by a huge ancient creaking bed; the bathroom was down the hall, and I shared it with the other occupants of the floor, whom I rarely saw as I worked such odd hours.

I was I suppose an unusual creature for a surgical registrar. My father had been the rector of a small parish in Dorset, and I was expected to follow him into the church. I had all the makings of a certain sort of priest—intensely solitary, much preoccupied with metaphysics, and passionately fond of poetry—and would undoubtedly, had I so chosen, one day have ministered to a flock of my own. But it was precisely in order to compensate for what I saw as the rather impractical tendencies in my character, and do some *real* good in the world, that I'd decided to go into medicine instead. After Oxford I'd taken the MBBS and then been appointed to the staff of St. Basil's while I worked for my MD. I was on call thirty-six hours out of the forty-eight, and was often up all night doing admissions then assisting in theaters till late in the afternoon. I won't pretend I was happy. I'd begun to realize I wasn't meant to be a surgeon, and I'd reason to think that my chief, Vincent Cushing, to whom I'd been attached since the beginning of August, was coming to the same conclusion.

Oh, he was a tough, bloody-minded character, did you ever know him? He was like your father. He had no sympathy for anyone less deft than himself, and he treated surgery like a branch of mechanics, this is what made him so difficult to work for. Theaters was up on the third floor at the end of a white-tiled corridor behind a set of swing doors, with a wash room where we scrubbed for surgery, which required three minutes with a hard brush on the backs of the hands, the palms, between the fingers and halfway up the forearms to the elbows, and this always left me chapped and sore. I never had a problem during the simple operations, when I was one of the two or three doctors performing and could stand over the incision with a clear view of all that went on, in fact I quite enjoyed taking out gallbladders, that level of surgery. It was the complicated procedures I disliked, where five or six doctors were involved and I'd have the tricky job of holding the retractors that pulled back the body wall so the surgeon could get in.

One morning I was desperately tired, having been up all night in Accident and Casualty, and I was assisting while Cushing operated. Though I was only an arm's length from the wound I was excluded from a clear sight of it by a wall of white-gowned backs all stooped over the patient on the table beneath a pair of large, powerful, circular lights. The procedure was a long one, the theater was hot, the atmosphere tense, and after an hour or so everything turned milky—I suppose I must have drifted off. Suddenly there came a loud rap. "More retraction!" barked Cushing, and I was abruptly jerked into the here and now. I gave more retraction. "Too much!" he shouted. "Who is that? Haggard? Wake up, man." The patient was under spinal anesthesia and Cushing was trying to find a bleeder deep in the belly. "Pull the bloody retractor," he cried, "I can't see what I'm doing. No no no no no, you're pulling too hard again, you'll rupture his spleen. Dear God what kind of idiots are they sending me now?" My face, behind my mask, burned with humiliation; impassive eyes gazed at me from other white-masked faces. I let my knees go slack, took a few rapid breaths, and stamped my right foot on my left to stimulate enough vascular tone to stay vertical and awake; fortunately there were no further mishaps.

Afterwards, in the wash room, Cushing eyed me with displeasure as he dried his hands. He was a stocky, impatient man who whistled tunes from the great operas while he operated. "What's the trouble, doctor," he said, "not getting enough sleep?"

"Frankly no, sir," I said. I was buttoning my white coat, about to go back down to the wards.

"Better get used to it. Medicine takes physical stamina, that surprise you?"

"I was aware of that," I said. Damn it, I *had* been up all night!

"You better be aware of it, doctor," snapped Cushing. "You won't last otherwise."

"If I could see what was going on," I retorted, "I could do my job."

"Don't bandy words with me, Dr. Haggard! You're going to have to learn to go days without sleep and perform competently, that clear?"

"Yes sir."

"Good. Because if you can't do that you won't survive. And get your hair cut, doctor!" And with that he flung down his towel and off he went.

The nights were the worst though. Exhausted, I'd write up a history of every patient who appeared, do a physical examination, a white-cell count, a red-cell count, and a hemoglobin, all in the musty closet of a laboratory at the end of the ward that stank of urine and chemicals. Hunched over a stained and battered workbench I'd light a Bunsen burner attached to an ancient gas cock by rotten rubber tubing, then boil the urine gently over the flame until a cloud of protein appeared. Test tubes cracked in the heat, urine spilled, and then, weeping tears of anger and frustration, I'd have to pour more into another tube and start all over again. My back ached from hours spent bending over a bed, a stretcher, an operating table, a lab bench. When I finally got off duty I'd trudge home to Jubilee Road, fall into bed and immediately be asleep, though at times I'd be too exhausted even for sleep, and instead I'd lie there in the darkness and ask myself, why? Why all this pain, all this sickness, what is the *point?* At these times medicine seemed as futile as life itself. For if all one's efforts proved negligible in the face of a steadily increasing volume of human suffering then it was hard to resist the implication of a random godless universe and us, its tenants, mere registers of sensation, specifically pain.

Hardly the most propitious of circumstances for a love affair, then, even if such a thought had crossed my mind, which of course it hadn't—I was always working, and as for your mother, she was a married woman, not only married but married to the senior pathologist and mother of a boy of sixteen! But as luck would have it we encountered one another again quite soon. It happened at the Cushings'; and I suppose you could say that that's when it all properly began.

What had she *done?*—this was what I asked myself as I stood in front of the mirror in the door of my wardrobe in Jubilee Road. Cushing had invited his registrars to dinner, and the senior pathologist and his wife would apparently be among the other guests. I had given little further thought to the woman at the funeral though now, at the prospect of actually meeting her, I experienced a tingle of expectation so visceral my fingers grew moist and gave me trouble with my collar studs. I had no idea what would happen, of course—all this was still inchoate within me, no more than a dimly sensed turbulence in the lower depths. But there was something, I knew there was something, and the picture I had of her lifting her chin as she turned her head in the church that afternoon, and caught my eye and *smiled*—it all came vividly back and aroused in me a powerful emotion I was reluctant to define.

So shortly after seven-thirty, in an elegant suit of evening clothes, with a white silk scarf thrown carelessly around my neck, I left the house on Jubilee Road and set out on foot for the Cushings'. It was a damp, windy night and I had to use my umbrella. This was before Spike of course, and I made good time down those long drear streets of high dark houses, with their hollow, haunted windows; I was still unsettled, and strangely excited. Daphne Cushing I'd already met. She greeted me warmly in the hall. "I knew you'd arrive at just the right moment," she whispered, linking her arm in mine and leading me across to the drawing room, "come in and have a cocktail. I expect you know everybody, we're all St. Basil's tonight." It was a large lofty room filled with dark furniture. Somber curtains hung over the windows. A fire had been lit and long thin flames leaped up from a solid mass of coal. "Ah, Haggard," said Cushing, looking in his dinner jacket like a little polished bullet as he emerged from a mur-

muring clutch of doctors and wives all in evening dress, "glad you could come. Somebody getting you a drink?" Wagner was playing on the gramophone.

My eye sought her, and found her, instantly. She recognized me of course. She was in an evening gown of oyster satin, cut on the bias and clinging like a glove to her slim form. She moved away from her companion as Daphne Cushing led me to her side. "Fanny, have you met Edward Haggard? He's Vincent's new registrar."

"No," she said, in a voice of smoky velvet, "I don't believe I've had the pleasure."

That night, dear James, your mother took my heart by storm— took it without a struggle. In those first moments I can't have been very articulate, I never am when I'm excited, I tend to become formal, but she understood. With a cocktail in one hand, a cigarette in the other, she lifted her chin and slyly asked me if I was always so disrespectful to the dead. Like you I am a small man, and I'd realized at once that she and I were within an inch or two of each other in height. Daphne Cushing, suspecting nothing, went off to see about the can- apés. "I don't imagine he minded," I said. She smiled that smile I remembered, roguish and conspiratorial, crushing out her cigarette in a large silver ashtray on a stand. As she leaned over, her gown rippled with reflected light from the chan- delier, and what a truly lovely woman she was, I thought— already I was fascinated by her, the pale, perfect skin, the slight, slender figure in the shining sheath of satin. Her dark hair was cut close to the head and gleamed in soft waves in the candlelight. She drew close to me and told me we were seated next to each other at table. Sharp increase of blood pressure in me, and then, laying a hand on my sleeve, she said: "And I don't want to talk medicine, or St. Basil's, or anything remotely connected."

I became aware for the first time of her perfume.

"We can talk about art, or football, or the weather, or what-ever you like," she said, "just not medicine or hospitals."

Suddenly I was at ease with her. She found it all as stuffy and tedious as I did. A quiet joy swept through me. "I'm afraid," I protested gaily, "I've thought about little else these last weeks."

"Then you must start now. You're not a complete philistine."

A few minutes later we went through to the dining room. She walked ahead of me, composed and assured, the silk straps of her gown snug against her small perfect shoulder blades. We were indeed seated next to one another, and the talk at the table, as she'd predicted, did revolve around mat-ters medical. But your mother would not allow me to listen, I was there, she said, to entertain her! She asked me about myself and learned I was preparing to take my MD. "And after that?" she said. We were eating soup.

"I suppose," I said, setting down my spoon and dabbing my lips with a napkin, "I shall go into general surgery. Or give myself over to a life of pleasure."

"Pleasure?" she said. She carefully buttered a fragment of bread roll. She gazed absently down the table. "That's rather Twenties of you."

"Oh?"

"I mean, I'd have thought pleasure was a worn-out idea, given the times, wouldn't you?" She turned toward me with lifted eyebrows and sipped her wine.

One often had to think quickly with your mother. She was easily bored, she liked sudden shifts of mood, it was a way she had of testing people. I knew what she was getting at of course, for all the talk at the time was of war. I was not optimistic. With our overextended empire, our faltering in-dustrial output—what chance had we of winning a war with Germany? Thriving, martial, boldly led Germany? I said as much, then added: "But tell me an idea that isn't worn out."

She looked away, apparently contemplating the question. The frown persisted, a delicate vertical wrinkling of the white skin of her forehead.

"Passion," she said.

"Passion?" I was something of a stranger to that idea! "I should have thought that passion, at least, was about pleasure—?"

"Oh no," she said quickly, "it's not about pleasure at all. Passion is very serious. I know you take it lightly, but you'll learn someday what a responsibility it is. It's the best we're capable of, civilized human beings."

Civilized human beings. How strange I would find it, later, to recall a time before I heard her say those words, express that ideal—there seems a curious weightlessness to it now, as though all existence prior to your mother was just a form of floating, a fantastic, ethereal, childlike condition that did end, yes, with the gravity of the responsibility of passion— but all of that was yet to come. "The best?" I said.

"What better?"

"But passion always dies," I said.

"Spoken like a medical man," she said, as our plates were removed. "For you, passion is a disease. It causes suffering, comes to a crisis, and dies."

She turned to me then with that wicked smile of hers and leaned forward, placing her hand on my arm. "Tell me," she said, in a low voice, again sounding like smoke and velvet, "do surgeons make good lovers? Too incisive, I should have thought."

"Try me,' I whispered, and immediately regretted it—I had drunk too much wine! I was much too excited! But she wasn't offended, far from it. She gazed at me a moment, then loosed a peal of laughter that rang round the room like bells. It stopped all conversation, and a dozen faces turned toward us. "I see you're amusing my wife, Dr. Haggard," said the senior pathologist, and conversation resumed.

•   •   •

All this I told you in my study that evening—not in so many words, but I think I gave you the essence of it. When I'd stopped talking you sat silently with your elbows on your knees, head down, staring at the floor. At least you looked up—and I was enormously touched to see your eyes glistening wetly in the muted lighting of that book-filled room. "She was beautiful, wasn't she?" you murmured.

"Yes," I whispered.

A trembling, tender silence. Then you sat up briskly, pushed a hand through the lick of black hair that had fallen across your forehead, and gazed at me with a frank, clear smile. "Thanks doctor," you said, "I feel better."

You left soon afterwards, but not before promising to return soon. I went back upstairs to my study and spent several hours quietly indulging the memories aroused by the evening's conversation.

Oh James. Love—adult romantic love—I have come to believe is an attitude of passionate devotion to an ideal. Your mother came to represent for me an ideal. She came to seem the very embodiment of grace. Grace: it was manifest in everything about her, it was the ineffable breath of being in all she said, and did, and thought, and felt—her spirit, in a word, she possessed *grace of spirit* and was as incapable of vulgarity as I believe any human being can be. I am a man and a doctor. The body sickens, it goes wrong, it stinks, it rots, it dies. This is where my work is, with the diseases of the flesh. It has become as essential to me as life itself that I animate the pitiful spectacle of sickness and pain with a meaning that transcends mere mortality. The love I conceived for your mother gave me the sole glimpse I have had of the possibility of such meaning, my one thin thread of hope: where before there was only the dark face of nature, with its absolute imperative of disease, suffering and death, now there was grace.

The irony of my life, if not its tragedy, is that I did not understand this until it was too late; only then, as I retraced in memory the vertiginous arc of our affair, and the desperate, terrible brutality of its ending, did I properly come to know what it signified.

The tragedy of my life, then, the failure to understand the nature of love, until it was too late. I don't think I really began to grasp it until that first autumn I spent in Elgin, when the wild winds started to blow. We were up on top of the cliffs of course, exposed to the elements, and I remember how I'd be elated, nightly, by the howling and wailing, sudden huge inexplicable crashes, and great gusts rattling windows and whistling down chimneys, flattening the fire. Around eleven I'd go down to the surgery and see to Spike, then back upstairs, to the back bedroom, which I'd decided to use as my study. I'd select something to put on the gramophone and stand by the window watching the sea, waiting for the morphia to bring relief. Then it would come, and my intellect, like some great bird tethered and pinioned to the earth too long, lifted, and climbed, and soon was soaring, and in the play and shift of vast vague ideas I'd stand there gazing out over the turbulent moonlit sea, and feel the familiar steady glow of peace aroused, the benevolence and serenity that in the normal course of events I rarely experienced, being afflicted so much of the time with pain. I became composed, where before I'd been agitated, I was able to concentrate all that had been scattered and in fragments, see the larger patterns, the higher truths—

Though it was not always so pacific, oh by no means—there were nights my mind played tricks on me, nights about which I have never spoken to you. I remember once, it must have been midnight or later, and the wind was howling, turning from the window back into the room, that dimly lit room of books and thought, and my eye being caught by some small movement in the *wall*, so it seemed. Those old upstairs rooms hadn't been redecorated for eighty years, so the plasterwork was everywhere overspread with a vermiculate network of fine cracks that pleased me in some curious way and that I'd always taken as the random effect of natural aging. Until, that is, the night I caught that movement out of the corner of my eye, and bending to inspect the wall discovered to my utter astonishment that the lines of the cracking formed distinct patterns, distinct *figures*—rich and various clusters of organic motifs, I mean, leaves and tendrils of the vine, in extended scrolls and spirals, and here and there bizarre figures, festoons of fruit, skulls, masks, snakes, and the longer I gazed into the wall, following the intertwining, convoluted lines of the pattern, and identifying newer and stranger grotesques half-hidden in its frenzied sweeps and swirls, the greater became my feeling of unease and excitement—the cracks in the plaster were no mere accidents of time, but *the product of conscious design.* This riot of elaborate organicism, these arches and lobes—they echoed, I realized, the detailing of Elgin's facade, they too expressed the wildness, the changefulness, the enduring vitality of the house—

Though in the morning, when I returned to the study, all I could see was random cracking.

Another time I was in the study late at night when I felt, from somewhere deep in Elgin's bowels, so it seemed, a massive, muffled *thump!* I was at my desk, writing. My head came up. Though it was muffled, there'd been enormous power in that thump—what was it? But before I could make any sense of it there came another one—and another—and another and another and another—and I sat there frozen at my desk, pen poised, in a state of total alarm. With every *thump!* the whole house seemed to shudder, the lights flickered, and for half a minute, maybe longer, it persisted, in a steady, measured rhythm, and I was struck by this single thought, that I was listening to the beating of a heart. But a monster heart—a huge monster heart, pumping and thumping through the shuddering, flickering structure in which I sat. Then it

stopped. As suddenly as it had started, it stopped. A silence—
and a sound, which I can only describe as a *sigh*—as though
the house, or some principle of animation (and respiration)
within it, was releasing breath. It was a long drawn-out sigh,
and it seemed to have an almost sibilant accent to it, a sort
of hiss, as it expired. But what a shock it gave me! I experienced terror, I admit it, there in that shadowy upstairs room,
there was a rapid increase in heart rate, a dilation of blood
vessels, I started to sweat and became aware of the contraction
of my sphincter. I thought the house was falling down! I
thought the entire cliff on which Elgin stood was crumbling,
that the sea, which had been eating into it for so many years—
so many centuries!—had, in hollowing it out, created such a
tortuous, complicated burrow of caves and sea chambers and
passages down there that finally the very foundations had
grown too weak to support the mass above, and the whole lot,
Elgin included, was falling into the sea! But eventually all
was still, and I wiped my clammy face and hands with a
handkerchief and asked myself, what was it? A moment's
thought, and I realized: the generator. Peter Martin had said
something about the generator, but at the time I'd paid no
attention, infatuated as I was with Elgin itself.

The morning after this ordeal I was weary and irritable,
there were deep shadows under my eyes, and in the skin
between and above my eyebrows were etched a series of deep
vertical slanting clefts, like the marks left by lightning on the
bark of a blasted oak. Mrs. Gregor was sensitive. She put my
breakfast before me without even rattling the teacup, but all
I wanted was a cigarette and the newspaper. I told her about
the thumping, and yes, she said, it would be the generator.
She'd get the man in to have a look at it. It was an old house,
this was the problem. Curiously though it endeared me to
Elgin all the more. Houses, I have come to believe, like love,
like nature itself, should not reassure, should not attempt to
soothe, or give comfort, but should, rather, *excite*.

But what was most vivid, those strange howling nights in

the autumn of 1938, to one peculiarly sensitive state of mind—
and it was a rare one, for numerous factors conspired to effect
it—was the first dawning sensation I had of a *presence* within
myself; becoming aware, for some fleeting passage of time,
mere minutes, perhaps, or hours, I never knew how long, of
a sort of *light* that burned in every cell of my body, a light
that did not merely illuminate my being but in a way consti-
tuted it, gave it organization, gave it harmony, meaning and
form—my *soul*, in a word, my spirit. The spirit came through,
and for the first time I knew myself in a physiological sense
to be more than the sum of my parts: an organism, yes, but
not merely that, there was spirit alive in the cells, there was
divinity in my nature, I was pure being created in the very
image of God—

Such were my nights, that first wild autumn in Elgin; my
mornings were more prosaic. Elgin enabled me to act—for
after a period of prostration and inactivity I had resolved to
work once more, to revive the sense of duty, of service, that
had gradually been dying those interminable nights I labored
in the wards of St. Basil's. I knew hospital medicine, and I
knew some surgery, but before I found Elgin I had never
practiced general medicine. Peter Martin came to advise me.
He told me that the backbone of the work was a group of
private patients, elderly retired mostly, who paid a guinea a
visit, though there was a sizable panel list too, for each of
whom I'd get nine shillings a year from the county. He said
that the main thing was to give people something to take
home with them. He used a Brighton pharmacologist for his
preparations, but he didn't have much faith in medicines as
such. "Palliative at best," he said, puffing away at his cigarette, then shuffled across the surgery to the glass-fronted
cabinet and took out a flask of yellow liquid. "Mist Explo,"
he said, "very popular." It was a concentrate made up from
crystals derived from picric acid which I could dilute, two

ounces to eight of water, and dispense to patients with a wide
variety of ailments. "Half a crown the surgery visit," he said,
"two shillings the medicine, tuppence the bottle."

"Mist Explo?" I murmured, thinking: mumbo jumbo, the
man's a witch doctor.

"Vast majority of people who'll come to you," he said, "*vast*
majority, doctor, have ailments that fall well within the scope
of the body's healing powers. Immense capacity to heal itself,
the body, but it's got to be persuaded."

Still I was skeptical. "You'll see," he said, turning away,
nodding, ash dripping down the front of his cardigan. He
dispensed digitalis for heart conditions but had little faith in
that either. "May prolong life a little," he said, and told me
a story about an old lady with congestive heart failure and
swelling of the legs so gross she could barely move. "Took
her digitalis three times a day with a quarter bottle of
champagne."

"And?"

"Died. Nothing I could do."

He showed me the three bottles of aspirin he kept in the
surgery, in one of which the pills were green, in another pink,
in the third yellow. "Make a great business of selecting the
most efficacious," he told me, "but they're all the same. We're
priests," he said, "that's our function. Give them faith in their
own healing powers. Let nature do the work."

Nature. As if nature were exempt from botches.

The morning of my first surgery the waiting room was almost
full. Everyone was eager to have a look at the new man, have
me inspect their malady. I realized only later that it wasn't
Mrs. Gregor's job to send patients in to me, Peter Martin's
habit was just to stick his head into the waiting room and say,
"Who's next then?" But when she brought me a cup of tea
in the surgery shortly before nine, without thinking I asked
her to send the first one in. She did as I asked; she didn't
want to make things hard for me.

The first was a stout young man in a loud checked suit, sweating profusely. He came in with an air of utter self-confidence, sat down heavily, leaned across the desk and shook my hand. "Morning doctor," he said, "my name is Watkins. I should like you to take me and my family on as patients. I ought to say straightaway, sir, that like a lot of other people I've been through hard times, in fact if it hadn't been for Mrs. Watkins I tell you straight I should've gone under, wonderful woman she's been. I may have run up a bill or two that should've been paid sooner but that's all over now. I'm in the scrap metal trade, and business is looking up at last. War coming, see? I shall very soon be able to hold my head up anywhere, and let me say right now that you shall be paid in full and prompt for your attendance. As soon as the bill comes in it'll be paid, I promise you that. I thought we'd better understand each other man to man right at the start, so I won't waste no more of your time. It's my balls. That's my trouble and my only trouble. Swell up with water every so often."

I reminded myself that I was here to serve. I looked up the man's file and found that Peter Martin had regularly tapped his hydrocele, a collection of fluid round the testicle. I told Mr. Watkins the next time he had trouble of that sort he should come in and I'd see to it. Apparently satisifed that our relationship was off on the right foot he vigorously shook my hand and marched out.

I saw several more patients before lunch. One disturbed me particularly, an ill-nourished young woman with pale lips and chlorotic skin who told me a sad tale of too many children in too small a house, and an unemployed husband depressed and drinking. Her own will to survive was clearly flagging. She was grossly anemic, so I prescribed iron, though this would barely begin to address her problems, and we both knew it. Another woman came in with a nasty case of pin knee—inflammation of the patella—from scrubbing floors. So I made up a kaolin poultice, poured boiling water on it and bound up the knee, then had her sit in the waiting room while the heat drew up the sepsis. She became upset. She was a char, she told me, and if she couldn't get down on her knees to scrub floors she couldn't work, and if she couldn't work she wouldn't eat. I told her just to sit still and when the time came I'd lance the abscess and all would be well. She went back into the waiting room and I called in the next patient. By the end of the morning I was thoroughly exhausted and Spike was throbbing painfully.

Mrs. Gregor wasn't ready with my lunch so I wandered out into the garden and down to the gate, where I lit a cigarette and turned back to look at the house. It cheered me. The sight of it lifted my spirits, reminded me why I'd chosen to come here. It was a windy day, the sky was clear, there was a strong bite of salt in the air, and Elgin was looking very gray, very lean and spiky, it seemed to be all juts and angles, all points and edges, less mass than plane. I smoked my cigarette and felt somewhat strengthened in my resolve; the first man, Watkins, had laid a chilly finger on my heart with his bland and cheerful "War coming, see?" I did see, oh I did. When I went back in Mrs. Gregor told me there was still someone in the waiting room. The woman with the pin knee! I'd forgotten all about her! I took off the poultice, and the knee has pussed up nicely, so with a sterilized needle I lanced it there and then, and sent her on her way.

After lunch I made house calls. I'd bought a motorcar from a man in Griffin Head, a dark green Humber that I was assured would be reliable. Nancy Hale-Newton was the widow of a colonel and lived in a large house called the Elms with her daughter Marjorie, a schoolteacher. Marjorie took me upstairs to her mother's sickroom. The curtains were drawn against the light and Mrs. Hale-Newton lay in bed, her complexion drained of all healthy color and turned a leaden grayish-yellow, the flesh so wasted the skin hung loose on her bones. A claw-like hand fluttered up from the counterpane and a cultivated but weary voice spoke: "Where's Peter Martin?"

I put down my black bag and Marjorie said, "Dr. Martin

retired, Mummy, don't you remember? This is Dr. Haggard."

"Haggard? Never heard of him. What happened to your hair, Haggard?"

"Good afternoon, Mrs. Hale-Newton," I said. "I'm Edward Haggard. I've taken over the practice from Peter Martin."

"I like Peter, he's a good man, he tells me the truth. You speak the truth, Haggard?"

"I try to."

"Evasive answer. You don't need to pretend with me, I've made my peace. Couldn't accept it at first, created a terrible fuss. Poor Peter, what a time I gave him! Face the darkness, Nan, he'd say, and I'd say, what darkness you old fool—I feel fine!"

The voice trailed off. Silence and shadows. I prepared a needle and asked the dying woman whether she wanted it now. "Yes," she murmured, "yes I do. I won't be going out just yet, Marjorie, I haven't finished with the injections."

On our way downstairs Marjorie Hale-Newton asked me what I thought her mother meant. I knew only too well. "She means," I said, "that she's at least getting pleasure from the morphia."

"Oh I know she is," said Marjorie. "She gets very impatient with me if I make her wait."

"Don't make her wait," I said. "Let her have it when she wants it."

Driving home that day I reflected that the practice of general medicine, and a firm discipline of work, and contact with ordinary people, with ordinary problems—this is how you treat a broken heart. Before I found Elgin I'd been constantly susceptible to terrible sudden powerful gusts of emotion that always left me devastated. For I missed your mother so intensely I could almost feel her presence—sometimes, if Spike was bad, I did feel her presence—and to suppress these attacks much psychic effort had to be expended. Occasionally

I succeeded, more often I failed. I found that if I tried to abort a stream of memories before it had progressed very far I could often spare myself a harrowing; though it soon became apparent that if I *did* suppress them, the feelings weren't dissipated but instead were merely dammed, as though in a reservoir, and when the floodgates opened—as invariably they did, sooner or later—then out it all poured, with torrential violence, leaving me weak, racked, sobbing, and unutterably wretched. To lose myself in hard work, far from London, among people who knew nothing of me or of her, and where there were no associations to trigger pain: this was how I thought I could get over it. I've never told you just how grim it really was, and with what success—or lack of it—I managed to deal with the loss of your mother. Why not? Why didn't I tell you how it really was, for me? Because, I suppose, you began to manifest your own pathology, and when that happened it preoccupied me almost to the exclusion of all else.

But this was the pattern of my days, morning surgery, house calls in the afternoon, evening surgery, on call for emergencies. I'd take one afternoon off a week and the occasional weekend. I soon realized that much of what Peter Martin had told me was essentially correct, that general practice involved a little surgery, a little medicine, and much reassurance and advice. I too became an advocate of Mist Explo.

And what, meanwhile, of my heart? Was it healing, as I'd thought it would, as a function of this fine big house, the care of a good woman, the practice of general medicine? As time passed I began to think it was. I began to think I was leaving the affair behind me, getting it out of my system. There were the odd twitches and twinges, but nothing I couldn't cope with. I was feeling better. I was forgetting her. Oh, I was fooling myself! I'd been briefly in remission, that's all, and this sad fact was brought home to me most vividly one afternoon that winter, on my way to see a patient.

I was driving along the seafront when I saw her. She was

turning up a side street, so the glimpse I had of her was partial and lasted no more than a second, but it was *her*, it was your mother—the way she walked, the way she dressed—she was in a black fur coat—the whole air of the woman—it was her, it had to be her, and I pulled over to the curb, climbed out of the car, grabbed my stick and hobbled after her in great haste, despite the howls of protest from Spike. Your mother! Here in Griffin Head! What was she doing here? She was here for me, obviously, she was *coming back to me!*

And of course it wasn't her. When I finally caught up with her she was, yes, an attractive, fashionably dressed woman of your mother's age, and she handled my apologies in the most charming manner, she was piqued and amused at my error, and even made a moue of mock chagrin that she wasn't whom I'd thought her—but she wasn't your mother, and I retreated, I limped off, cursing myself for a fool, for it wasn't, I confess, the first time it had happened though it was the first time I'd been so utterly convinced that it was her. It shook me badly, the whole experience, and late that night I was still thinking about it, thinking about the moment when with beating heart I'd touched her shoulder and she'd turned, though by that time, in my imagination, she'd become your mother, it was your mother who'd turned, her face open and shining, and pressed herself against me, and gripped the collar of my over-coat, and touched my face, and whispered hello, and why should the memory of her clutching my collar and pulling me to her like that have affected me so, was it the slimness of her fingers and the way they tugged at me like a child's? Oh, I did myself no good that night, no good at all, limping round Elgin and weeping like a boy as I tortured myself with the idea of the woman in Griffin Head that afternoon being her, of her coming back to the car with me and returning with me to Elgin—I showed her round the house that night, I took her (slim phantom) into every room, then later we walked to the cliff and stood gazing at the sea, and I remember every word we said to each other, for I've lived every moment of it a hundred times over, and wrung from every moment every last ounce of sweet feeling it offered before passing on and allowing the hours to unfold to their own exquisite pattern. Near dawn I drank a couple of glasses of gin, which calmed me, and then I was able at least to contemplate sleep.

Your mother. Or rather, *not* your mother—frequently, in the days that followed my encounter with the wrong woman, I limped back and forth across the upstairs back bedroom in a state of rage—rage at my own folly, my own ineptitude, my own damn weakness, impotence, fatuity—had I not left London precisely to prevent this sort of thing from occurring? Had I not bought Elgin precisely because it was untouched by memories of your mother, because it was free of those associations so rife in London, stabs of loss that came with each chance glimpse of a bit of the world once shared with her? I knew now there'd be no easy relief from the pain aroused from within, the pain I'd foolishly thought almost extinct. At every passing moment, so it seemed, in the days following, some faint cool shadow rose unbidden into consciousness, the image, perhaps, of her going before me into dinner at the Cushings', or slipping off a shoe, in the quiet of the saloon bar of the Two Eagles, to rub a silken foot against my calf, or murmuring to me with languid affection from my bed in Jubilee Road—time, I'd thought, would lay these inner ghosts, and surely, to have left the city where the affair had taken place, surely this must help the process of time, help begin to heal the rawest of the wounds, ease the more ferocious, the more savage and implacable of the hurts I had sustained? But no, apparently not. Apparently I was not yet to enjoy the luxury of a simple melancholy, not yet to know resignation, and the ability to recall the loved one's memory with tenderness rather than pain. No, apparently I was to twist and thrash and flail about a little longer.

I remember one day sitting at the table picking at my lunch (since Spike I'd become a very light eater), feeling weary and dispirited and wondering if I'd made a ghastly mistake in taking on the practice, the house, all of it, and I remember glancing up at Mrs. Gregor as she quietly poured me a cup of tea. Her calm face cheered me. She knew I was in pain; though she said nothing, I could tell she knew, and I felt her concern, and her sympathy. She seemed to be telling me that all would be well. And I remember thinking, no, I will not be lonely. I will not allow myself to be overwhelmed by hopeless longing for something that has ceased to be real. But even as I thought this a small voice said, oh, but it is real—your feelings are real, your pain is real, your loss is real—and as if he'd been waiting for just this to happen, Spike delivered an especially vicious jab, which sent me hobbling back to the surgery.

Later I again tried to rally my spirits, and reflected that if I was to avoid sinking into a bog of maudlin emotion I'd have to develop a firmer mental discipline. It occurred to me that I couldn't simply wait for time to heal me, I would have to set about deliberately healing myself, for it was absurd to be the slave of feeling. Feeling, I told myself, is only one facet or dimension of experience, and by what law must it predominate over the rest?

For several days I held to my resolve. I did not permit myself to think about your mother. When I did, when I found myself caught up in some sweet passage, intoxicated with some memory, I abruptly shut it down, and turned my attention elsewhere. It was not easy, nor was it altogether successful, for if I banished her from my waking mind she merely waited till nightfall, and it was very much harder to keep her out of my dreams.

But I tried. And eventually there came a period of several days when I did not suffer. I began to think it was working. I began to think that my refusal to indulge the reveries and

memories and night-dreams that thronged about the doors and windows of consciousness, beseeching entry—my refusal to admit them, I thought, was gradually stilling the storm and allowing me to inch toward peace once more. Peace—peace of mind—where I could contemplate your mother and the few brief months we'd had without having to wage this constant terrible warfare with the armies of my own unconscious mind, whose sole objective so it seemed was to lay waste to my heart and leave me howling for the woman I loved like an orphaned child amid the rubble of a bombed city.

Oh James. A lifetime remembered in a bottle of gin; a tragedy in a grain of morphia. How clearly I see it all now, this drama, this story—the design of the thing a journey, of still-uncertain destination; or perhaps a wheel, within whose spokes and arcs pain and suffering appear not as manifestations of futility but as the ground or soil or compost of the spirit whence new growth springs: for we rot and rise, and without pain there can be no light. And the figures, the characters, all etched in sharp relief against a blood-red sky: your mother, Ratcliff, yourself—me—the others, less vivid, whose fates are somehow intertwined with these. One, curiously, was a dying boy I treated in St. Basil's, a young workingman called Eddie Bell, who was in the last stages of tuberculosis. He shouldn't have been on a surgical ward, but we'd found a lump in his lung and taken out a rib. Not that it did much good. The disease was progressing faster than the thorax could heal, and Eddie grew paler and thinner by the day.

I suppose it's not surprising that I should think of him now, for he, like you, would die in my arms. But oh, poor Eddie! There was something about the boy, and the way he faced death, that made a deep impression on me. I'm a doctor, I've seen a good deal of death, but there are always those who shatter your detachment and wring your heart and make you pray for a miracle. Eddie Bell was a clean, decent lad with a wife and a baby, and it seemed the cruelest thing that he should be taken so young. One night I was at his bedside when he coughed suddenly and blood came welling into his mouth. He struggled up, this thin, white ghost of a boy, ethereal, almost, against the sheets, and spat it out to keep from choking. It made a dramatic splash of claret on the bed-clothes, and I called for a nurse. We screened his bed and I wiped away the rubbery clots of blood and mucus from his mouth while the sheets were changed. "Will it be tonight?" Eddie murmured, when I had him comfortable again, and I couldn't lie to him, I nodded, and said: "Yes Eddie, maybe tonight." There was no way to stop the bleeding, so no point in giving a transfusion. Close to dawn I made up a needle of morphia. "Doctor," he said—he was very weak, and I had to cradle him in my arms in order to give him the injection— "before you give me that, promise me there'll be no post-mortem. I told my wife I'd come to her clean and unscarred."

I promised, of course I did.

Then I gave him the morphia and he became soporific. The bleeding continued until his poor wasted lungs could no longer gather enough oxygen to sustain life, and his skin whitened to the color of an embalmed corpse before my eyes. I laid him back down and covered him with the sheet. Just as I emerged from between the screens Cushing appeared at the end of the ward, accompanied by McGuinness, my fellow registrar. Down they came, white coats swirling, with Sister beside them, and we gathered round the bed. "I'll be curious to see what happened to that abscess," said Cushing. "Get him down to Pathology, will you, Haggard? Tell Ratty Vaughan we want to have a look at the lungs."

All I could think of was the promise I'd made to Eddie just a couple of hours before. I mentioned it. Cushing snorted; he told me it was a damn silly thing to do, making promises to a man who wouldn't last the night. "Oh, promise him the world, if you want to," he then said, "but don't for God's sake think you have to keep it."

"But is a postmortem really necessary?"

This was not wise. McGuinness gazed at the ceiling, Sister slipped off down the ward. "You imagine, Dr. Haggard," said Cushing, in tones of the iciest courtesy, his eyes bright with scorn, "I wish to look at the boy's lungs for fun?"

"No sir."

"To divert myself?"

"No sir."

"Thank you. I'm gratified at the high regard you appear to hold for my sense of professional responsibility."

Oh damn you, Cushing, I thought, as I weathered a few more blasts, damn you and your hard cold surgical medicine, what room is there for caring and humanity and compassion in your sort of medicine? I left the ward a little later. I had twelve hours before I was on call again, and I intended to sleep. It was just striking noon as I came out onto the steps of St. Basil's. The day was wet and dismal. I stood there in the drizzling rain, exhausted, depressed, and without an umbrella. I turned up my collar and prepared to run for the bus. "You'll catch your death," someone said. I turned. It was your mother.

She was wrapped in a black fur coat with a huge collar and pouch sleeves, holding a large umbrella, and on her head a closely fitted, dark green, turbanlike hat jabbed with a parrot's feather. She'd been in the hospital, she said, "doing good works." Her eyes were moist as though she'd been crying; she seemed a sad, rather fragile creature in all that black fur, but even as she looked me over, looked me up and down, a smile began to form, and her spirits visibly rose. "You look ghastly," she said. "Shall we go and have a drink?"

The hotel was an elegant Georgian building where they seemed to know her well. She surrendered her umbrella, but not her fur, and led me across a marble-floored hall to a large, comfortable lounge furnished in the baroque manner. We settled ourselves in a pair of wing chairs with curved legs, beneath a high ceiling divided into panels containing foliate and shell motifs. A waiter silently materialized beside her chair. "What will you have, doctor?" she said, opening her coat. I asked for a gin and tonic, and she'd have one too. Then she sighed, and said, "All this rain, I do find it so depressing. I wanted to tell you how much I enjoyed meeting you the other night, was it very dreadful for you?" As she said this she groped in her handbag for cigarettes.

"On the contrary," I said. I could feel the fatigue and depression of the last hours lift. I lit her cigarette for her. "Thank you darling," she said—darling!—then: "What have you been up to?"

"Practicing hospital medicine," I said, "but I wouldn't want to bore you with that."

"Oh," she said, "I don't think you could bore me, a man who'd dedicate his life to pleasure." A small smile as she glanced at me through half-closed eyes, then, before I could reply: "Who was the last patient you saw?"

"Eddie Bell, plumber's mate. Consumption."

"Poor fellow," she said. "How is he?"

"Dead," I said, as the gins arrived.

The waiter was bending over the table between us, setting down the glasses. For several moments we did not speak. The waiter moved away.

"Sorry," I said, "didn't mean to be blunt."

"Oh don't worry about that," she said. "Living with Ratcliff all these years, death is an old friend." She sipped her gin. "I daresay he's told you that the science of medicine is built upon the postmortem?"

"I'm afraid your husband was never a teacher of mine."

"Lucky you. I'm sorry, I don't mean to embarrass you with my disloyalty." She looked away. There was a brief silence. She really had the most exquisite profile, the clear brow, the small fine nose with its delicate, paper-thin nostril, the white white flesh of her throat! I told her more about Eddie Bell, and the promise I'd made him, and what had happened when Cushing came.

Her eyes settled fondly upon me. I thought there was languor in them, though in fact (this she told me later, when our early impressions of one another were an eager topic of conversation) she was conscious not of languor but of admiration. She thought I'd been brave to stand up to Vincent Cushing, and she liked me for it. "How marvelous," she sighed, "to hear a doctor speak about medicine as a moral activity."

"Clinical work," I said. I think I understood the drift of her thinking, and felt slightly alarmed—I hadn't meant to impugn Cushing's *morality!* I made some demurral, said something vague about the need for research; ironic, considering my recent run-in with the man. She wasn't having any of it. An impatient snort of scorn. "But don't you wonder," she said, "what it is makes men spend their working lives poking through the diseased bits of dead bodies? God, there I go again. Don't answer that. Here I am telling you all my secrets, it must be the drink, it always goes to my head before lunch." She asked me what the time was. "So late!" she cried. "I had no idea! I must fly!"

We parted on the steps of the hotel. The rain had stopped and a watery sun was trying to break through the clouds. Suddenly the turmoil of London was upon us, the buses and taxis and crowds, and suddenly I felt extremely weary; I had been almost two days without sleep. Your mother was drawing on her gloves. "I did enjoy that," she said, turning to me. "Oh, you're exhausted. Take a taxi home, please."

"Maybe I will," I said, though I knew I wouldn't.

"Goodbye Dr. Haggard."

"Goodbye Mrs. Vaughan."

We shook hands.

Reflecting, later that night, on our conversation, I thought of what your mother had said to me about Ratcliff. And I wondered—could I tell you about that revealing disclosure of hers, without alarming you unduly? For how odd it was, I'd thought, that she should have said what she did about your father's work, and with such passion! Or so it had seemed to me at the time (of course I knew nothing then of your parents' marriage)—my story had aroused anger in her not toward Vincent Cushing, but toward her husband, toward Ratcliff. Could I say this to you? Would it help? Or were you (it suddenly occurred to me) on *his* side? Later she told me that she'd been late for her lunch appointment and had then wandered round the National Gallery all afternoon, "somewhat *distraite*," she said, though at the time she couldn't think why. She didn't get back to Plantagenet Gardens until after six, and when she walked in through the front door your father was coming down the stairs dressed for dinner. "Darling, have you any money in your pocket?" she said. "I've a taxi outside."

"Leaving again?" said Ratcliff.

She could be very funny sometimes. She told me how, on her way back into the house, Ratcliff had called her from the drawing room, where he was standing in front of the fire turning the pages of the *Lancet*. She paused in the doorway— I can imagine the expression on her face, her fingers busy with the delicate task of removing her hat—as Ratcliff put to her his big question. "Had you forgotten the Piker-Smiths?" he said, without looking up. And of course she had! She had completely forgotten the Piker-Smiths! She hadn't been in the kitchen all afternoon, so Iris would be hysterical and the meal a fiasco! Ratcliff let the question sink in then gazed at her over the top of his spectacles. But she wouldn't give him the satisfaction, she told me. "Of course not," she said. "Fascinating couple. He told me such an interesting thing about bowel tumors last time, I must remember what it was. Who could forget the Piker-Smiths?"

"Now where were we?"

You'd telephoned to ask if you could come up to Elgin and

talk to me more about your mother. It was almost two weeks since our last conversation, and it had occurred to me that you might not come back. You arrived just after my late surgery, rather breathless, having come all the way up the hill on a bicycle. It was a lovely evening, shortly after the battle of Dunkirk, I remember, for black smoke from blazing oil tanks had been blowing across the Channel all day, though by the time you appeared the wind had changed direction and the evening was glorious. As you pulled off your bicycle clips and then, panting and smiling, pushed a hand through your disheveled hair, I suggested we take our drinks outside. "Lovely," you said.

We sat in the old white wicker chairs out on the paving stones by the back door, a low table between us and on it a bottle of gin, a bottle of tonic, two glasses and an ashtray. The sun was going down, the sky was a mellow symphony in pastel shades of blue and gray with one solitary rag of cloud angling down toward the sea, its underside lit by a vivid pink rash. Beyond the paving stones the garden was a blowsy profusion of unmown grass with a large rosebush overflowing its trellis and heavy with white flowers. "Where were we?" you said. "We were at a dinner party, doctor, and my mother was being witty."

Oh dear, I can be so clumsy. There was such harmony and contentment in that evening hour, as we watched the sky change color, and the sun descended to a sea of polished steel, I forgot my decision to let you make the running—I was, I realize, too fervent in the depiction of my feelings, it is a failing of mine. I told you how, at the end of the evening, as I was getting into my overcoat in the hall, she had approached me and asked me with a small smile, with just a hint of *innuendo* in it, if I was off in pursuit of 'fresh pleasures.' "No," I told her, "I've had quite enough pleasure for one evening."

"You must take me with you next time," she said, "I never seem to get any pleasure anymore." At that moment your father came up with her fur coat. She thanked him, then said:

"I was just telling Dr. Haggard how we never seem to have any pleasure these days."

"Pleasure?" said Ratcliff, glancing at me with a jovial expression that can hardly have been sincere. "My wife has never shown an interest in pleasure, she's much too busy. I hope you're not corrupting her, doctor."

I know a growling animal when I hear one; James, this was a man with a threat! "Oh, I know little about pleasure," I said, having no desire, at the time, to antagonize the senior pathologist. "I'm just an amateur."

"An Englishman and an amateur!" cried Ratcliff, with that familiar bark of laughter. He had a cigar between his teeth and he was mellow with brandy. "Like myself." Here he laid a hand upon my shoulder, a gesture apparently of warm male complicity, but I knew better.

"I'm surrounded by amateurs," murmured your mother, "are there no qualified sybarites in the house?"—at which point Daphne Cushing came gushing in and the whole thing collapsed into babble and chat.

But what I remember, when I described this scene to you, was the troubled expression that appeared on your face. Had I gone too far? Had I hinted inadvertently at what must only be gradually revealed, had I given it all away? And it was only then that I properly realized how difficult it would be to tell you the story of our affair, for no child can listen dispassionately to an account of his mother's infidelity. But because it was essential (I felt) that you understand, I knew I had to do it, but with a sort of opaque clarity, a delicate, oblique candor . . . I paused, and you rose to your feet, took a few steps down the path and stood there silently gazing at the sun as it sank behind a horizon line sharp as a blade. Without turning you said: "So did she throw herself at you?"

"Oh good God no!"

Had I given you that impression? I pulled myself out of my chair and went to you. You were blushing wildly, angry and confused like a hurt child—I felt a wave of warm protective sympathy rise within me, and I caught you by the shoulders. "James, James, no, it wasn't like that, forgive me, I didn't mean to suggest that for a moment, there was nothing like that, nothing like that at all"—and I gazed into your eyes with as much earnest conviction as I could muster, and held your shoulders firmly, and at last saw you soften. "Believe me," I whispered.

You wanted to be convinced; you shrugged off the terrible suspicion that had sprung into your mind. "Sorry."

"Nonsense," I said, dropping my hands and limping back to my chair. "Nothing to be sorry for. Finish your drink. Have another."

"No," you said, "I must be off." You hesitated. "Doctor, I don't know if you'd be interested, but there's a sort of a do on up at the mess."

Now you were reticent, embarrassed at what had just happened between us—you were still blushing! Oh James, I warmed to you more with every moment we spent together— you had her face and her grace but you had yet to acquire her composure. "Are you inviting me to a party?" I said.

"Well, yes, actually."

"Where and when?" I said, and when you told me I said that if I wasn't on call I would certainly come. I was flattered; I was also curious to see how you were with the rest of the squadron. I'd met a couple of the other pilots and they seemed a good deal more hearty than you, they lacked that moody complexity that so intrigued me about you. Was this, I wondered, a source of discomfort to you—were you the butt of humor—did they pull your leg—?

What happened next? She came to my room. I was never able to tell you about her coming to my room—how could I? Though maybe you guessed. It was late 1937, autumn had slipped into winter, the weather was damp and chilly and the frail and elderly with their rheumatism, their influenza, their arthritis came tramping through the doors of St. Basil's, seeking care. One night I was in the flat in Jubilee Road, having been on duty for forty-eight hours straight. The gas fire was lit but it wasn't enough, and I was wearing a jersey, a cravat, and my lined paisley dressing gown. I'd had a perfectly bloody day. Cushing had told me I'd never make a surgeon and again I'd seriously asked myself if he was right. There was a certain untutored deftness with fine instruments that I seemed simply to lack. I paced the room, hands plunged deep in my pockets, smoking, worrying, trying to stay warm. Someone knocked at the door. "Come in, Desmond," I shouted.

The door opened. "It's not Desmond"—those familiar tones—and I whirled round: it was your mother. We were immediately in each other's arms—her very *being there* shattered whatever thin crusts of reserve and propriety still stood between us! We clung to one another. "Something has happened," she whispered.

"I know."

Something has happened. Dear James, never, I think, can three simple words have engendered such joy in a man's heart. We clung to one another in the middle of the room, rocking slightly; eventually we came apart. For a moment or two we hovered there, stranded in some odd void between intimacy and decorum: something had happened, yes, but whatever it was, it was yet to be assimilated. She took my face between her fingers then turned away. She drifted to the window, pulled aside the curtain, and glanced out. I think I must have offered her a drink.

We sat in the armchairs, pulled up close to the gas fire. She kept her coat on and wrapped her fingers round her glass and stared into the thin hissing flames. Usually so voluble, she was now silent and I, with my initial excitement checked, rather, by her strange, distant mood, watched her, and waited, ready to take my cue from her. "I'm sorry it's so cold in here,"

I said at last. She glanced up. "Were you listening to the news?" she said.

"Yes. I'm rather afraid we're in for it."

"War with Germany. What a beastly idea."

"I'm so glad you came. I keep thinking about you."

"Yes, I know." She frowned.

"You know?"

She nodded. "It's happened to me as well."

I wanted to take her in my arms there and then and cover her perfect face, and her throat, and her breasts with kisses. She reached for my hand. She held it in both of hers and gazed at me with great seriousness. "What are we to do?"

I saw no problem. "Celebrate?"

She wasn't amused. She stared into the gas fire. Then she shook her head and rose abruptly to her feet. "I must go," she said.

"No, don't."

"I must. This is foolish. What can come of it? I shouldn't have come here, it was a stupid impulse."

"It was a wonderful impulse. Please sit down. Five minutes."

She hesitated. "Five minutes."

Five minutes.

Traces of her perfume clung to my dressing gown. I noticed it as soon as she'd gone, as I wandered about the room, touching things, my thoughts and emotions in turmoil. I brought the material to my nose, and smelling her perfume awakened the memory of touching her, the warmth of her slim body beneath the fur coat when I first slipped my hands in under it. I became aroused all over again, and felt suddenly trapped, so I threw on my hat and overcoat and ran downstairs and out into the blustering raw night and began to walk.

I never knew quite where I walked or for how long. All I could recall, later, were dark streets of large houses lost in

gusting sheets of rain, water streaming in the gutters, the
occasional bowed figure hurrying by in the blur of a streetlight,
umbrella slick with rain—striding forward through the night,
my hat pulled low over my forehead and my overcoat flapping
about me, I did not feel the cold and damp, for I was wrapped
in the heat of erupting emotions that didn't even *begin* to
subside until I turned at last into a small pub called the Two
Eagles, not far from Jubilee Road, and stood at the counter
of the saloon bar, dripping wet and still in high excitement,
and bought a large gin. Only then did I articulate it: I love
her.

This produced dazed bewilderment, the very idea of it, and
I found a small table near the fire—the room was deserted—
sat down and took off my spectacles to wipe them on my
handkerchief, and gazed at the burning coals and told myself
again: I love her. I contemplated the fact. How odd it was.
Funny really. How had it happened? Small miracle, considering, but there you are, there you have it. I love her. At last
I looked up, looked around, realized how wet I was; then the
clock behind the bar caught my eye. I should have been at
St. Basil's twenty minutes ago!

The ward was in darkness when I got there, and silent but
for some wheezing and snoring and the odd soft moan.
McGuinness was with the night sister in her office. He had
little to tell me, and when I'd apologized for keeping him
waiting he struggled into his overcoat and prepared to leave.
"Wet out, then," he said; I must have looked like a drowned
rat. "Filthy night," I said vaguely.

Filthy night—yes, to McGuinness it would look like a filthy
night, to all the world it was a filthy night, but to me, to
Edward Haggard, no, not a filthy night, a golden night, a
blessed night. In the hours that followed I would find moments here and there, little islands of grace amid the darkness
of sickness and injury, when this immense miracle of the heart
became once more vivid to me. For the first time in my adult
life I knew I loved a woman.

It began to rain again shortly after midnight, and it kept up almost until dawn. The ward was quiet, and I took some minutes to stand on the steps between the great portals at the hospital entrance, my white coat whipping about my legs, and my mind spreading out across the city like a vast winged god. Strong winds blew; there was no moon, only heaped banks of low cloud, and the streets of London flashed and shone in the downpour; every few moments the wind flung volleys of rain at the windows of sleeping houses, and embers hissed in deserted fireplaces as the rain found its way down chimneys. It tumbled in torrents along gutters and into drainpipes, it went flooding down drains. What few people were about in the city scurried with their heads down from doorways to cabs, their umbrellas ravaged and broken in an instant. It was the same storm system that had been lashing the south coast for days now; in the capital, citizens turned uneasily in their beds, ancient race memories awoken by the violence of the weather battering at their windows and doors. Your mother has described to me her state of mind that wild night. She did not attempt to sleep. She sat on the padded stool in front of her dressing table, she said, removing her makeup, in her silver robe. A fire burned in the grate, two table lamps gave off a low, warm glow. The room was deeply carpeted, the curtains were thick. There was warmth, safety and comfort in this room, but the fingers of danger plucked at her throat—and she *liked* it, she told me, she liked it, it made her feel alive. A curious mood, she told me, with this excitement, this restlessness upon her, and from time to time she went to the window and pulled aside the curtain and watched the storm sweeping about the houses opposite, and all along the pavement the bare branches of the big old chestnuts flailing in the wind. Then she turned and wrapped her arms about herself, and closed her eyes, arousing in herself the memory of deep and recent sexual pleasure.

For I had been a good lover to her. She had risen from the armchair and wordlessly taken my hand and led me into the bedroom, where without haste, and keeping her eyes upon mine, she had begun to undress, and I of course had done the same. It was with some care that she laid her clothes and underwear on my chair. Then we climbed in together under the sheets. My heart rate was very high indeed. I took her in my arms and her skin was soft as silk against my own. I began kissing her face and her throat, and when I lifted my head from her breasts, she saw (she told me later) my eyes, and never, she said, did she imagine she would forget their expression at that moment, the utter glut of feeling, the *love* that was in them. Something in me cried out when I entered her, and in the few timeless moments that followed I knew a sense of fusion and completeness that I had never experienced before, and never will again until I die. It was the first time I had properly made love to a woman.

Later, in her room, she heard Ratcliff coming up to bed, heard him cross the landing at the top of the stairs, then go straight to his room, and this was unusual, for it was his habit to tap at her door and open it a crack and whisper to her to sleep well. She liked that he did that, she told me, but tonight he did not, and this made her feel grateful and uneasy at the same time. Suddenly the world seemed fragile. Suddenly it all seemed to shiver, as though great explosions were occurring three streets away. She leaned against the wall of her room, she said, pressed her body full against it, to feel how solid it was. She sat down at the dressing table and stared at her own reflection. We must be careful, very very careful; we must never make a mistake; there are ways of doing these things. There is danger here, but we can control it. All this she told me later.

By the next morning the storm had blown itself out and she awoke to a world that felt as fixed and stable and permanent as ever. She breakfasted alone; Ratcliff had left early for the hospital, and you were of course away at school. She ate a finger of buttered toast with just a smear of marmalade and drank a cup of coffee—I was avid for every detail of those hours! The alarm she had known in the night had dissipated, she told me. She felt gay and light-headed. It was a damp cold morning but the sky was clear.

Oh, but the imagination of a man in love is a florid jungle of lush, fast-growing forms of life! I had made love to your mother. Now, without yet fully grasping the essential complexity of the situation, I began to indulge in richly textured daydreams about her. She was a figure of shimmering loveliness to me. She was beauty itself, she was perfection; I lived only to see her again, and though this didn't happen for some days the waiting, at first, was less harrowing than you might imagine: my intoxication with the very *idea* that I loved her had not yet passed. So vast, so strong was this feeling, and so enamored was I of it, all else was mere detail, and beneath notice; I was in a state of bliss.

I remembered a gesture she made, a way she had of lifting her chin and at the same time glancing at me through half-closed eyes; then the smile would come, the humor of recognition, for it was a joke, we decided, that we had seen each other, and recognized each other, and in effect said to each other: I have known you all my life and here you are at last. And I wonder now—had I known that the comedy would play out as it did, would I have behaved differently? Would I have fled from her and flung myself into medicine with a passion I no longer felt, become absorbed in medicine and so hidden from her? I don't think I would. Remember Hopkins, the poem about the mind having mountains, cliffs of fall, "frightful, sheer, no-man-fathomed"? At the end there's this:

> Here! creep,
> Wretch, under a comfort serves in a whirlwind: all
> Life death does end and each day dies with sleep.

Well, no creeping for me! No comfort for me in the whirlwind! This was my feeling. Your mother and I had the same soul. We were drawn to one another by a force inexorable. It could not have happened other than it did. She'd told me that "it" had happened to her too, and this was all I needed to know; so exalted did this make me feel, her actual presence would almost have been too much; it was enough to sustain the feeling.

I see myself in the flat in Jubilee Road. I should be sleeping, but cannot. I pace up and down the faded carpet, I stop at the window and pull back the curtain and peer out—perhaps she will come to me again, perhaps I will glimpse her alighting from a cab below—? At that moment a cab does turn into Jubilee Road, and moves toward the house, and suddenly I'm convinced that *this is her*—this is her, coming to me again—but it passes without stopping and I let the curtain fall back, pace the carpet once more, pause by a sketch of a seascape at sunset. I would like to go back to the Two Eagles and order a large gin and so live again the moment when it first dawned on me that I was in love, but I cannot leave the room for fear that she will come while I am away.

I fall dispiritedly into an armchair and doze for a while. I am awoken by a knock on the door. I leap to my feet—cross the room—throw wide the door—it is Desmond Kelly, the landlady's husband. What did that friendly man see? He saw the door wrenched violently open, and standing there before him, one hand on the doorknob and the other clutching the doorframe, as though the entire structure would otherwise collapse, a wild-eyed Englishman in a dressing gown. Desmond Kelly was sympathetic. He understood the essential incoherence of the human condition. "Should I come back later, doctor?" he murmured in that soft lilt of his (he was a Cork man, and a Republican).

"What is it?" I cried.

"The wife says will you be wanting the room done out in the morning?"

"Yes!" I cried. "No letters, Desmond? No messages for me?"

"Nothing," he said, dramatically. "Not a single one, doctor."

I pushed a hand through my hair and frowned. "Thanks," I said, and turned sadly back into my room, deflated and forsaken. The lover is a comic figure, truly, but love can change its nature. It has the germ of tragedy in it.

Time passed. Not a lot of time, by normal standards, but by the clock in my heart—ages, eons, very eternities. I was desperate to see her again. I needed to nourish my love upon her being, as though my love were a ravening parasitical creature which if it could not feed upon her would feed instead upon its host, causing agony. I was in agony. Missing her was no state of tranquil melancholy, it was active, it was fiercely energetic. There came a moment when it occurred to me that she had not been in touch with me because she was dead. This idea rapidly turned to certainty and I began to grieve for her, and now —cruelest of cruel ironies—I felt that I had lost her before I had even known her—grief without even the consolation of memory! The problem was, I couldn't reach her. The idea of writing to her or telephoning her—any such move was dangerous, hadn't she told me not even to try?

And meanwhile I continued to work, functioning as best I could. An elderly prostitute called Belle Sylvester was found in an alley in a coma one night and brought into St. Basil's. It was our turn receiving from Accident and Casualty so I had to work her up. A first, cursory examination on the ward gave me no real clue as to what was wrong, though after I'd eliminated all other possible causes of coma, meningitis suggested itself. I was compelled, reluctantly, to perform a lumbar puncture.

The night sister wheeled screens round the bed then turned the unconscious Belle Sylvester on her side and bent her double, knees to head. She was a big woman, fleshy and pink. I settled myself on a chair at the bedside, frowning, uneasy— I dislike lumbar punctures, they're so damn tricky. I scrubbed the skin at the puncture site, painted it with antiseptics, then laid sterile cloths across her broad back, leaving one small patch uncovered. I picked up the big spinal needle and then, with as much delicacy as I could, inserted it. It seemed to be sliding in nicely, until suddenly—and this was what I'd been dreading—there was a horrible scraping sound—I'd hit bone. I lifted my head, looked at Sister and withdrew the needle. "It's impossible," I muttered, sitting up straight for a moment, unbuttoning my white coat and sweeping the skirts back, then hunching forward on the chair to again slide in the needle, "with her bent double like this—to aim the needle—accurately—*damn!*" Again the scraping sound—again I withdrew. I wiped my brow, took a few deep breaths, tried to shake off my fatigue. For just an instant I thought of your mother, and my penis stirred in my trousers. The problem was that if, in my search for the minute box canyon formed by the bony arches of the vertebral column, I plunged the needle in too deeply, I'd pierce a vital organ and kill the woman. I inserted the needle once more, and this time was rewarded by a pulpy feeling. "Yes," I murmured. I withdrew slowly, allowing a few drops of cerebrospinal fluid into the barrel of the syringe, then rose to my feet; the image of your mother again sprang into my mind, and for a second or two I was elsewhere.

Your father was talking about dead bodies. "This is hypostasis, gentlemen," he was saying. "Note the discoloration of the skin." He was a fat, confident man who smoked cigars to mask the smells of the cadavers with which he worked. "Begins to happen about thirty minutes after death, and takes six to eight hours till it's done. Caused by the blood gravitating downward and suffusing the lower capillaries, leaving the upper surfaces of the body pallid. Starts off pink, then rapidly darkens. Ends up purple." He gestured at the gaping cadaver before him with brisk, choppy hand movements, like a man conducting an orchestra. "Another peculiarity of the body in death, gentlemen, is the appearance of a network of bluish veins, dendritic in structure, just below the surface of the skin. Generally occurs when putrefaction is rapid." He paused and spent a moment, frowning, relighting the cigar. "Note too the shedding of the skin and the formation of adipocere. This happens when fatty tissue changes to fatty acids. You'll also see bloating as a result of methane generated by decomposition, you'll see liquefied eyeballs, you'll see blistering of the skin, you'll see dazzling changes of color, maggots, you'll even see corpses bursting open. You can never really rely on the dead to do what you expect; it all depends on temperature, moisture, insects, bacteria, oh, a host of factors."

I was down in Pathology to hear what they'd found in Eddie Bell's lungs. Your father was in the postmortem room, standing at a dissecting table in a black rubber apron, his sleeves rolled up, large hands ungloved, talking to half a dozen medical students. On the dissecting table (steel, with a central channel and a hole where body fluids were hosed down) lay the pale cadaver of Eddie himself, with his thorax split open. Also in the room was a glass-fronted cupboard containing instruments (knives, saws, bone forceps), a row of metal hooks with rubber aprons hanging from them, and a table with steel bowls for specimens, at which your father's assistant, a balding, weasel-faced fellow called Miggs, was busy with a slice of Eddie's lung. It was a small, cramped, low-ceilinged basement room with a narrow barred window at the top of one wall through which a little light was admitted, and a view of feet crossing the courtyard outside. It was cold, and stank of formalin. "Pathology makes physiology possible," your father was saying, "in the sense, gentlemen, that organic functions are revealed only when they fail." Standing there patiently, waiting till he had a moment for me, I remembered your mother's words. "Don't you wonder," she'd said, "what it is that makes men spend their lives poking through the diseased bits of dead bodies?" I could hear her voice, see her eyes, feel my lips upon her silky skin; and James, at that moment I experienced my first real spurt of antagonism toward your father.

I've often wondered—what kind of father can he have *been* to you? You were a complicated boy, sensitive, poetic—what did he do to you, this butcher of a man? It doesn't surprise me that you identified so closely with your mother, you recognized her grace and were drawn to it, and repelled (though you may never have admitted this to yourself) by your father and his death trade, everything he stood for. But if by some chance—and these were my thoughts after the evening when you'd asked me if she'd "thrown herself" at me—if your sympathies did, somehow, lie with him—then you'd see me in the blackest light. So if I were to tell you everything, as I intended to, I knew it must be done gradually, not all at once. I must slowly paint a picture of your parents' marriage, a portrait which, if subtle enough, and accurate enough, would lead you irresistibly to an understanding of your mother's unhappiness—the causes of it—and my own effort, ultimately unsuccessful, to relieve it, and offer her the life of hope and joy she deserved, and from which your father blocked her. This as I say was my intention, and if I haven't fulfilled it the fault lies not with me, but somewhere in the tangled chain of circumstance and accident that has brought us here, now.

The tangled chain. I lift my head. My eyes are streaming tears. Hangars at the edge of the airfield, long low structures growing indistinct as the light begins to go. Figures moving across the grass toward us, waving their arms; faint shouts reach my ears. Over on the far side the ack-ack gun, the dispersal hut, behind them trees, a church spire, all smudged against the evening sky. Hard at times to believe there's a war on, up here on the Downs, among these grassy rolling hills where sheep, and old stone walls, and the odd copse of oak and elm are the features of the country: this is farmland, grazing land . . .

In retrospect the whole sequence of events—all that's happened since I first began to practice medicine down here—it all seems merely a sort of prelude to your arrival. As though I was sent here so as to witness—what, exactly? Was it just a rare and curious medical phenomenon, what started happening to your body, entirely explicable in scientific terms? Or something much stranger, more glorious? Even now I waver. Even now I cannot be sure. What I believe in the morning I doubt at night. What I'm sure of at night is fantastic in the morning. As is the idea that I was *sent here*. I am a doctor, finally, but must that necessarily preclude a belief in fate? In some higher plan? Some design? At times I'm inclined to think not. At times I'm inclined to doubt the tangled chain, the random weave of circumstance and accident. At times I'm inclined to believe that the whole point and meaning of my life has been to lead me to *this precise moment*—here—with you—at twilight—in the shadow of a blazing Spitfire.

It was the spring of '39. I believed I was recovering. My first dreadful winter in Elgin had passed, the weather was improving, and I tried to get out of the house as often as I could to walk on the beach and breathe the good sea air. That spring I discovered a method of managing the wooden staircase down the cliff that Spike seemingly could tolerate. It involved leading with the good leg, descending sideways, and making frequent stops. It was time-consuming, tiring, and uncomfortable, but it was worth it: the beach was usually deserted in the early evening, and I could ramble along at my leisure, poking with my stick at shells and seaweed and odd bits of fishing gear that had washed up with the afternoon tide. There was a flat rock I liked to sit on to smoke a cigarette and watch the sun go down, and stretch out the bad leg and give Spike a rest, and think about the day, and watch the shadows lengthen and the sea grow dark, as the crags and hollows of the cliff face behind me turned black in the twilight. I wouldn't go back the way I'd come, but by a path that ascended fairly gently to the road, then up the road to the top of the cliffs and so to Elgin.

Though Spike would make me pay for my exertions. The evening would find me in severe pain in the gloom of the surgery. I'd have at hand a steel bowl, kidney-shaped, in which lay my big hypodermic needle; and an ampoule of morphia. I'd tap it smartly then snap off the top. Draw up the fluid into the syringe—a squirt or two to expel the air—and from the lifted needle droplets fountain in the twilight. With my jacket draped over my shoulders I perch there on the edge of my desk and roll up my sleeve, and tie the rubber tourniquet till the veins of my inner arm bulge against the skin. A quick swab, fist clenched tight, then the needle slides in and the plunger is carefully depressed. After a moment or two the syringe clatters back into its bowl and the tourniquet is tossed onto the desk. Still with my sleeve rolled up, still with my jacket draped about my shoulders, I make my slow way upstairs. Somewhere in the house a clock faintly chimes the half hour; otherwise all is still.

I remember there was one evening that spring that I found myself dressing for a dinner party being thrown by Hugh Fig and his wife. I had no desire to attend the thing, but saw no way of getting out of it—and I wonder now, *why* must it all cling to memory, every damn detail—why can't I *forget?* Because, I suppose, this was the first dinner party I'd attended since the Cushings', and so completely had my heart and mind been colonized by memories of your mother there was little in the world that didn't trigger pain. I remember opening my wardrobe and taking out my dinner jacket and becoming acutely aware of the last time I'd worn it—but what a different man gazed back at me now from the mirror in the wardrobe door! I was in my vest and trousers, my braces hanging down my thighs, my stick hooked on the chair nearby, and what a

skinny specimen I'd become, I thought, as I regarded the
ravaged, wild-haired, too-large head atop the bony narrow
shoulders and the sunken hairless chest; and I remembered
the days before Spike when I was not thin but wiry, when
hard work maintained a distinct musculature of my small-
boned frame, when your mother, at least, despite my ill-
proportion, had seemed to like the look of me. Hard to imagine anyone liking the look of me now, I reflected. Now I
looked puny. I looked like a shrimp, a crested shrimp.

But oh, no maundering tonight, Spike had been silenced
and even as I started dressing I began to feel expansive. I
slipped on my dress shirt, and buttoned it, and as my fingers
deftly attached with studs the collar and cuffs I saw the familiar
transformation begin, the familiar magic that this ritual never
fails to perform, the metamorphosis of a shrimp into a man
in evening dress. I pulled on the trousers and the patent
leather shoes and tied the black bow tie. Cummerbund? I
thought not, from a conviction that the evening's company
would have scant appreciation for good tailoring. A last glance
at myself in profile in the mirror, and what was that lovely
thing of Max's?—"all delicate spirits assume an oblique attitude toward life."

Some minutes later I heaved myself in behind the wheel
of the Humber and turned out of the drive onto the coast
road. The sun had set, and the sight of the sea fired my senses
with exhilaration: it was a skin of rippled black satin, with the
moonlight washing over it like golden oil. As I drove I wound
down the window and listened to its calm voice, its subtle
symphony, the slur and hiss as it rolled and murmured and
slapped at the rocks beneath the cliffs. On the other side of
Griffin Head I pulled into the driveway of the Figs' villa.

Out of the car, up to the front door, barely had I rung the
bell than a housemaid opened the door and then Hugh Fig
hove up behind her, welcomed me warmly, and led me across
the hall. Great big lanky man, like a heron. I liked him.

"What's your poison, doctor?" he said. What did Barbey say about the British? "A people of the north, lymphatic and pale, like their mother the sea, but loving to heat their blood at the flame of alcohol." Lovely.

"Gin and tonic, if I may."

There were three or four people in the drawing room. Hugh introduced me first to his wife, Jean, a tense woman of about forty with a slightly yellowish discoloration of the skin that suggested a liver complaint of some kind. As we shook hands I wondered idly what her urine looked like. The other couple were the Piker-Smiths, Harold and Vera. The name rang a bell. He was a doctor, a dull man with a practice in Wimbledon. She was tall and thin, had teeth like a horse, and gushed at me with enormous volubility. She shook my hand powerfully and bent toward me like a tree bowed by the wind. "Dr. Haggard!" she cried. "I've so been longing to meet you! I think we have people in common." It then came back to me that her husband had been attached to St. Basil's. "Fanny Vaughan—don't you know Fanny?"

I did not respond—I could not respond! A moistness sprang to my eyes. She had hit the mark with her very first arrow. That one remark did for me for the rest of the evening.

I arrived back at Elgin shortly after ten-thirty and immediately made for the surgery. Then I went upstairs to the back bedroom, hung up my dinner jacket, untied my bow tie and unfastened my collar. I went to the window. The first sensation was one of profound relief: I had escaped those dreadful people, and as I stood there gazing at the moonlit sea the terrible sense of loss and yearning that had been aroused by Vera Piker-Smith's question softened. I leaned against the window frame, shifted my weight onto my good leg, laid my head against the windowpane and with my right hand gently thumped the wall a number of times as a sort of dry, tormented, sobbing noise came from my throat. Oh God. When

was it that I had become such a fool of love? It had been at
that funeral, the seed had been sown that day, that's when it
had started to grow, down in the dark soil of my heart, and
me all unsuspecting until it burst forth, sturdy and vigorous
in its maturity—oh *God!* I lifted my head, shook it briskly
and blew the air out of my lungs like a walrus. The wind had
died, the moon was hidden behind a patch of black cloud;
the sky was alive with stars. I could stay in the house not a
moment longer. I seized up my dinner jacket from the back
of the chair, and my stick, and with as much haste as I could
manage I clattered down the stairs and out through the back
door onto the path that led through the gate at the bottom of
the garden to the edge of the cliff and the staircase down to
the beach. I had never attempted it at night, it was only in
the last week or two that I'd discovered that Spike could in
fact manage the descent at all, but in my desperation to get
out, get *away*, get down to the water, to be anywhere but
cooped up in Elgin with my damn memories, my damn *feelings*—it didn't occur to me that descending the staircase at
midnight would offer any more of a problem than it did at
dusk.

And at first it didn't. Still in a state almost of panic I hauled
Spike down the first dozen steps before pausing to catch my
breath. I was suddenly and intensely conscious of the darkness, first, and second, of the sound of the sea crashing onto
the beach far below me, and that its black and heaving surface,
the gleaming rocks, the shelf of pebbles and the stretch of
hard damp sand, all of it was but dimly discernible by starlight
alone. But what came to me then even more vividly was the
powerful sense of having entered an unknown and possibly
dangerous region, the cliff face so familiar to me by daylight
now a black mass of shadow into which my excited mind began
immediately and in spite of myself to project its terrors. For
the first time the cliff face felt alive, alien, hostile—benev-
olent watchers by day, these bulwarks, now they were mon-

sters, living gargoyles, rearing and looming for a thousand years, and it seemed to me that by leaving the top of the cliff and beginning this descent I had abandoned all light and security and given myself over to—what? The dark? The night? I laughed aloud, but the thin sound of it was quickly swallowed, leaving me as desolate as before. I began once more to descend.

Oh what are you doing? I asked myself. Isn't there something ridiculous about all this—you feed your obsession with the woman with morphia until you're unable to think of anything else, you can't sleep, you can't even stay in the house—as though Elgin were your own head, your own mind—as though by escaping Elgin you can escape the thoughts and feelings and memories that roil and turn endlessly, endlessly *in* that mind—it's not romantic at all! But down I went anyway, sideways, like a crab, good leg first, then Spike, then the stick, good leg, Spike, stick, and then I began actually to savor the terror that this plunge into a black unknown aroused in me. Was I mad, I wondered, voluntarily to push myself further and further into the darkness—my vulnerability increased with each step I took. But vulnerability to what?

There are close to a hundred stairs in that steep staircase, divided into nine unequal flights, each flight following a particular tack down the cliff then changing direction as the face of the cliff dictates, a short platform facilitating each change of tack so the structure seems to zigzag down, a fragile business of sticks and nails clinging to the great broad bulk of the cliff like a centipede. I did not pause again until I was halfway down; I turned to see how far I'd come, and the top of the staircase, a few uprights and a length of railing, stood out sharply over the lip of the cliff against the starry sky. Then I looked down: still the moon was hidden in a bank of heavy cloud, and the sea, the beach, all was black, though a faint gleam of frothing showed around the humped black rocks where the tide crashed against them and rolled hissing up the sand. A few minutes later I was painfully clambering off the staircase and scrambling down the last few yards of a boulder-strewn gully and onto the beach.

The cliffs made of this stretch of beach a crescent-shaped cove, and there was a powerful sense, with the sheer walls behind me, and the tide hissing across the sand, of being embosomed in a small dark watery pocket of the night. I'd turned up my collar and hunched my shoulders against the wind, my one hand gripping my stick, banging it into the pebbles with every forward step, and the other hand stuffed in my pocket clenching and unclenching to the steady rhythm of the jabs of protest coming from Spike, and the pulse of the sea, and the ebb and flow of my own emotions; and as I raged along I suddenly saw my relationship with your mother for what it was—not, as your father would have it, the infatuation of a foolish and deluded young man with a sophisticated older woman, not that at all, nothing could be further from the truth. The reality of our relationship could never be under-stood in such terms, as your father thought, no, in a condition of romantic love it is the *soul* that speaks, it is a discourse of soul with soul, and all else is behavior, even the sex. For what is sex after all but a cleaving together and a fusion? It is the making of the two into the one, the recovery of a *lost unity*, and this is what I saw that night, that she and I were—are—two parts of a single whole. This of course is no new idea, this is not original with me, it is a Platonic idea, it arises in the very dawn of our civilization: I am a fragment, a broken thing; I am incomplete and unfinished. Blindly I groped my way through the world, seeking, though I did not know it, for that which would complete me. She completed me, but I lost her. And having known fusion and wholeness it became impossible to live without it—I'd rather *never have known* that such a condition was possible.

And then I thought: so what can I hope for now? There is only the one: for I love not out of need but from the recog-

nition of the profound spiritual communion I share—with her!
Only with her! This is why I left London and why, even
though I was still a relatively young man when I did so, her
loss marked in a sense the end of my life. But I chose to go
on; I chose to follow my calling, I chose to serve, and the full
weight of that decision was borne home to me that night, as
I turned at last, and retraced my steps, and struggled painfully
back up the staircase from the beach. For the steps that lay
before me, each of them demanding that Spike be lifted,
howling, and set down, lifted and set down, those steps were
like the days that remained to me, each one of them bringing
its demands, its labor, its pain—and no sweetness in recom-
pense, no peace, no love, no rest, no grace. No grace—until,
that is, you came.

That night on the stairs I saw a toiling unto death. And I
saw that all I had to relieve the burden of that toiling were a
few weak dim shadows of love: poetry, I mean, and music,
for it is the nature of art to be a shadow or echo of love, an
attempt to represent love, but an attempt doomed to produce
only melancholy, for it carries within itself the lack or loss of
that to which it aspires, which as I say is love. And that is all
the solace that remains to me—this I realized, climbing back
up to Elgin that night—all I have are the husks and shadows
of love, I who once possessed the thing itself.

And I do do my work, I am treating my patients, I am taking
morning surgery each day, and making my house calls in the
afternoon. Whatever I may have lost, and I have lost much,
I have not lost this, my commitment to service, to duty. I do
my work, I read the poets, and I watch the changing arc of
the sun in the sky as spring turns into summer, and the evening
shadows thicken, and you, dear boy, lie dying in my arms—

That night marked an important change in my thinking about
your mother. After that night I no longer attempted to sup-

press my memories, nor the feelings that were inevitably excited by their arousal. I understood that our love affair would influence me profoundly—define me probably—for the rest of my life, and this being so, I chose, freely, not to forget. I would not, I decided, allow the memory to atrophy, to wither and fade, I would keep it fresh, I would nurture it, make of it an object of worship and construct an altar in my heart where I could perform, nightly, my devotions. I'd realized you see that I was one of those rare men who, having loved, come to understand love as the most significant spiritual activity a man can undertake. Love, for me, is not ephemeral, it is not a transient emotion, a passing state, a passage or flight into madness or ecstasy; I see it, rather, as an exalted or even *sacred* condition, a condition in which all the highest and best of human faculties are exercised. Your mother had said to me the night we met that passion was not a sickness, not a disease, but was, rather, the best we were capable of, civilized human beings. Ironically, it was I who came to embrace the idea, while she—

It was hard, nonetheless, in the days following the Figs' dinner party to cope with the memories that now intruded constantly into my thoughts. I remembered her clothes, her conversation, the way she ate, drank, laughed—it all came bubbling back into consciousness at random moments and despite this decision I'd made it never failed to distress me. One morning I was examining an old man with a lung condition, bending over my patient with a stethoscope, when suddenly I saw your mother's wrist—a slender, rather bony wrist, a delicate stem, otherwise unremarkable, but it was stamped indelibly in the fabric of my memory and was enough to make me leave the room and spend a minute or two mastering the sudden overwhelming movement of grief within myself. At times like this I lost faith: why couldn't I abandon her, I wondered? After all I'd suffered, why hang on like this? I could so easily call up the negative: ponder the hurts I'd suffered directly or indirectly through her; stir up a good smoky blaze of resentment and so attempt to find relief in the fact that it was over, that I had escaped the constant turmoil of violent feeling she aroused in me—why not do it, I asked myself, why not vilify the woman, know her as the source and agent of all the misery I had gone through in the last months? Hating her, I thought, would be easier than continuing to love her like this.

But I couldn't do it. I tried, but I couldn't. Why not? Why not just summon her image and hold it up to a distorting mirror—no beauty is so flawless that from a certain angle, in a certain light, it cannot be rendered grotesque, and the power to effect such a transformation resides always with the observer—why not? But I couldn't spoil her; the horror of spoiling was, to me, more terrible even than the daily anguish of missing her, missing her so acutely and with such convulsive unhappiness that at times I felt death would be preferable: no, the horror of spoiling exceeded the pain. The pain I could endure, I *would* endure, but to spoil her, to blacken her, to violate her image in my heart—this I could not do. Why not? Because—and here I sighed, recognizing the exquisitely mordant irony of it all—because I loved her. And that would never change.

No, that would never change—that never *has* changed, as you better than anyone can confirm. How could I otherwise have welcomed you with the warmth I did, were there any trace of bitterness or anger in my heart? Or worse, had I forgotten her, or grown indifferent? I loved not *what* she was, but *that* she was. You see, inasmuch as everything your mother had ever touched was for me impregnated with power (the fly-in-glass was then, and still is, at all times in my right-hand trouser pocket) then how much greater by extension the power of the being whom she had not merely touched but created?

Though what she created they have now destroyed.

•   •   •

Poor darling boy. Poor *ruined* boy, with the light of Heaven in your dying eyes—sleep. So what was I to tell you—that it was *Ratcliff's* fault? No, that would be too much, too soon, I decided. Too much truth. Go slow, I told myself. Find out what the boy is made of. What he can take. More than ever it was vitally important to me that you understand, for in some curious way I felt that I owed it to *her* that despite all you had to deal with, despite having to carry the secret of your disease—you should have the truth; and that if I told you the kind of woman she was then you, like me, could carry her flame and her spirit forward, and thus she would never die, not truly die. Not an ignoble impulse, I think? Though sadly, you had no opportunity to grasp what it was I was trying to tell you before you came flaming from the sky like a dying god and now I shall be left, again, to be the sole witness and carrier, not only of herself but of you also, or rather of her *in* you, fused in you.

A vast aeroplane hangar with a bowed roof of corrugated tin and massive sliding doors painted blue—this was the first thing one saw, coming up to the station; and in its shadow was the pilots' mess. In time I came to know it well, that one-story prefabricated structure with its few functional armchairs, bare wooden floor, its scattering of tables and a bar that ran the length of one wall, hanging above it like a trophy the propeller from some unlucky German bomber. At the other end of this long narrow room stood a battered upright piano, and I remember going past one day on my way to the sick bay and being startled to hear, drifting in the morning air and mixing incongruously with the smells and sounds of aeroplanes, the melancholy notes of a favorite Chopin nocturne. Looking in at the window I saw a young pilot called Johnny Hart sitting at that battered piano, a cigarette between his lips, and last night's beer glasses still on top. I was rather moved.

But the first evening I was invited up to the mess it was not Chopin that was being banged out on that old upright, far from it—the pilots were having a party, a party to which you, to my delight, had invited me. I'd been concerned, I remember, about your relations with the other pilots, about how a complicated, sensitive boy like yourself was treated by those rough hearty men. I needn't have worried. Squadron spirit was unlike that of any other tight-bonded community of men I'd ever known or been part of. For beneath the raucous shouts of laughter, and the incessant pounding of the piano, beneath it all I discerned a thread of intense mutual devotion, an inarticulate intimacy, born, I guessed, of constant shared danger and the proximity of sudden violent death—a form of *love*, though of course I would never have said such a thing to any of you, you'd have been embarrassed and scornful at the very thought of it.

You were at the bar when I came in. You saw me at the door and immediately came over to greet me. "Hello doctor," you said warmly, taking me by the elbow, "come over and have a drink with B Flight." You introduced me to three or four pilots, clean, brisk, affable young men smoking pipes and drinking beer, standing in the familiar RAF stance, legs apart, hands plunged deep in the side pockets of your tunics. I was given a large gin and asked a few questions, but conversation soon veered round to aeroplanes, and crashes, and senior offices, and I listened with pleasure as the RAF slang rolled off your tongues—your kites and prangs, your pieces of nice, your swank, your Spits, your curtains. It was clear to me that you were different from the other men; that evening I saw that they sensed it too, and that it provoked in them a certain deference toward you, a certain gallantry, as though they understood that this slim youth was special. You never joined the group singing at the piano, you preferred to stand with the pipe-smoking talkers at the bar, narrow-shouldered and slim-hipped, a small smile on your lips and one of the other young men at all times in attendance by your side, murmuring remarks, lighting your cigarettes—and it was hard for me not to think of some other evening, some other room, and the same small figure in a black fur coat, glancing at me with a lazy smile through half-closed eyes—

For she had come again, as I knew she would, and she had come bearing gifts—a volume of poetry and a bottle of gin. Poetry was to become one of our shared passions; I introduced your mother to the lovely lines

Ay, in the very temple of Delight
Veil'd Melancholy has her sovran shrine . . .

She loved the ode, and often had me read it to her. It was quite unfashionable, then, to like Romantics, but we didn't care. But yes: at last she'd come. I had been growing more frantic with each day that passed, each day with no sight of her, no word from her, I was going mad; imagine my relief when I got her note telling me when I could expect her. I stood at my window gazing down into Jubilee Road with mounting impatience; eventually I saw a taxi pull up outside the house, saw the door swing open, saw a slender black oxford, a stockinged calf, the hem of a skirt, the woman herself. I was down the stairs and at the front door before she could ring the bell and rouse Desmond Kelly from the back of the house. She was just ascending the steps, carefully, for it was icy out, with one gloved hand on the railing and the other clutching her parcels to the breast of her fur. Her hat was an elegant affair with a narrow brim that swept forward low over one eye. She lifted her face to me; her skin was whiter than ever in the cold air, her eyes slightly damp, very blue, and sparkling. "Hello," she said; we embraced in the hallway, rather gently, as though careful of damaging one another.

She ascended first, and for the briefest sliver of time a

strange shadow fell across my soul. Lambs to the slaughter: the phrase sprang into my mind from nowhere, as I climbed the staircase behind her, though of course I did not voice it. In my room she made straight for the gas fire and stood there with her back to it, pulling off her gloves. I hovered. "What can I give you?" I began.

"Well," she said, "first take these"—she handed me the parcels—"and now you can hang up my coat, though on second thought it's rather reckless of me to surrender it. I'll keep it on for the moment." That *smile!* "The book and the bottle are for you."

I then had business with book and bottle. "It's been perfectly beastly," she began; "thank you darling," as I gave her her gin. She was sitting in an armchair now, her legs crossed, one ankle pulled in close to the other, in a beautiful dove-gray suit cut on tailored, mannish lines, with broad shoulders and a straight skirt, and the big black fur of course, I could never get that bloody room warm enough for her!—when after only a moment she stood up and came across to my chair, and leaning forward cupped my face in her hands and stared a long, searching moment into my eyes, and told me she was sorry I'd been miserable, she never ever wanted to make me miserable again, though she thought she probably would.

I didn't know what she meant.

"Oh darling. Use your imagination."

The moment passed, she sat down again and began talking. "I was too distraught for words," she said, as I leaned across to light her cigarette, and she blew smoke at the ceiling. She knew we had to take great care, for Ratcliff must never find out, but it made her simply wild not to be able to see me, her clever, noble, handsome lover with the terribly difficult decision to make about his career. "I've been thinking about it," she said, "and I don't think you should go into surgery. I know surgeons. They lose sight of what matters. Their patients are unconscious when they do their real work. You're

so good with people, I think you'll be much more use in
general medicine."

"Good with people?" It had never occurred to me that I
was good with people.

"Good with me. Darling, it's so *cold* in here!"

I was moved, deeply, that she would think about me and
my problems. "I know it is," I said, "I'm afraid there's nothing
I can do to get it any warmer. Would you like to go somewhere
else?"

"Oh?" She stood up and wandered to my bookshelves,
touched the spines of this and that. I was standing by the fire
now with one hand in my pocket, the other gripping my gin.
My heart was racing. "I've found a nice little pub," I said.
"Very quiet."

She moved back to the fire. "You look like a schoolmaster,"
she murmured. She took the gin from me and put it on the
mantelpiece, then put her arms around me. She pressed herself gently against me. I closed my eyes. One hand at the
small of her back—the other in the silky-soft hair at the back
of her neck—her perfume in my nostrils. She pushed her
thigh between mine. "What pub?" she breathed into my ear.

"The Two Eagles," I whispered, moving my hand up and
down her back, under the jacket of her suit, feeling how soft
the silk of her blouse was, and how soft the skin beneath.
"It's warm too."

"And quiet?"

"Always empty."

"No one goes there?"

"Only me."

"It'll be our pub."

Our lips touched. She kissed me. It was the softest kiss
imaginable. I was already deeply aroused. I felt a dampness
in my underpants. She pulled gently free of me. My heart
rate was high, my respiration shallow. I was very happy indeed
in a very foolish way. All I wanted was to keep holding her,

forever. That would be enough. I told her so. "Shall we go to bed?" she whispered.

Afterwards she sat in the armchair in front of the fire and I sat on the floor with my head on her knee. Still we sustained that impossibly exquisite tension—how rare it is, and how sweet! She felt it too, she told me; she thought: this is a gift, where did it come from? "I remembered your eyes being green," I said.

"They go blue in the cold," she said, and we laughed! How we laughed! It wasn't the least bit funny, but such was our happiness that laughter was at least an outlet. Then we drank more gin; it made no difference; we were already drunk. "Did you look at your book?" she said. It was Keats. I opened it at random. "She cannot fade, though thou hast not thy bliss," I read, "For ever wilt thou love, and she be fair." It sobered us a little. I lifted my eyes from the book and gazed at her; she turned her head aside.

She told me later what happened when she got home that evening. In the cab, she said, she sat powdering her face and feeling wicked and guilty, but at the same time she was aware of other, stronger emotions, emotions that were associated with me, my idealism, my love. They flourished quietly, she said, in the darkness of her heart, but sitting in a cold cab on the way home to Plantagenet Gardens and Ratcliff—she was miserable.

But then, she said, her mood changed. All at once she realized she need not feel so terribly maudlin about it all. Some little flicker of domestic cruelty, or indifference, from Ratcliff—the mere memory of such a flicker, she said, a pin-prick, no more, of marital distaste such as she had felt a thousand times—that had been stimulus enough, given the delicacy of her moral and emotional condition at this point; I forget precisely what it was. Whatever it was, she thought again of me, and the anxiety vanished. It all comes of understanding renunciation, she said—how easy it is to renounce one's pleasure, but how resilient, compared to the tedium of self-mortification, is its memory. She would banish her guilt, she said; Christmas was coming, you would be home, it was hardly the time to have the specter of adultery hovering about the place.

It was with this figure uppermost in her mind—the hovering specter of adultery—that she paid off the cab and let herself into the house. The light was on in Ratcliff's study. "That you?" he called as she closed the front door softly behind her.

She stood before the mirror in the hall, taking off her hat. "Yes it is," she called back.

"Come in and have a nightcap."

Oh God. She'd dreaded this. He sounded genial. She'd hoped to be able to slip quietly up to her room, and nine nights out of ten this would have presented no problem; nine nights out of ten the study door would be closed, with him wrapped in his precious solitude like a larva in a cocoon. Tonight of all nights he was genial. All too easy for me to reconstruct what followed; your mother talked to me at length about Ratcliff, for I was always intensely curious to know what went on between them. She stood in the doorway with her hand to her mouth, covering a false yawn. "No nightcap for me, Ratcliff," she said, "I'm exhausted."

"Come in for a moment," he said. "I want to talk to you." A flicker of alarm—about *what?* He was in his leather armchair, a scotch in a cut crystal glass at his elbow, the standard lamp directed onto the book in his hand. He was in his gray velvet smoking jacket and Moroccan slippers.

She went in. She wandered along his bookshelves, keeping her back to him. She pulled out a volume at random and idly turned the pages. The carpet was thick beneath her feet, the lighting warm, the traces of an after-dinner cigar still faintly lingering. "How is Brenda?"

"Much as usual."

"Pleasant evening?"

"Oh fine. Ladies' night out, you know." She turned to face him, still with the book in her hand. "We talk about our husbands, analyze their manly qualities."

He frowned. Oh why do this, she thought, why provoke him? This is what happens in marriage, she told me—one snipes away constantly, resentment never sleeps. "I wanted to talk to you about James," said Ratcliff. "I suppose it can wait till the morning."

She heard the touch of chill in his voice. "I'm sorry, dear, I didn't mean to be beastly. I'm tired, I think I'll go up."

He nodded. She put down the book, crossed the room and kissed his forehead. "Sorry," she murmured, and came behind his chair and began gently to massage his temples.

"Ah," he said, "that is exquisite."

"Headache?"

"Since about two this afternoon. Nothing works on them anymore."

She continued to massage his temples, his forehead, the nape of his neck. He had grown fat in recent years; her fingers kneaded a thick roll of flesh at his collar. She often told me how distasteful she found it to have to touch him. He groaned with pleasure. "Nothing gives me relief, but you can.'"

"Poor thing. You work too hard." It was a familiar conversation.

"I know. That is good, my darling." She felt the knotted muscles beneath the soft fat, felt them slacken as she worked out the tension with her fingers. "I'll come to you later, may I?" he said quietly.

"I don't think so tonight. I'm very tired."

"As you wish." Again that sudden chill; that *ice*.

"Goodnight Ratcliff," she said. It was typical, she told me, that his tenderness, so rarely aroused, should vanish with such abruptness if he sensed the slightest rebuff. But he made no effort, he hadn't for years. He was fat, and he always smelled of formalin. It was a smell that made her think of pathology

labs, and cadavers. He came to her smelling of death, she
said, cigars, whiskey and death. She went upstairs to her room
and sat at her dressing table. She opened a jar of cleansing
cream and began gently working it into her skin with the tips
of her fingers. She felt calm and sad and now her conscience
didn't trouble her in the slightest.

All this flickered through my mind in the few moments I stood
at the bar of the mess half listening to a fighter pilot tell a
tale of high adventure in the sky—and at the same time watching your face. Oh, but you loved being among them, this was
clear, you reveled, in your quiet way, in the company of these
dashing, handsome, brave young men, you took a keen delight
in all the robust, physically affectionate conviviality they displayed though without, somehow, ever fully participating in
it—you looked on, for instance, when, quite late in the evening, the squadron formed a human crocodile that then
crawled about the floor snapping at the skirts and trousers of
the visitors. It seemed clear to me that you were a strange
one, temperamentally, for a fighter pilot—there was an aggressively competitive streak in almost all the pilots I met at
the station that you seemed to lack, and naturally I wondered
what happened when you climbed into the cockpit, if it man-
ifested there. It was only later that I understood that you
lacked it almost entirely, that aggressive drive, and that it was
probably in order to compensate for that lack, and to prove
to yourself you were a proper man, that you'd become a fighter
pilot in the first place.

   During the course of the evening I was introduced to the
station medical officer, and the next morning I drove up the
hill and offered him my assistance, an offer which he gratefully
accepted. Many of my older patients had died by this time,
others had been called up, and I had time on my hands; also,
during the extended period of despair I had gone through in
the autumn and winter I had not perhaps been as attentive

to the practice as I might have been, and it was not flourishing. But now my spirits were lifting, and I was eager to work once more. I remember that I parked outside the sick bay, but before going in I stood a moment at the edge of the airfield, leaning on my stick, and gazed across the grass at the squadron sprawled in deck chairs by the dispersal hut on the far side. It was a warm clear day, the sky was deep blue with just a few high plump pillowy clouds, and you looked the very picture of languid nonchalance, there in your deck chairs, dozing in the sunshine. Sunlight glinted on the Perspex cockpit hoods of the Spitfires lined up wingtip to wingtip on the grass nearby, but even as I watched you a head appeared out of the window of the dispersal hut, there came a single shouted command— and you scrambled. Now there was nothing languid about you at all! You went sprinting across the grass (exhilarating sight!), buckling parachute harnesses over flapping leather jackets, your trousers tucked into heavy flight boots, on your heads close-fitting leather helmets, the chin straps undone, the goggles on top, and within seconds you were clambering into your cockpits and gunning your engines. Then one by one you bumped across the grass, flames leaping from your exhaust, and within a few seconds you were airborne, in formation, and rapidly climbing!

As I was leaving the station an hour later I saw a solitary Spitfire come in to land, and watched the pilot haul himself out of the cockpit and tramp silently across the grass, having perhaps witnessed (I imagined) a man going down in flames who an hour ago was playing chess with him. Curious thing, that you should be stationed in the hills above this most moribund of seaside towns, your presence, I remember, seemed to me at times like a whisper of dark necromancy, as though spirit were somehow being breathed into a corpse.

Not surprisingly my dealings with your father in the hospital became increasingly uncomfortable. I didn't like to condemn

the man out of hand, but it was hard, in light of what your
mother told me about what went on in Plantagenet Gardens,
not to bear real animus toward him. One day shortly after
Belle Sylvester died (she never came out of her coma) I was
down in Pathology watching Miggs do a craniotomy on the
woman. After dissecting the scalp, and folding back the flaps
of skin, he sawed round the exposed skull and cracked it off
with a head chisel. How he enjoyed his work, gruesome little
man! He grinned at me in his weaselly way when the crack
came. "Like a walnut, eh?" he murmured. He lifted it off
with a flourish. Underneath I could clearly see that the dura
was covered with a sugary-looking fibrinous exudate, and I
knew my diagnosis was correct. Meningitis. Nothing I could
have done.

Leaving the postmortem room I almost collided with Ratcliff, also on his way upstairs, wearing a black rubber apron
under a starched white coat flapping open. He had a cigar
between his teeth and his manner was brisk. "Ah, Dr. Haggard," he said. "Get any joy from the woman?"

For an appalled instant I misunderstood him, but it was my
patient he meant. "Much as I expected, doctor," I said. I
attempted to give the impression of being in a great hurry,
which indeed I was. "Don't rush," he said, "we'll walk up
together. This is a teaching hospital, we're an intellectual
community, we should always make time to talk. You know,"
he said, as we made our way along the windowless corridors
of the hospital basement, past the incinerator room, beneath
lagged pipes that wheezed and seeped, "a lot of you people
upstairs have strange opinions of what goes on down here.
No, you needn't be polite, I know what gets said. But let me
tell you what the great Romberg Snoddie told me, many years
ago. It's the *pathos* that conditions the *logos*, do you see what
I mean?"

Pathos and *logos?* Suffering and science? Strange way he had
with small talk, your father. I was aware of the smell of for-

malin—the smell of death!—as I murmured something, I forget quite what, some half-remembered scrap of morbid anatomy.

"Precisely. Now answer me this: what is medicine?"

We were climbing the steep stone staircase that ascended by two stages to the ground floor. The wooden handrail was attached to the wall with brass fixtures; it had been worn smooth by generations of doctors and lab assistants and medical archivists and janitors. What is medicine? I should have been in theaters five minutes ago; Vincent Cushing became furious if he was kept waiting. You father didn't wait for my answer.

"Science of life," he said, as we paused on the landing halfway up for him to relight his cigar. "But life, doctor, can only create a science of itself by means of dysfunction and pain."

"Ah," I said. This glee with which he had buttonholed me—did he, it suddenly occurred to me, *suspect* something? My unease intensified.

"I analyze the dysfunction," he said, "you deal with the pain. Am I right?"

"I suppose so."

"Complementary activities. Therapeutics can only arise on the basis of pathology, I daresay you've heard that before."

"Yes indeed, Dr. Vaughan."

"Don't patronize me, Dr. Haggard."

This came out very sharply indeed. I stopped and turned, as your father shouted with brief laughter and clapped me on the shoulder. "Don't lose sight of the *pathos*, doctor," he cried, and strode away across the lobby.

Later, when I was having lunch with McGuinness in the junior common room, I mentioned what your father had said. "Odd birds, pathologists," said McGuinness, "very odd indeed. Never met one I liked. Now what sort of a doctor wants to hang around the tombs all day? In some cultures they keep the corpse in the house till it rots. I think there's something primitive makes a man go into pathology. I pity the wife."

"Oh?"

"Imagine living with Ratty Vaughan."

Things were quiet on the ward that day, and I had leisure to reflect on McGuinness's words. What was it, after all, that inspired a physician to devote his career to cadavers rather than living human beings? A deficiency in the emotional sphere, without doubt. I began then to see your father's behavior at home in a much clearer light. He was a senior pathologist, but he was also an emotional primitive; and the idea that such a man should be married to an exquisite, delicate woman like your mother—I found it hard to contemplate, it made me so angry. It still does. For you see, I believe he didn't merely destroy her chance to be happy, I believe he destroyed yours too.

Was it pressure from Ratcliff I wondered that led you to join the RAF and become a fighter pilot? He was so utterly and aggressively male, with his leather aprons and his booming voice and his big cigars, it was not difficult to imagine him imposing his own particular twisted ideal of masculinity on his son. At times you seemed so young, practically a schoolboy, and I was impressed—I was *awed*, rather—to think of the work you did in the sky each day. I'd look at that fresh boyish face, the clear eyes with their thin dark brows converging to a delicate arrowpoint at the top of that small straight nose, and around your red lips no sign yet of the weary irony that inevitably comes to stamp the English face—you should have had no more to think about than Latin prep and cricket bats and the spirit of the Upper Sixth! No, not hard to imagine Ratcliff wanting to make a "proper" man of you, and you succumbing, giving yourself over to it with gusto, in fact, afraid of admitting to him and perhaps even to yourself just how deeply unsuited you were by nature for the work of a

Spitfire pilot. Though I never doubted your love of flight—
that was always clear to me, the way your eyes lit up when
you talked about it. Once you told me that to be earthbound
was in a way to be blind, so I asked you if you thought *I* was
blind.

You paused here. "No, I don't think you are," you said.
"You're not caught up with petty things. You have an imagination. I think you're a pilot in spirit."

"I'm flattered."

You blushed. "Sorry, was that impertinent?"

"No, dear boy," I cried, "it was not! I'm delighted you
should think me a pilot in spirit—I'm afraid I feel like a
crippled shrimp much of the time."

I meant it, too; I treasured the compliment, I kept it close,
like the fly-in-glass your mother gave me for Christmas . . .

. . . the Christmas of 1937, when we were deeply in
love . . . but forced by circumstance to keep our love out of
sight, and to meet always in quiet places, where we wouldn't
be known—love in the shadows. I remember describing to
your mother my strange, uneasy encounter with your father
on the stairs in St. Basil's, and I remember that she'd smiled.
"That sounds like Ratcliff," she said, and I was bewildered
by the warmth that accompanied her words—was it affection?
Nothing, surely, as strong as that. Familiarity, yes. Boredom,
scorn? So hard to know. Your parents had been married for
seventeen years, and I'm aware that complex patterns of feeling evolve over lengthy periods of intimacy, but even so—
oh, I didn't know what to make of it.

She wouldn't be able to see me until after Christmas; she
urged me to get away for a few days, she thought I needed a
rest. I only had twenty-four hours off, I told her. But I did
have an uncle, my mother's brother, an old man who lived in
a small town on the south coast, and he'd written to me in
November inviting me to lunch on Christmas Day. At your

mother's prompting I now accepted the invitation, though with some misgivings; I'd have preferred to indulge the emotions of my lover's heart in London, I'd have liked to fan the flames of my unceasing obsessive desire to be with her sitting alone over the gas fire in Jubilee Road. I see now how important it was that I go; for had I stayed in London I would never have known Griffin Head, nor renewed acquaintance with an uncle I hadn't seen since I was a boy.

Christmas in St. Basil's. The wash room up in theaters had been decorated with bunting and streamers and everyone felt festive. As we scrubbed for surgery there was energetic talk about Germany, and the growing tensions between us. I realized, powdering my hands, the easier to draw off the rubber gloves afterwards, that my attitude to the prospect of war had changed, that I no longer felt the same grim fatalistic sense of relish I used to feel, for now the future held promise for me. Now I feared the upheaval and destruction that war would bring—now I had something to lose. And so, I realized, had the rest of the surgical staff, this was clear from their conversation. Cushing of course had the last word. "It all goes to demonstrate," he said, when we'd gone through to theaters, and were about to begin a complicated visceral sympathectomy, "that the British, politically speaking, are split down the middle." We stood with our forearms bent upward, hands pointed to the ceiling, as the scrub nurse gowned us, tying the bows behind our backs. "Rationally," said Cushing, "we adhere to democratic principles. Emotionally, imaginatively"—hemostats clicked, sutures were snipped, the wound was a forest of loop-handled steel instruments—"we indulge a rich appetite for costume and ritual. Hence our adoration of the monarchy. It's a damn sight more benign"—here he cut the first of the small preganglionic fibers emanating from the thoracic and lumbar cords—"than what the Germans do. Where we have royalty"—now he frowned, barked out a few terse orders, called for more retraction—"they have the Nazi party." Then he began talking about diastolic blood pressure, and the arteriolar vasculature, and the operation went forward. Speak for yourself, I thought. It wasn't royalty I was worried about, it was your mother. If war came—as it probably would—and we lost it—as we probably would—what place would there be in that new world for love?

My uncle's name was Henry Bird and he lived in a small white villa overlooking the esplanade in Griffin Head. Oh, I need hardly describe the town to you! Often enough we've amused ourselves on the subject of Griffin Head—only through your eyes was I ever able to see the place with humor and affection, before you came I was bitterly unhappy here. It is an Edwardian sea resort, and in the years before the war its residents were elderly and invalid for the most part, retired to the coast after careers in the professions or the stock market or banking in London, or in the colonial or diplomatic service abroad. Peace and quiet is what the place offered them, and convalescence in comfort. A dozen or so hotels and boardinghouses catered to the small number of visitors who came during the summer, but there were few attractions for the more vulgar type of holidaymaker, hence the town's reputation for a particularly stagnant form of English gentility.

I went down on Christmas Eve. A frail but spirited man, my uncle Henry, he'd spent his life as a sort of glorified manservant to a wealthy member of the local aristocracy, since deceased, who'd apparently been generous in her will. Intensely sociable, charming and effusive, and marvelously elegant in a dark blue suit with a white shirt and a pink bow tie, he greeted me with great warmth—"Lovely to see you, dear boy!"—and made us each a powerful cocktail. Sitting in his small, neat drawing room I listened with half a mind as he talked happily about his antiques. My arrival had coincided with a wild winter storm: salt-drenched gales scoured the buildings along the front, and waves broke against the seawall with such force that columns of water were hurled thirty feet high then dashed to white spray and foam. I gazed out of Henry's bay window and felt a sort of correspondence of the elemental wildness outside with the turbulence in myself: this, I thought, rather savoring the conceit, is the weather of my heart. Pathetic fallacy I daresay, but no less powerful for that. Over game hen with mashed potatoes and brussels sprouts, and a nice little claret he'd been saving for the occasion, and a rich plum pudding, and nuts and dates and cheese and port, I listened to Henry as he lingered among his memories of the old days in the great houses. "Life is very different now of course," he murmured, mellow and maudlin with port. "So much has changed." He sighed. "Sometimes I lie in bed at night and listen to the waves turning far out to sea, and I think it's all a dream, only the sea is real."

After lunch we went for a walk. In our hats and overcoats we made our way down to the front, down through the old part of the town with its steep narrow cobblestoned streets that aroused in my imagination pictures of Griffin Head as it must have been in the 1700s, a smugglers' haven of peglegged old salts in cocked hats and earrings. The wind drove salty rain into our faces and flattened our clothes against our bodies and forced us to clutch our hats tightly to our heads. With some difficulty we managed to cross the esplanade and stand in the gale on the seawall, watching the waves exploding and crashing, one after another, then falling away, sucking and dragging at the loosened shingle piled against the battered wooden groins that sliced the beach into sections and streamed with seaweed. Henry's scarf I remember fluttered about him like an ensign. He grinned wildly at me and shouted remarks I couldn't hear.

After a few moments of this we turned our backs to the wind and pushed eastward along the empty seafront toward the pier, which was almost lost in a haze of spray and rain. Beneath dark, lowering clouds gulls rose and wheeled and screamed in the wind. Henry wouldn't go out along the pier, so I staggered out by myself and stood gripping the railing behind the pavilion at the far end, as the violence thrashed and gushed about me. My head was soaked and streaming with salt spray, a wonderful sensation. I turned and gazed inland, saw through the scrim of hazy rain the stormswept little town clustered on its hill in tiers, the old part at the bottom, the neat terraces of white Regency villas higher up, and higher still the Gothic Revival mansions brooding behind tall hedges and old trees. Despite the blurring of the weather the effect was one of strong vertical accents, of sharp outlines and jagged profiles, and I exulted in the rather odd, wild, toothy beauty of it all, for it was, as I say, somehow expressive of my own condition and feeling. Further to the east the cliffs stood out against the angry sky, a few proud old houses on the summit; one of them was Elgin, though of course I didn't know this yet; beyond, the visible world was lost in the gloom of approaching dusk.

After we got back to the house Henry told me, over tea and hot crumpets, a curious story about the town. To the west of Griffin Head, he said, there was once a church which stood sixty feet back from the edge of a cliff. Over the years the sea ate steadily into the cliff, until the destruction of the church seemed imminent, and it was desanctified and abandoned. The stonework crumbled, the tower and south wall collapsed, and ivy crawled thickly over what was left. Not surprisingly an atmosphere of melancholy desolation grew up around the place, and there were reports of unearthly forms flitting among the ruins. Then one wild night in the winter of 1925 a great storm tore out the cliff and took the remains of the church with it, and the next morning the stones were strewn all along the beach. What disturbed the local people was not the loss of the church, that had been expected for years; no, what disturbed them, said Henry (whose spirits had been quite revived by our walk), was that the sea had bitten

into the graveyard, and in the face of the new cliff could quite
clearly be made out the forms of human skeletons. They're
still there, he said. "Come down and see me again, dear boy,
and I'll show you the bones."

A melancholy aura pervades any institution at Christmastime.
Despite the best efforts of the staff, asylum bonhomie only
serves to point up what is lacking: all that is intimate, familial
and domestic. When I came into St. Basil's late that night I
encountered an atmosphere of gray gloom. The train journey
back from the sea had already done much to destroy my ex-
ultation of the afternoon. My compartment was dirty and un-
heated, and I'd sat peering out into the darkness and smoking
cigarette after cigarette, and trying not to shiver, for my overcoat was still damp despite Henry's gallant attempt to dry it
in front of the fire. Only a few more days till I saw your mother
again, but even that thought failed to ignite my imagination,
so overwhelmingly antiromantic is the effect of traveling by
rail in the south of England in winter. Sharing the compartment with me was a weary young woman with two children
who had consumed far too much sugar earlier in the day and
were now, predictably, suffering the consequences. We were
all suffering the consequences. I was never so glad in my life
to see Victoria Station. Back in Jubilee Road I huddled on
top of the gas fire in my paisley dressing gown with a cup of
hot tea laced with gin and felt sorry for myself.

The days between Christmas and the New Year have always
seemed to me a sort of black hole in the calendar. Days of
desolation. But about halfway through Boxing Day I found
myself thinking of your mother's impending visit, and so near
did it suddenly seem that I felt the familiar surge, the visceral
tingle and warmth, and my spirits began to rise. There was a
letter for me when I got home from St. Basil's on the twenty-
ninth, in that by-now-familiar hand: would I meet her in the
Two Eagles? I was disappointed that she wasn't coming to

Jubilee Road, but I understood why, the cold of course. Perhaps we would come back afterwards.

I was there early, and she was late—and the twenty or so minutes that I sat alone provided several intense jabs of panic, as I considered the possibility of her not appearing. But at last she arrived, rather flustered, rather distracted. "A large gin, darling," she said, "I need it."

"I thought you weren't coming," I said. "I thought something had happened to you."

"Really? What would have happened to me?" She was opening her cigarette case. Her eyes never left my face as she put the cigarette between her lips. I pulled my matches from my pocket, and as she leaned forward to the flame her eyes were still on mine. "Sorry," I said, "am I being silly?"

She inhaled deeply and shook her head. A pale hand fluttered across the table and settled on my sleeve for a moment. "You're not being silly," she said with seriousness. "Thank you for worrying."

"I'll get your gin."

When I sat down again she said, "I have a present for you."

"I have one for you too," I said. "You look tired, has it been difficult?"

"I'm not sleeping well," she said as she groped in her handbag. "I don't know why."

"Things awkward at home?" For a moment I glimpsed in my mind's eye the face of the senior pathologist, and heard his ringing baritone—"It's the *pathos* that conditions the *logos*, doctor!"—and then McGuinness's acid tones—"There's something primitive makes a man go into pathology—*I pity the wife.*" She brought out a small object wrapped in green tissue paper. "I don't imagine you'll like it," she said, "I just thought of you when I saw it, so I bought it. It was an impulse."

"An impulse," I said, as I took it from her. She hadn't answered my question about things at home, but great tenderness was aroused at the idea of her thinking of me on seeing something in a shop window. That I should be present in her mind when we were not together, as she was in mine—to be told this, actually to hear it from her lips rather than simply wondering if her response to me mirrored mine to her—it affected me more strongly than I'd imagined possible. We had said so pitifully little about our feelings! Yet all the time, in the obscure depths of the heart, something had been growing: love. The growth of love. I unfolded the tissue paper and discovered wrapped within it a piece of glass shaped like a pebble, flat on the bottom, with a fly inside it. "Good God," I said, "now how did they get it in there?" I held it up to the light. Whole and perfect, a common housefly, *Musca domestica*, was suspended in the glass as though frozen in flight, as though the air through which it moved had solidified abruptly about it, trapping it to eternity. As I turned it in my fingers daggers of light flashed and splintered from the smooth curved surface. "Isn't it curious?" she said. "Do you like it? I thought it might make a paperweight. Or you could clench it in your fist in moments of fury."

"I'll keep it in my pocket," I said. I put it back on the table, in its crumply nest of tissue paper. "It will bring me luck."

"Of some description."

I stepped round the table and stooped to kiss her lips. She turned away slightly and gave me her cheek. Her hand came up and touched the side of my face. The kiss lasted a second or two; then came a brief flurry of confusion, me losing control, kissing her neck, then abruptly sitting down and pushing my hand through my hair while she, with a small smile, watched me. "I know," she said. "It's difficult. I'm sorry, darling." I shook my head and lifted my drink slightly, to her.

When it came time to leave she still hadn't answered my question about things at home. I rose from the table and slipped the fly-in-glass into my trouser pocket, where through the material I could feel it hard against my thigh.

Later that evening I was in my room getting ready to go to

St. Basil's. I was changing my shirt in front of the mirror in the door of my wardrobe, the fly-in-glass on the table behind me with the desk lamp shining directly upon it. When I'd briefly lost control in the Two Eagles, and kissed her neck, she'd said, "I'm sorry. It's difficult, I know." But what had she meant—*what* was difficult? Sustaining our passion under clandestine conditions? Or something else—not going back to Jubilee Road to make love, perhaps?

Then a little later she'd suddenly felt sure she could hear Ratcliff in the next bar. I'd listened, and heard him too; he was talking about the role of the pancreatic hormone in glucide metabolism. We'd stared at each other, aghast, for several moments—I went up to the counter and cautiously peered round into the next bar—to find a group of commercial travelers telling each other jokes. This of course was symptomatic of the deeply furtive nature of our relationship, and it troubled me. Never had I imagined that when I met the woman I was destined to love she would be married to another man—not just another man, but another doctor, a colleague. Oh, but Ratcliff Vaughan was an odd, cold creature, I told myself, barely human, a *pathologist*, for the love of God! Whatever went on in Plantagenet Gardens, it hardly bore thinking about, this sad, lovely woman and that primitive. With these thoughts running in my head I attempted again to tie my tie; my fingers were shaking and I couldn't seem to get the bloody thing right, and I hate more than anything an ill-tied tie.

The tie was tied, but still I didn't move away from the wardrobe mirror. Oh God. Possibly my whole thinking was wrong. Do you know the feeling—you may not be old enough—the ghastly lurch of shock, I mean, that comes when, having thought about a thing for days on end, and then suddenly encountering a point of view in which previously unimaginable categories are employed, all values abruptly shift—?

Ten minutes later I left the house and made my way up

Jubilee Road (it was a cold, windy night) toward St. Basil's. I was on Accident and Casualty, but my shift was happily uneventful. Around two o'clock I admitted a man whose hand had been horribly crushed under heavy machinery during night work in a factory. I called McGuinness in, for the damage was extensive. As I applied Vaseline dressings to the wound I thought about the commercial travelers in the Two Eagles; suddenly—it hurts me to remember this—suddenly the affair with your mother, viewed against the reality of a man in pain and in danger of losing his hand, seemed so foolish and indulgent that I felt myself ridiculous. But it *mattered*, this I could not deny, *she* mattered, I loved her and *love* mattered— how then could it be ridiculous? Yet it was. I felt the hard lump of the fly-in-glass in my pocket. Love is what we crave, but it vanishes like a dream on exposure to a certain sort of reality, such were my thoughts in the few moments it took me to apply a pad of Vaseline gauze steeped in bactericide to the bloody mangle of flesh and bone.

Then McGuinness appeared; examined the damage; turned to me and shook his head. We took the man up to theaters. The procedure is straightforward: you have to leave a flap of skin so there's something to sew back over the stump, then with a heavy amputating knife you saw off the mess below the level of the flap, toss it all into a pail (whose contents later go down to the incinerator room in the basement) and stitch up what's left. It was the first time I'd cut a man's hand off, and it made me shiver. We were clever though. We saved his apposition. He would still be able to hold things with his thumb and forefinger, the only digits he had left on that hand.

When I left St. Basil's the next morning I was tired, but clear once more in both my heart and my conscience, for a sustained bout of surgical activity had dissipated the anxiety that the meeting in the Two Eagles had aroused. Now here's an odd thing. Did you know (though how would you?) that in some doctors, surgical work has an aphrodisiac effect? I find this hard to understand. Amputation, especially, fills me with distaste for all bodily functions, and when I came away from the wards my desire was generally for nothing more physical than a volume of poetry and a glass of gin. So it was that morning. I got back to Jubilee Road, changed into my pajamas and dressing gown, and after a few minutes with Keats slipped into deep dreamless sleep. I was awoken in the late afternoon by a knock on the door. It was Desmond Kelly, with a letter from your mother. Delicately scented, in that neat spidery hand of hers, it said she was sorry for being such a bore yesterday evening, would I forgive her? She loved me and would see me again very soon.

Soon we were meeting at every opportunity. It wasn't easy for either of us; your mother hated telling lies, while for me, getting away from St. Basil's for even an hour required that another doctor cover for me, usually McGuinness, and though I invented a story about an elderly relative who was desperately ill he soon became skeptical, and a joke grew up around "Dr. Haggard's sick auntie." In fact it was Henry I had in mind.

But though it might involve just twenty minutes in the Two Eagles, or a teashop, each meeting served to sustain the taut string of feeling that bound us together. We would sit at the very back of the teashop and hold hands over the hot-buttered teacakes, and murmur our small talk, our lovers' talk, while under the table our knees touched, and your mother would slip off a shoe and rub a small silken foot against my calf, which instantly aroused me. Encounters like this served only to inflame my impatience to be alone with her again. Naturally I never went to Plantagenet Gardens, she always came to Jubilee Road. I've told you about that room, it was a large, untidy, high-ceilinged room with a few big pieces of dark battered furniture. There were books and papers in piles on the floor, and a skull for an ashtray. On the wall, among my landscapes and sunsets, hung an elegant framed Vesalius print my father gave me shortly before he died.

That scholar's room now began to change. It began to reflect your mother. The harsh glare of the overhead bulb gave way, with the arrival of a pair of pale blue ceramic lamps, to a low soft shadowy glow. She brought a beautiful Persian rug on which we lay together in front of the gas fire. She hung a length of fabric across the bedroom door, replaced the sheets and installed candles. Pots and bottles of unguents apeared, creams and lotions and perfumes. My quarters were gradually feminized. My cell became a boudoir.

This then was our private sanctuary; our intimacy, our love, our passion, all found expression here. Your mother was at times voracious, feline, avid for me; at other times slow, voluptuous and careless; she was a woman of many moods. I remember her nested in the pillows and linen of my big bed in a superb state of languor, her elegant clothing in immodest disarray, a pale lovely creature suffused with the glow of profound physical pleasure. I remember too how sometimes we'd be together in the Two Eagles and such would be the impatience generated by her urgent sexual need of me that we would hurry back to Jubilee Road even if only for eight or ten minutes, and barely get the door shut behind us before we were on the floor and pulling off her silvery silk underpants. Afterwards I'd lie back and smoke and stare at the ceiling and feel a sort of swimmy, dissolving sensation sweep over me like mist. I'd weep a little and then laugh in an abashed sort of way as your mother, heavy-lidded and indolent, lay in my arms and gave me little kisses and murmured endearments, darling, sweetheart, precious Edward. She told me how deeply it excited her when I became excited, how this being so fiercely desired aroused desire in her, and how my silence, and my intentness, made me seem a stranger to her, and how it alarmed her but fascinated her that my sexual character differed so dramatically from my social self.

She had never (she said) felt herself the object of such passion before.

A brief period, then, of almost unblemished bliss. What blemishes there were were the blemishes all lovers know. Everything was so fraught! I remember once we argued about Hitler. "So alarmist," she remarked, glancing at a man's newspaper as we left the Two Eagles after a swift drink one evening, "all this talk of war with Germany. Hitler doesn't want war."

"Not this year, certainly," I said. We were standing on the pavement looking for a taxi.

"Not any year," she said. "I think he's created order and stability in the country. He won't risk that."

"But the man's a monster!" I cried. "He's a megalomaniac! A murderer!"

"He's an authoritarian," she said, "and that's alien to this political culture, but they do things differently in Germany."

"They most certainly do."

"Their history hasn't given them the experience of democracy that ours has."

"Darling, it's not about history!"

"Can anything be said to be not about history?"

"Yes. Fascism."

I suppose the same argument occurred over thousands of dinner tables every night, in the months before Munich, before Prague. But for us to argue, even about politics—it left me feeling utterly desolate, as though I'd lost her. I was miserable until I saw her again. She dismissed it with an airy wave. "Oh darling," she said, "we were just talking about Hitler. What a sensitive soul you are—you mustn't take it so seriously."

But I did. My life now contained only two types of time, time with her and time without her; one paradise, the other hell. There were the small agonies: waiting for her, and becoming panicked if she was late. This was torment. I would

try and explain her absence to myself until at last it became
impossible not to assume that disaster had occurred and she
was lost to me forever. Then she would appear, and find me
affecting pathos, trying to hide my joy at seeing her, and so
wasting whole, precious minutes of the few fleeting hours we
were to be allowed. There was my tendency, too, after each
meeting, to dissect and analyze every word and gesture she'd
made, examining each in trembling apprehension that it signified on her part impatience, or boredom, and therefore imminent rejection. There were even moments (the man with
the mangled hand was one) when I *doubted*—when the whole
fragile tissue of feeling became somehow unreal and I could
not hold on to it, though the doubt vanished the instant I saw
her.

But we grew careless. Caught up in love's dream, feeling
invulnerable, and touched with grace, we grew careless. Perhaps it was inevitable. Perhaps we needed, unconsciously, to
precipitate a crisis—perhaps we *had to!* I don't know. I don't
know what made her come to the hospital that night. She was
at times subject to black moods, to brief attacks of melancholy,
and I've come to believe that Ratcliff provoked this unhappiness in her, that he was the source of her pain, and that she
came to me for solace. I did what I could, believe me, I felt
for her, and it was torture for me to see her suffer, as it's
torture to see *you* suffer, precious boy—! But I was on the
ward one night when a porter appeared and told me that a
Mrs. Piker-Smith was waiting to see me downstairs.

I hurried down to the lobby; it was your mother of course.
She was in the black fur, and a close-fitting black hat with a
net veil spangled with tiny black stars. "I shouldn't really
leave the ward," I whispered. She lifted a gloved hand and
laid a finger against my lips.

The lobby of St. Basil's is an echoing, pillared hall with mar-
bled floors and portraits of governors past and present hung

on the walls. By day it is like a railway station, milling with people, a din of noise; by night it is silent, and thick with shadows; deserted but for a cleaner with her bucket and mop. From the back of the hall a stone staircase descends by two flights to Pathology, Medical Records, and the incinerator room. Beside the staircase, against the back wall, and hidden from view by a pillar, stands a wooden bench, and I followed your mother, tiny veiled figure in a huge black fur, heels clicking on the tiles, across the lobby and behind the pillar to this bench. We sat down. She turned to me, lifting the veil and folding it carefully back upon her hat. Her face was in shadow, for little light penetrated the space behind the pillar. Her lipstick looked black in the gloom. I tried to take her in my arms but she pulled away, turned her back to me and groped for cigarettes. I lit two, gave her one, and we smoked; all evening, she said, she'd been restless and on edge. Her voice had a sort of somber, breathless urgency to it. Ratcliff had gone to some function at the Royal Society of Medicine, leaving her alone in the house, and eventually she'd been unable to read any longer and had gone up to her room, intending to put on her coat and go for a walk. It was then that the idea of visiting me at St. Basil's had come to her.

After a first recoil of shock at the audacity of it, and the risk involved, it had occurred to her to wear her veil. Entering the hospital and waiting for me in the lobby had aroused anxiety, but now, she said, she felt calm. She leaned toward me, threw away her cigarette, and this time allowed me to kiss her. The pervasive hospital smell, bleach and antiseptic, mingled in my nostrils with her perfume. I took her gloved hands and in a low voice told her I wanted to spend all night with her. She seized my face and kissed me several times, small, rapid kisses, murmuring no, telling me that I must get back to work and she must go home. I lost control at that point, and so did she, and kissing, now, with passionate urgency, we fumbled at each other's clothing, pulling at buttons and clips, and we managed, somehow, to get my trousers open, and her skirt pushed up, and still in the big fur coat she climbed into my lap and there on the bench at the back of the lobby of one of the great London teaching hospitals we made hasty passionate love that left us dazed and panting and clinging to one another in disordered lethargy and I (as usual) began to cry, which aroused your mother to the realities of the situation, so stroking my head and making little tender clucking noises she gently pushed me away and readjusted her clothing and by the flame of her cigarette lighter attended to her face in the mirror of her powder compact. My own excitement subsided. I buttoned my trousers and retrieved my stethoscope from under the bench. I became aware of how peaceful the lobby was, the stillness and silence curiously restful, as though we were in a cathedral. I turned back to her. The flame of her lighter trembled as a small draft crept among the pillars, and the obscure, flickering reflection of her face was for an instant eerily distorted in the tiny glass of the compact. Satisifed, finally, that no trace of the recent brief passion remained, she snapped it shut. "Now back to work," she whispered, and we rose to our feet. After a last embrace I made off through the shadows.

Suddenly, footsteps! From the staircase appeared Miggs with a rack of test tubes, and I saw your mother turn toward him. "Evening, Mrs. Vaughan," he said, without apparent surprise, and passed on. Good God, her veil! She'd forgotten about it! She hadn't replaced her veil!

Later she told me about the journey back to Plantagenet Gardens. Miggs had seen her—this thought was of course uppermost in her mind, but the odd thing was, instead of feeling acute alarm she felt exhilarated—why? Because she was adrift in love's dream, and nothing could touch her because nothing else mattered—was this it? Or was there some other reason, some perverse longing for crisis, or the ecstasy of the abyss—James, I *don't know!*

• • •

Perhaps you do. Perhaps you understand her better than I do.
We didn't ever solve the problem of how to talk to each other
about her, did we? After the evening you asked me if she'd
"thrown herself" at me I realized it was impossible—that is,
that the son of a beautiful mother could share with that woman's lover any sort of common language with regard to her, or
not, at least, in any *direct* way. I couldn't speak to you about
the sexual expression of our love. I could never tell you what
happened to me just by *looking* at her—watching her walk
into a room in front of me, a tearoom, the saloon bar of the
Two Eagles, even watching her cross to the window in Jubilee
Road—she was so straight and slim and lovely I yearned for
her with every cell of my body. She'd turn and she'd see it
in my eyes, and seeing it, she would feel the desire aroused
in *her*, and then we would be in each other's arms. I loved
her as a woman, her skin, her small perfect limbs, her lips,
her hair. She loved me as a man, she adored this ill-propor-
tioned body of mine, she adored my penis, adored its en-
gorgement, thick-veined and large-headed—not unlike
myself!—her fingers were skillful with my trouser buttons,
and the mere touch of them upon the fabric quickened my
arousal such that by the time she pulled me free of my clothing
I would be as eager for her small soft tender mouth, her little
teeth, as she was for me, and this lasted only long enough to
become so intolerably exquisite that nothing would do but
that I be inside her, and this she would effect with those quick
deft fingers and then we'd cling together and be one until
orgasm swept us onto another, higher plane—small wonder
afterwards that I cried! None of this I could ever tell you,
though I wanted to, for it was the direct erotic manifestation
of our spiritual communion.

As, in a way, are you.

I remember it was Mrs. Gregor who first set me thinking,
after you'd been to tea one afternoon. She'd brought us up a

tray and on it a plate of macaroons and a Dundee cake. I've a sweet tooth myself and will often work all day on a piece of chocolate, so I didn't notice that between us we ate all the macaroons *and* the Dundee cake—but Mrs. Gregor did, she was fond of you. "That young man likes his cake," she remarked, when I came back in from seeing you off and found her in the hall putting on her coat in front of the mirror. I was about to go into the surgery. "Oh?" I said, and I don't know why this is—call it a doctor's intuition—but I paused there and paid close attention to what she was telling me. Some sort of warning bell went off, I suppose. Mrs. Gregor was straightening her hat. Without taking her eyes off her reflection in the mirror she said: "I'd thought that cake would do us another week."

"Did we eat it all, Mrs. Gregor?"

"I don't know that you did much of the eating, doctor. You've never been much of a one for Dundee cake."

I went into the surgery and closed the door behind me. So. One more thing I knew about you. You resembled your mother, you blushed easily, you flew Spitfires—and you loved sweet things. I think at some level of my unconscious mind I began to form a hazy, tentative hypothesis. I stress unconscious; it was weeks before I had a clear clinical picture. But I think even in the first days of our friendship I was alert to the symptoms that would eventually organize themselves into a diagnostic pattern, a dramatically disturbing pattern, not only for you but for me, too, as your friend and physician.

Yes, perhaps I should have spotted it sooner. Oh, but it was a cold, cold winter, this last one, the coldest in forty-five years and never have I had such grief from Spike since the early days—my God he was vicious! I understand why, of course—damaged bone grinding against its seating in the pelvis—but that does little to help. Nor was it just late at night, as is generally the case, this winter Spike was active all day, and all night too. I was forced to rely rather more extensively than usual on the morphia; I needed a shot just to get through morning surgery, and another after lunch for afternoon rounds, if I was to be any use to my patients at all (what patients I still had). So it was not an easy winter, and the effects of it lasted through the spring and into the summer. Which makes me wonder if I shouldn't have realized sooner that something was seriously wrong.

Daffodils were coming up in the parks of London—Nazis were marching triumphantly into Vienna—and for your mother and me the first augurs of disaster made themselves known. It can't have gone unnoticed that I was less single-mindedly focused on my work than I'd once been, and it wasn't just the hours here and there when I slipped away for trysts with your mother while McGuinness covered for me. All doctors make these arrangements, if they're to have any private life at all. No, it was more a matter of attitude. My heart wasn't in it anymore, and this sad fact was demonstrated to the entire hospital with the ghastly mess I made one morning of a simple appendicectomy.

It's a delicate thing, opening a man's belly. You draw the knife across the skin, the flesh parts, you clamp the severed vessels, sponge the blood, suture and tie, cut through the yellow fat beneath, then the fascia, clamp, sponge, suture, tie, then the peritoneum, and so on. But I went in with such force I cut right through the fascia with the first stroke of the knife, opening numerous blood vessels, and then, while tying them off, somehow sewed the end of my rubber glove into the wound. I was rather shaken by this, and botched the rest of the operation. The patient recovered, eventually, but he had a complicated convalescence and became enormously distended, with the result that the nursing staff referred to him as "Dr. Haggard's pregnant man." What particularly irritated Vincent Cushing was that the rubber glove story went all over St. Basil's, and as I was part of his team he was subjected indirectly to ridicule. This rankled.

He called me into his office. He stood gazing out of his

window onto the courtyard below, his pudgy little hands clasped behind his back. "Dr. Haggard," he said at last, "you've been on my service for six months."

"Yes sir."

He turned. He frowned. Then: "Surgery is the most exacting branch of medicine."

Another pause. He went to his desk and sat down. I was anticipating more of the same, but instead he looked up at me and said, "I can get you transferred to the medical service tomorrow, and you would go with a strong letter of referral." Good God, was I being *sacked?* This was a shock. "Is that what you want, doctor?"

"Actually no, sir," I said, "not at all. I would like to finish my residency with you."

"I see." Pause, cough, frown. "Why, then, doctor, have you apparently lost your taste for the work? You know what's required of you."

"Yes, I do." I pushed a hand through my hair. "I've been preoccupied. I know I shouldn't let it interfere but I'm afraid it has. It won't happen again."

"Preoccupied—?"

"Family problems."

"Oh?"

"My uncle has been ill."

"Something serious, I take it."

"Cancer. Inoperable."

"I'm sorry. You're close to him?"

"My people are dead, sir. He's my only relative."

He was a hard but not a heartless man, he said, and he maintained high standards on his service because it was his responsibility to train able surgeons—though I hadn't forgotten the business with Eddie Bell. "I do sympathize," he said. "At the same time, as I'm sure I need not remind you, the physician has not the luxury of dwelling on his personal problems while he is attending patients."

"I know."

"You may make a surgeon, Dr. Haggard, I don't rule out the possibility. Frankly I'm unhappy with your performance. I shall be watching your work closely in future."

That was all. I was not a happy man as I walked away from Cushing's office. I seemed on the point of throwing away a career in surgery for love of your mother. This must not happen, I told myself, though the truth was, in my heart I didn't care. I didn't care. All professional ambition had paled and withered in the shadow of this grand passion, and I'd have happily exchanged a lifetime of surgical work for twenty-four uninterrupted hours alone with her.

I did try, in the days following, to do better, but it wasn't easy. My mind wandered constantly. Faced with a suppurating abscess, I saw the smooth white skin of your mother's breast. Removing a dirty dressing, and finding a black patch of necrotic tissue, I imagined placing delicate kisses on her belly. Encountering death, I remembered her clinging to me and gasping with pleasure on a bench at the back of the hospital lobby. Wherever my eye fell, wherever I saw disease, or injury, or death, I also found hints and glimpses of beauty, and the difficulty lay in keeping my attention on morbidity when all my soul cried out to love.

But what place was there in this world for love?

I learned later that Ratcliff had found out almost immediately about your mother being in the hospital that night, but waited some days before asking for an explanation. Why did he wait? From what she told me I had the impression that he must have been frightened of the truth, of discovering just how dissatisfied she was with the marriage, in other words how badly he had failed her. But then, as the days passed, and she still did not allude to it, he must have worried at it with growing irritation. It was either of no importance, I imagined him thinking—which was unlikely—or else she was concealing it from him. But if she was concealing it, she must have known that Miggs would talk, in which case she would surely have brought it up, in order to allay any doubt or suspicion on his part, and this she had not done.

April came, the sky was pale as pearls, and the trees along Plantagenet Gardens were hazy with buds. It was on a warm evening in April, your mother told me, that Ratcliff first attempted to face the rift that had for years been opening between them, and which in recent months had widened at such an alarming rate. The dining room was a somber room, not a room that invited intimacy, and your mother had always disliked it, though recently, she said, she'd often thought of *me* there, and this, she said, had changed its associations, had superimposed upon the shapeless mass of memories of desultory meals with Ratcliff the idea of *love*, where it shimmered like a mist over a swamp: at this table, and upon this chair, she had sat thinking of her lover, and now the furniture glowed.

Ratcliff of course knew nothing of this. "Have you," he began, "thought any more about Scotland this summer?"

The last time he'd brought up the subject your mother had felt distinctly irritated at the idea of leaving London, and said something vague and noncommittal. "Scotland," she murmured now, setting down her knife and fork and touching her lips with her napkin; Iris had served them a nice shoulder of lamb. "No, I haven't. We should discuss it when James is here, I suppose."

"Oh, I doubt we'll see much of him this summer. I've told him he can start flying lessons."

"You haven't! Oh Ratcliff."

This was a shock. To think of you flying aeroplanes—you were still (in her mind) a child. She said this to Ratcliff. "No he's not," he said. "He's not a child anymore. We have to accept this."

"But it's so dangerous!"

"He has to try it. If he can't fly with our blessing, he'll fly without it."

And then a curious thing happened. All her resistance to

the idea, the surge of maternal anxiety it had provoked—it all just evaporated, leaving her strangely indifferent. Let him fly, then, she thought. If he wants to fly—if Ratcliff wants him to fly—so be it. She gave a small shrug of her shoulders. "Very well," she murmured, reaching for the mint sauce. Ratcliff frowned at her as he tore a bread roll part. What did this mean, this sudden lapse into unconcern? (She was in love, of course, that's what it meant, and like me could think of little else.) "Then you don't object?" he said.

"What does it matter if I object or not? You seem to have decided the issue."

"Frances, what *is* the matter with you these days?" A note of exasperation here. "You seem to care about nothing anymore. Don't you owe me the courtesy of an explanation?"

She raised her eyebrows at this. "Frankly I don't think I do." She gazed at him across the table and after a moment he took off his spectacles and rubbed his eyes with his thumb and index finger. She caught a faint whiff of formalin. How pregnant must have been the few seconds of silence that followed that candid gaze! What a complex private history underscored that silence, the long years of emotional negotiation they had endured to reach this present state of mutual balanced toleration! The membrane of marital order could take so much stress and no more, to this they had both been sensitive for some time, neither of them willing to see it torn. But something had changed, this much was clear, and Ratcliff persevered. "Something has happened," he said. "I don't know what it is, and I'm not altogether sure I want to. But you do owe me this, you know, you owe me at the least a modicum of candor."

Again she lifted her eyebrows and said nothing. Her silence seemed to infuriate him. "Well? What do you say to that? What's your answer?"

"What's your question?" she retorted. She felt suddenly terribly weary, she told me afterwards. It was all so tedious, so predictable.

Ratcliff sighed. He poured himself more wine. Iris came in to clear away the dinner plates. They generally went straight from the main course to cheese and fruit and coffee, if they had no guests. When Iris had left the room Ratcliff said flatly, "What were you doing in the hospital the night I was at the RSM?"

"Was I?" she said. "Could I have the grapes, please, Ratcliff?"

"You met Miggs. He told me, of course. He thought it odd that you should be there at that time of the evening. So do I."

"For God's sake!" She was certainly not going to be cross-examined like some errant medical student! "How dare you speak to me like that! How dare you sit there and tell me that you and Miggs find my behavior odd! What else does Miggs say about me?"

"I don't discuss you with Miggs. As well you know. I merely ask: what were you doing in the hospital?"

"And I tell you, I resent bitterly—*bitterly*—the implication that I was 'doing' anything that would oblige me to give you an explanation."

"Nevertheless I ask you for an explanation."

"And on principle I refuse to give you one."

They were both bolt upright in their chairs, she told me, tense and furious. And what happened then, I wanted to know? Your mother gave a slight shrug. He backed off, she said. But why, I cried? It seemed most peculiar. I expect he doesn't really want to know, she said. She described how he sank back against his chair. "All right," he said, tight-lipped now, controlling his anger. He folded his napkin precisely, rolled it tight and thrust it into its ring. "We'll talk about it later."

"I'm going upstairs," your mother said coldly. "Please ask Iris to bring up my coffee."

"Frances."

She paused at the door.

"I apologize for losing my temper."

She went out without another word. She hadn't heard the last of it. Oh, it was becoming much too complicated, she wished it were all simple again. Damn him! Damn him for smelling a rat!

"Oh damn Ratcliff. What a bloody nuisance. Were you very upset, my darling?" It was eleven o'clock in the morning of a fine day in the middle of April, and your mother and I were in my flat in Jubilee Road. She'd been undecided whether she should tell me about it, and had said nothing immediately; but I'd quickly realized that all was not well, and after some concerned probing she'd told me everything, or almost everything; actually I'd begun to suspect that she never gave me a full account of what went on between herself and Ratcliff, perhaps because she could not convey the deep and subtle pattern in the fabric of that long, complicated relationship, its contradictory figures of attachment, resentment, and neglect. It made me feel desperate, being excluded from the hermetic web of her marriage. What I never really grasped was the idea that love may languish, even die, while attachment endures. By this stage I fervently desired her to leave Ratcliff and live with me, at whatever cost; but though I may have hinted to her of this I had never put it to her in frank and unambiguous terms.

There were flowers on the table, a large bunch of tiger lilies that she had brought. She had introduced flowers into my flat early in the relationship. They were leafy-stemmed, bulbous lilies, the speckled, pale orange petals folded back to allow the trembling stigma to thrust forth stiffly amid its cluster of slender, anther-tipped filaments, and a strong shaft of morning sunshine had unerringly sought them out where they fountained in profusion from a simple white porcelain vase, also introduced into the flat by your mother.

"Was I upset? Yes, I was very upset. He made me feel like a criminal."

"I wish—"

"Yes?"

"Nothing." She was sitting in an armchair and I was on the Persian rug with my back against her legs, gazing at the ceiling. Our fingers were interlaced, probing and playing with one another. "Do you think of leaving him?"

It was asked tentatively. "Oh darling," she murmured, "what would I do?"

"Live with me?"

She said nothing, though our fingers continued to speak. Each of us sensed what would be involved in pursuing this line of thought. I was nervous, and classified it as faintheartedness, and despised myself for it. I knew that the conversation must be had soon, and when that happened I would take my courage in both hands and properly propose the very thing that now gave me such anxiety even to think about. "What's to be done?" I said quietly.

"I don't want to think about him," your mother said, and slipped out of the armchair and knelt on the rug beside me. "Lie down," she said, so I stretched out on the carpet with my hands clasped behind my head. I was in a sleeveless V-necked argyll jersey and gray flannels; she was in an elegant pale green tweed suit with boxy shoulders and a snug felt hat. She unbuttoned my trousers. Easing her skirt up over her thighs she carefully settled herself athwart me. She gazed down at me through half-closed eyes, and the smile on her lips was the one I remembered from that funeral. Her fingers were busy with the clips of her suspender belt. I rubbed the head of my penis against the soft skin of her inner thigh, above the top of her stocking. "What do you think you're doing?" she murmured. "Now don't get me all messed up, I'm having lunch with someone."

"I'm giving you a physical."

"Oh you are, are you." She lifted herself slightly and made some adjustment to her underwear such that I was able to slip just the crown inside her. "That's all you're allowed," she said, "it's more than you deserve."

I pushed up slightly—a small intake of breath. "Stop that," she whispered. Her eyes were closed, her chin lifted, her lips parted. "I'll be late."

Another small push: exquisitely tantalizing! "Who are you having lunch with?" The gas fire hissed in my ear.

"Mind your own business." Still with her eyes closed she suddenly sank down on me with a long soft groan. A tide of warmth swept through my body. "I'll have you struck off for this," she breathed. Ominous words.

As you lie here in my arms, as these memories sweep by, as the story unfolds, movement by movement, opening in my mind like a complex flower—I am filled with foreboding. For as with the clouds of war, so were the clouds of ending, of parting, of sorrow drawing close. "Love is a growing, or full constant light"—this I had experienced, and it had filled my heart with glory—"And his first minute, after noon, is night." That night now approached.

Betrayal. I am not exempt, none of us is. I betrayed Henry Bird, and the first inkling I had of it came the day after your mother and I made love on the floor of Jubilee Road. It came from Peter Martin. That morning a milkman had found yesterday's bottle still standing on Henry's doorstep. He'd raised the alarm, a policeman had broken in through the back door and discovered the old man unconscious on the kitchen floor. He was admitted to the cottage hospital and had not yet regained consciousness. "I am his physician," said Dr. Martin, "and he is not taking any medicine that I am aware of, so I think we may discount an overdose. I don't have to tell you," he went on, "that it's probably a stroke." I thanked him and hung up. The news shook me badly. It was not that Henry should have had a stroke (at his age cerebrovascular disease was common), it was, rather, the fact that I had been telling people he was seriously ill, so as to pursue my love affair. It was pure coincidence of course, so I told myself, but I couldn't escape the irrational conviction that this was my doing—that by imputing disease to the old man I had actually brought it on—*I* had made him ill.

Peter Martin telephoned me the next day. "I think," he said, "we can safely say he's had a massive cerebrovascular accident. What would you like me to do, doctor?"

I could picture it all too clearly, Henry lying in bed in the cottage hospital, his skin white as china, his hair fine as silk, looking as though he were fast asleep and dreaming of great houses. For a moment a wave of guilty sorrow almost overwhelmed me. Peter Martin broke the silence. "He seems," he said, "a little wheezy. I think perhaps we're seeing the early signs of pneumonia."

I understood what I was being asked. Pneumonia—the old man's friend. "I wouldn't advise giving him sulfonamides," I said.

"No, there's no point. You'll be coming down, then?"

"Yes."

"Then I look forward to meeting you. My house is Elgin, it's up on the cliffs."

There was nothing more to say. Henry was to be allowed to die in peace, and I would see to the funeral arrangements. I hung up the telephone feeling very bad indeed. A week later the pneumonia carried him off, but I didn't go down to Griffin Head to make the arrangements, nor did I attend the funeral. I was in traction.

It was a wet, windy night and the pub was almost empty. A girl stood behind the bar drying glasses and gazing across the room in an abstracted, unfocused manner. She was miles away.

The few lamps hanging from the ceiling in dusty globes emitted a gloomy, yellowish light redolent somehow of weariness and loss. A woman with Parkinson's sat at a table by the fire with a glass of stout, which she lifted to her lips with the trembling fingers of both hands. The clock behind the bar ticked mournfully; no one spoke. I was exhausted, having been on call for seventy-two hours, and your mother was in very low spirits indeed. I was much in need of sleep—failing that, of conviviality, stimulation—but none was forthcoming, and with what little energy I could muster I made an effort to cheer her. I set my elbows on the table and leaning forward took her hands. Her eyes briefly registered irritation, then softened slightly. Something in her sad face strained toward me but failed to emerge or connect. I had never seen her like this. "Tired?" I said.

She pulled her hands free and shook her head. "No. Oh I don't know, it's all such a bore."

"What's the matter?" It was not easy for either of us, with Ratcliff so suspicious. She touched her hair, looking not at me but off to one side, unable to meet my eye. "I start to wonder if it's worth the trouble," she said, "I can't"—she paused, and produced a sort of sigh, as though it was an effort just to voice the words—"I can't endure much more of this." Still without looking at me she groped for my hands. "What about me?" I whispered. Was it the end? A flurry of rain suddenly lashed the window and she startled nervously. After a while she began to speak calmly. "I don't have the strength for it, darling. He knows how to wear me down, and he'll do it, he'll drive you away no matter what you do. No matter how much you try to hold on to me he'll drive you away. He doesn't know who you are but he knows that you exist, and he won't tolerate it. He's too strong for me."

"Then leave him!"

"Oh darling." She lit a cigarette. There was impatience and scorn in her voice. "Leave him for what? To live on a registrar's

salary? Love in a hut. Not even that. You couldn't continue
at St. Basil's if you lived with me. Use your imagination."

I was silent, reeling.

"You don't even light my cigarettes anymore. It can't go
on, you must see that."

"No!" A cry of pain, this. She turned to me and her eyes
briefly filled with tears. "I'm sorry, my darling, but we must
be sensible. There's James to think of too."

After that there was no getting through to her. She didn't
have much time. We spent another ten minutes in that dreary
pub and a grim ten minutes it was. No sort of intimacy seemed
possible. I tried to arouse in her the familiar bonds of affection—complicity—recognition even—I just wanted her to
recognize me, give me back a glimmer of something real—
but it was as though her real self had sunk like a guttering
flame and all there was in its place was this ghastly brittle talk
of being sensible, and that deadness in her eyes and voice as
though the words she was speaking were detached from all
meaning and emotion. Never had she shown this face to me
before. Not only was she showing me the face, she was using
it as a screen for an emptiness, out of which issued nothing
but this lucid unfeeling talk of ending it. Only once did she
show any emotion, connect with me at all, and that was when
she pleaded with me not to try and make her change her
mind. It would only make things worse for her. Anyway, I'd
be better off without her, she said. I'd be well rid of her, she
said, she'd only cause me pain—and she made me promise.
There in the shabby little saloon bar of the Two Eagles, as
an old clock ticked and a lonely old woman with shaking hands
sat mumbling to herself in the corner, I gave in and promised
her I wouldn't try and make her change her mind. Why did
I do it? Because at that moment, worried, exhausted, and
depressed as I was, I saw no way out. So I promised. I only
broke that promise once, but oh, with what disastrous
consequences!

Now things began to move rather quickly. The following afternoon your father performed a postmortem on a body pulled out of the Thames just below Lambeth Bridge. It had been in the river for at least two months, and the stench of it quickly spread through the entire hospital. It took him little more than an hour, by which time he had the entire heart and slices of all the other organs laid out on a tray that went into the refrigerator, covered with a damp cloth, for gross examination in the morning. Most pathologists wear rubber gloves for dissecting cadavers, but not all. Some prefer bare hands. Your father was a bare-hands man. Although there was a risk, if he cut himself while handling a diseased organ, of acquiring whatever infection that organ harbored, he believed that rubber gloves interfered with his sense of touch and hence with the accurate interpretation of the pathology.

Upstairs on the surgical ward I was as aware as everybody else of the stink of the floater and it did nothing to relieve the cloud of gloom under which I had labored since the meeting with your mother in the Two Eagles. I couldn't accept that I wasn't going to see her again. I simply didn't believe it. We'd been tired and depressed, I told myself, we'd feel differently in a day or two. I also had the worry of Henry. So I shambled about the hospital with my hands plunged deep in my pockets, head bowed and shoulders slumped, a picture of dejection and a far cry from my usual brisk self. Perhaps, I suddenly thought, she was feeling the same, perhaps she too found it impossible to think of us not meeting again? I was making dressing rounds with Sister, going from patient to patient, taking off old bandages and putting on new ones. The work was straightforward, and my mind drifted as I snipped at soiled and bloody dressings with my bandage scissors. Perhaps I should telephone her at home? It was risky, but this was an emergency. I needed to see her. Ratcliff was obviously still at work, the smell rising from the basement was ample evidence of that.

I was wrong. Ratcliff was back at Plantagenet Gardens when the telephone rang. He had come home twenty minutes earlier and without announcing his presence gone straight into his study. He didn't want to see your mother immediately. There had been tension between them for days now, which neither had attempted to relieve. I would imagine that all he wanted, after dissecting a floater, was to have a drink and listen to a little Mozart. Then the phone had rung. He'd heard her pick it up upstairs. From an impulse that he did not attempt to resist he reached for the telephone on his desk and very gently took the receiver off the hook and brought it to his ear. He heard your mother saying it was impossible (what was impossible?) and a man's voice saying that he only wanted an hour, and he was so shocked that he replaced the receiver almost immediately. But he had heard two names. One was his own; the other was mine.

Dinner, I would guess, was a strained affair that night. Having recovered from the first impact of moral shock aroused by hearing his wife making illicit arrangements on the telephone, Ratcliff had probably had to consider carefully what he ought to do next. Your mother once told me that in his way he was a passionate man, but that he placed no value on the expression of passion outside those situations in which he felt it appropriate. It was appropriate in the context of marital sexuality, he thought. It was appropriate on occasion when one fought the necessary battles that a responsible professional life demanded. It was not appropriate in politics, nor was it appropriate in the situation in which he now found himself. So he had not gone storming upstairs to confront your mother with what he had heard. He had, instead, as a reasonable man, tried to think beyond his anger. The impulse to revenge must be discounted. The desire to punish her was no basis for action, and by the pure exercise of will he waited out the first turmoil of hurt and rage so that he could decide what was best. There was also, I believe, his reluctance to face the truth, to acknowledge the extent to which he'd failed your mother.

By the time he heard the bell for dinner he'd resolved to say nothing. I don't believe he wanted to abandon his marriage. And I think it more than likely that he applied to this unhappy situation his own principles of pathology. Function was being revealed by failure. The *pathos* was conditioning the *logos*. He could not live with your mother in a state of emotional estrangement anymore. For too long he'd allowed them to live parallel lives. This present dysfunction proved it. He would expend every effort to recover the health of his marriage, and he expected to succeed—hadn't he always succeeded in carrying out his intentions, once he had properly formulated them? He knew your mother (he thought), he knew her weakness, he understood her in ways she did not understand herself. So he thought. Or so, at any rate, I imagine him thinking.

So there they sat at dinner in that somber dining room, where only the ticking of the clock on the mantelpiece, and the clatter of cutlery, broke the charged silence between them. They were having fish. He asked her if she would like a game of chess after dinner, but she'd promised to go round and see Brenda for an hour. He nodded and said no more. Your mother did not linger for coffee, but excused herself and went upstairs to put on her hat. Ratcliff was in his study when she left the house ten minutes later. Perhaps it saddened him to think of her doing damage to their marriage. Perhaps it saddened him to think that he was in some way responsible for that unhappiness. But now it had become a problem, a difficult, delicate problem of erasing the source of the unhappiness, undoing the damage, and bringing her home again.

He telephoned Brenda, ashamed of himself, I daresay, for doing it, but doing it all the same. Brenda improvised bravely. Fanny had said she might drop in but she hadn't appeared yet. So she was in on it too, thought Ratcliff, as he replaced the receiver. Then he sank back in his armchair, pressed his palms together with his fingertips just touching his lips, and frowned. Edward. Edward. Where had he heard the name recently? Who had been talking to him about someone called Edward? Then he had it: Vincent Cushing. One of Vincent Cushing's people had sewn the end of his rubber glove into a patient's stomach: Edward Haggard. Good God, he knew the man! They'd even sat at the same dinner table, at Cushing's house! Haggard had been at the other end, making Fanny laugh all night!

Ratcliff telephoned St. Basil's. He asked if Dr. Haggard was on duty. Yes he was, but he wasn't on the ward. He'd gone out for an hour. Would he like to speak to Dr. McGuinness? No, said Ratcliff, that wouldn't be necessary.

I was walking with your mother down a deserted street of decaying Georgian houses behind the hospital. It was a cool evening. The sky was not black, rather that curious shade of dark blue that makes you think of the hour before dawn. Strips of cloud scudded across a gibbous moon like rags and streamers chasing some ghostly night parade. Your mother had linked her arm in mine, and drawn in close to me, pressing against me as we walked. I'd told her about Henry Bird, who lay unconscious in the hospital in Griffin Head, and just talking about my fear that I'd caused his illness made it seem absurd. "Probably an aneurysm," said your mother. "It was there in his brain long before you even met me." She was not angry that I'd broken my promise and telephoned her. She told me she liked it that I needed her. Ratcliff never needed her, she said, he was self-sufficient, always in control. He had never shown weakness. Why should this make her unhappy? It stifled her. His strength stifled and limited her, such that she felt needed only by her child, by you, and even you were slipping away from her now, slipping into manhood and all that went with it.

How sad she was that night, almost as if she knew what was about to happen, all the horror. I hadn't dared to ask her if she'd changed her mind, so I didn't know if we were going on as before, or if these were our last moments. We stopped beneath a lamppost. Cupping her cheeks in my hands, my fingers still smelling of antiseptic, I kissed her eyes and forehead and the tip of her nose and felt again the familiar, potent, unsteady wave come coursing through me and leave me trembling, for it was at times too much, what I felt for her. The streetlight bathed her features in a yellowy radiance, her parted lips, her eyes searching my face, the frown of anxiety and unhappiness. "Darling Edward," she murmured. We walked on. The scene is etched in my mind.

When she let herself back into the house the light in the study was on and the door was open. "Is that you?" Ratcliff called, and she paused in the doorway of the study. "How is Brenda?"

"Brenda's fine."

"And Anthony?"

"I didn't see Anthony."

"Like to sit down and have a drink?"

"I think I won't, Ratcliff. I'm going up."

"As you please."

Anger then, surely, a black surge of it that he must have controlled only with the utmost difficulty. She wouldn't even sit down and have a drink with him. But he did control it. He had determined the course of action he would follow, and he was not going to sabotage it with rash outbursts, no matter what the provocation.

At this point, of the three of us, only Ratcliff fully understood what we were moving toward, only he knew that these in a sense were the last days. Your mother must have suspected, but we'd parted on a somewhat ambivalent note. As for me, what was about to happen, what Ratcliff was about to do, would come as the most violent of shocks, and have the most far-reaching of consequences—I feel them to this day.

Oh God.

So was this why you abandoned me, was this why you renounced me, threw me over, left me broken, in *all* senses broken—shunned, ignored, wretched, friendless, alone? Surely not, surely you would not so easily surrender what we had, yet you did, you allowed him to drive a wedge between us—!

Oh God.

He called you into the study again, didn't he? Isn't that how it happened? He called you in—you didn't want to see him then, he'd already hinted to you that he'd found out, and I imagine Brenda had telephoned by this time and told you about his calling her—so you must have known what was up. He was standing by the fireplace. "What is it, Ratcliff?" you said, and you avoided his eye as you crossed the room to the cigarette case on the low table, and busied yourself there. You were in gray that evening, the gray dress of soft wool, long-sleeved and tightly belted at the waist, which I loved—you moved across the room in that clingy dress, that sheath of gray wool, and stood frowning as you lit your cigarette and Ratcliff started in on you. *Why* did you give in to him? Oh, he is a man of strong will, I know, I've experienced the force of his personality, I've seen him storming down the corridors of St. Basil's so I do understand how intimidating he can be. But you are strong also! And didn't you think of me—that I was *with* you, and could give you all the support you might possibly need? All you had to do was stand firm in front of him for those few minutes, defy the man, refuse to crumble before his inquisition—why, why, my darling, need that have been so difficult, when you *knew* I was waiting, and you *knew* the strength of my commitment—? But you did. You allowed him to overwhelm you, and though I have been shattered and destroyed by this I bear no anger toward you. You were not strong enough—I understand. He told you he knew you weren't at Brenda's; he was bluffing, but you weren't to know this.

Oh God—

Oh God, not you, darling boy, your *mother!* Your *mother!* Oh my angel, my precious boy—

I have a picture in my mind of your mother coming into your bedroom, late at night, and you sitting at your table with a lamp focused on the model aeroplane you're building, and her standing there in the doorway, smoking, her dark form framed by the light from the upstairs landing, watching, silently, as with slim precise fingers you delicately assemble a wing—

Flight—how you loved flight—

And do you remember the evenings we had in Elgin? When we talked of ideas like the spirit, and the higher will, and service? And the quest for the infinite? You'd come after evening surgery, perhaps share the cold supper Mrs. Gregor had left, then we'd go upstairs. I'd read to you in the study, or we'd simply talk. Often we wouldn't turn the lights on, we'd watch the sunset smoldering on the horizon, burnishing the lip of the sea. I'd offer you a drink, but generally you refused. Oh, there was something in the atmosphere of that large, empty house, with the last glow of sunset, the gloom, the poetry we'd shared—a coming together of influences that was intoxicating for both of us, do you remember? I once told you facetiously after we'd read a little Swinburne together that we were bound to win the war because we were so much crueler than the Germans, and when (a little bewildered I suspect!) you asked me why I thought so, I clapped shut the Swinburne, waved it in the air, and cried: "That's why!" That made you laugh, didn't it!

Oh, and I'd pace the room, I'd limp up and down, talking of this and that—in a certain sort of mood, with a certain sort of listener, and among my own books, I'm the kind of man who can talk for hours on end without once repeating himself, or failing to entertain, and you of course know how to listen, I always appreciated that in you, and listen you did, you gave me the sympathetic ear I needed, you encouraged me to wander, intellectually, from topic to topic, and occasionally, inevitably, I'd drift into areas of purely personal concern. I remember once showing you a picture I was particularly fond of, a reproduction of a romantic painting of a heap of icy debris in an empty polar vastness, and telling you that landscape was a state of the soul; and when you looked doubtful I said painting should never be an act of imitation but rather a refusal to imitate, because art, after all, must finally aspire to passion—and you said, "Passion?"

I paused in my pacing, I limped to the window and gazed out. "She believed it was the best we were capable of," I murmured, "civilized human beings."

"Who did?"

This was asked in the softest of tones, it was the merest breath from the shadows. I said nothing. I leaned my forearm on the window sash, then leaned my forehead against my arm, and allowed my weight to rest on my good leg as I looked out at the sea, from which the last of the sunset had by this time vanished entirely. Neither of us broke the silence. You knew who I was talking about. I said this. You said, "She thought there was nothing better than passion? Physical passion?"

The moral asceticism of youth. "I don't think it was quite as simple as that," I said, turning from the window and facing you across the darkness. "I don't think you should judge her harshly."

"She never wanted me to fly," you said. You were all in shadow at the far end of the room, in an old high-backed wing chair of Peter Martin's. "She tried to convince me there wouldn't be a war."

"She loved you," I said. "She wanted to protect you. It's a mother's natural instinct."

"I asked her if she was against fascism. She said of course she was, but she was against war too."

"And?"

"I said she couldn't be against both of them."

It suddenly came to me, and with devastating clarity, that I was losing you. That after tonight you would never come back. You'd reached some sort of decision about your mother and the part I'd played in her life, and there was no more you wanted to know, even though I had barely begun the task of explaining it to you. "I don't think she really understood what was at stake," you said, and for the first time I heard in your voice, and in your thinking, the unmistakable tone of Ratcliff, and my heart sank. The idea that you would carry with you, perhaps for the rest of your life, Ratcliff's idea of her, and his contemptuous dismissal of our love affair and all that it meant—it was unthinkable. I flailed about in my mind for some means, any means, to prevent this happening. "Did your father talk to you about her illness?" I said.

I saw you turn toward me in the gloom. A pause.

"Why do you ask?"

"I wish I could have seen her, that's all."

"But why?"

I gave a slight shrug and turned back toward the window— oh, I had promised myself never to bring this up with you, but I was desperate, desperate not to lose you! "It's nothing," I murmured. "These cases—these obscure kidney condi- tions—they're complicated. Tricky to diagnose properly."

Again a pause. "You think she was diagnosed wrongly?"

"No no no. No, I'm sure everything was done that could be done. I'd have liked to examine her myself, that's all."

What did you make of this? I couldn't tell; you were of course far too delicate to impute to me a dishonorable motive. Silently the moments passed, and I hated myself for what I was doing—sowing a seed of unease, this was what I was doing, planting suspicion in you, suspicion that would only fester until it brought you to me again.

You rose to leave soon afterwards, troubled, I could see, by our conversation but unsure just why. I shook your hand at the front door, and you were always so sweet when you left me, rather formal, rather apologetic for having taken so much of my time. As if I had anything better to do! You mounted your bicycle, and I watched you wobble off down the drive in the dusk, wheels crunching on the gravel, small and slim and upright in the saddle. Just where the drive turns out onto the coast road you turned to wave and you saw me there in my black corduroy jacket and snowy white shirt, a silk cravat at my throat, and I lifted a hand, standing in the doorway of my dark, soaring, narrow house, then turned and went inside and closed the front door behind me, and so into the surgery to see to Spike. All this, of course, before our relationship became one of doctor and patient.

Doctor and patient . . . I am aware, at times, of the grandeur of my spirit. At such times I find it absurd that it is housed in this puny frame, which has become, since Spike, a ruin. This is why I fell in love with Elgin, it offered a structure adequate to me, for I am not a small man *spiritually*. It is a jest of nature and an irony of circumstance that I am trapped in this flawed and puny frame, though never, I think, has it been brought home to me so clearly, until I met you, or rather, until you began to suffer your peculiar glandular disturbance, just how far this tendency in nature for botch and error can go. For my concern that you understand the nature of my relationship with your mother was soon to be overshadowed by my concern for *you*, for you and what started happening to you as you continued daily to face violent death.

My last real encounter with your father occurred as I emerged, one afternoon, into the hospital lobby from the basement stairs, hard by the bench where your mother and I had made love. He was in a dark green leather apron under his white coat, about to descend. He stopped dead and glared at me.

I believe the sight of me enraged him. I believe he had worked himself into such a state of jealous rage he was unable to control himself. He seized me by the arm. He called me an odious worm. He said I was furtive, insidious and contempt- ible. He said I couldn't begin to understand the mischief I was creating, the harm I was doing: all this he hissed at me in a low voice that attracted no one's attention, a cigar between his teeth, all the while gripping my upper arm so hard I couldn't get away from him. It was when he accused me of harming your mother that I made my retort, and given what I've told you, you will understand that I acted with restraint, much good it did me. All I said was, words to the effect that it was *he* who'd harmed her, and that he wasn't worthy of her. He fell silent. He let go of my arm and turned away, then suddenly turned back and with a sort of vicious swatting mo- tion he slapped me with the back of his hand, very hard. The speed of the attack took me completely by surprise. I am a small man, and it knocked me off balance. My spectacles flew off. I remember thinking, in that first fraction of an instant when the mind operates with a sort of mad clarity, that I could regain my balance by flailing my arms about. So with white coat flapping, and stethoscope leaping wildly off my chest, and canting steeply backward, I windmilled there at the top of the stairs, but to no avail. I fell badly and hit the landing halfway down.

Of the fall itself I have no memory. One moment I stood flailing at the top of the staircase, the next I was lying in a heap on the landing, and when I tried to move there flared in my hip pain such as I had never before experienced, and would never have thought possible. Even as I lay there, nau- seous, unwilling to attempt the smallest movement lest it bring back the pain, I was perfectly aware of what had hap- pened, I had a clear picture of the pathology, it was quite obvious, really, after a fall like that: the neck of the femur was fractured. I'd broken my hip.

I suppose I must have passed out then. A dim awareness of faces and voices, of being loaded onto a stretcher, carried upstairs, and everything that jarred the hip had me crying out with pain. It wasn't until I was on a bed that someone gave me a shot of morphia and then, mercifully—nothing. The last thought I had, as the needle went in, was the phrase "pin and traction."

A broken hip is pretty straightforward. You open it up, dissect away the muscle, and bang in a steel pin. It's called a Smith-Petersen, and it holds the broken ends together. During cold weather, or when I'm tired, or if I've been on my feet too long, it'll produce inflammation in the femuro-pelvic joint, where the neck of the thighbone fits into the pelvis. Then it hurts like the devil, and that's when I need a shot of morphia to keep me cheerful—you know how I am when Spike's not behaving. And if it hadn't been for your father knocking me down the stairs that day I'd never have known the pleasure of Spike's company.

The ironies began crowding in on me thick and fast now. Not least among them was being admitted to St. Basil's as a patient, and then being assigned to a bed on my own surgical ward, with McGuinness my attending physician. It was a Nightingale ward, fifteen beds down either side of a long, high-ceilinged room, each with the patient's fever chart attached to a clipboard and dangling from a hook at the foot of the bed. The floors were parquet, and squeaked, the walls were painted pale green to shoulder height, white above, and there were three large windows down each wall with potted plants on the sills. The smell of antiseptic permeated everything. It was a busy place, patients shuffling about in dressing gowns, being wheeled off for this test or that—nurses running up and down—ward rounds morning and evening, when McGuinness would move from bed to bed with Sister—and twice a week grand rounds with Cushing himself.

God how I came to dread the sound of his footsteps as he

came clattering upstairs from the senior common room! I'm
well aware of the attitude surgeons hold toward fracture patients, they're a nuisance, frankly, tedious and time-consuming and not very interesting. They need X-rays, cast changes,
adjustments in traction, there are always a thousand small
things to be done for them, and you can never relax, for
although pinning a hip is the most common procedure on
fracture service, once you've started the operation the chances
of infection increase in almost direct proportion to the length
of time the incision is open. The body will tolerate the pin
only as long as there's no infection around it, so if infection
does set in it can't be cleared until the pin is removed, and
then you have to start all over again. So you must get it right
first time and pretty quickly too. Cushing took a sort of grim
relish in pointing all this out to me.

But the dominant feature of the period immediately after
your father attacked me was the pain. Cushing operated the
next day, whistling Puccini throughout, I'm told, and then I
was put in traction, my leg suspended from the knee with
weights attached to the ankle to stop the muscles pulling the
pin out of alignment. The pain began with each return to
consciousness, built rapidly to a peak, where it held with such
excruciating intensity it had me twisting from side to side
doing everything I could to keep from screaming, and not
always succeeding. McGuinness would be sent for (it all
seemed to take forever), but when he finally appeared, and
made his way down the ward to me, rather than feel relief at
his approach I would grow ever more frantic and by the time
he reached my bed I'd literally be *begging* for the needle, and
not even the twitch of contempt in his face could silence me,
that's how bad it was.

Oh, never presume to judge the severity of another's pain!
Never presume to judge what can be borne—dear boy, I need
hardly tell *you* this. McGuinness would sit at my bedside,
frowning, as he drew the fluid into the barrel of the syringe,
and he'd murmur: "Calm down, man, you'll get your shot"—

and even in my bleary wretchedness I could read his mind, he was thinking it contemptible that a man (and a doctor) should humiliate himself like this on a public ward. I didn't care. I just wanted the needle. At last I'd feel the prick, then the prickle, then I'd begin to sweat, my mouth would go dry, the pain would ease, and I'd lie there, soaked in sweat, gazing up at the Balkan frame of steel bars and pulleys over the bed, and in the now misty remnants of consciousness I'd breathe a prayer of thanks. Soon I'd drift into a shallow, restless sleep.

I gaze out over the airfield now and try to shake off the shame that clings to the memory of those days. It was terrible, terrible—the indignity of being dependent on the nurses for bowel and bladder functions. Being unable to turn over in bed, or reach for a book or a cigarette. Crumbs getting into the sheets. But worst of all, the pain. I tried to keep the injections down to two a day but I always needed more. I tried to control it—I bore it as best I could—but when it began truly to bite, when it climbed to that crest and simply *did not break*—then I'd feel my willpower loosen and shred like the fiber of an old rubber band. McGuinness would come, eventually, his face a mask of professional neutrality but I could see the pity and scorn it concealed. With wordless efficiency he'd give me my shot and after a moment or two the pain ebbed away, the lights grew brighter and I'd start to feel better, though curiously it wasn't that it disappeared, it was still there but it had lost the power to dominate consciousness to the exclusion of all else, it didn't matter, somehow, it didn't *hurt* anymore.

I'd know then a sense of expanding wonder; voices on the ward seemed to come from a thousand miles away, I'd think of your mother, and my heart would grow tender. Even then, you see, even in that utter extremity of suffering, she was with me, she was my inspiration, and I have come to believe that without her—without the knowledge that she was in the world, loving me—which I took on faith, she never visited me of course—without that, those early days would have been impossible. For I believe (Peter Martin taught me this) that spirit can be mobilized to a therapeutic end. My will to heal, to create a bony union in my femur, was in those first days grounded in the idea of your mother, so in a very real sense it was *through her* that I was able to inspire the resources of my body to fuse the fragments into a whole.

But they were strange and terrible, those days and nights in traction. I once awoke in darkness to the certainty that the wires of my Balkan frame were the spars and rigging of a ship, an eerie death ship about to cast off and carry me over a subterranean sea to some island of the dead from which I would never return. I struggled to get off the ship and in my panic managed to set the whole frame shaking, the whole complicated system of weights and pulleys, and in the process damn nearly tore Spike clean out of my hip. The night sister later told me that it was only with the greatest difficulty that they were able to subdue me and settle me down with a needle, for in my efforts to get off the ship I'd somehow found the strength of ten men.

When finally I was allowed out of bed, and started hobbling up and down the ward on crutches, I was a gaunt, gray, hollow-eyed creature, listless and ill-tempered, prone to headaches and itching and sudden waves of pain—and my hair was shot through with this wild streak of white. Because of the pain, and the morphia injections I had to have to control it, my arms were like pincushions, the punctures crowded together in rashes. I'd already been told that Henry Bird was dead, which did little to help, but as I say, at this stage I still believed in your mother, and remembered our last conversation, when she'd so deftly dispelled my feelings of guilt about him. I was even able to handle the shock of having Vincent Cushing come and tell me quite bluntly that I wouldn't be required on his service any longer. Even this I could cope with, for I'd already anticipated Ratcliff talking to him, urging my dismissal—and getting his way, for of course he shared with Cushing a near-impregnable position high in the hierarchy of St. Basil's. The

shame of it was, of course, that I couldn't say a word in my
own defense. I couldn't accuse him of knocking me down the
stairs, because that would have dragged your mother into it,
which was unthinkable. But yes, I could cope with it, because
I thought she loved me, believed in me, and was waiting for
me.

I was in traction for six weeks, and it was another six weeks
before I was able to bear weight on the leg. I changed. During
those terrible weeks, I changed. The gaunt gray man who
limped out of St. Basil's in the summer of 1938 was a very
different creature from the passionate fellow who'd stood his
ground that spring and told the senior pathologist what harm
he was doing his wife. Suffering leaves its mark; what is it
Wordsworth says?

> Suffering is permanent, obscure and dark,
> And shares the nature of infinity.

My suffering was certainly permanent; as to its darkness and
obscurity, your mother's rejection was the single worse shock
I had to bear—all of it I could have endured without faltering,
had she remained true. She did not; and though my love did
not abate in the slightest—it grew stronger, in fact—I was
forced to go forward alone. This tempered me. It matured
me. I aged many years in those short weeks, learned much
about the spirit and about that pear-shaped, fist-sized, four-
chambered bag we call the human heart. Poetry, you see, was
my great aid, in those dark nights, to know that what I was
experiencing had been experienced before, and by men who
could transmute that experience into beauty:

> Most wretched men
> Are cradled into poetry by wrong;
> They learn in suffering what they teach in song.

James, fallen angel: this is my song.

•   •   •

I still possess the letter she sent me. I'd intended one day to show it to you, but I don't suppose it matters now. It was shattering. I believe it would have devastated me even if I'd been in rude good health. It would have devastated any man. It didn't say much. We were never to see each other again. I was to keep my promise not to try and make her change her mind. It could never work for us—surely, she wrote, I must have known that? She had a son, a home, a marriage. It was over. No tenderness. No word of love. The first time I read it was like being struck full force in the face with a bucket of cold seawater. Spike started up immediately, and I had to shout for McGuinness though he'd seen to me only an hour before. What was I to do? What could I do? I smelled the hand of Ratcliff all over that letter. It was all too easy to imagine her situation: he would answer the telephone, intercept the mail, watch her like a hawk; any attempt on my part would only make things worse. I wasn't afraid of Ratcliff, don't think that. Despite what he'd done to me, don't think that. But I was afraid of what he might do to your mother, should I disobey her instructions.

I did on one occasion telephone her. It was the middle of the afternoon, so Ratcliff was almost certainly down in Pathology. I made my way on crutches to the end of the ward and the public telephone. In my dressing gown and slippers, and weak with pain and apprehension, I dialed the number. It was picked up on the fourth ring. "Yes?" she said. How flat her voice was. Devoid of expression, achingly, pathetically empty of feeling—this was what he'd brought her to. "It's me," I said, "can you talk?"

"Who is it?"

"Edward."

"Oh." A long pause. Then: "Yes?"

"I got your letter. I know you didn't mean it."

"I'm afraid I can't talk to you," she said in that cold, dead voice, and hung up the receiver. She was sealed off from me, in some grim prison of Ratcliff's making. The next afternoon a rather sinister thing happened. Lying on my bed I realized that he was standing at the end of the ward in a black rubber apron with his sleeves rolled up, staring straight at me. Then he was at my bedside! "You little fool, she doesn't want you," he hissed, "don't you understand that? *She doesn't want you!*" I tried to raise my head from the pillow but could not—the effort exhausted me—I was drenched in sweat—a wave of nausea swept over me—and when I opened my eyes again he was gone. She'd told him, then. I didn't try to reach her again.

Oh, I thought about it. I thought for a time it was my duty to reach her, to somehow get her away from Ratcliff and make her see what he was doing to her; I couldn't forget the tone of her voice when she'd said, "I'm afraid I can't talk to you." They echoed in my head, those dead flat tones, during the pain-racked days and nights I spent in St. Basil's, they devastated me, and it was a week before I finally began to attempt to accept the fact that I had to let her go. I have to let her go, I have to let her go: up and down the ward I'd hobble on my crutches, the words like the chant of a mob in my head, you have to let her go, you have to let her go—armies marching across Europe, and as they marched they chanted, you have to let her go, you have to let her go. "But I *cannot* let her go!"—I awoke one night with this scream on my lips, and woke the ward (what's worse I woke Spike too), but it did no good, those marching armies just kept on and on: you have to let her go, you have to let her go.

Eventually I was discharged from St. Basil's. I was getting about with just the aid of a stick by this time; the pain was still bad, and the scuffed leather medical kit I carried containing needle and ampoules was, if not the center of my existence, certainly necessary for my sense of security. I'd accepted the inevitable, and felt as though a loved one had died: I was in a state of mourning. My interest in the outside world was nil, and I was incapable of activity. I spent my days and nights shuffling wretchedly about my room in Jubilee Road, glancing into volumes of poetry only to toss them aside with weary indifference. I knew I would never love again. I would never do anything again. All I could do was grieve.

I told myself to forget her, but I thought about her constantly. Everything reminded me of her. The lamps. The rug. The fly-in-glass in my trouser pocket—I kept it over on Spike's side, they somehow seemed connected, Spike and the fly. I'd take it out a dozen times a day and turn it in my fingers till the sobs came, till the grief racked me anew, and that would get Spike going, and I'd have to reach for the scuffed leather medical kit to deal with the pain, for the one pain unfailingly engendered the other, as though a current flowed from heart to hip, and hip to heart. The Keats she gave me, which we'd read from together in front of the fire—it was practically crystalline with associations, as was the porcelain vase, the flowers (I never let Mrs. Kelly throw out her flowers)—dead now, these many weeks, and their water stinking, but I gathered the brittle fallen petals in a saucer and gazed at them for hours on end: *for she had touched them!* Her voice was in my dreams, though I hardly slept at all, but the semiconscious daze I'd slip into, after relieving Spike—it was then that I was most susceptible to her presence, the sound of her voice, her footfall on the landing outside my door—I'd heave up out of my chair at dead of night, and with the grotesque gait, part limp, part lurch, of the agitated cripple, haul myself over to the door and fling it wide and there'd be—nothing!

Nothing. I sank deeper into listless depression. It occurred to me that if I brought up the memory of every occasion on which we'd been together—what we'd done, what we'd said—I could somehow rob them of their power to ravage and devastate me. I could defuse them. It did no good. Worse: it exacerbated the pain, which got Spike going, so I'd have to have a shot, and then I'd hear her, and so it started all over again.

I was going mad.

I had to do something—good Good, I had to make a living! I forced myself to face facts. A career in surgery was no longer a possibility, so I had to think about general medicine. Positions in London were few, but I could easily enough find work as an assistant in some country practice and make five hundred pounds a year. And given all that had happened, given my state of mind, the idea of getting out of London actually roused, for the first time in weeks, a small faint flicker of interest—until, that is, the reality of country practice came home to me. Was this really the best I could hope for? The promising young doctor who'd won a coveted place at one of the great London teaching hospitals—was I now to become an overworked, underpaid assistant to some country doctor? It rather looked as though I was.

This provoked fresh despair, lassitude, self-reproach. I was worthless and despicable, and I deserved all the misfortune that had befallen me. I had never been anything but worthless and despicable, and it was impossible that your mother could ever have loved me. She was right to reject me. I was incapable of love, I was incapable of achieving anything of value, I was petty, narcissistic, dishonest, weak, and my one sole aim had always been to hide my weakness—this seemed undeniably true, for apparently I was now addicted to morphia as well. It only surprised me that I should have had to be brought so low to recognize it.

The salient feature of those days, then, a profound dissatisfaction with myself which, when it became particularly acute, set off Spike, which then had me reaching for my medical kit, and in the brief dreamy hours of release that followed your mother would become vividly present to me, which would set the whole sorry train in motion once more.

The dead, flat creature caught in a prison, and powerless to escape, was not, I then realized, your mother—it was me. No wonder she rejected me. Such were my thoughts. And any pity I may have felt for her, should, I saw, in justice, have been directed toward myself: it was *I* who was weak and powerless! Thus I railed at myself, thus did I make myself suffer, and in the process derived a sick, self-punitive gratification. It occurred to me at one point that if I died your mother would then, at least, be forced to acknowledge what I'd felt for her, and what she had sacrificed. Oh, I was an open wound, and without sleep I could not heal.

I realized that the first thing was to get off the morphia. Spike hurt, this was a fact of life, even after bony union was effected in my hip; and he hurt worst as I fell off to sleep, when my muscles relaxed and the damaged bone ground like a drill against its seating in the pelvis. A needle relieved that hurt, not only relieved it but brought in its train waves of peace and serenity—nonetheless I couldn't use morphia as a crutch for the rest of my life, with God knows what effect upon my moral and intellectual functioning. So I stopped. One morning I just stopped.

At first all was well. I had risen at my usual time and gone without my morning shot, and spent the next hours looking at the newspaper. It was around noon—twelve hours after the last injection—that I began to grow uneasy. I became aware that a feeling of weakness had gradually crept over me. I began to yawn, then noticed that I couldn't stop shivering. I pulled a blanket round my shoulders. I seemed to be weeping, though not out of misery, it wasn't true weeping, it was, rather, a hot, watery discharge that had begun pouring from my eyes and nose in a copious stream. I crawled into bed—that huge creaky bed I had shared so often with *her!*—and fell into a restless sleep.

Throughout that warm summer afternoon I tossed and

turned under the sheet and was tormented by grotesque dreams. I saw Ratcliff bearing down on me in his black rubber apron, his face a rictus of rage and in his hand an amputation knife. I found myself on the steel table in the postmortem room with Ratcliff and Miggs and Cushing sniggering down at me. My thorax was open, my insides were piled neatly on my chest, and my penis was rolling around on the floor. I got up on one elbow, concerned to recover my penis, and my insides slithered off and fell on the floor and they all laughed.

I awoke at six in the evening: eighteen hours since the last injection. I couldn't stop yawning—I yawned so violently I feared I would dislocate my jaw. Armies of ants crawled about under my skin. Huddled in my blanket with the tears pouring from my eyes, and a watery mucus from my nose, I managed with difficulty to smoke a cigarette. I was shivering uncontrollably. At one point I struggled to the fireplace and peered at myself in the mirror. My pupils were dilated and the skin of my face was pimpled like gooseflesh. Suddenly I felt violently sick. There was no time to reach the bathroom down the hall, I had to make do with my chamber pot. The vomiting was explosive. Its contents were streaked with blood. Kneeling there over my bloody flux I opened my shirt and saw the skin of my belly knotted and corrugated as though a nest of vipers were writhing beneath it. Diarrhea soon followed. But I did not crack.

The hours crawled by. I called your mother's name, it gave me strength. I was doing it for her, this was the only way I could go on with it. By the next morning I was in truly pitiful condition. In a desperate attempt to relieve the chills racking me I had gone back to bed and covered myself with every blanket I could lay my hands on. My whole body shook and twitched beneath this mountain of bedclothes, though the pain not only in my hip but in all my muscles prevented me from getting sleep or even rest. I clambered out of bed and for a while I limped back and forth across the room, attempting to get warm. I opened a book and tried to read; hopeless of course. With tears of frustration and misery I climbed back into bed: the sheets and blankets were soaked through to the mattress. Then came a knock at the door! Filthy, unshaven, befouled with vomit, I called through the door: "Who is it?" My voice was a weak, fluty thing, like an old man's. I was only just able to keep the concerned Desmond Kelly from coming in to see what was the matter.

Time passed with excruciating slowness, and no relief came. I could neither eat nor drink, and in the course of that second day I became weaker and weaker as my bodily reserves were consumed and vitality slipped away. I thought then that unless I found relief I would surely die; and that seemed a heavy price to pay for dispensing with a crutch. Shortly after noon I broke. I cracked. I barely had the energy to drag myself out of my armchair and with trembling fingers make up a needle. But thirty minutes later (so rapid was my recovery) I was downstairs, shaved, clean, and joking weakly with Desmond Kelly about the terrible noises he'd heard from my room in the night. Eight hours after that I felt again the unease that had ushered in the nightmare, and I decided to prolong my holiday from hell. As I have ever since.

Three days later there again came a knock at the door. It was early evening and the light was starting to go. Desmond Kelly stood there with a letter. I tore it open. It was from Hugh Fig, the solicitor in Griffin Head. Apparently Henry's will had been read: everything was left to me, including the house. I looked up—gazed with a dawning smile into the mild, sad face of Desmond Kelly—and in that moment knew I was saved. In the midst of my darkness had come this one pure blessed shaft of grace. Despite all I'd done to him, Henry had kept faith with me. Grace, unbidden, had entered in, and my next steps were obvious, certain, and natural.

I felt my vital energies rekindled—I felt I could act again! I said this to Desmond Kelly. "So you can, doctor," he said.

He wasn't surprised. A wave of euphoria rose within me. I seized him by the hand—a wild, mad fellow I surely appeared, gray-skinned and unkempt, my mood careering crazily from profound depression to violent excitement in the space of a moment. Desmond Kelly was imperturbable. He knew the human heart.

I decided to go down to Griffin Head without delay. I telephoned Hugh Fig and told him to expect me the following afternoon. He asked me if I wanted to stay in my uncle's house—*my* house, as it it now was. No, I told him, I would prefer not to; could he recommend a decent hotel? Oh, the Ship, he said, you'll want to stay in the Ship.

Late the following morning finds me threading my way through the crowds at Victoria with as much of a spring in my step as Spike will allow. The day was warm and I was in my linen suit, which I hadn't worn once that summer, having barely been out of the house and when I did go out having little concern for my appearance. Not so now! I was freshly shaved, I was wearing my good Panama, dark glasses to hide the shadows under my eyes—yet another sleepless night, though this time it was excitement that kept me up—and a light summer raincoat thrown about my shoulders. I had my stick, my ticket, my light traveling bag, and Spike was under control. I felt like a man on the threshold of a new life. I felt as though a great journey was beginning—as indeed it was, a journey that has led me to this moment, this airfield, this duty, this end—this oddly glorious end—

I bought a newspaper from a vendor in the station. The situation in Czechoslovakia was critical. I sat by the window, smoking cigarettes, my stick clasped between my legs, my bag on the overhead rack. How beautiful England looked that day! Glimpses of the Downs, lush green rolling hills with smooth humped backs, like burial mounds, and the sheep cropping at the grass in the sunlight. Fields of golden corn, a high blue sky and a warm sun, sleepy villages, great estates—what did I care for dark portents of war, those unknown people in that distant land? Then comes that exhilarating moment, the first smell of salt in the wind. You leave the hills and descend to the coastal plain, there's the lighthouse, the cliffs, the sea sparkling beneath that deep blue sky, and at last you're steaming into Griffin Head itself.

I took a taxi into town and after settling in at the Ship made my way to Hugh Fig's office on the front. We discussed the disposal of Henry's house, and the handsome portfolio of stocks he'd left. It was all quite straightforward. We concluded the business and then, just as I was about to leave, Fig asked me if I remembered Peter Martin. Of course I did, I told him. I'd talked to Peter Martin on the telephone several times during Henry's last illness. He was the GP. What Hugh Fig said next was to have a profound impact not only on my life but also, I believe, on yours. "Peter Martin," he said, "is an old man. He's frankly too old to handle the work by himself much longer. It occurred to me that you may know someone who'd be interested in buying the practice."

I paused, with my hand on the doorknob—and you know what happened next, I went up to Elgin and I fell in love with the house; I fell in love with the house and made of it a museum of nostalgia, a temple to the memory of your mother, where I worshiped her spirit and would undoubtedly have continued to do so had you not appeared and drawn me back into the stream of life. Was this why you came to me? Was this your purpose, to show me the possibility of a life after death? Of a reconciliation of spirit and nature? Of a *reunion*?

Though ever since our last conversation, when Ratcliff's tone was in your voice, I'd felt as if I was losing you—losing you as I'd once lost her! And the prospect had hit me harder than I'd ever have thought possible. So I'd sown my seed of unease. By raising a question about your mother's illness I had instilled a doubt in your mind that would, I hoped, eventually draw you back to Elgin. Not that your doubt would be ill-founded;

I had reflected often in the long watches of the night as to what occurred during the last weeks of your mother's life. Doctors are notoriously unreliable in the diagnosis and treatment of their own families, this is well established. How much more so, the doctor whose wife has deceived and betrayed him? Ratcliff Vaughan was a cruel, aggressive man—did he dismiss your mother's early symptoms (and in kidney disease these can be oddly oblique)—as "nerves"? Did he, consciously or otherwise, allow her to sicken, and all the while reassure her, and you, that nothing was really wrong? The diarrhea, the fatigue, the loss of skin tone—all just "nerves"? Did he punish her thus for betraying him? It is not inconceivable. So when I sowed my seed it was not out of sheer gratuitous mischief; I had serious grounds for suspicion.

For I'd seen her myself in the spring of '39, and nothing had been wrong with her then. A woman at a dinner party had thrown me into a storm of misery merely by mentioning her name—"Fanny!" she'd cried. "Don't you know Fanny?" That's what brought it on, that's what brought on the fever once more.

It was the day Hitler entered Prague. She wasn't expecting me. She wouldn't have seen me had she known I was coming. It was almost a year since the night we'd walked down an empty street behind the hospital, beneath a gibbous moon, . . . I'd driven up from Elgin after breakfast, reached London at noon, and parked under a budding chestnut tree on the other side of Plantagenet Gardens, having stopped at a telephone box a little earlier to establish that Ratcliff was in St. Basil's. I had no clear idea what I was going to do. Wait for her to come out, perhaps, or march up the steps and stand beneath the portico, between the pillars, and press the bell, stand there until the heavy black front door swung inward and admitted me to a house I had never entered before, a hallway with a polished wood floor, a large mirror over a side table—

I sat in the Humber smoking cigarettes and watching the

door. At one point a middle-aged woman in a shapeless brown coat came out with a basket over her arm and went off along the pavement. Now she is alone, I thought. I must still my racing heart, compose myself, get out of the car, cross the road, knock on the door—

It was at least half a minute before she opened it. "Edward," she said—not coldly, but with surprise, curiosity, a flicker of annoyance—then: "What happened to your hair?" I don't remember what I said. I had thought of her so often, since we last met, that actually to be with her paralyzed me. I remember in my confusion noticing the few fine wrinkles at the corners of her eyes—her skin was as clear and white as ever, her eyes still shone with liquid light, but I didn't remember those fine lines before. I think it may have been the sunshine. It was a bright day. What did she see? A ruin. "May I come in and talk to you?" I said.

A slight frown. "I suppose so."

She led me down the hall. Walking behind her had always aroused me, and it did so now. We went into a drawing room with aquamarine curtains, silk-shaded lamps, and richly patterned rugs on a gleaming wood floor. French windows were open at the far end, spilling sunlight into the room. On the coffee table stood a vase of flame-colored tulips. On the mantelpiece a silver cigarette box. She took one and lit it. "I can't give you any tea, I'm afraid," she said, "Iris has gone shopping."

"Yes, I saw her."

"Oh you did. Edward, what is it you want? It's really not very convenient to have you here."

The sense of transgressing was so strong I found it hard to speak. I am never articulate in situations of high emotion. "There's something you must know. It may make no difference to you at all, but I must tell you."

An intake of breath. She found this tedious. She found me a nuisance. A bore. This deflated me. I had not anticipated such coolness in her. I'd thought she might be angry, but not cool. Not bored. "Well?"

How to say it? How to make an impression on her? In a sense it didn't matter. I already knew it was hopeless. She would throw me out in a moment, but I was *with* her, and that was enough. Angry, indifferent, scornful—it hardly mattered. It was her. "It hasn't been easy for me. I haven't been able to forget you."

She was sitting on the sofa, half-turned toward the French windows, smoking, waiting. Not looking at me. A tissue of small sounds filled the room, a bird, a clock, a voice from another garden. What we call silence. "I have a practice on the south coast now," I said. "I have a house. I make a reasonable living." No response. I didn't say I have a morphia habit. "I live quietly, I do two surgeries a day and house calls in the afternoon." Nothing. Christ, what was I *saying?* "But I don't feel anything," I cried, "I can't take pleasure in anything, I'm not properly alive, all I know is you're not with me and all the rest is empty, useless, dead, without meaning—" I paused, and realized I was standing in front of her fireplace with my arms in the air, like a man giving a harangue. She was turned toward me now so I said, with all the love in my heart: "Won't you come and live with me?"

She frowned. She leaned over to stub out her cigarette then rose to her feet. She gazed into my eyes, shaking her head slightly, like a mother half-amused at the mischief of a favorite child. She took my hands in hers. "You shouldn't have come here," she said quietly. "It could be difficult for me. You didn't think of that, did you?"

I felt a fool. No, I hadn't thought of that. Blinded by the intensity of my feelings, I'd behaved clumsily, I'd made her life difficult. "I didn't think you'd let me see you otherwise."

"I probably wouldn't have."

She dropped my hands, turned away, sat down again on

the sofa. The sunlight from outside made a sort of gray gloom at this end of the room. "I'm sorry," I said.

"Sit down," she said. "Darling, what could have come of it? Really? All that secrecy. It became so wearying, telling lies. It drains one's vitality. It never adds up to anything. We just fanned the flames, and it was torment because we couldn't ever be together."

"But we were together!"

"Oh no we weren't. You must realize this. The only way of dealing with love is being together for a long time, the world shut out, being in bed together all night long, waking together in the morning. All we had was a furtive hour here or there—it was making us both miserable."

"But what could we do? You wouldn't leave Ratcliff."

"How do you know?"

"I asked you."

"You weren't very insistent."

"What do you mean?"

"You didn't try and take me from him."

"I'm trying now!"

She lifted her eyebrows. "Oh," she said, turning away again, "what good does talking do?" She rose from the sofa and walked down the room to the French windows, where she stood in the sunlight with her arms folded, gazing out into the garden. I came up behind her, slipped an arm round her waist and pressed myself against her. "Oh my love," I breathed, "my heart—"

"No, Edward." She deftly disengaged herself and moved away. "I think you'd better go now."

"What am I to do? Now you tell me I could have taken you from him!"

"Oh, maybe you could have, I don't know. We had an affair. It's over now. Go away—get on with your life—get on with somebody else. I'm sorry for what happened to you but there's no more I can do."

I sank into a chair and stared at the floor, elbows on my knees and hands dangling. Her words had devastated me. A moment later she pulled me gently to my feet. She gazed into my face with a worried, tender expression. "You're a sensitive man," she said, "I always loved that in you. You're a real doctor, Edward, and that's rare. Find someone to love. Please, darling."

I shook my head.

"You must."

The doorbell rang and we spun apart. The mood shattered, it was as if we were scrambling out of a pit of blackness, back into everyday life. She went out, closing the door behind her. "You see what I mean?" she said when she came back a few moments later, as I tried to take her hands again. "No, you must go now. Really, Edward, I insist. Go now. And please don't visit me again."

At the front door she took my face in her hands and kissed me softly for several seconds on the lips. Then she opened the door and I left. I sat smoking in the car. A little later I saw her go out; she did not see me. I did not follow her. I sat there all day and watched the house. She came home late in the afternoon. Night fell and a pale moon, like a claw, filtered its light down through the branches of the chestnut trees. I drove back down to Griffin Head feeling that I had done myself no good, that I had simply fueled the flames of my misery. But I glorified in the smell of her perfume on my fingers.

It was just after the declaration of war that I learned of her death. It came as a dreadful shock. It was a Saturday, and I was alone in the house when the letter from McGuinness arrived in the afternoon post. I stood there in the hallway with the letter in my hand and then for some reason I turned and limped down the passage to the kitchen. Mrs. Gregor had washed the dishes and stacked them beside the sink on a kitchen towel, and rather than use a second towel to spread them out on—how odd that I should remember this, of all things—she had made an unsteady pyramid of cups and plates and glasses and cutlery that even as I looked at it seemed to tremble and be on the point of collapsing. The floor was swept and the table was clear apart from a little heap of eggshells, potato peelings and other organic rubbish in the middle of a sheet of brown paper. This puzzled me; not being a gardener I took a few moments to realize that this heap of rubbish was compost for the garden, my first thought was of some kind of offering.

I went out into the scullery and looked at the Wellington boots and watering cans and piles of yellowing newspapers, and then I went outside and walked down the garden and through the gate and so down the path to the edge of the cliff. The light was just beginning to go. I stood and gazed out at autumn sunlight on a calm sea, seeing how it spilled onto the surface in a great broad swathe made up of countless shards and scraps of light, closely packed at the center so as to form a dense blanket of silver and only at the edges breaking into its constituent fragments. The difficulty somehow lay in understanding the activity of the light on the water, in iden- tifying a pattern in the constant movement of the waves, the endless dancing and shifting as the current lifted the blanket of light and then rolled on, leaving it to settle once more— thus does the stricken mind clutch at distraction.

How long I stood there I don't know. After a while I became aware that long washes of pale blue and mauve were angling into the splotchy molten mess of golden radiance where the sun was going down while above it, high and flecky, its point to the west, an arrowlike cloud formation had appeared. After some minutes the mauve and blue bands turned a smoldering pink which grew deeper in tone as the sun touched the horizon and then went down. I seemed to awaken at that point, and as dusk rapidly descended I made my way back up the path to the house. Into the scullery I came and slammed the back door behind me—and heard a frightful crash from the kitchen. Mrs. Gregor's pile of dishes had fallen off the counter and shattered on the floor. I stood gazing in horror at the mess and then fled limping to the surgery. It was nephritis, McGuinness said. Kidney failure. She was ill for some weeks and then sank rapidly. She died in St. Basil's. Nothing anybody could do.

I attended the funeral. The ghastly echo of that other occasion, the day I first saw her—saw her and knew her and loved her! For the church was the same—many of the mourners were the same—and yes, I arrived late—but not accidentally this time, not because I'd been up all night in Accident and Casualty, but because I didn't think I'd be welcome. I slipped into the back of the church after the service had begun. A few heads turned, a few familiar faces—the Cushings were there, McGuinness, the Piker-Smiths. What was different though was the presence of so many uniforms. Almost all the men were in uniform and quite a few of the women (not me of course, Spike kept me from active service). Ratcliff had joined the RAMC, and from the partial glimpse I had of him up at the front of the church he looked, in khaki, more aggressive than ever. English funerals I've never found particularly conducive to grief but this one was. For me. Not for anyone else that I was aware of, but for me. I wept throughout, noiselessly, without once attempting to stanch the flow and careless of the opinion of my neighbors. I stood there with my hat in my hand, my stick hooked over the pew in front, and allowed the tears to course freely down my face.

How good it is for the heavy heart to weep! I have wept often for your mother, in varying moods and circumstances, but never I think have I been as cleansed and refreshed and *emptied* by my tears as I was at her funeral: I voided my grief, that day. I had been in shock you see, ever since I learned of her death, and had failed fully to acknowledge that grief. Now it came pouring out of me in a hot, steady stream that continued to flow even as her coffin was borne slowly down the aisle to the strains of the *Dies Irae*. Oh, it cut me like a knife to see her coffin, to think of her pale perfect body — no, not perfect, not perfect at all anymore, diseased, rather, spoiled and diseased—but I could not tear my eyes away, I gazed with mounting horror as it was borne down the aisle toward me—and then I saw you.

I saw you. Or I saw, rather, among the coffin-bearers, a young man in the uniform of an RAF pilot-officer, recently commissioned and wearing his wings. A small man, delicate of feature, his dark head lowered in grief—I knew this must be her son, and I found myself staring at you with a fierce intentness, so fierce an intentness, in fact, that you sensed it, and lifted your head, and stared, for an instant, straight into my eyes—straight into my *soul!*—before dropping your head once more. You don't remember the look we exchanged that day; I have never forgotten it. The afternoon you came to my surgery and said: "I believe you knew my mother"—I remembered it then, for there was, in your face, in the church that day, an expression of feeling that precisely and exactly mirrored my own. I felt between us a current of communication, and when soon afterwards I slipped away (I did not linger long among the mourners) this was what I carried away with me, the memory of meeting your gaze and finding replicated in it my own passionate experience of grief and loss. No, you may not consciously remember it, nonetheless it formed the foundation of the friendship we erected round her memory, like a tabernacle round a host—

But that didn't happen for months. First would come the winter, and oh, such coldness I remember that winter! It was the fiercest in forty years and we certainly felt it in Elgin. The generator broke down repeatedly and the wind howled in round those warped old window frames, so we had to close up most of the house and put in paraffin heaters. The rooms on the seaward side, including my study, were too cold to be used, though I still liked to go in late at night, in my overcoat, and for an hour or two watch wild seas hammering at the cliff. Mrs. Gregor had seen many winters in Griffin Head but none as bad as this, she said.

Whenever I had the chance I went down to the lonely, bird-haunted wastes of Elder Harbour, a large natural inlet created by inroads of the sea, from which the tide ebbed through a channel in the shingle beach, leaving marsh, mud flats and small streams. The wind howled about me as I trudged along, gulls dipped and screamed overhead, beneath lowering gray clouds, and the smell in the wind was of salt and rank fish and cord grass. Mrs. Gregor had told me about a great gale-driven tide that had swept across the marsh flats one winter when she was a child, flooded a farm on the other side of the coast road and drowned all the pigs. The ruin of an old wind-mill loomed at the desolate western end, much of the brick-work crumbled on its seaward face, and within the spars and ribs of the sails the latticework was splintered and smashed. The shaft no longer turned. In this mill the local kidney rock was once ground for cement, and on the sands nearby I came upon scattered lumps of the stone, grayish and finely grained and laced with translucent yellow veins composed of calcite crystals that for some reason struck me as beautiful, and which I collected and brought back to Elgin. I kept one on my desk in the surgery, and an old man told me that the cement it yielded was so hard that modern drills wore out on it and paint would stick for only a short time even if a sticky surface was applied first. Dead. Dead. But there could be no end (I thought), it was not the living woman I loved but her spirit, and that was unchanged and unchangeable. What is the life of the body against the life of the spirit? All too easy to see her flesh a pile of rank matter heaving with worms, not only

her, all of us, you, me, all of us. Life is a squalid little farce
if it offers no higher meaning than this—?

I continued to function, morning surgery, rounds after lunch,
evening surgery, on call at night. It was a cold winter and
Spike was vicious. My need of morphia to control the pain
was at times intense, but never did it interfere with the con-
scientious discharge of my duty. I am a man of robust character
and never permitted my judgment or competence to be im-
paired. Nonetheless that winter my need was acute, and I was
forced to raise my dosage and shift from intramuscular to
intravenous injection for quicker effect. I kept a supply of the
drug in the surgery, in a cupboard under lock and key. An
inspector from the Home Office did drop by, unannounced,
one morning, but the books were quite in order. In fact—as
I was quick to point out to him—I prescribed a good deal of
morphia to my patients, the practice including many elderly
persons among whom cancer was common. The tolerance for
morphia of patients like these—Nan Hale-Newton was a case
in point—increased (I told him) over time, and often quite
rapidly: it was not rare that a quarter-grain dosage would have
to be raised to three grains within a matter of weeks. For this
reason I always had to have a large supply on hand, and the
man from the Home Office was satisfied that no illicit pre-
scription was occurring.

January was a month of gales, high winds, and angry seas,
and Elgin was battered continually by storms. One wild night
I heard glass breaking overhead, and went up to the top floor
to investigate. There were rooms up there that I hadn't visited
since the days I was first in the house, rooms in which Peter
Martin still had furniture stored. Only one light worked, on
the landing. I limped along the dusty creaking boards and
into each of the rooms, where sheeted furniture skulked like
pale fat phantoms in the shadows. In the corner bedroom at
the end of the corridor two panes of glass had been blown in.

When I opened the door the gale caught it with great force and flung it back on its hinges against the wall, and then went howling down the corridor as though trapped and bursting for its freedom. There was nothing to be done until the morning, but I didn't go back downstairs. I sank into a sheeted armchair and remained there for many hours, such was the lassitude that overtook me during the long nights, this winter.

There was a lot of death about this winter. A number of my elderly patients succumbed to cancer though Nan Hale-Newton hung on grimly. Jean Fig died. She had first been to see me after that disastrous dinner party, when the mention of your mother's name had thrown me into such a passion of misery. In the clear light of day she'd looked even iller. Her skin still had a distinctly yellowish-green tinge, and the bags under her eyes were quite as deep and dark as my own. Jaundice perhaps? After a few polite interchanges I asked her what appeared to be the problem. "I do hate to bother you, doctor," she said, "it's probably nothing at all." She'd be a handsome woman, I remember thinking, if she relaxed a little. Why was she so tense, so angry—was it Hugh? He'd always seemed perfectly affable to me. "I'm always tired but I can't sleep," she said. "And I get these attacks of diarrhea, but I never know when they're coming." Probably, like most women of her class, she suffered in a hell of quiet desperation. "I threw up after dinner and I had to go to the bathroom five times during the night. I just don't know what's wrong with me."

"We best take a history then," I said, with some effort summoning my brisk warm physicianly manner, "and then I'll examine you."

Jean Fig's history shed no real light on her complaint. The usual childhood illnesses, a fractured metatarsal at the age of nineteen when a horse trod on her foot at a gymkhana, married at twenty-three, no children. "Why no children?" I said.

"We can't," she said. "We've tried, but we can't. I don't know whether it's my fault or Hugh's. He says it's mine, but he never says why he thinks so."

I then asked her to go behind the screens and get undressed. "What, everything?" she said.

Fifteen minutes later she was again sitting across the desk from me. I had probed and prodded and palpated, I had listened to her heart and her lungs, I had tested her reflexes and taken her pulse, which was a bit on the quick side, but apart from this I couldn't find a thing wrong. "Probably a mild attack of gastritis," I said. I made her up a bottle of Mist Explo. "Come back and see me in a couple of weeks, will you?"

"What exactly is gastritis, Dr. Haggard?" she said, taking a few coins out of her purse.

"Not serious," I said, "mild inflammation of the mucous membrane of the stomach. Should settle down pretty quickly."

"And would that make me tired?"

"It might." I screwed the cap on my fountain pen and took off my spectacles and rubbed my eyes. I hadn't slept.

"And look." She lowered her head. "You see? I'm losing my hair."

I frowned. Probably neurotic. Not enough sex, not enough love, too much quiet desperation. She was drying up like a forgotten apple in a neglected bowl. Impossible, I reflected, to fathom the hell that existed behind the facade of an English marriage—hadn't I seen the example of your parents? What vile tortures, I reflected, what unspeakable cruelties were unleashed when the last guest left and the front door closed and like a black and pestilential fog intimacy once more descended! "Let's see what happens when that gastritis clears up," I said. Though I supposed it might be equally possible that when the last guest left and the front door closed ecstasy erupted, sensual joy, active love. Caring, candor, and affection. Unlikely, but possible. I made a note in my desk calendar, and we both rose to our feet. "Good morning, Mrs. Fig."

"Good morning, Dr. Haggard. And thank you."

When I saw her next there was little improvement. Still that worrying yellowish tinge to her skin, and no real change in her inability to keep food down. I examined her again, and again failed to find anything wrong. I felt more sure than ever that the problem was not organic at all, but psychological. Again I delicately broached the subject of her relations with her husband. It was hard for her to be frank with me, but after some gentle prodding she admitted that Hugh had indeed become distant from her, had withdrawn from her, and that they'd lost a connectedness they'd had for years, a connectedness she treasured for it was, she thought, what love is. "I'm sure it's all my fault," she said, "feeling ill all the time, having no energy, losing my hair—what husband wants to come home to a creature like this?" By then the poor woman was in tears. "I'm trying to make an effort," she said, "but it does no good. He acts as though I'm not even there."

And sex?

"Sex?"

The question embarrassed her. She had to be coaxed. But at last I got her to speak. In the past, she told me, they'd made love regularly, three or four times a month, and they'd always shown each other physical affection, hugs and strokes and so on. But all that had stopped, and she thought her own ill health had as much to do with it as Hugh's neglect: she was always so tired she had neither energy nor desire, the only desire she had was for sleep. Even so she had made an effort, she had tried, despite her exhaustion, numerous times to initiate lovemaking, but Hugh wasn't interested. She had assumed he was preoccupied with his work, and she'd tried to get him to talk to her about it, but this had failed to elicit anything either. Probably it was just a phase he was going through. Men were such odd, incomprehensible creatures, she said, and it was so hard to make them *talk*.

"I see."

I was now completely convinced that her anxiety about her marriage was contributing to her ill health, which in turn was affecting her relations with her husband—she was caught in a vicious spiral, the distressed mind producing physical symptoms which then compounded the original problem. I told her all this.

"I'm doing it to myself?" she said, a note of annoyance creeping in here. "I'm making my own hair fall out? I'm turning my own skin yellow?"

"I think you probably are," I said.

For a moment I thought she might tell me to go to hell, but she didn't. Pity. It would probably have done her good. I sold her a bottle of Mist Explo and sent her on her way.

Jean Fig's condition continued to deteriorate and eventually, after consulting her husband, I decided she should be admitted to a private asylum in Bognor Regis. Hugh visited her every weekend, but her condition worsened. I was later told by the superintendent of the asylum that she had for some time before her death refused to see a doctor, claiming that none of us knew what was wrong with her. A tragedy. She was buried in the graveyard in Griffin Head, and I found myself more moved by her funeral than I'd expected to be. Hugh Fig was dignified and manly in his grief.

Was it nephritis, I now wonder? Kidney disease? And I think quite probably it was.

In the meantime of course war had been declared. We were at war. I remember reading the paper at breakfast the morning of September the fourth. Mrs. Gregor said little, as usual, but it was not hard to know what was going through her mind. I like a lightly boiled egg for my breakfast in the autumn and winter months, with half a slice of dry toast and two cups of

tea—like yourself I've always been a light eater. As I read
the paper that Monday I kept an eye on Mrs. Gregor, on the
assumption that what she felt the country felt, for she'd always
seemed to me to be a sort of weather vane in this regard. That
morning there was purpose and vigor in the way she set the
water on the stove to boil—spooned tea into the teapot—
sliced the loaf for toast. She was eager, I could tell, to get
the job started and get it done. No more waiting-and-seeing,
no more hoping for the best. She was ready.

And you? At the time I had no idea that our lives were
moving inexorably closer, though there was perhaps something, that morning, that made me think of your mother with
a more vivid apprehension than usual, she seemed more distinctly *with me,* at the outbreak of war, than she had for some
weeks—was this a premonition of her imminent death? Or
was it, I wonder now, the first dawning glimmer of awareness
I had of your approach?

The old people seemed not to share the general mood, the
grim sense of purpose I detected in Mrs. Gregor. They remembered too well the horrors of '14–'18. The intimation of
personal mortality made the prospect of mass death abhor-
rent—this I could understand: the scale shifts, the private end
becomes insignificant in the epidemic. It seemed to the old
men and women who came into my surgery that morning that
a sickness was upon us, and what galled them most was the
warmth of its welcome; but they had neither the will nor the
strength to resist. Then, as I went through the town on my
rounds that day—and what a beautiful day it was, the weather
was warm and clear and windless for the first days of war—I
saw a gaggle of evacuated London schoolchildren down on
the beach, East End children, dressed in rags, with grubby
faces and grazed knees, screaming with pleasure as they scam-
pered barefoot from the incoming tide—they'd never seen
the sea before. Further along, soldiers were digging up the
beach to fill sandbags. When I got home in the late afternoon

Mrs. Gregor was busy with brown paper, sticky tape and drawing pins, blacking out the windows of the rooms I used at
night. It depressed me not to be able to gaze out of the study
window, so I took to going up to the top-floor rooms and used
them for my nocturnal sea-gazing.

Actually I do know what you were doing at the outbreak
of war, for you've told me. Practicing battle climbs to thirty
thousand feet, where oxygen hissed into your face mask from
a black steel cylinder behind the armored bulkhead. Firing
your guns into the sea and raising a jagged plume of foam on
the water. Cloud flying and night flying, air drills and battle
practice, and getting to know Spitfires—and how you loved
Spitfires! You were never able properly to explain to me the
joy of flying a Spitfire, but I think perhaps I understand. You
told me how you once climbed through twenty-seven thousand feet of cloud, passed out, dived for four miles, and recovered consciousness just in time to pull out of it and climb
again—in any other aircraft you'd have bought it, you said.
Curtains.

My second winter in Elgin. I continued to sustain my love
upon the idea of your mother but it was difficult, those long
cold nights, not to grieve for the woman herself. Now I truly
haunted Elgin with her memory, it served to keep her spirit
alive. Late at night I would hear her voice in the top-floor
corner room, and despite the frigid chill that hung in the air,
and turned my breath to smoke, I'd be aware, as I came
hobbling along the passage, of vague ineffable wisps of her
fragrance, and when I opened the door and went in I'd be
certain she'd been there. These delicate impressions of her
presence enabled me to sustain her, though it was only possible in the long watches of the night, when no other human
presence interfered.

During the day I continued to practice medicine, though
with no great effectiveness I fear. That winter no bombs fell,
though we had certainly been expecting them. We knew what

had happened to Barcelona, buildings flattened, streets filled
with dead and dying, the sky black with enemy aeroplanes—
but no, no bombs fell, and the only war casualties I had to
deal with were caused by the blackout. Hardly a night passed
without someone falling down a flight of steps or walking in
front of a bicycle. One man was brought in with a broken leg
after toppling off the platform at the railway station; fortunately no train was coming. Another broke his nose when he
walked into a tree. Treating these casualties of the blackout
I found it impossible not to think of your mother in a bed in
St. Basil's, with you and Ratcliff standing over her. What was
her last thought? Had it been of me? Had she called out my
name—had your eyes flickered to Ratcliff's—had there been
a frown, a shake of the head—?

Dear James. I sometimes think your coming to Elgin saved
my life. That long, terrible winter after she died was almost
the end of me. I had lost her a second time, I was doubly
bereft, and it was barely possible at times to keep going. The
night I climbed down the cliff, and raged along the beach in
the darkness—that night I'd resolved to keep her flame alive
in my heart, and console myself with poetry and memories,
the husks and shadows of love. But after she died at times
the flame guttered, and I lost faith in the ongoing viability of
her spirit. Then I would storm around Elgin crying my despair,
my fury, my grief, my loss. I would give up medicine, I cried—
I had done my service, I could do no more—*non serviam*, it
was enough. Oh, it was a cold winter, the coldest of my life,
and it should have marked the end of the story. The flame
had burned brightly, then died; all that was left was work and
death. Until you came. Your coming marked an end to that
terrible bleak season—

I knew who you were. The afternoon you appeared in my
surgery, I knew who you were. I'd been reading Goethe,
Faust, I remember—"eternal womanhood leads us above"—
rather prophetic! But yes, I knew who you were, I'd seen you

at her funeral—and oh, the change your coming was to make
to my life . . . The story was not over, after all; there was
another chapter yet to be written, a final flourish, and why?
You, that's why; because you had come. You aroused feelings
in me I thought I would never know again. This limping
shadow I'd become, with broken hip, broken heart, broken
hopes—I seemed now to step into the light of day, to come
properly to life once more. Blood coursed in my veins, my
heart beat with fresh life, there was zest and vigor in all I did.
Mrs. Gregor remarked on the change; she said she'd not seen
me looking so well since I'd first come to Elgin. I could tell
she approved. She disliked my melancholy, and the irregular
habits it encouraged. All that spring you visited me in Elgin,
and I awoke happy in the morning, and not even the stretch
of bad weather we had in June could dampen my mood. There
was rain and fog, clouds and thunderstorms, all of which
served to incite Spike to particularly vicious flare-ups, all of
which I dealt with as I always have, but even Spike I could
now tolerate with benign resignation, with grace.

Whenever I was up at the station I took the opportunity to
look for you in the mess or the dispersal hut. The strain on
all you fighter boys was palpable now, as you waited for the
onslaught that we knew was bound to come. In the past weeks
Hitler's armies had swept across Europe smashing everything
in their path. Holland and Belgium had crumbled. France fell
in a matter of days. Fears of an invasion on the south coast
of England began to be voiced with increasing frequency. But
first would come the air assault, and what you boys wanted
more than anything was to get on with it. Such courage you
displayed, such heroism—I felt privileged to witness it,
though of course I never said this, for if there was anything
you hated it was being what you called "romanticized." But
why shouldn't I romanticize you? You were romantic in the
original sense of the word. You engaged the enemy in single
combat, man to man. You were gallant. You were chivalrous.

You were brave. Why not romantic? You were knights of the air; and you, dear James, you were *my* knight, my gentle, parfit knight, you were one of that brave doomed breed sick with nostalgia for something worth fighting for, something worth dying for—

But what for me was most remarkable, at the time, was the sense I had of being liberated at last from grief. My spirits were rising, and not mine alone; there was a new feeling abroad, I had detected it in Mrs. Gregor, for there had come, with the fall of France, and the knowledge that we now stood alone, a sense of exhilaration combined, curiously, with a desire, albeit oblique and perverse, for things to get worse, to get as bad as possible, until we were, as a people, staring directly into the abyss, so that *then* we might fight back—we seemed to need to have it confirmed that the situation was hopeless before the impulse of resistance could be properly aroused. Oh, they were extraordinary days, and I was no less affected by the mood of them than anyone else, though my exhilaration was not provoked just by the threat of invasion, no, I was exhilarated for different reasons, for reasons of my own. For this was the period when you were visiting me regularly in Elgin.

And then—disaster. James, did I have to lose you as well— was it inevitable? I'd already had my forebodings, and sown my seed of unease, for I was desperate to keep you coming back; but I had not been wise. You did come back, but on your face an expression I'd never seen before, a sulky, boyish resentment touched with real anger. You'd stood at the front door of Elgin taut and coiled like a spring, and I brought you straight into the surgery. "Drink?"

"No thank you. I came to talk to you about what you said about my mother."

"Oh?" Frowning, my eyes averted, I busied myself with cigarettes.

"Yes. You suggested she wasn't treated properly."

"Did I say that?"

"That was the impression you gave me."

"I certainly didn't intend to."

"Then why did you say you wished you could have seen her?"

"Not because I felt she was being treated incompetently."

"Then why?"

"Why do you think?"

You stared at me furiously, and I was reminded—dreadful memory!—of your father's expression when he attacked me in St. Basil's. "You said kidney conditions were tricky to diagnose."

"So they are."

"So why would you say that unless to suggest she was being treated incompetently?"

"Do you think she was being treated incompetently?"

"I?" This caught you off guard.

"Yes you. Weren't you concerned?"

"If I was concerned I spoke to my father."

"And?"

"He told me everything was being done that could be done."

"But you weren't sure."

"Why shouldn't I be sure?"

I shrugged. "You're so angry about it now."

"Don't you think my father would have known if there was any way to treat her?"

"You've spoken to him again?"

"Yes I have."

"And what did he say about me?"

"He said—"

"What?"

"You were not her attending physician. How could you know?"

"I expect he said more than that. I expect he told you I

was unreliable and untrustworthy and that you should have nothing to do with me."

You glared at me and said nothing.

"All the same you've come back to tell me this. Why? Because you suspect there's something in what I say. You're not convinced your father's telling you the truth."

This was going too far. Face ablaze you rose abruptly to your feet and left the room. Damn! Damn damn damn! I had misjudged you—misjudged how much in thrall you were to Ratcliff. A moment later the front door banged behind you. I sat there smoking until forced by his clamoring to attend to Spike.

Then three days later I heard the news that I suppose unconsciously I'd been dreading all spring: you'd been injured. I was in the surgery seeing to Spike when the call came through. It was the adjutant from the station. "B Flight?" I cried—that was your flight—"Who?"

It was you.

Five minutes later I was in the car and turning out onto the coast road. The alarm I'd felt on hearing that it was you—the vehemence of it surprised me. In my imagination I saw your Spitfire cartwheeling across the airfield, smashing itself to pieces and you lying in the wreckage broken and dying. Then the adjutant told me there'd been heavy flak over Dover and you'd caught some of it chasing a Dornier down. "Badly hit?" I said.

"He got out of his kite by himself," he said, "but he's not happy."

The station sick bay was another of those single-story prefabricated buildings clustered in the shadow of a hangar. The main room had half a dozen beds, three down each side; off it was a side room where the medical officer worked, and it was there that I found you. You were standing at the window, and as I came hurrying in I noted the ragged rip in your

trousers, just below the waist but well to the right of the spine.
Blood had stained the fabric around the wound. "James," I
cried, "you've been hit!"

You turned stiffly toward me, wincing, clearly in some pain.
Your face was set in hard and hostile lines. "Stung a bit," you
said curtly.

"Let's have a look at it then."

The great worry with such penetrating injuries is the spinal
cord, the risk of damage to the vertebrae. Your tunic came
off easily enough, and your trousers, but your shirt and underpants were stuck to the wound with dried blood and I had
to pull the fabric smartly from the flesh, which made you
wince. I sat in a chair and you stood with your back to me,
in the light, while I examined the wound. It was narrow,
ragged, and deep; it seemed probable that a small piece of
shrapnel had embedded itself in the muscle of your upper
buttock but without affecting backbone or fatty tissue, so there
was no immediate danger of infection. I would need to get
an X-ray to confirm it, of course, but I didn't think we had
to worry about tetanus. I told you all this. There was an
examination table on the far side of the room. "Lie down
flat," I said, "and I'll clean you up. Have to give you a shot
of something, I'm afraid."

"Do your worst," you murmured, climbing gingerly onto
the table as I prepared the syringe. I injected into the muscle
close to the wound; I noticed as I did so that the texture of
your skin was like your mother's, there was the same silky
feeling when I touched you. I paused a moment to let the
anesthetic take effect—and to my great annoyance, unex-
pected and unwanted, grief arose, and I had to turn away,
hold myself rigid as the wave passed through me. After a
moment I was under control and I forced myself to concentrate
on the work at hand. Then I was stitching the wound, and
James, were I stitching the face of a beautiful woman I don't
think I'd have taken more pains about it. I closed it all coarsely

with catgut, then sewed the superficial skin with silkworm gut and completed the job with stitching so fine your flesh would carry no scar. It was fastidious, time-consuming work, but had it been your mother on the table I would have made every effort; I could do no less for you. I doubt your father could have done as elegant a piece of stitching.

Eventually it was finished, and you climbed down. I was washing my hands. "No more flying for you for a while," I said, glancing at your reflection in the mirror over the sink. You were shuffling across the room, the neat cluster of stitches stark against the white flesh of your upper buttock. You reached for the dressing gown hanging on a hook on the door, and for just a second, as you pulled it on, I caught a glimpse, in my mirror, of the front of your body. Frowning, I turned round, picked up a towel and dried my hands. I was puzzled at what I'd seen. There appeared to be something rather peculiar about your penis.

That night in Elgin I thought again about what I'd seen, and I was concerned. As a doctor, I was concerned. As a man, however, as a *friend*—I was wounded by the coldness and hostility you'd displayed. Though I could at least console myself that you'd have to see me once more, if only to have your stitches out. When that happened I would treat you, I decided, with brisk neutral professional courtesy. You could make the first approach to reconciliation, as and when it suited you. *If* it suited you—

I was in the surgery when you came into my waiting room a few days later. I had your X-rays on the desk in front of me. There was, indeed, as I'd suspected, a fragment of metal lodged in muscle in your lower back, but there was no point in trying to dig it out as it posed no risk of infection. I brought you into the surgery and asked you to get undressed; I was still curious about what had seemed, in the brief glimpse I'd had of you in the sick bay, to be some slight genital abnormality.

You emerged from behind the screen, and I watched you closely as you moved across the surgery. I had you stand in the middle of the room. What I saw, as I rose from my desk, was a small, pale, perfectly made young man with black hair, narrow shoulders, slim hips, and an almost complete absence of body hair. There was a tendency to infantilism of the sexual organs; there was also a slight convergence of the lower limbs toward the knees, and imperceptible, perhaps, to any but the trained medical eye, mild gynecomastia with slight enlargement of the nipple. It instantly suggested nascent glandular disturbance, which was worrying. I approached, frowning, pulled over a chair and examined you more closely. Your skin, I again noted, was oddly smooth to my fingers. I paid particular attention to the penis, plump and soft like a child's, and the testes, cupping them in my hand, weighing them. Froehlich's syndrome, perhaps? They were rather small. You grew suddenly impatient. "That's enough of that," you said. I rose to my feet, and you stepped swiftly over to the examination table and lay down flat on your stomach. At the time I had no real knowledge of the pathology, though I was aware that shock, or violent emotional upset, could produce disorders of the endocrine system. "Had any bad shocks lately?" I murmured as I started taking out your stitches.

Muffled snort from you. "Plenty of shocks in this war."

"Ah."

You were dressed again and sitting across from me on the other side of the desk. Tricky things, endocrine disorders, and I wasn't certain just what would happen next. My concern was that it might get out of hand, and I thought you should see a specialist. But when I mentioned this you very curtly ruled it out, the mere suggestion of a visit to London. You told me, with some impatience, that the squadron was way below full strength; the new pilots had barely had more than a few hours' experience in Spitfires, and needed constant help and surveillance; and anyway, you said, there was little to defend these shores but the few fighter squadrons that remained operational. This was no time to disappear up to London to see specialists, you said, and anyway why? You felt fine. There was nothing wrong with you, beyond a bit of shrapnel in your back. Your duty lay here in Griffin Head, on this point you were adamant.

I understood of course your need to deny what must have been extremely disturbing to you, these curious changes occurring in your body. I began to tell you about the pituitary gland and its secretion of estrogen: if your pituitary was malfunctioning there should be no delay in seeking specialized help. But you wouldn't hear of it, you angrily cut me off before I'd properly made my point. Not until it was over, you said. "What, the war?" I cried.

"No," you said, "the Battle of Britain."

The Battle of Britain. It was the first time I'd heard the phrase. Now that the Battle of France was over, the Battle of Britain would begin. It would be fought in the air, for in order to invade England Hitler must get his army across the Channel unmolested by the RAF; he must wipe out the RAF first. So I shouldn't have been surprised that you chose to stand and fight. You were putting your country first.

The next days were not easy for me. I had been sleeping badly, so I was tired, which made Spike vicious, which in turn interfered with my rest. I spent much time pacing my study through the long watches of the night, from time to time going down the path at the back of Elgin to stand on the cliffs and watch the searchlights. You were constantly on my mind. I pictured the dispersal hut: little more than a shed really, with a stove in the middle and a pipe going out through the roof, a few old armchairs and couches scrounged from various barns, a table with a telephone on it and a few charts and notices tacked to the walls. On warm days you'd drag the chairs outside onto the grass at the edge of the airfield, otherwise you'd be clustered round the stove with your feet up reading newspapers or novels or playing chess, ready to go when the phone rang and the word came through to scramble. How was it for you? Those others, they had only Messerschmitts to worry about, the threat they faced was clearly defined. Their enemy came from across the Channel, from Germany. Not yours; you had an enemy within you, but what *was* it, exactly? Was it Froehlich's, as I suspected? Your fat distribution was certainly feminoidal, but it lacked the marked deposit on lower belly and thighs that one associates with Froehlich's. Perhaps, I hazarded, the constant anxiety of warfare, as experienced by the fighter pilot, could cause endocrine disturbances of such severity as to effect visible changes in the body's sexual characteristics—?

Several days passed, and you did not come to see me. I looked for you whenever I was up at the station, but for some reason you were never around. Then one afternoon, just as I was leaving the sick bay, I saw a Spitfire coming in to land that I recognized as yours, and after it had taxied to a stop I limped across the grass to meet you. You heaved out your parachute and jumped down off the wing. You seemed distinctly displeased to see me; you gave me a brief nod then turned your back on me. "James," I said, in as pleasant and reasonable a tone as I could muster, "why don't you come down to the surgery tomorrow. I'd like to have another look at you."

You ignored me. You began talking to your fitter about your guns. I persisted; wasn't your welfare my responsibility now? "I've dug up some gen that might interest you," I said.

"I'm on ops tomorrow," you said, your back still to me.

"Can't let it go too long," I said.

At last you turned to me. You flung off your flying helmet and began angrily wiping your hands on an oily rag. "Look

doctor," you said—and your eyes were flashing with anger!—
"why don't we just forget all about it? I'm all right, do you
understand?"

"Up to you," I said. "But I can't believe this isn't preying
on your mind. Talking it over might help."

"It certainly would not help," you snapped. "Now please
excuse me, I have an aeroplane to see to."

"But James," I cried, "you're sick!"

You turned to me. "Not me, doctor," you said shortly.
"You."

That was all we said. I was unwilling to put pressure on
you; I thought it quite possible that the best thing for you
might be just to get on with your war and not pay undue
attention to what was, after all, not a life-threatening condition. But I did notice that it was progressing, I could tell by
your skin, your voice, your general demeanor. Impossible of
course to know what was happening elsewhere to the body,
I'd need to examine you for that, and there seemed little
likelihood, the frame of mind you were in, of your permitting
that. But I could imagine how alarming it was, seeing your
body behave so oddly, and in all probability having to deal
with urges and desires that issued from what must have felt
like an alien creature within you.

Meanwhile it was becoming clearer to all that command of
the air was the necessary precondition for invasion. The Luft-
waffe was attacking the RAF by day and by night, in the air
and on the ground. Only when the RAF was knocked out
could a landing in England be undertaken. Churchill said that
the future of civilization depended on you. If you failed, he
said—that is, if the RAF failed to repel the German air assault,
which would open the way to a landing on the south coast—
the world would sink into the abyss of a new dark age made
sinister by the light of perverted science.

This then was the end of the brief idyllic phase of our friendship. I saw much less of you after the Battle of Britain began;

you were on two-minute alert from dawn to dusk, and had little desire to spend your evenings in Elgin. I can understand why. You were in a state of physical and emotional exhaustion, and cared for little but sleep, and the company of other fighter pilots, for they alone shared what you were going through. Not everything. Only I was aware of your medical predicament, the mutiny of your disturbed and raging glands. Late at night I pored over books in the upstairs back bedroom and thought about you, puzzled over what it meant, that you seemed to be growing paler, softer, quieter by the day. Eventually it became clear to me that I had stumbled upon a pathological phenomenon previously unknown to medical science. The effect on the endocrine system of acute, sustained emotional pressure had never been properly studied, presumably because the conditions necessary to provoke it—intense, high-speed air combat for instance—had never existed before. I suspected that fear—specifically, the constant terror of sudden violent death—could produce, in individuals of a certain predisposition, disturbances of the pituitary gland that could cause changes in the body related to the secretion of hormones. It was a new syndrome, perhaps even a new disease, a disease unique to modern warfare. But I could only write it up if you'd allow me to examine you, take a history, attempt treatment—and this, clearly, you were not prepared to do. Perhaps if you would ever let me examine you again I could do a proper case study and write a monograph. Publish an account of the diagnosis and treatment of the disease. *Name* it, even—*Haggard's disease?* But no; ignoble thought; I pushed it out of my mind. You were suffering, that was all, and it was my duty to relieve that suffering.

In August the weather improved. It was clear, still and warm, a lovely English summer, but these were the worst conditions for an overworked, undermanned air force whose pilots were close to exhaustion. Every day you went up five, six, seven

times. The sky over Griffin Head was crisscrossed with con-
trails that unraveled like rolled bandages as Spitfires fought
Messerschmitts escorting bombers whose targets were the air-
fields of southern England. Casualties were heavy. The station
was attacked again and I was there. It was one of those warm,
cloudless days, utterly tranquil—until, that is, the message
came over the loudspeaker: "Large enemy bombing formation
approaching Griffin Head. All personnel not engaged in active
duty take cover immediately." I looked up but I couldn't see
or hear a thing in that clear blue summer sky. All round the
field men were running for shelter. A Spitfire came past me
with a roar to take off downwind and it was then that I saw
them, a dozen black shapes shining in the sun and coming
straight on. I stood transfixed, fascinated, mesmerized—this
was the enemy.

Then came the rising scream of the first bomb—I came to
my senses—and threw myself onto the grass, covering my
head. Through my fingers I watched the Spitfire take off, and
it occurred to me that you might be flying it. It was about
twenty feet off the ground when suddenly it catapulted upward as though on a piece of elastic, came down on its back
and plowed along the runway upside down. The next moment
a load of dirt hit me and then I heard someone shouting,
"Run, for Christ's sake!" I peered round, spitting dirt out of
my mouth, and saw the adjutant standing in the door of a
shelter and waving wildly at me. Somehow I got myself over
there. My first thought was of my black bag, somewhere out
on the field; my second was of you, and whether you were in
the crashed Spitfire. I started to ask where you were, but the
scream and crump of falling bombs made it impossible to be
heard. The air was thick with dust and the shelter heaved
with each explosion, and for several minutes I believed that
you were dead, and that I would shortly be dead also. Then
the bombing stopped. There was a moment of utter silence
in the shelter before we emerged into the fresh air.

The runway was torn apart. It was full of gaping holes. There were mounds of earth everywhere. A lorry lay on its side by the dispersal hut, one wheel torn off. Smoke drifted in the still, silent air. The Spitfire had come to a halt halfway down the runway, where it lay upside down but not burning. An ambulance was racing across the grass toward it. "Whose aeroplane?" I cried.

"Johnny Hart, poor sod," someone said.

"Right," I said. Not yours! Then I saw my bag, apparently undamaged, sitting on top of a large gobbet of dirt. Off I limped, with Spike screaming like the blazes in my hip. There was nothing I could do for Johnny Hart. He hung limp in his harness, upside down with a broken neck. All I could think was, it might have been you. It might have been you. Then: it would be you. One day, it would be you. Not perhaps upside down with a broken neck, but plunging in flames into the Channel, going out in a blaze of glory . . . The life expectancy of fighter pilots in the Battle of Britain was not long.

By night I watched searchlights slicing across the darkness, and heard the bark of the ack-ack guns. Sometimes I'd walk down through the back garden to the edge of the cliff, and in the warm night air gaze out across the Channel toward the French coast, and sense there the waiting evil. I feared for you. I telephoned the station every evening and discreetly inquired after you. I came up at every opportunity, and it was a mark of the stress you were all under that your banter grew rougher as your stamina declined. I didn't mind, of course I didn't, I understood the pressure you were under. You'd be lounging about in battered armchairs, maps stuffed down your flying boots, uniforms creased and baggy, no collar and tie of course, just a piece of silk tied round your neck. You were the long-haired fighter boys, scruffy, cynical and brave, England's last hope. And you, dear boy, you lounged there too, as though to the manner born, you were fighting and surviving with the best of them, and only I knew how sick you were.

• • •

No, you never came to see me in Elgin anymore. At first I didn't mind, for I knew what you were up against, all of you. Then I faced up to the fact that there was more to it than this, and that you were deliberately avoiding me. What made it worse was your unfriendliness up at the station. You were aware, whenever I came into the mess, or the dispersal hut, that my eyes would always seek you first, but you no longer met my gaze. You turned away as though I were a stranger. On one occasion you slid down into your armchair, stretched your legs out, tipped your cap forward over your eyes and pretended to be asleep. You barely troubled to conceal a yawn. Later, when I thought about it, I realized why you were acting this way: you were angry with me because I *knew*. You had suddenly shied away, withdrawn from me, because you couldn't admit to this physical embarrassment that must every day be growing more pronounced, more inescapable.

This was painful to contemplate. It was obvious to me how desperately you must need not only treatment but a sensitive ear, how you must be craving affection and understanding. Who else could you turn to? Certainly not Ratcliff. But I could have been of real help to you, for I had an idea of what you were going through, and could grasp the horror of it all. I look at what nature has given me—I am not a tall man, in fact my body is barely bigger than a child's, and yet I have a man's head, full-sized, with a great shock of hair that spills from my brow in the manner of the late Beethoven and does nothing but emphasize the ill-proportion of my anatomy. Since Spike my gait is wretched, I shuffle and limp, I have gray skin, and this curiously vivid streak of white in my hair that springs up off my forehead like a fountain of ice. When I think that this botched and crippled structure is the frame for the spirit that burns within it, burns with a passion and at times a grandeur that few men know—it's a joke, a travesty, and as a result I have learned to cultivate impotence, of a sort, as a way of life.

But you! You were still a young man—and I remembered what it was to be young, to be fit and strong, to live in a young man's body. When a young man's body is functioning properly there is no better place on earth than inside it.

Oh, but I missed your friendship too—was it wrong to think of myself? I was no stranger to loss and loneliness, God knows I drank deep enough of both in the wake of your mother's rejection. To lose you, however, so soon after finding you— I was quite desperately disheartened by this. I remember stopping at the Elms and going in to see Nan Hale-Newton. She was still hanging on; though riddled with cancer she wasn't letting go, she hadn't finished with the injections, as she told her perplexed daughter Marjorie. It always did me good to see her, I admired the ferocity of her determination not to surrender to the darkness until she chose to do so. "In my own good time, Haggard," she would tell me, "that's when I'll be going out." Marjorie was a good and devoted nurse, and as a result was turning into a spinster, but if Nan felt any guilt at being the instrument of her daughter's progressive desiccation she never expressed it. "That girl's getting to be an old maid," she'd sniff, after Marjorie had left the sickroom and I was preparing the needle.

"It's your fault," I'd say (we spoke candidly, she wouldn't tolerate any other sort of conversation).

"Nonsense. Marjorie's got a mind of her own. Let her go out and live her life. Nobody's stopping her."

"No, nobody's *stopping* her."

"No one has to do what they don't want to."

"So what would happen to you?"

"Me?" A muffled hoot. "What does it matter about me? An old bag with one foot in the grave, what do I matter?" She refused to acknowledge Marjorie's predicament.

So I turned into the Elms late one afternoon after visiting the station and being cruelly reminded yet again that you had spurned me. Marjorie took me up and left me with her mother.

"So what's the matter with you?" The voice had turned into a dry, hoarse rasp but it had lost none of its authority. The curtains were drawn, the room was full of shadows, and also of that awful pervasive smell of a failing, diseased body, inactive too long; broken vessel of a still-vigorous flame. Her eyes glinted in the sunken skull, a few dry gray wisps of hair framing it like a halo. "What's on your mind, Haggard, spit it out. No, let me guess. It's that young pilot of yours."

I'd told her about you. Not everything, but who you were, who your mother was.

"Has he been shot down?" she said. "I hear them up there, killing each other."

I said you had no time for me anymore.

"Not surprised! Why would he pay any attention to an old cripple like you?"

For some reason, I don't know why, fatigue perhaps, this was too much. I was unable to suppress a sob. "Oh for God's sake man," said Nan Hale-Newton. "Come on, where's my injection? Here I am suffering the torments of the damned and you're blubbing like a gel."

She was right of course. I opened my black bag. A little later she was breathing gently and her eyes were closed. Spike was being a bloody nuisance so I broke open another ampoule and relieved my own pain. I sat there by her bed, my breathing in unison with hers, my face softened by the same sad smile, until after half an hour or so Marjorie came up to see if there was anything wrong.

A curious thing happened on my way out of the Elms. I came downstairs with Marjorie and saw standing on the hall floor a large cardboard box full of Nan's clothes. Marjorie noticed me staring at it and said: "They're for the evacuees. I don't suppose you're going past the church, doctor?"

"What?" I was transfixed—there was a fur coat in that heap of discarded garments *exactly the same color as your mother's.*

Marjorie repeated her request. "Yes," I murmured, "yes of course I will."

"Somebody should have the use of them," she said. "Mummy won't wear them again."

I dropped off Marjorie's box of clothes at the church, but not before I'd taken out the fur coat. That would go home with me to Elgin.

Often I stood at the edge of the airfield and watched you land. I'd see the cockpit hood pushed back as you brought the aeroplane down, I'd see you glance out, your goggles pushed up on top of your flyer's helmet and the strip of silk at your throat fluttering wildly in the wind. What a beautiful machine it was, with its trim deceptive frailty, its wickedly simple lines! The ground crew would be waiting, the fire tender, the ambulance. You'd cut the engine and the Spitfire would seem almost to float down, then you'd lift the nose just a hair, bump down on all three wheels, and let the aeroplane run off its speed. You'd disconnect the radio and oxygen leads, release your safety straps, then swing your legs up and over onto the wing—and that's how I'll remember you, squinting at the sun from the wing of a Spitfire, and only I aware of the bizarre physical transformation you were undergoing. Though if you saw me you'd walk off in the opposite direction.

Why so cruel? Was it only because I knew about your condition? Perhaps there was more to it than this. Perhaps it was because you were your mother's son. It daily became clearer to me that I had to do something. You were suffering exquisite misery, and only I could relieve your pain. It was my duty. Oh, but these were hard times and I began to feel terribly dispirited. I began to feel I would never know anything but loss. There was one night that I reached for your mother in the darkness—in my mind, I mean, for it had become a habit over time to feel for her presence in memory and feeling, if not in physical reality, when I was alone and melancholy late at night—and she wasn't there! She wasn't there! I could summon the image of the woman but it was a bare, stark memory, no more, it was bereft of emotion—I felt nothing!

I had never known this before. To fail to feel—this truly was loss, and I was bewildered, frightened, dismayed. I'd been in the upstairs corner room among the sheeted armchairs, watching the moon on the sea; the black fur coat was draped about my shoulders, it reminded me of her, it helped me identify myself with her living spirit—until now! I left the room in high panic and came down the stairs in a very frenzy of alarm, down through the darkened house. Into the study, and a frantic groping in the drawer of my desk—not there! Down the next flight, good leg bad leg stick, across the hall and into the surgery, and just as I thought, I found it in the drawer—the fly-in-glass. I stood in the darkened surgery and clutched it tight, and as I'd hoped and prayed it would it began to generate comfort, in the form, faint at first, but slowly gaining power, of pain. The old pain, pain the familiar. The ache, the bite of the pain—it was Spike remembering, not I, it was Spike who held her memory and all the associated emotion—Spike it was who held the slim phantom close, held her clinging to the pin in my hip like a plasmid substance, translucent, faintly shining, trembling to life now in the darkness, and I sank into my chair and reached for my black bag, relieved that the crisis was past. The idea came to me then that memory was less a faculty of the mind than of the body, for with the easing of Spike's pain so did the memory of your mother cease to harrow me with hopeless longing.

And then I had the most peculiar and vivid sensation: I felt her presence. Not as I'd felt it before, when by dint of sustained reverie I'd aroused a wisp of her perfume, the sound of her voice—at those times there seemed only the most delicate membrane separating the construct of aroused memory from her actual presence, only the thinnest of veils—no, it was not the willed evocation of her, which invariably brought in its wake tears of frustration as I railed against my inability to break through and make of the phantom a woman—it was not that, it was a tranquil, unstrained conviction that announced itself calmly and that filled me with the sure knowledge that she was, yes, viable still in the world, and inhabited the body of her son: she had come back to me.

I rose from my chair and pulling the fur snugly about me I climbed the stairs to the top of the house, where I could gaze at the sea and attempt to assimilate the idea. The profound physical likeness of mother and son, and your emergent womanhood—I had been quite wrong to think exclusively in terms of glandular disease. Explanation—*pathos* and *logos*—could not begin to encompass what was happening to you, the miraculous change that was even now being effected by the movement of her spirit into your body.

A long night, as I pondered all this, but eventually for a few short hours I slept. When I awoke, the whole tissue of thought and wonder collapsed. It all seemed the most preposterous nonsense. The doctor within me spoke, he scoffed with skepticism—movement of spirit in the world? A fevered imagination, erotic obsession exacerbated by morphia—the boy was victim of glandular disease and suffering agonies of confusion as a result—this was my concern, my sole concern. So said the doctor. And so did he believe, as he went about his duties that day.

But come nightfall I was no longer sure. Watching the searchlights sweeping across a black sky, feeling the pressure of ideas that owed little to the cautious half-truths of empiricism, I was convinced again that the soul of a dead woman cried out to her lover through the body of her son. I stood in front of the window, wearing the fur, and saw her gazing back at me; and I knew I was right. It was many hours until I slept; and when at last I did slip away I dreamed a very curious dream.

·   ·   ·

There was a Heinkel in trouble in the sky over Griffin Head. It was one of a group that had crossed the Channel with an escort of Messerschmitts. The squadron scrambled and attacked from the rear, from above, out of the sun; the German fighters took evasive action, going into half-rolls and vertical dives with the Spitfires in hot pursuit. I heard the crackle of machine-gun fire and stopped the car (I was up on the Downs for some reason) to get out and gaze at the sky inland to the north, but all I could see were trails of vapor. The Heinkels, separated from their escort, turned for home and in close formation made for the coast at twelve thousand feet. Somebody on his way back to the airfield—was it you?—spotted them from above and dived straight down in a quarter head-on attack. You got the slowest of them in your sights and let go with all eight guns in several short bursts. Smoke poured from the port engine and the bomber began to lose altitude. At about eight thousand feet it jettisoned its bombs. To no avail; it crashed into the sea and went down in seconds. None of the crew got out. A stick of bombs fell on the outskirts of the town, and several houses sustained extensive damage. One of them was Elgin.

There is a way the body has of postponing pain, of going into shock in the immediate aftermath of trauma. The mind will function in a similar fashion when it must protect itself from too fierce an assault of feeling. This, in the dream, seems to be what happened now: my initial reaction was one of bemusement. Two hours earlier I had left a house. I returned to a smoking ruin. At first I didn't perceive how severe the damage was. There was an eerie silence and the air had a sort of sharp and tremulous clarity. I stood in the driveway, leaning on the door of the Humber, and gazed at the facade of the house, which seemed almost intact—the windows had been blown out, and the roof badly hit, but an initial impression of solidity was there. But slowly my eye moved upward and settled on the strange skeletal pattern of charred rafters arching against the blue afternoon sky like the bones of some prehistoric creature. Several were still burning. Everything was so still! But even as I stood there a clutch of slates went suddenly slithering down and clattered into the wreckage within with a sound like clanging steel. I became aware of the myriad noises of Elgin settling and dying, heaves and groans that were almost human, splinterings and smashes as stresses and pressures were redistributed, realigned. It then occurred to me that the real destruction must be at the back, so I limped round the side of the house, through that oddly trembling, pristine air, picking my way over shattered glass and slates and masonry.

And this was where the bomb had hit. It was as though a huge bite had been taken out of the back of the house. The back porch, the back kitchen, the scullery, the kitchen itself— the rooms above—utterly destroyed. The blast had knocked the walls out sideways. Small fires burned here and there. Strange thing, the way the unconscious mind works, for I perceived not wreckage but fragments of order. Splintered stretches of flooring sagged drunkenly against stumps of walls but here was a table, rubble all round it, and a cup and saucer intact on top. Here was a bundle of newspapers neatly tied with string. Here was the kitchen stove and on it a pot with a wooden spoon, though the pot was full of broken slate. The floors above had fallen in and I came upon part of the wall of my study, and hanging in the middle a painting, undamaged, of a wanderer above a sea of mist. I gingerly picked my way through, my black bag in my hand, still incredulous, as though I were on my way, as usual, to the front of the house for afternoon surgery. And then I saw Mrs. Gregor's shoe.

Spike began to shriek in my hip and I had to sit down. I sat on a kitchen chair amid the rubble and the small fires and opened my black bag. I dissolved a tablet in a teaspoon over a match and managed without mishap to fill a syringe, though my hands were less than steady. A few moments later, composed, somewhat, I leaned over and picked up the shoe. The tears came. Smoke drifted in thin gray coils into the clear air. A woman's shoe speaks volumes. Mrs. Gregor's was a stout brown sensible shoe, well worn; it was still laced up. It was broad in the instep, for she had a wide foot. Once I held your mother's shoe, some long-ago afternoon in Jubilee Road. Your mother's foot was slender and small, she had a delicate foot. She had a delicate ankle. I remembered kneeling on the rug in front of the gas fire, with her curled up in the armchair, after we had made love, and discovering such perfection, such beauty, in her foot and ankle. At some point I heard the squadron overhead. During the last weeks, whenever I heard Spitfires passing over the house, even if I was seeing a patient I excused myself, and limped off down the passage into the kitchen, and out through the back door, and lifted my eyes. Now again I heard the squadron, and I marveled that one among you carried within his slender androgynous frame a spirit of courage, and innocence, and youth, and beauty, and hope. Then I lifted my eyes; sitting on a kitchen chair in the ruins of Elgin, clutching a dead woman's shoe, I lifted my eyes to Heaven and dreamed I saw an angel.

An angel—what did *this* mean? What was happening to me— was I going out of my mind? Was I being driven mad by loss and starting to confuse reality with the products of my own grief-torqued imagination? That I could even picture you, poor sick boy, an angel—and an angel you had certainly appeared, hairless, translucent, with tiny breasts and a boy's genitalia, evanescent in the daytime sky and soaring upward like a diver returning to the surface, and *radiant*—your whole figure *suffused* with light—I sat up violently in bed, Spike awoke with me, and I stared, unseeing, horrified, hands clasped to my face, at the back of the bedroom door. What was happening to me? I arose in haste, shaved hurriedly and made my way downstairs to the kitchen; Mrs. Gregor was at the stove melt-

ing a lump of lard in the frying pan. The sight of her gave
me comfort. I sank into a chair and groped in my pockets for
a cigarette. "Egg, doctor?" she murmured.

There was a newspaper on the table, and a pot of tea. "Fine,
Mrs. Gregor," I said as I stared unseeing at the war news.

"Sausage, doctor?"

"I beg your pardon?"

"Sausage? Shall I do you a sausage?" She had turned from
the stove and was holding up a large pink pork sausage. The
idea of food was intolerable. I rose unsteadily, left the kitchen,
and hobbled down to the surgery. The morning was quiet; I
had no patients to see, thankfully. At about noon, somewhat
recovered, I heard Mrs. Gregor wheeling her bicycle round
to the front of the house, and from some stray impulse I came
out into the hall to the front door, whence, unobserved, I
watched her lift herself onto the saddle and pedal off down
the drive. The sight gave me pleasure, inasmuch as I was
capable of pleasure, I don't know why; oh, I suppose the
residue of what I'd felt in that dream, on finding her shoe in
the ruins of Elgin—I was relieved that that good woman had
not died after all, and more to the point, still cared enough
about my welfare to appear daily in Elgin.

Later I drove to the Elms to see Nan Hale-Newton. I told
her about my dream. She'd never been bombed, she said,
but she'd lost houses, knew how painful it could be. But only
bricks and mortar, after all, this was her line. Not Elgin, I
said, that house wasn't just bricks and mortar. Nonsense, she
snorted. Then she said an astonishing thing: "You should
marry the woman."

"What woman?"

"Your housekeeper."

"Mrs. Gregor? *Marry* her?" I was bewildered. How on earth
had she jumped to this conclusion?

"Oh, look at yourself, man. You're ill. You're coming apart
at the seams. You never eat. Forever mooning about that damn
boy. Marry the woman, you need someone to look after you.

She'll have you, but not for much longer. Marry her while
you still can." Then she sighed. The room was full of shadows.
"I'm tired," she said, "I dream about water." I said I didn't
know what that meant. We sat there in silence.

I hesitate to tell you what occurred that night. Drawn, irresistibly, to be near you, I drove up to the station. Being now
unofficially attached to the medical officer's staff I was admitted by the sentry and parked the car by the sick bay. I
knew where the pilots' quarters were; what I hoped to do
there I cannot now imagine, simply I was drawn to you like
a moth to a flame. Oh, the idea of it now, I shudder at it—I
see myself skulking in the shadows of the big silent hangar—
there was a moon that night, and little cloud, which made
concealment difficult. I see myself darting past the Spitfires
in the gloom of the hangar, tiny limping figure in a black fur
coat scuttling across a vast space of shadows and aeroplanes.
Down the side of the hangar and across to your quarters,
another of those prefabricated structures with its corrugated
tin roof gleaming dully in the moonlight. I paused, panting,
in the shadows. Somewhere within, I knew, you slept. What
did I intend to do now? Come to you in the darkness? Hardly!
It was mad, mad! But I did not go back, not immediately. I
sat on the grass, in the shadows, with my back against the
wall, feeling connected with you through mere contact with
the building in which you slept.

I returned to Elgin in the early hours of the morning, and
went to the surgery and took out your X-rays. For a long time,
I don't know how long, I gazed at those shadows, those dim
visual echoes of your physical being, and lodged within, the
clear hard outline of your shrapnel, your Spike, our material
linkage.

The following afternoon I drove up to the station as usual. I
parked by the airfield and sat in the car smoking cigarettes.
I saw several scrambles before the adjutant came over and

asked if he could help me with anything. Nothing, I said. He then told me, with some tact, that my presence was making the pilots uneasy. "You know how superstitious they are," he said. "Would you mind, doctor?" I left the station. I knew where you'd be later: there was a squadron party in the mess.

It was a mild warm evening. Searchlights scissored the darkness, and the night was alive with the boom and clatter of big guns. I walked on the beach, I stumped up and down in my fur, raging in my distraught mind against the prospect of the darkness to come, as the sea hissed and murmured on the Griffin sands, and when, exhausted, and in severe pain, I came into the mess I found that the party was already raucous; the pilots were celebrating. But in all the hilarity there was now a barely concealed tone of fatigue, of desperation, of hysteria even. Five, six, seven times a day you went up. You were losing pilots hourly. The onslaught was relentless. It didn't let up. Wave after wave of them, Dorniers, Heinkels, with their escorts of Messerschmitts—I had seen them, those black aeroplanes shining in the sun, crosses on their wings, droning steadily onward, and committed to our destruction— they were the very manifestation of evil! Of course there was frenzy in your carousing, it was the song of death you roared round the piano.

I approached. You watched me coming toward you. I daresay I seemed absurd to you, I certainly seemed absurd to myself—a tragic figure on a tiny scale, this was me, suffering the agonies of the damned but for what, exactly? "Hello doctor," you said wearily, and turned toward the bar.

"Hello James." My angel! I stood beside you and waited to be served. I offered you a drink but you refused. I ordered a gin. There were loud voices, shouts of laughter, a scrum of large bodies in blue uniforms, but we seemed curiously insulated from it all, you and I. "James," I said, as I busied myself lighting a cigarette, and keeping my eyes averted from you, "have I hurt your feelings?"

The cigarette was lit. I exhaled smoke, took a sip of my gin and only then glanced at you. You were gazing at the rows of bottles behind the bar, and I didn't know what to make of your expression. You lifted your glass to your lips. "You know, I'm only concerned for your well-being. If I've been tactless, in some way—"

Your eyebrows lifted a fraction.

"If I've alarmed you unduly—"

Did I detect a smile?

"If I gave you the wrong impression—"

Now there was a delicate snort of irony.

"I have. I've frightened you, I can see that. No need, no need at all. We have a number of possibilities. There are hormone treatments I can prescribe. We should talk about it though. You must let me examine you again."

"Oh no." This was spoken firmly, with utter conviction. At last you looked at me. You turned squarely toward me, your fine black eyebrows drawn together in a delicate frown and anger smoldering in those clear dark eyes, and said, "I don't know what it is you imagine I have, but I can assure you there is *nothing wrong with me.*"

So this was it. You were still denying it, pretending it wasn't happening. Pushing it away, blocking it out. This I could understand. "James," I began—I would have to speak tactfully; I'd have preferred to conduct this interview in my surgery, if you'd only allow it—"let me explain to you something about the pituitary gland."

You shook your head slightly and turned back toward the bar. The disease was progressing, this was clear to me, and for an instant my composure seemed about to desert me—I was fascinated at the sight of you in that uniform, knowing what I did about the body within. Suddenly—it was the strangest thing, nothing like this had ever happened before— suddenly I felt a distinct movement of sexual feeling toward you, a movement of *passion*. I picked up my drink, pushed a

hand through my hair, perhaps I even flushed a little, I don't
know—such confusion I felt at that moment! I was then aware
of some hilarity close behind me and turned to see a pilot
mincing across the floor with one hand on his hip, then pausing, glancing over his shoulder, and saying coyly, to the delight
of the whole mess—"Care to examine me, doctor?" Spike
shrieked—I turned back to the bar, downed my gin and ordered another. Silly boys. I threw a quick oblique glance in
your direction. You were moving away from the bar, a drink
in your hand, a cigarette between your teeth, a lick of black
hair flopping over your forehead, grinning.

A little later, in Elgin, tranquil now, not expansive but
tranquil at least, I stood at the window of the top-floor corner
room and listened to the thunder of the guns and saw you in
my mind's eye at the bar in the mess, a scrap of silver silk
knotted about your throat. It was the last time I saw you whole.

The next days passed in a sort of daze. I continued to go
about my duties, what duties I still had, and every afternoon
went up to the station. Around Griffin Head all the signposts
had been taken down, all the street names removed, so as to
confuse the Germans when they came. And we needed no
reminding that when they did come it was on the south coast
that they'd be arriving: Griffin was the front line. The town
was a cat's cradle of mines and barbed wire; huge cement
cylinders had been put in the roads to block the progress of
armed enemy convoys, and sentries were posted everywhere,
manning pillboxes; they had two machine guns between the
lot of them. The barricades thrown up to block a German
advance were pitiful—clumsy jumbles of barrels and tree
trunks and old iron bedsteads, and at the crossroads where
the coast road met the main road the police had dumped a
hundred tons of broken glass, as if for a medieval siege. I told
Mrs. Gregor what I thought, and she warned me not to talk
too freely; you could be fined, or imprisoned, for spreading

"alarm and despondency." One man was heard saying it would be a bloody good thing when the Empire was finished, and got a year in gaol. At Winchester an officer billeted in a rectory was denounced as a spy by the vicar's daughter because he didn't pull the chain after going to the lavatory. The girl said his behavior was "un-English."

Invasion. This is what happens to a community facing invasion. As I sat smoking in my car by the airfield I reflected on what was about to happen to us, what would happen when they arrived. Evening was already coming when I saw you scramble for the seventh or eighth time that day, saw you climbing into the west, into the sun. What place I wondered for us in the Third Reich? I, a cripple, and you—you, a brave sick gallant boy giving your life for a hopeless cause—

This is what I imagine happened. In line astern you ran into them at eighteen thousand feet. Badly outnumbered you turned head-on to them, hauled hard back and swept clear over them in a steep climbing turn and in those seconds they lost the advantage. Your wingman let go a burst of fire at the first one, who sheared off toward you and you knew he was yours. Fierce unwavering concentration, sweat on your brow and knuckles white as you kicked the rudder over to get him at right angles then let go a four-second burst with full deflection—and grim relief as you saw him come through your sights and the tracer hammered home! For a second he seemed to hang motionless, then a jet of red flame shot upward and he spun down into the sea. Then a blur of twisting machines, tracer bullets beading and crackling, the sudden glint on metal of the setting sun. Another went down in a sheet of flame on your right as a Spitfire went by in a half-roll. You were weaving and turning and trying to gain height when you saw another one below you climbing away from the sun so you closed in to three hundred yards and gave him a two-second burst and saw fabric rip off the wing and black smoke pour from the engine but he didn't go down. Angry now you put in another burst and at last saw red flames shoot upward as he spiraled out of sight. And then—a moment's inattention. Why? Sun in your eyes? A flicker of terror? Jab of pain from your shrapnel? Whatever: it was *then* that you felt a terrific explosion, so strong it knocked the stick out of your hand and the whole aircraft shuddered violently. But it didn't start burning so you headed for home.

With what excruciatingly tender care did you nurse that Spitfire back to Griffin Head! What did you think about? Could you think about anything but the job in hand? Did you think about me? The cockpit only burst into flames as you touched down. I was there waiting for you. I was the one who saw you standing on the wing engulfed in flame, then falling, and I the one who reached you first and smothered the flames with my fur. And I who with needle and ampoule killed the pain of a body too badly burned to live. Final irony, yes, I killed you, but I killed you because I loved you. To save you suffering.

And now you lie here in my arms, and I sit stroking this poor charred head, this seared and blistered and stinking black head as they come lumbering toward us through the dusk. Pressed against my chest, mouth open and fighting for breath, and gazing sightlessly up at me—darling boy what have they *done* to you! You couldn't live like this, your face burnt off and seething with infection, all beauty destroyed—

I lift my eyes and look away; my face is streaming tears. Yes here they come, and what is it they're shouting, fool? Fool, yes—fool of love—

Your poor *hands*—like your father you wouldn't wear gloves, and see what's happened to them now, they're clawing. You had such lovely hands, you had your mother's hands—

They've stopped some yards off and stand there strangely spectral in a twilight shimmering with heat from the blazing aeroplane—and what a noise they're making! Fuel, they're shouting—not fool, *fuel*, fuel tank, the fuel tank's going to blow!

Then with a shock of violent exaltation I feel the sudden nearness of her spirit. Again she has entered your body, she has entered this ruined dying body and as passion swells, and Spike howls, I fumble in the black bag with my free hand for the needle. Your black lips parted, a gasp, a sigh, a word. My face down close, what is it you're saying to me? I press my mouth gently to yours and probe for your tongue with my own, probe with tiny darting flickers till I taste in your terrible burnt head the fresh sweet wetness of the living tongue within—

VINTAGE CONTEMPORARIES

WHERE I'M CALLING FROM
by Raymond Carver

The summation of a triumphant career from "one of the great short-story writers of our time—of any time" (*Philadelphia Inquirer*).   0-679-72231-9

THE HOUSE ON MANGO STREET
by Sandra Cisneros

Told in a series of vignettes stunning for their eloquence—the story of a young girl growing up in the Latino quarter of Chicago.

"Cisneros is one of the most brilliant of today's young writers. Her work is sensitive, alert, nuanceful . . . rich with music and picture."—Gwendolyn Brooks
0-679-73477-5

ELLEN FOSTER
by Kaye Gibbons

The story of a young girl who overcomes adversity with a combination of charm, humor, and ferocity.

"Ellen Foster is a southern Holden Caulfield, tougher perhaps, as funny . . . a breathtaking first novel."   —Walker Percy
0-679-72866-X

NOTHING BUT BLUE SKIES
by Thomas McGuane

Thomas McGuane's latest novel, chronicling the fall and rise of Frank Copenhaver, is set in a Montana where cowboys slug it out with speculators, a cattleman's best friend may be his insurance broker, and love and fishing are the only consolations that last.

"So sizable in vision and execution, so funny, so tragically and truly about America . . . that one is moved to stand and applaud."   —*Boston Globe*
0-679-74778-8

THE JOY LUCK CLUB
by Amy Tan

"Vivid . . . wondrous . . . what it is to be American, and a woman, mother, daughter, lover, wife, sister and friend—these are the troubling, loving alliances and affiliations that Tan molds into this remarkable novel." —*San Francisco Chronicle*

"A jewel of a book."   —*The New York Times Book Review*
0-679-72768-X

VINTAGE CONTEMPORARIES